A THEORY

of Love

KATE CHRISTIE

SECOND GROWTH

Second Growth Books
Seattle, WA

ISBN-13: 978-1-7289310-1-2

DEDICATION

To AG, my champion in spectacles, who has worked with me for nearly a decade to make sure I don't let fear of what *might* be keep me from what *could* be.

ACKNOWLEDGMENTS

I owe many thanks to the able Margaret Burris, copy editor extraordinaire, who dropped everything to read through a late draft of *ATOL*. Margaret, your attention to detail is unparalleled—and much appreciated. Any errors contained in the following pages are mine, likely the result of last-minute changes uploaded in the cover of night.

CHAPTER ONE

Eva DeMarco sat at the bar, trying not to stare too obviously at a group of women playing pool in the next room. This was her first time at a women's bar since college, and while hairstyles and clothing had changed in the past decade, not much else seemed different. The women around her were still mostly in their twenties, still cradling pint glasses and the occasional bottle of beer, still interacting mainly with each other and sending anyone else in their vicinity guarded glances. Just sitting here adjacent to the scene drama, Eva was remembering why she had stayed away for so long.

Of course, her now-defunct hetero marriage probably had something to do with her extended absence from the queer social scene, too.

"We don't have to stay if you don't want to," Alexis said, leaning in to be heard over the top 40 music playing throughout the Thistledown, one of Seattle's sole remaining lesbian bars.

"No," Eva said, and forced a smile at her best friend. "This is fine. It's good."

One drink, she promised herself, letting her gaze wander again.

Earlier that day, she had been thrilled when Alexis had suggested they blow off a writing session for dinner and drinks on Capitol Hill, Seattle's alternative neighborhood. She might have been less elated if she'd realized where the drinks portion of the evening would lead, but when their after-dinner stroll brought them past the Thistledown and Alexis had lifted one perfectly plucked eyebrow at her, Eva had nodded gamely. *Why not*, the pint of Elysian IPA coursing through her bloodstream had seemed to ask.

1

Oh, right—because she was a recently divorced thirty-something academic who hated the bar scene, her mind had supplied only after they were seated. Still, it was better than a non-gay bar. Straight men had always flocked to Alexis, drawn in by her warm brown skin, springy curls, and the perpetual smile on her face. They rarely stuck around for long, though. Like Eva, sunny-seeming Alexis was a proud nerd whose conversational repertoire revolved around Marxist theory and the status of women's labor under capitalism. Most guys hitting on women in bars wanted to discuss these topics about as much as they wanted to talk about someone else's children. Or their own kids, for that matter.

The music washed over her, and Eva sipped her second IPA of the evening as Alexis guided the conversation toward familiar topics: Alexis's husband, Tosh, and his two kids from his first marriage; Eva's mother and her continued adjustment to life in assisted living; the upcoming fall quarter at their respective universities; and, of course, their current joint research project: cultural attitudes toward readers and writers of romantic fiction.

Eva wasn't sure which fact startled her more these days—that her marriage had failed or that she'd abandoned her Serious Research Interest in the visual arts to study the contemporary romance novel. As an untenured assistant professor, it would have been safer to stick to what she'd been hired for. But the losses of the past few years had piled on one after another, and she'd awakened one day to realize that the world around her no longer looked or felt the same. Light and color seemed darker, and somewhere along the way she'd lost pleasure in the things she'd once loved.

Soon after that, Alexis had dragged her to a therapist who had assured her that the profound emptiness she felt was to be expected and would one day pass. In the meantime, whatever distraction helped get her through her grief was perfectly acceptable: taking anti-depressants, bingeing TV shows, reading romance novels.

Eva had been with her up to that moment. But—"Romance novels, really?"

"And what exactly is wrong with romance novels?" Gayle, the therapist, had asked, gazing at her over the top of her tortoiseshell glasses.

"You know."

"I'm not sure I do."

Eva had huffed aloud, irritated that she was being forced to confront yet another uncomfortable truth about herself. Which was arguably the point of therapy, but still. She already felt badly enough about her life. Did she really need to interrogate her culturally-instilled attitude about a widely disparaged form of fiction? As Gayle continued to stare at her, Eva had realized that yes, in fact, she did.

That night, Gayle had emailed her a list of novels and authors to try, and Eva had chosen a title at random: *Outlander*, the first book in Diana Gabaldon's time-travel series about a World War Two-era woman who ends up stuck in the eighteenth century Scottish Highlands. The novel was intriguing, well-written, and sympathetic. In other words, nothing like Eva had expected of the genre. After one too many of her exhortations to give the novel a read, Alexis had finally succumbed. Soon they were sending each other articles to help "unpack" their culturally-conditioned biases toward romantic fiction, and voilà: two Serious Research Interests left by the wayside in favor of the defense of women's reading and writing.

Their drinks were nearly empty when Alexis's gaze narrowed on the other room.

"What?" Eva asked, glancing over her shoulder. "Do you see one of your students?" The bar was twenty-one and up, but that rarely stopped a determined underage drinker.

"Sadly, no," Alexis said.

Sadly? But of course—as a straight, married woman with tenure, Alexis had nothing to fear from being seen at a lesbian bar in downtown Seattle. The resulting gossip would probably only inflate her scores on RateMyProfessors.com.

"Don't look," Alexis added, "but there's a woman at the pool table who keeps staring at you."

With difficulty, Eva tamped down her kneejerk reaction to glance around again. Instead, she took another pull on her beer and only then let her gaze wander toward the pool table where a group of athletic-looking women was socializing. She didn't see anyone glancing her way—until, suddenly, she did. The woman in question was tall and attractive, short blonde hair falling over her forehead in a way that looked casual yet artful, dark blue button-up rolled to her elbows, skinny jeans hugging what appeared to be long, muscled legs. Their eyes met and Eva quickly looked away.

"How do you know she's not staring at you?" she countered, because that was a common enough occurrence in their shared history.

"One way to find out." Alexis slid down from her bar stool. "I'll be right back."

"Wait!" Eva caught her shoulder, fingers digging in. "You are not going to talk to her!"

Alexis glanced at her. "Of course I'm not. I do, however, have to pee. If I'm right, *she's* going to come talk to *you*."

Before Eva could wrestle Alexis back onto the stool, she slipped out of reach and all but skipped away.

Fantastic. Now Eva was alone in a lesbian bar with a hot woman eyeing her from across the room. She peeked toward the pool table again in time to see said hot woman pass her cue stick to someone else. Wait, was she heading this way? Oh, god, she was.

For one absurd moment, Eva considered fleeing. But Alexis had left her purse behind, and the odds of Eva being able to safely extricate herself from the bar stool with both of their purses in hand seemed fairly low. Instead, she took another drink from her pint glass and stared down at her phone, even though she already knew there were no new texts or emails. Unlike some people in her department, Eva had checked her email religiously while on leave for the past year. She'd published, too, a paper that she and Alexis were scheduled to present at a conference and a book chapter that was in the final stages of revision. Publish or perish, or so the saying went.

Out of the corner of one eye, Eva saw the attractive woman pause beside her.

"Could I get another Alaskan Amber?" she asked, her voice low and surprisingly soft-spoken.

The bartender handed her a bottle of beer. "What's the name on the tab?"

"Cass," the woman replied. "Thanks." She stepped closer to Eva. "Excuse me, but you look familiar. Have we met before?"

Even as Eva looked up into the woman's striking blue eyes,

she inwardly cringed at the cheesy pick-up line. "Um, no, I don't think so."

"Really, I think I might know you from somewhere. Do you hang out here a lot?"

"This is actually my first time," Eva said, trying to bite back a smile. "So no, I don't come here often."

The stranger—*Cass*—was smiling now too, and lo and behold, she had a dimple. No wonder her pick-up game was terrible. All she had to do was flash that smile and any would-be object of her affection would promptly melt at her feet.

"I'm not trying to pick you up," Cass said. "I promise."

"In that case, I'm not sure if I should be relieved or offended." Eva clutched her pint glass, mildly amazed at herself. Was that actual flirting? If so, then kudos to the makers of the Elysian IPA, really.

"Not that I *wouldn't* hit on you," Cass backtracked. "I mean, I'm sure anyone would be lucky to get to know you."

"You're sure of that, are you?" Eva crossed one leg over the other and hid another smile as Cass's gaze dropped to her skirt before skittering quickly back up. "All right, then. Maybe we have met. What do you do?"

"I coach rugby." The other woman's eyes took on a fixed quality that implied she was steadfastly refusing to look at Eva's legs.

Rugby—was that the one where the ball looked like a football but the players didn't wear pads? "I've never been to a rugby game," she admitted. "So it can't be that. Where are you from?"

"San Francisco."

"I've never been there, either."

"What do you do?" Cass asked, picking at the label on her beer bottle with a neatly shorn fingernail.

"I teach," Eva said automatically, even though she hadn't been in a classroom in more than a year.

"Where do you—?"

Before Cass could finish the question, an even taller brunette bumped into her from behind, arms sliding around her waist.

"Cass," she all but whined, "you said you would be right

back."

"And I will be, Amy," Cass said, her voice unreadable as she slipped out of the new arrival's grasp.

Eva glanced down at her pint glass. It would seem Cass already had a date, which meant she really hadn't been hitting on Eva. Yep, not embarrassing at all.

The brunette cut her gaze to Eva before turning away. "Don't be too long," she cast over her shoulder.

Silence reigned as they both watched the other woman sashay away. Finally, Cass said, "Sorry about that."

"No problem." Eva swallowed the rest of her drink in one go and slid carefully from the barstool, hand on her purse. "I actually have to go."

"You do?" Cass asked, her brow wrinkling adorably because of course, everything about her was adorable from the tip of her perfectly coiffed head down to her old-school Converse sneakers.

"Yes. My girlfriend isn't feeling well," she announced, and then paused. She and Alexis had referred to each other as "girlfriend" more than once, much to the dismay of Alexis's easily embarrassed pre-teen stepdaughter. But the term took on different connotations when invoked in conversation with an actual gay girl at a lesbian bar.

"Your girlfriend," Cass echoed.

"Alexis," she supplied, because her brain had decided that verisimilitude would make the lie more believable.

"I see." Cass's focus shifted to a spot beyond Eva's shoulder, her expression unreadable again.

Crap, Eva thought as her "girlfriend" materialized beside her. So much for a quick escape.

"Hi," Alexis said, the wattage of her friendly smile immediately casting Eva's sick-girlfriend excuse into question.

And this—this right here was why Eva didn't do the bar scene. But in for a pound, or whatever the stupid saying was. "Hi, honey," she said, sliding her arm around Alexis's waist.

To her credit, her best friend's expression didn't change. "Are we heading out?"

"Yes. I was just telling Cass here about your headache." She gazed meaningfully at Alexis, who barely hesitated before nodding.

They had used this excuse too many times to count in the early days of their friendship in New York's Greenwich Village.

"Silly migraine," Alexis told Cass as she reached for her purse. "Probably it was the disco lighting."

"That can happen." Cass's gaze returned to Eva. "You know my name, but I didn't catch yours."

"Oh, sorry. It's Eva." She waited for the inevitable comment about Adam, but it didn't come—maybe because they were in a lesbian bar.

Cass's eyes narrowed a little, and then she smiled again and held out her hand. "It's nice to meet you, Eva."

"You, too." Even Cass's hand was lovely, with smooth skin and a callused palm that probably came from throwing a rugby ball around all day. Did she wear little shorts that showed off her— attributes? Eva squeezed her hand without meaning to and then quickly let go as Cass's eyes flew up to hers.

"And I'm Alexis," Alexis added cheerfully, still not working very hard at selling the migraine story, in Eva's opinion.

Cass bowed her head slightly. "Nice to meet you, Alexis. I hope to see you both again soon." And with that, she flashed her killer dimple at Eva one last time, turned her adorable attributes around, and walked away.

Alexis waited until they were out on the sidewalk, the noise and light of the bar receding behind them, to inquire, "Do you want to tell me what that was about, *honey*?"

Eva hunched her shoulders as they paced toward Twelfth Ave. "Just me being me."

"I'm going to need a little more context."

Eva sighed and began ticking off the key conversational points. "She said I looked familiar, I accused her of picking me up, she insisted she wasn't, I refused to believe her, and then a woman who I'm pretty sure was her date showed up to stake her very obvious claim."

"At which point you invented a girlfriend to save face?"

"Exactly."

"Oh, Eva, I love you," Alexis said, laughing as she wrapped her arm around Eva's neck and tugged her close.

Eva hid her face in her friend's shoulder as they walked. "See?

This is why I'm better off alone."

"No way. Your first time back out on the dating scene and a gorgeous woman chats you up? I would say tonight was a complete success."

"And I would say you've lost your ability to interpret reality," Eva said.

But she didn't argue any further. Cass the rugby coach might not have been her type (or vice versa) but she had certainly been attractive, and for a few minutes there, Eva had felt a long-dormant part of herself threatening to awaken. Maybe life after divorce wouldn't require her to live alone with a clowder of cats, as Alexis had put it. Her dog Harvey would probably have something to say on the matter of sharing their home with feline interlopers, anyway.

"Not to change the subject," Alexis said, "but you're still coming to movie night this weekend, aren't you?"

"As long as it isn't *Captain Underpants*. I'm not sure I can handle that many fart jokes again." Alexis's stepson might be Eva's favorite seven-year-old in the Seattle metro area, but his taste in films was abominable.

"In that case, consider yourself lucky..." Alexis paused and then finished, "that the only male in your household currently is Harvey. How's he doing, anyway?"

"Good. I think he's finally stopped waiting for Ben to come home." Eva didn't comment on the subject change. She knew that having a conversation with her could be like walking through a minefield. Mostly she was glad that Alexis was willing to keep trying. "Speaking of, I think I might head out."

Alexis slipped her arm through Eva's, trapping her at her side. "Not until we've sobered you up, my friend."

Which, right. It had been ages since she'd consumed enough alcohol to have to worry about driving herself home.

For the next hour, they traipsed all over Capitol Hill because, "Studies show that exercise helps your body metabolize alcohol, Eva." Once they were suitably exercised, they stopped for coffee at one of the dark, eclectic shops on Broadway because supposedly consuming caffeine also helped you sober up. When Eva asked Alexis why she knew so much about mitigating the effects of alcohol, her research partner reminded her that while both the

University of Washington and Edmonds University were known for their top-notch academics, U-Dub was also legendary for its students' partying ways.

At last Alexis deemed Eva sober enough to make the drive back to the Seattle suburbs, and they backtracked to their cars parked on a side street near the Elysian Brewery, where their night out had begun.

"So," Eva said as they paused beside her ancient Subaru Legacy. "Thanks for tonight, even if I did make an idiot of myself at the Thistledown."

Alexis tilted her head, curls falling to one side. "I still say that woman was into you."

Eva paused, remembering Cass's eyes on her bare legs and the warmth she had felt wash over her at the idea of someone as attractive as the rugby coach being even a tiny bit interested. But then she remembered the second woman, Amy, glaring at her. Even if Cass had been interested, she wasn't free any more than Eva, still nursing her divorce wounds, was.

"I don't think so," she said, shaking her head.

"We could go back sometime soon," Alexis suggested. "You know, see if we run into her again?"

Yes, Eva's mind supplied. "No," she said. "I do not have the time or energy to get involved in some ill-advised entanglement, and you know it."

"Ill-advised entanglement?" Alexis shook her head. "Methinks the lady doth protest too much."

"Seriously, Lex, let it go, okay? Pinkie swear you won't bring it up again." She held out her hand, pinkie extended challengingly, and smiled as Alexis emitted the distinctly unfeminine guffaw that had first drawn Eva to her in graduate school a dozen years earlier.

"Eva," she whined, covering her mouth as she always did after one of her graceless laughs managed to escape.

"Let's go, Hammond. Time's a-ticking."

Sighing in what Eva hoped was amused exasperation, Alexis hooked their pinkies together. "Fine. I swear."

"Word of honor?"

"Oh my god, white people are so weird! *Word of honor.*"

"Excellent," Eva said, and turned to manually unlock her car door. The power lock had been broken for close to a decade. Probably she should get around to having it fixed one of these days.

Alexis's goodbye hug was as warm as ever, and Eva didn't want to let go. But eventually, she had to pull away and climb into her car, where she waited to turn on her engine until Alexis was safely inside her Volvo wagon three spaces away. Then, with a final wave, Eva headed for the freeway.

As she drove the thirty minutes north to her house in the Edmonds Bowl, the popular neighborhood just up the hill from the ferry terminal, she didn't, for once, dwell on how strange it felt to be heading home by herself. For the first time in recent memory, she didn't think about what she'd lost or about the dreams that would never be realized. She thought instead about the warmth of Cass's palm against hers, of the deep blue of her eyes in the low light of the bar, of the odd weight in her voice as she'd said she hoped to see her again soon.

Even though Cass appeared to be involved with someone else and their brief meeting had ended in actual shenanigans, Eva couldn't help wishing that they really would get a chance to see each other again. She couldn't remember the last time another person had sparked even a frisson of interest, let alone the genuine attraction she'd felt toward Cass. As she pulled into her driveway from the alley and parked under the carport, Harvey's whines audible through the back door, Eva conceded that maybe Alexis's suggestion they make a return trip to the Thistledown wasn't a completely terrible idea. And then she was entering the neat and orderly bungalow, and Harvey her forty-pound lapdog was slathering every inch of available skin with kisses.

She dropped her purse and key on the kitchen counter and herded him into the living room. There, she collapsed on the couch and urged him up beside her, winding her arms around his neck to keep him from bathing her face, too. A boxer-Boston terrier mix, he could sometimes be an irksome blend of high-strung and bully breed.

"I missed you, too, buddy," she said, smiling as he wriggled impossibly closer.

Alexis was right. She was lucky to have Harvey, lucky that Ben hadn't fought her for custody of the dog they had rescued together.

She wasn't sure she could have taken such a battle—which was probably why Ben had let her keep him.

She leaned her head on the back of the couch, rubbing Harvey's smooth, fawn-colored coat. At least memories of her failed marriage didn't hurt as much as they once had. The sensation reminded her of when she'd had her wisdom teeth removed in college. The initially bloody, painful gaps had eventually healed over, but for years she had noticed a sense of loss when she poked her gums with the tip of her tongue. Until, one day at last, the empty spaces had felt like they'd been there all along.

"We'll get there, Harve," she murmured, rubbing the white blaze on his chest, and was rewarded with an onslaught of kisses to her chin. One of them wholeheartedly believed it, anyway.

CHAPTER TWO

"Why am I going to this shindig with you, again?" Cass's brother asked as she shooed him out of his house and into the passenger seat of her Jeep.

"Because Maya got stuck at the hospital and told me to make sure you didn't bail to play *Legend of Zelda*," she replied, depositing the bakery bread and quinoa casserole on his lap.

Matthew settled the dish more comfortably. "Yes, but what I'm wondering is why *you* don't want to bail to play *Legend of Zelda*."

Cass had to admit this was a valid question, seeing as they had whiled away many a late night engaged in such endeavors. Often Maya, his significantly better half, joined them when she wasn't working a late shift.

"One word, my dude," she said as she rounded the front of the Jeep. "Potluck."

Not only would there be free food and booze at this shindig, as her brother had called it, but it would also be nice to spend some quality time with colleagues in a beautiful setting. Not that she had a certain colleague in mind, because she didn't.

"Where's Amy?" Matthew asked.

"She flew back to Oakland this afternoon." Cass turned the key in the ignition.

"I thought she was staying for a few more days."

"She had to get back early." Cass guided the Jeep away from the curb, stubbornly refusing to meet her brother's gaze.

"Let me guess—even though you were clear about not wanting a commitment, she asked for one. Am I right?"

Cass responded with her usual maturity when it came to his irritating smugness: "Shut it, asshat."

"I told you, Cassiopeia, very few people do casual well. When are you going to learn to listen to me, baby sister?"

She rolled her eyes both at his nickname and at his chosen term of endearment. Pejorative? Whatever. He was all of 16 minutes older than she was, a fact he never let her live down. "I don't know, bro. Maybe when you learn that I don't need relationship advice from someone who married his college girlfriend? I have more experience with women than you do, in case you've forgotten."

"Hard to forget when you remind me so much," he grumbled. "Sometimes I really wish you were a guy. Then we could just measure our dicks and be done with it."

"Ew!" She wrinkled her nose at him. "Kindly keep your dick comments to yourself."

"I thought polyamorous people weren't uptight."

"I'm not poly. I just don't want a committed relationship right now. There is a difference, you know."

"Sure, Jan."

She wanted to smack him—let's be honest, she usually wanted to smack him—but they'd arrived at the banquet facility, and it wouldn't do to be seen brawling by the people they worked with. She parked the Jeep and headed toward the entrance, not waiting to see if Matthew followed. She loved this event space. Located on a bluff overlooking Puget Sound, the Eagle's Nest featured concrete floors, rustic wood beams, and an oversized fieldstone fireplace with a natural wood mantelpiece. It also offered a veritable wall of windows with sweeping views of Whidbey Island and the Olympic Peninsula.

Cass had attended several events here since moving to Edmonds the previous summer, and had to admit that views like these, along with loads of quality time with her brother, had helped ease her transition to Washington State. When she'd first arrived, she'd missed San Francisco and her old life there like crazy. Now, more than a year later, she no longer obsessed about going back to California the way she once had.

"Food first, conversation second?" Matthew asked as they entered the banquet facility's main room.

"Go ahead. I'm going to have a look around."

"Suit yourself," her brother said, and headed toward the banquet tables arranged at one end of the building, potluck offering in hand.

"And don't tell everyone you made the casserole this time!" she called after him.

His only response was an evil laugh. Typical.

Cass surveyed the crowd. Couples and families were seated at round tables while others stood in small groups near the fieldstone fireplace. She'd been running late after the rugby team's first preseason scrimmage, so she wasn't surprised to see most of the tables already occupied. She wasn't the only one who enjoyed a good potluck.

"Cassidy," she heard a familiar voice call, and turned to see her boss beckoning to her from beside the fireplace. She sighed inwardly even as she started toward him. This was supposed to be a social event, but no doubt he had a burning techie question that couldn't wait until Monday. That was the thing about working for Baby Boomers. They often expected their employees to not only accept but actively enable their unhealthy approach to work boundaries.

"Glad you made it," Steve Henry said when she reached him. "How was the scrimmage?"

She winced. "Don't ask." The women's club team was only in its third season, and while they had made gains since Cass had arrived the previous year to help Mike, the head coach, they still had a ways to go.

"Well, I'm sure they'll improve under your tutelage," Steve said.

"At least they have nowhere to go but up."

They chatted about the current gorgeous weather and the rugby team's fall match schedule, and then Steve appeared to zero in on someone in the distance.

"There she is," he said to Cass. "I was hoping to introduce you to someone I don't think you've met yet."

At that moment, the crowd parted and Cass glimpsed a woman approaching, plate of food in hand, gaze trained on the person beside her. A person who, Cass realized, was Matthew.

"Eva," Cass's boss said, waving at the petite, dark-haired woman.

Eva glanced in their direction, and as the smile on her lips froze, Cass felt her own heart rate pick up unaccountably. Or not entirely unaccountably. Because, holy crap—it was her.

Until that moment, Cass hadn't been certain that the woman from the Thistledown was, in fact, Dr. Eva DeMarco, junior faculty member of the Edmonds University Department of Sociology. Her photo on the department website showed her from a distance atop a rocky summit, dark brown hair gathered in a ponytail, sunglasses hiding her features. A Google search had turned up only a private Facebook page with the same picture and a pixelated group shot from a university event. Dr. DeMarco wasn't big on social media, it seemed.

Steve touched Cass's elbow, leading her forward to intercept the pair. "Matthew, how are you?"

"Good," her brother said as he shook the hand that Steve, dean of the College of Arts and Sciences, extended. "I was actually bringing Eva over to meet my sister. Cass, this is Eva DeMarco from Sociology. Eva, Cass is in her second year in the Master's program in your department."

"This is the graduate assistant I was telling you about, Eva," the dean put in. "Cassidy, Dr. DeMarco is rejoining us after a year away. I believe she might require some assistance with the new college website."

There was a pause during which Eva continued to eye her, expression still frozen. Tentatively Cass held out a hand. "Hi, Dr. DeMarco. It's nice to meet you."

"Um, right. You, too." Eva bobbled her plate momentarily before taking Cass's hand.

Her skin was as soft, her hand as small and perfect in Cass's grasp as it had been the week before at the Thistledown. She let go as quickly as courtesy allowed. Crushing on a professor was not a good idea, especially not when the professor in question had a gorgeous girlfriend.

"You two have been in touch before, haven't you?" the dean asked.

As Eva's eyes widened, Cass hurried to say, "I think we emailed a few times last year, didn't we, Dr. DeMarco?"

15

As the graduate assistant (GA) for Edmonds University's College of Arts and Sciences, Cass had been tasked with helping port the HTML-based college and department websites into the university's new dynamic content management system. She had emailed everyone in the Sociology Department during winter quarter while completing the bulk of the site transfer.

"That's right." Eva nodded, her expression settling into something minorly less alarmed. "Please, call me Eva," she added.

"Okay. My friends call me Cass."

Eva didn't respond, only looked down at her plate, which Cass noticed carried a generous helping of the quinoa casserole she had made the night before.

As the silence once again lengthened, Matthew gave Cass a look she could easily read: *Why are you being such a douche?*

"No Maya tonight?" the dean enquired.

"Unfortunately not. She had to work late at the hospital."

As he and the dean chatted about the time constraints on labor and delivery nurses at Swedish, one of Seattle's largest hospitals, Cass stole a look at Eva, only to find her gazing up at her from under her eyelashes. Cass's pulse accelerated again. She could honestly say she'd never met a professor as attractive as Eva DeMarco, with her deep brown eyes and her shiny dark curls cascading over her shoulders.

"So, Cassidy, do you have any time to spare for Eva this week?" the dean asked. "I'd like our faculty to be up to speed with the new systems before classes start, if possible."

Cass tried to salvage her already meager professionalism. "Um, yeah. No problem. My mornings are open this week. Is there a day that works better for you, Dr.—um, Eva?"

"I'm sure that isn't necessary," Eva said. "I wouldn't want to trouble you."

Before she could explain that it was her job to train faculty and staff members on the university's new systems, the dean interceded again, his usually laidback tone firm.

"There are some tricks to getting your schedule integrated with the new learning management software, Eva. Fortunately, Cassidy here is a real whiz with computers. Talk about fortuitous timing—we got lucky when she decided to do her graduate work at Edmonds."

Matthew elbowed her subtly, his way of saying he was pissed their mutual boss was singing her praises and not his, and Cass once again resisted the urge to smack him. She *was* a whiz with computers, thanks to her years of working in the tech industry. If Matthew had ever deigned to think about something other than astrophysics, he might be able to customize Drupal modules on the fly, too.

"In that case, I'll have to check my schedule," Eva said, her voice as stilted as her smile.

"Excellent." The dean's gaze sharpened again. "There's Ron. Enjoy yourselves, everyone. And again, Eva, welcome back."

He moved away, but Cass barely noticed. She was too busy pondering the faint flush tingeing the professor's olive skin, the muscle twitching in her jawline. Was she massively closeted, or was she simply annoyed that a student knew more about her than she wanted?

Matthew glanced between them again, brow creased. "Do you guys already know each other?"

"No," they said quickly, almost in unison.

"Only from email," Cass added, careful not to look at her brother. One look in her eyes and he would know she was lying.

"Riiight." His voice dropped suddenly. "Wait. Cass, tell me you didn't... I mean, she isn't...?"

As Eva's gaze flew to him, Cass followed suit. Only her look, she was sure, carried more irritability than alarm. Freaking twin telepathy. Though she hadn't used names, it was clear now that she should never have told her brother she'd run into an Edmonds professor at Seattle's best-known lesbian club.

"Weren't you going to get a plate, Mattie?" she asked. As he started to protest, she grabbed his elbow, her grip punishing. "Maybe you could get me one, too."

After a thankfully short, entirely non-verbal battle of wills, he nodded disgruntledly. "Whatever you say, *sis*." He started to turn away but stopped. "It's nice to see you, Eva. Really. I'm glad to hear things are going well for you."

"Thanks, Matthew," she said, her voice softening slightly. "It's good to see you, too. Tell Maya hello for me?"

"I will." And with a last scowl at Cass, he turned away.

The fact that her brother knew Eva wasn't surprising. With only 7,000 students, Edmonds University was hardly the largest school around. But physics and sociology were highly divergent fields, as Cass well knew.

"Don't worry," she said as her brother disappeared into the crowd. "He's not going to tell anyone where we met. I'm not, either."

"Well, that's good to hear." Her voice was uncertain, her eyes less warm and sparkly than Cass remembered from the bar. "I thought you said you were a rugby coach?"

"I am. I'm the assistant for the women's club."

"Why do you need a graduate assistantship, then?" Eva asked.

"Part-time assistant coaches don't qualify for tuition remission."

"Ah. Sounds like it's a good thing you have those legendary computer skills to fall back on, then," Eva said, and then looked away as if the semi-flirty comment had surprised her, too.

Cass gazed about the banquet room, wondering if Eva's girlfriend was nearby. "I'm sorry about the Thistledown," she said, though she wasn't entirely sure what she was apologizing for.

"You have nothing to be sorry about," Eva said. "I'm the one who… Anyway, I appreciate you keeping the details to yourself. As open-minded as Steve might be, that's not a conversation I want to have with my boss."

"I know what you mean." Cass hesitated. "So is your girlfriend here? Alex, was it?"

"Alexis." Eva paused, small white teeth worrying her lower lip. "Actually, I have a confession to make—"

Whatever she was about to say was interrupted by the blurred human form that chose that moment to crash into Cass.

"Yo, yo, didn't you hear the locomotive coming, Trane?"

What was it about people invading her personal space any time she tried to have a conversation with Eva DeMarco?

"Jace," Cass said, smiling despite her irritation as she slapped hands with her overzealous greeter. The smallish guy was beaming up at her, his glasses slightly askew as always, fleece zipped all the way up to his chin also as per usual.

Jace MacKenzie grinned sideways at Eva. "Hey, Eva. It's good to see you."

"You, too, Jace. I wondered if you'd still be on campus."

"What? Of course! Although I only have a year left to finish, so I guess it's this year or never."

Eva appeared to rein in a smile—a common enough expression around Jace, Cass had learned. "And on that note... It was nice to officially meet you, Cass. I'll email you about getting together. For the training session, I mean," she added.

"Absolutely. I look forward to it." Outwardly Cass's smile remained steady, but inwardly she face-palmed. One didn't typically look forward to a work training. It wasn't a date.

Eva's head tilted slightly but she said only, "See you both soon."

"See ya, Eva." As she drifted away, Jace turned back to Cass and thumped her shoulder enthusiastically. "Dude, how was your summer?"

"Really good. You?" she asked, but she was staring after Eva, replaying their brief conversation in her mind as she watched the other woman take a seat at a nearby table occupied by several other members of the Sociology Department. Cass could hear the group's greetings from here, tinged with warmth and something else she couldn't quite identify.

"Can't complain," Jace said. "Got a ton of research done up in Alaska for my thesis. So, Trane. Hanging out with Professor Hotty McHotty, hmm?" he asked, wiggling his eyebrows.

"Don't be a jackass."

"What?" Jace held up his hands. "I didn't come up with the nickname."

"That's so not the point."

She tamped down on the impulse to ask what Jace knew about Eva. When it came to university politics, it was always better to hold your cards close to your chest. Cass had learned this from years of watching her parents maneuver through a variety of faculty and administrative positions at Sarah Lawrence College and Columbia University. Matthew was also in the family business— *The Academy*, as they all pronounced it in suitably stodgy tones— along with several of their cousins. That was one reason Cass had decided to go back to school. She was tired of being the only Trane of her generation without a graduate degree.

Jace, however, didn't need to be asked to volunteer what he knew: "Eva and her husband split up a while ago. I heard by the time their divorce became final, Ben was already living with Tina Gardner from Psychology. They were the resident faculty scandal until Flesche got accused of harassing that girl."

"Wait. She was married to Ben *Miller*?" Cass asked, automatically checking the room for the history professor. He was a faculty rep on the Edmonds University Tech Committee, which Cass served on as a grad student rep. He'd been the first committee member to befriend her, and she'd even tagged along with Matthew and Maya to a dinner party at Ben and Tina's house over the summer.

"She and Ben were a spousal hire right before I started," Jace said. "I don't know who the university wanted more, her or him. Although he already has tenure, so you do the math."

Jace was an excellent source of college and department gossip. A part-time employee of the university's IT department, he'd been trying to finish his Master's in environmental science for the past six years. Given that students only had seven years to complete a Master's degree at Edmonds, he would be cutting it close.

At that moment, Matthew returned with a plate of Cass's favorites—quinoa casserole, kale salad, Asian noodles, and even a chocolate chip cookie from PCC.

"Oh, I love those!" Jace said, already edging away. "Later, Trane twins!"

Matthew didn't bother replying. He simply leaned into her shoulder and murmured, "Eva DeMarco? Seriously?"

"What? I didn't do anything." She shoveled a forkful of noodles into her mouth.

"Why do I find that hard to believe?"

She fixed a smile to her lips and all but hissed, "Seriously, can we not do this here?"

"Fine. I'm going to mingle," he said. "I've only got an hour in me tops, though."

"Mom and Dad wouldn't approve of your attitude, Dr. Trane."

"Good thing they live three thousand miles away."

Cass couldn't help but agree.

Without Maya to guilt-trip them for their eat-and-run tendencies, they completed a brief circuit of the room and then left the party, though not before convincing the student bartenders to hand over unopened bottles of Alaskan Amber on their way out. Cass had assumed they would head home for an evening with her video game console, but her brother apparently had other plans.

"Want to break into the planetarium?" he asked as she started the Jeep.

"Want to be unemployed?" she countered.

"I have a key…"

"It's not breaking in if you have a key, dolt."

"Is that a yes?"

She sighed, pretending she wasn't thrilled by the idea. "I guess."

"Nerd."

"*I'm* the nerd, Mr. Married-with-a-PhD-and-tenure-track-position-before-thirty?"

"You're just jealous."

Cass laughed as she guided the Jeep up the hill toward the campus observatory. "That'll be the day."

"Penis envy is a real thing, Cass."

"Dude! I already told you to stop talking about your dick! Besides, if you had ever taken a humanities course, you would know that Freud was wrong about anything having to do with women."

"I know," he said, smirking. "I just like to piss you off. Freud would call that, what, sibling rivalry?"

"No, that was Alfred…" She realized he was messing with her yet again and flipped him off. Not as satisfying as smacking him, but she was driving along a rather tall bluff. Better to be safe than smashed into tiny bits on the rocks below.

A few minutes later, Matthew was silently exhorting her to tiptoe past the observatory front desk where a student worker was glued to his phone, and Cass was questioning her life choices. *Were* they breaking in? Could they lose their jobs if they got caught? Maya would blame her, no doubt. She'd said more than once that Cass was a bad influence, and Cass was pretty sure she hadn't been joking at least one of those times. Matthew had his wife conned, just as he'd convinced their parents that he was the golden boy and Cass the classic black sheep. Sadly, their parents hadn't taken much persuading.

"Tell me that's not a skeleton key," she whispered as Matthew tried and failed to unlock the door to the planetarium.

"Shh," he shushed her. Which, she noticed, was neither confirmation nor denial.

The key finally worked, and after giggling their way past the squeaky outer door and into the inner sanctuary, Cass stared up at the dome while Matthew headed for the projector situated on a podium behind the last row of seats. The circular room was lit only by a thin line of red lights that stretched beneath the arced ceiling from one marked exit to the other. Cass didn't mind the dark, though. The cool hush of the space reminded her of snowy nights at Vassar College, where she'd done her undergraduate degree what felt like a hundred years ago now.

Vassar's observatory, a gift from the Class of 1951 back when the Seven Sisters school was still all women, had been one of her favorite places to visit when school got to be too much. The observatory might not have a planetarium, but it did offer weekly open nights when visitors were encouraged to gaze at the stars through the two large reflecting telescopes, each in its own separate dome. Cass had loved looking up at a tiny corner of what she understood to be a nearly incalculably large universe, her own problems immediately dwarfed by the sense of gargantuan perspective the view afforded. That was one of the things she'd missed while living in San Francisco—starry skies. Here in Edmonds she was fortunate to see stars often. Or, at least, when the Washington skies were clear enough to afford a view off-planet.

"Here we go," Matthew said, his voice tinged with excitement.

"Are you sure we should be doing this?" she asked, looking back at her brother. "Mom and Dad will kill me if we get in trouble…"

Matthew nodded as he made his way down the aisle toward her. "It's fine. I actually just got asked to cover Astronomy 211 this quarter, so I can come in here anytime under the guise of course planning."

Jerk, she thought, for letting her worry like that. Then again, he had invited her to a private planetarium show, so he wasn't all bad.

In the middle of the center row, they popped the caps off their beer bottles and leaned back in the comfy chairs. The dome lit up with a 3-D map of the universe while the speakers vibrated with Neil deGrasse Tyson's deep tones, and even though it wasn't at all how Cass had expected the night to go, it was pretty great. Just as well then that Maya had gotten stuck at work. If she'd come to the potluck, Cass doubted Matthew would have proposed ducking out early. But some woman caught up in the messy, often dangerous process of becoming a mother had needed help, so Maya had stayed late as she often did.

The space show was in an instrumental section, images from NASA's Saturn probe, Cassini, playing overhead in black and white, when Matthew said, "Cass."

"Yeah?" She didn't look away from the video feed of Saturn's hexagon-shaped cloud system. Really, how did such a geometrically perfect object exist in nature?

"Be careful with Eva DeMarco," her brother said.

Now she looked at him, taking in the serious angle of his eyebrows. "What do you mean?"

"It's not my story to tell. Just, trust me, okay?"

"There's nothing to worry about," Cass assured him. "I'm only here for a few more months. Besides, she's a professor and I'm a grad student. We're not actually allowed to hang out." She didn't mention Alexis. No one seemed to know about her, and Cass wasn't about to out Eva, not even to her brother.

Matthew waved a hand. "You know that policy is meant to prevent sexual harassment and power imbalances. Relationships between professors and grad students are a time-honored tradition. Just, not her, okay?"

Before Cass could reassure him that she had zero intention of getting involved with anyone at Edmonds, the narration resumed, drawing her attention back to the dome. As an animation showed the Cassini probe's Grand Finale, the spacecraft's suicide descent into Saturn's atmosphere, Cass forgot about Eva DeMarco and other earthly conundrums. This was compelling entertainment, watching the NASA folks who had worked on the same project for two full decades tearing up as they witnessed the purposeful destruction of the machine they had shaped their careers around.

It wasn't until later, after she and Matthew had returned home and chatted with Maya about college gossip and the latest obstetrics case, after she had made the brief walk to her apartment in her brother's detached garage and settled in for the evening, that she remembered Matthew's cryptic warning. Ben was a friend of his. Was Matthew simply referring to the messy end of Eva and Ben's marriage? Either way, it wasn't any of Cass's business. She had come to Seattle to get her life back together; she couldn't afford to get distracted at this stage of the game.

The last few years had been challenging, it was fair to say. First, she'd been laid off from the tech firm she'd worked at since moving to San Francisco. Then she'd blown her shoulder and had to quit the All Blues, her pro rugby side, in what was looking more and more like a permanent end to her playing career. At least she'd had COBRA to cover her medical costs. Otherwise she would have been considerably worse off. But even so, with the dissolution of her longest-term relationship since college following close on the heels of her injury, she'd been only too happy to take the coaching gig at Edmonds, especially when Matthew offered to help her get into graduate school. Not only had being here allowed her to rehab her shoulder and enjoy some quality time with her brother and Maya, it had also, as a plus, gotten their parents off her back. A Master's might not compare to a PhD, but it was a graduate degree. Hopefully they would finally stop dropping hints about her failure to live up to the family name.

Their expectations were a bit unreasonable, Cass had always thought. Fewer than ten percent of Americans earned graduate degrees, for Christ's sake. At least Matthew had never bugged her about education. That was why she hadn't hesitated before accepting his invitation to live in his garage while nursing her assorted wounds. And in fact, it had been lovely to hang out with him and Maya again, especially now that he wasn't in grad school. The fact that she was helping them out financially by renting out their garage apartment only made the whole endeavor more palatable. Her presence in Edmonds had come with an expiration date, though. As soon as she finished her coursework in winter quarter, she would be heading back to the Bay Area to look for a job while she finished writing her thesis.

Despite this longstanding plan, none of her California friends seemed to believe she would return. Boone, her best friend from the All Blues, had said to her during a video chat recently, "You're totally going to fall in love with some girl up there and stay, I can feel it. You're never coming back to the Bay Area, are you?"

"Of course I'm coming back," she'd replied, forcing herself to sound positive. "Seattle is temporary. My real life is there."

That may have been the case when she'd left Oakland the previous summer, but was it still true now? She wasn't sure anymore. Recently, she'd felt happier in Edmonds than she could ever remember being in California, but that was probably because Matthew and Maya lived here, too. Besides, the life she had built in the Bay Area had essentially crumbled around her, so it wasn't a fair comparison. She might prefer forests and mountains to cities, but Western Washington simply wasn't her style.

Whenever she said that in Maya's earshot, her sister-in-law would tease her, "Oh, so you're too cool for this school, huh?"

And she would reply, "Basically," while dodging her brother's attempt to flick her as hard as he could.

It wasn't that she was too cool, though. It was more that she'd grown up in the suburbs and had fought hard to escape her hometown's judgmental, closed-minded attitude. Edmonds didn't have anything close to a vibrant queer community, and while downtown Seattle was only a half hour away, Cass was too busy with school and rugby for anything but an occasional night in the city. Then again, she would be done with school soon, which would give her more time to explore Seattle and its surroundings. This past summer had been awesome, working normal hours on campus during the week and taking weekend ferry rides to the Peninsula or camping out on the flanks of Mount Rainier with her brother and Maya, who were still learning their way around Washington, too. The Pacific Northwest was as beautiful as Matthew and Maya had promised. There was nothing to say she couldn't stick around spring quarter or possibly even a little longer to experience more of what the area had to offer.

An image of Eva DeMarco standing atop a rocky outcrop, the Cascade Mountains or possibly the Olympics stretching green and white behind her, flashed into Cass's mind. Resolutely, she pushed it away. If she was going to return to her old life stronger and healthier, her mojo and her shoulder both fully restored, she didn't need to be thinking about a woman who was not only already taken but also a dozen different kinds of wrong. The last thing either of them needed was a messy affair.

Assuming someone like Eva would even be interested in her. And that, Cass thought as she opened Twitter for one last pre-bedtime scroll, was an awfully large assumption.

CHAPTER THREE

Eva loved her office. Old Main, with its classic Renaissance Revival style and ivy-covered brick facade, was the iconic face of Edmonds University. As the oldest building on the Frederick Law Olmsted campus, it had housed classrooms and administrative offices since the university's founding as a normal school in the 1870s. For Washington State, Edmonds U was practically ancient. That was one of the things Eva loved about the school. She had grown up in the Northeast, where cobbled streets, Gothic architecture, and other remnants of the eighteenth century were commonplace. The Northwest, meanwhile, was strip malls and bungalows, conspicuous design and industrial neighborhoods, rustic decor and misappropriated native art. To her, the university felt like an island in an ocean of clashing construction.

Not that the campus didn't have its own share of mismatched buildings. It had been around long enough to collect an assortment of Renaissance-style edifices with the occasional sleek, glass-walled structure juxtaposed against a Gothic tower. The sometimes eclectic architecture reflected the school's changing focus over the decades. Ed U, as the locals called it, may have started out as a seminary to educate teachers, but by now most of the departments on campus looked down their noses at the School of Education. Education was not considered a "truly academic" field of study the way history and literature, chemistry and physics were. The same could be said of sociology. Like education, Eva's chosen field occupied a gray area in the academy. That was the real reason she and her colleagues had been marooned on the fourth floor of Old Main, where the air conditioning was flaky and some of the classroom windows hadn't been cleaned in years. But Eva didn't mind. She wouldn't have liked the industrial architecture of the art building, or the modern glass and concrete slickness of the biology and chemistry buildings, connected by an intricate walkway designed to resemble DNA and RNA chains.

When she'd first considered extending her leave the previous year, she'd checked to see if Steve would give away her office. The room on the fourth floor of Old Main might be small, but it faced the arboretum to the east and received abundant sunlight—when there was sunlight to be had. In Western Washington, sunbreaks were nowhere near as plentiful as Eva was used to after decades on the East Coast.

"Of course I won't give your office away," the dean had promised, gazing at her across the conference table in his spacious suite in College Hall, the lines of his face arranged in the familiar expression of sympathy she had grown to both appreciate and detest. "It's here when you're ready to return, and so is your position."

He hadn't been dean of the College of Arts and Sciences for very long. Otherwise, he might well have given away both her office and her position. The state and federal medical leave acts had only protected her for six months. Mostly, she knew, she had Steve Henry, "the man with two first names" as she, Ben, and Tina had always jokingly referred to him, to thank for the university extending her leave as long as they had.

Today, though, instead of the pleasure she usually took in climbing the creaky stairs to her floor, each step felt almost shaky, as if her nervousness had somehow spread to the building. Her customary beginning of the year jitters felt more intense this time around. She'd always loved teaching, even as a lowly graduate student tasked with grading the huge introductory sociology courses at New York University. But the last couple of years had changed her so much that now she wondered if any of her former self had survived. Did teaching rely on muscle memory? Would it come back as easily as pedaling a bicycle did? She wouldn't know until she actually stood in front of her first class the following morning, and that was the unnerving part.

As she made her way along the wide, high-ceilinged hallway, she clutched her bag tightly, squinting in the near distance. There.

A figure in black jeans and a gray collared shirt stood outside her office, arms folded, gaze fixed on the nearby notice board. Like the hallway, it too was almost empty, but soon enough it would be besieged with brightly colored notices of environmental club meetings, scholarship notices, and international travel opportunities, oh my.

As Eva approached, the dark-clad person turned and smiled at her. Cass, early for their meeting. Eva tried to catch her breath—from climbing four flights of stairs, not from the prospect of spending the next untold minutes with Cassidy Trane. Her horror at discovering that the attractive woman from the Thistledown was in fact a student from her own department had abated somewhat since the potluck, but it still lingered in the back of her mind.

"Eva," Cass said. "Good morning."

Her cheeks were pink, her hair swept back in a casual style that Eva imagined either took two minutes or two hours to get just right. With her sleeves rolled up to the elbow, she seemed ready to tackle the day. Eva was a morning person herself, but she was accustomed to academic types who had picked their line of work not only for the chance to be immersed in their intellectual passions but also because the hours were, frankly, attractive. Then again, Cass was probably used to early morning workouts. Eva didn't imagine that the women's rugby club team had much sway when it came to scheduling practice times.

"Good morning," she replied, and smiled briefly before focusing on her door lock. Like the rest of the building, it was ancient and mysterious. The trick to turning the reluctant mechanism seemed to shift weekly. She inserted her key and jiggled it for a good ten seconds, keenly aware of Cass looking on. But the other woman didn't say anything, and Eva was grateful. Ben would have taken the key from her with an impatient huff, certain he could do a better, faster job. Usually, he could.

At last the lock succumbed to her ministrations, and the door swung open. The mingled scent of lemon, lavender, and books greeted her, and she paused in the doorway to breathe it in. She still couldn't believe sometimes that this was her life, that she actually got to do what she loved best—teaching—while studying whatever academic puzzle captured her interest.

Behind her, Cass waited quietly, as if sensing her happiness tinged with mild terror at returning to start a new quarter after such a long leave. *Happiness*—there had been a time when even her office in Old Main hadn't made a dent in the pain and rage spiraling through her, bringing her down, down, so far down. But she knew her own strength now, and that, she had decided, was the silver lining in the storm cloud that had temporarily swallowed her.

"Come on in," she said, waving Cass forward. "Thanks for making time for me this morning. I tried to follow the instructions in your email, but alas, I am definitely not the technical type. That's why I have a Mac."

Cass stopped inside the door, glancing around the small space. "A Mac? In that case, I might need your help navigating. I'm a PC woman myself."

She'd called herself a woman. Okay. Eva hadn't wanted to make assumptions about her gender identity given the way Cass presented, but there'd been no obvious opportunity to ask about pronoun preferences. At least Eva wouldn't have one more thing to trip over. She very much wanted to respect other people's gender identities, but she was still getting used to employing they/them as a singular. After a year of being either mostly alone or with people her mother's age—other than her regular Saturday movie nights at the Hammond-Nakamura residence—she was definitely rusty.

Eva pulled her spare office chair up to the desk and motioned Cass into it. "Do you need my password?"

Cass settled on the hard-backed chair that Eva had liberated from a classroom her first year at Edmonds. "No, you'll be doing most of the typing. I find that people usually retain things better if I talk them through the motions." She paused while Eva sat down beside her on the padded swivel chair. "Besides, you're not supposed to give out your password, Professor. Don't you read your Edmonds Tech Committee minutes?"

As she turned the computer on, Eva willed away her blush at Cass's teasing tone. "Only if I absolutely have to."

"I'm shocked," Cass said.

"No, you're not."

"No, I'm not."

A moment later, the home screen flickered into view. Eva

logged on, and Cass began to explain the mysterious ways of the university's website. While she might not know her way around a Mac, Cass appeared to be accomplished at simplifying the steps needed to navigate Edmonds's new content management system. Eva had no idea what a Drupal module was, but Cass's clear explanation and insistence that Eva take notes on important processes—like how to update her biography, CV, and the list of publications on her department profile—meant she didn't need to.

Only fifteen minutes later, Eva's profile had been updated, her personal page was populated with her fall quarter teaching and office hours schedule, and Cass had even managed to link her Canvas and Drupal modules. Whatever that meant. Probably Eva should have listened more closely to why that was important, but it wasn't her fault that Cass smelled like vanilla, or that her skin emanated the sort of warmth that Eva wanted to sink into, or that in the light from the window, Cass's eyes were even more bewitching than the night they'd met.

Eva closed her eyes briefly, remembering that she had all but accused the woman beside her—the *student* beside her—of trying to get into her pants. She had also made up a girlfriend, but that was easy enough to fix. In fact, as soon as they were done, she would whip out the awkward semi-apology she had practiced on her way to campus, one that didn't include admitting in any way, shape, or form how attractive she found Cass.

"So that should do it," Cass said, her voice rising at the end in a slight question.

Eva snapped her eyes open and smiled weakly. Jesus, she needed to get a grip here. Alexis was right. She had been a shut-in for far too long.

"Hey, you!" As if she had been magically conjured, Alexis chose that moment to appear in the doorway, her easy greeting breaking off as she stopped and stared. "I'm sorry, am I interrupting something...?"

"No!" Eva said way too forcefully, and scrambled to her feet. Her decision to not tell Alexis about Cass's presence at the potluck was returning to bite her in the butt—as it was always, she could now see, going to do. "Cass here was just helping me with my university accounts. We're done, aren't we?" she added, swinging back to Cass.

"Yeah, we should be." Cass rose and smiled at Alexis, extending her hand. "Hello again. Alexis, right?"

Alexis stepped farther into the small room and shook Cass's hand, a shit-eating grin hiding just out of sight, Eva could tell. "That's right. It's nice to see you again, *Cass*." She shot Eva a veiled look that let her know she had a serious amount of explaining to do.

Normally, Eva loved it when Alexis stopped by, especially this week when she could use all the support she could get. Right now, though, she was questioning that aspect of their friendship.

"So do you work on campus, too?" Cass asked.

"Not this campus. I teach at U-Dub. I was just swinging by to drop off Eva's favorite Northwest treat." She held up a small box decorated with the pink and brown Cupcake Royale logo.

How had Eva failed to notice this all-important item? The shop around the corner from Alexis's house in Madrona made a salted caramel cupcake to die for.

"What do you teach?" Cass asked, her brow slightly furrowed.

"Sociology," Alexis said, as if she were stating the obvious. Her eyes flew to Eva, full of silent questions.

"Is that how you guys met?"

"Yes. We met in grad school," Eva said, hoping her own look told Alexis to let her do the talking.

"NYU, right?" As both women looked at her, Cass gestured toward the huge Mac on the small desk. "It's on your profile."

"Oh, right. My profile."

Alexis lifted her eyebrows at Eva and tilted her head toward Cass with an easily interpreted non-verbal exhortation. She was right, of course. This would be the perfect opportunity to resolve the misunderstanding Eva had prevaricated the night they met. She could explain that she had invented a fake girlfriend to extricate herself from an embarrassing social situation, reference a research point on the prevalence of lying among strangers, and they could all laugh it off. More importantly, they could move on with their lives and never again speak of The Dread Thistledown Incident. The speech Eva had rehearsed, however, was not something she wanted to have an audience for. Bad enough Cass would have to hear it.

Cass's phone buzzed. "Excuse me," she said, and headed out into the hall where Eva could see her typing rapidly with her thumbs.

Unfortunately, she could also see Alexis in the foreground staring at her, eyebrows still raised in another easy-to-read demand: *What the freaking hell?* Eva ignored her, choosing instead to watch Cass pocket her phone and return to the office that had never felt quite this small.

"Everything all right?" Alexis enquired.

"Yeah. Surprisingly, the English Department skews more Luddite than technical. I should probably head over there."

"Not before you try a cupcake," Alexis announced, opening the box and holding it out to her. "There's salted caramel, triple chocolate, and red velvet."

"That's kind of you, but I shouldn't," Cass said, her avid stare fixed on the box belying her words.

"Come on," Alexis said, smiling. "If you don't take one, then one of us will have to eat two…"

"Really," Eva added, nodding. "You'll be doing us a favor. The last thing I need today is two cupcakes."

"Well, in that case…"

Cass's gaze seemed to linger on Eva a tad too long before she reached into the cupcake box. Eva watched to see which pastry she would claim and almost sighed in relief. Red velvet. The perfect choice because Alexis was a chocolate connoisseur and even Cass's adorable dimple wouldn't have saved her if she'd dared to steal— *ahem*, if she'd chosen the salted caramel.

Eva watched as Cass bit into the cupcake, vanilla frosting and tiny red and white sprinkles adorning her lips before she licked them away. And, right. Eva looked back at the box in Alexis's hands, trying to blot out the image of Cass's mouth.

"Oh my god, this cupcake is *amazing*," Cass said.

Okay, but was that slightly breathless hitch in her voice really necessary? Eva reached into the box and selected her own cupcake, hoping the salty sweetness would be enough to distract her from untoward thoughts.

"Told you," Alexis said smugly around a bite of the triple chocolate.

"Seriously," Cass said as she glanced between them. "How do you guys not weigh like a thousand pounds?"

"Willpower," Alexis said.

Something Eva needed to work on developing more of herself.

"I have to run," Cass said a little while later, still licking cupcake crumbs and icing from her fingers. "But thanks. I think that cupcake made my day."

"Glad to be of service," Alexis said with a typically nerdy bow.

"Thanks again for the computer help," Eva added, smiling. Then she held up a hand to her mouth, remembering that she probably had chocolate crumbs in her teeth.

"You're welcome," Cass said, her own smile warm. She glanced at Alexis as she moved toward the door. "And nice seeing you again, Dr....?"

"Hammond. But please, call me Alexis," she added. "I hope we meet again."

"So do I." Cass turned away, but then she paused in the doorway. "Actually, if you guys aren't doing anything next Saturday, we have our home opener against Portland U. It's a double header with the men's team, and it would be nice to have a crowd for the women's match. Besides, there's usually a pretty decent community showing at our matches."

It took Eva a moment to realize that she meant the LGBTQIA community. Another opportunity to right that wrong impression...

"We'll be there," Alexis promised.

"Awesome. Good luck with classes tomorrow, Eva. Let me know if you need any help."

"I will," she said, ignoring Alexis's *I bet you will* snort that she prayed only reached her ears.

With a final smile, Cass left the office, her shoes squeaking against the newly polished floor that Eva knew would lose its sheen as soon as the student body returned to campus in full force.

Not that she should be thinking of any student's body.

As Cass's footsteps faded, Alexis turned on Eva, her delighted grin finally escaping. "Um, hello? Do you perchance have some news to share? Something to do with, oh, I don't know, the hot woman from the bar hanging out in your office?"

Eva slumped in her ridiculously expensive ergonomic chair and expelled a long breath. "I was going to tell you…"

"No, you weren't," Alexis interrupted, laughing, "or you totally would have! What was she doing here? Spill immediately or I am no longer your best friend."

"Lex," she whined, peeking up from under her lashes.

"Nuh-uh, missy," Alexis said, dropping onto the small love seat near the window. "That look doesn't work on me. Now give me the dirt, or I won't ever bring you cupcakes again."

Cupcake deliveries were nothing to joke about. Eva straightened in her seat. "Fine. Remember the department potluck you cancelled on last minute?"

"No! She was there?"

"Yep." Eva shared the story, leaving out the part about Cass's brother apparently figuring out how they had met. The less said about that, the better.

"Carly has such bad timing!" Alexis exclaimed when she'd finished. Her stepdaughter had picked the previous weekend to request Alexis's help for the first time ever in their relationship. True, it had been for academic assistance on a project she'd left until the last minute, but who didn't procrastinate?

Well, Alexis, actually. And Eva. That was one of the things they'd bonded over in graduate school—completing projects on time. Or, you know, early.

"Now it all makes sense," Alexis said. "She really did think you looked familiar that night, didn't she?"

"It would appear so."

"Correct me if I'm wrong, but it would also appear that she still thinks you and I are a couple. Why haven't you told her we're not?"

"I was just about to when you showed up with your stupid cupcakes," Eva groused.

"How dare you. Cupcake Royale cupcakes are not stupid!"

"Fine, I take it back."

"Good." Alexis cradled the meager remnants of her cupcake. "I would never let anyone besmirch your name, *mon petit chocolat.*"

Accustomed to her best friend's weirdness, Eva brought the conversation back to her own disaster of a life. "I still can't believe I flirted with a student. In my department, no less."

"Are you kidding? This is perfect."

"How is me making a fool of myself with a student perfect, Lex?"

"You didn't make a fool of yourself. Although you have carried the fake girlfriend bit a tad too far. But even with that minor hiccup, the big picture is nearly ideal."

Eva stared at her. "What are you even talking about?"

"Hear me out. We've got several tropes going on here," Alexis said in her excited researcher voice, and started to tick them off on her fingers. "The meet cute, check. Forbidden relationship, check. The jock and the nerd—"

"Lex!" Eva was not generally a violent person, but she slapped her friend on the arm. "My life is not a series of tropes! Jesus. I never thought I'd have to say this to you, but you've read too many romance novels."

Alexis pushed up her glasses. "Very funny. But come on. This is kismet at work, Eva. Can't you feel it?"

The thought might have occurred to her once the shock of seeing Cass at the potluck had worn off. But: "Even if she was interested, I can't risk getting involved with a student. The dean and my chair have been incredibly understanding, but as you know, I was supposed to have my tenure review last year. That means I have to be on perfect behavior this year."

Alexis waved a hand. "She's interested. Trust me."

"Why, because you're such an expert on lady love?"

"I have queer friends!"

"Name one."

"You."

Eva scoffed. "I meant queer friends in actual queer relationships."

"Tom and Angelo." At Eva's skeptical eyebrow, she added, "They're neighbors. You don't know them."

"Neighbors? Let me guess. They're middle-aged tech executives with teenage twins."

Alexis's eyes widened. "How did you know that?"

"Seattle demographics, my friend. And unlike you, I actually am queer. But whether or not Cass would ever think of me that way, it wouldn't work. She's a grad student, which means she probably has no intention of staying in Edmonds."

"I'm not saying you should marry the woman," Alexis said. "In all honesty, a short and sweet affair might be just what you need."

"Alexis!" Eva felt her cheeks warm. "I don't do short and sweet affairs, especially not with students when I'm under tenure review!"

"There's always a first for everything. Besides, I still think you're taking the student thing out of context. She's not in one of your classes, and she's what, twenty-nine or thirty?"

Eva shrugged as if she hadn't abused her Banner access only the day before and looked up Cass's date of birth in the university database. She'd turned 31 on the 14th of July—Bastille Day.

"And you're not advising her thesis, are you?" Alexis pressed.

"You know I'm not advising anyone's thesis right now."

"Then seriously, the rules don't apply here."

Eva sighed. "Lex, I need you to listen to me. Can you do that? Because I cannot risk getting involved with Cassidy Trane, and it would be great if you could support me on this."

Alexis stared at her for a long moment, and then, at last, she capitulated. "All right. I hear you, and I support whatever you choose. You know that."

Eva did know that. In fact, she was absurdly grateful for Alexis's support over the past few years. Without her best friend showing up to drag her out of bed at times and merely out of the house at others, Eva wasn't sure she would be back at work now—or, possibly, ever. It sounded dramatic, and Eva normally wasn't about the drama, but Alexis had remained at her side throughout the Series of Unfortunate Events, as Eva darkly referred to the occurrences that had recently beset her. Ben, meanwhile, hadn't known what to do with her grief, a fact that irritated Alexis to no end. That was why even though Eva had let go of her marriage with both hands, Alexis was still harboring what amounted to a sizable grudge.

Which, if Eva was being honest, was fine with her.

"Thank you," Eva said, and rose, pulling Alexis up and into a hug. Her friend melted against her with a surprised laugh. "See? I do appreciate you, even if you did somehow manage to turn me into a hugger."

"It wasn't easy," Alexis allowed. "I swear, you are the literal definition of a WASP."

"Hey! My people are Episcopalian, not Protestant."

"Oh, sweetie." Alexis pulled back and patted her cheek. "Those are the same thing. So. It turns out I have the morning free. Any chance I could convince you to go over the latest round of *Trollops* edits Penelope sent?"

Penelope Graves and Tristan Van der Streek were co-editing the book Eva and Alexis were writing a chapter for, *The Romance Novel in the Academy: Tropes, Trollops, and the Rhetoric of Romance*. Their own chapter title was *Romancing the Canon: Pride, Prejudice, and Patriarchy in the Denigration of Women's Fiction*. They had advocated for a different subtitle—*The Phallus-y of Pride and Prejudice in the Denigration of Women's Fiction*—but in the end Penelope and Tristan had rejected it. Eva and Alexis still referred to the chapter as "*Phallus-y*," and one or both of them would likely find a way to include the original working title in an interview or conference panel. As Alexis liked to say, you couldn't keep a good subtitle down.

Eva started to calculate how much time she would need to get ready for the two classes she was scheduled to teach this quarter, "Research Methods: Design" and "The Sociology of Popular Culture." Then she stopped. She had been mostly ready for both classes to start for weeks now.

"I believe I could be persuaded," she told Alexis, wiggling her eyebrows suggestively.

"You are such a nerd."

"Hello, Pot. Kettle here."

"You know you just made my point, right?"

Eva opened the desk drawer that contained her special stash of red pens. She was a pen snob, Ben used to say. She only used Pilot gel rollers, a fact that Alexis, also a self-professed pen snob, claimed to appreciate.

Soon they were seated side by side on the love seat that took up most of one wall, matching chapter print-outs on their laps. Eva tapped her red pen against her thigh as she read through the comments Penelope had forwarded them from the requisite three peer reviewers. Writing an academic book chapter was nearly as complicated as taking part in a College of Arts and Sciences curriculum development meeting: difficult to get anyone to agree about anything. Penelope and Tristan had already asked for two rounds of edits, and now the peer reviewers were basically infighting amongst themselves. Eva could genuinely say she had not missed being forced to submit to consensus decision-making during her unofficial sabbatical.

And yet, despite the final editing hoops they were currently maneuvering through, Eva was excited about this book. Romance novels, which consistently sold more copies than any other type of fiction, constituted the only genre written, edited, published, and read predominantly by women. At the same time, it was the genre most derided by critics and other readers, the lone genre whose audience's intelligence and ability to separate fantasy from reality were regularly maligned. Eva was a trained sociologist and a long-time feminist, and even she had fallen prey to those cultural assumptions.

Like Eva, Alexis had started her career focused on an acceptably academic research interest. Her doctoral thesis on the immigrant experience in the urban north had been rock-star quality, and a follow-up book on the American-born children of immigrants had earned her tenure at 34. But while Steve had supported Eva's shift in research interests almost from the start, Alexis had said more than once that her dean probably would have tossed her out on her ear if he could. As the lone black woman in her department, she should be studying the school-to-prison pipeline, he'd lectured her more than once. Or the impact of American slavery on the splintering of contemporary African American families. And so on and so forth, never recognizing his own racial bias.

Beside her, Alexis nudged her and pointed at a comment that took up three quarters of the margin. "Is this guy serious with his 'readers shouldn't be encouraged to fantasize about a hero they would put a restraining order on in real life' bullshit?"

"I know, right?" Eva said. "It's like he's not comfortable with women fantasizing about men who are fundamentally unlike him."

They exchanged a look, a matching smile starting at the corners of their mouths. "Fucking straight white men," they said in unison, shaking their heads. And then they turned back to the print-out, red gel roller pens held at ready.

Really, though, had Eva been any better in the beginning? It still made her wince to remember how she'd had the gall to lecture her therapist about why romance novels weren't worthy of the title *literature*.

"They're formulaic and overtly sentimental," she'd argued during that first session, parroting the criticism she'd absorbed at some unknown point. "And talk about predictable. Girl meets boy, girl loses boy, girl gets boy back, and they ride off into the sunset, happily ever after."

"I'm afraid I don't see what's 'wrong' with enjoying a fantasy that at its heart revolves around unconditional love and happy endings," Gayle had said. And then she'd moved in for the kill: "Have you ever read a romance novel, Eva?"

She'd hesitated before admitting, "No." As Gayle continued to stare at her, eyebrows raised, Eva had realized that she was holding onto a culturally-conditioned bias for no reason other than that it was familiar. Like a freshman in an intro sociology class who refuses to acknowledge their own racial bias, she was defending widespread attitudes about the value of romantic fiction without conducting her own research.

A week later during her second session with Gayle, she'd recognized another truth: "Romance novels are stigmatized." And then, unexpectedly, tears had sprung to her eyes. "Like…" She'd trailed off. Therapy sucked. Better to go through the world ignoring the hard things—or so her mother's side of the family had always counseled.

Gayle had handed her a box of tissues. "Like?"

Eva sniffled and hunched forward, a tissue clenched in one fist. "Like me."

"In what way?"

"A romance isn't really literature just like a woman who can't bear a child isn't really a woman."

"I know plenty of women who would disagree with both assertions."

"No, it's the culture asserting that, not me."

Gayle had looked at her over the top of her glasses, her voice gentle as she asked, "Are you sure about that, Eva?"

Later, Eva had slid into the passenger seat of Alexis's car and let herself be driven back to Edmonds, where Harvey was waiting alone in the house Ben had recently moved out of. She and Harvey weren't really alone, though. Alexis had appeared on their doorstep shortly before Eva's first therapy session, armed with a suitcase and Tosh's blessing to stay for as long as she needed to. A weekend had turned into a week and then into two despite Eva's attempts to kick her out. Alexis wasn't having any of that, not since Eva had admitted that she'd considered the idea of suicide. Theoretically only, you understand. Just an academic interest, a sort of *hmm, wonder how I would do it.* An entirely hypothetical question.

She would never actually take her own life, she'd tried to assure her friend. She was aware that suicide destroyed the lives of those left behind in a cruel ripple effect, one that she would never want to be responsible for. But whether or not her interest in the topic was anything more than academic, Alexis had given her the option of either (1) checking herself into a psychiatric unit for seventy-two hours; or (2) starting therapy, taking the pills her doctor had prescribed, and being babysat by her best friend for the indefinite future. Eva had chosen option two.

There was a reason, she'd soon learned, that people took anti-depressants to get through a bad patch. She'd never dreamed she would be one of those people, but in hindsight she was glad she had agreed to go on meds because within just a couple of weeks, the world had begun to regain some of its light and color. Not a lot, but enough that she could look back on the moment she'd considered the supposedly academic question of how she would go about ending her life and shudder at the darkness that had threatened her so guilelessly. Now, almost a year and a half later, she was drug-free and felt more resilient than ever. For that, she owed Alexis more than a heartfelt thank-you. Really, she'd often thought, she owed her friend her life.

Straightening on her office couch, Eva tried to refocus her thoughts. That was the flip side of building your career around a topic that was personally gratifying: Sometimes the political could become almost too personal.

"You okay?" Alexis asked beside her.

"Fine," Eva said, offering her a smile before turning back to the work at hand.

These days, she was pretty sure she meant it.

CHAPTER FOUR

The taste of red velvet cupcake was still sweet on her lips when Cass paused in the hallway not far from Eva's office and Googled "Alexis Hammond sociology." The first link led to an academic conference from two years earlier, but the second was pay dirt: Alexis's department profile on the University of Washington website. Cass read the text slowly, her brain only stumbling when she reached the final sentence: "Dr. Hammond lives in Seattle with her husband, the distinguished historian Dr. Toshishiro Nakamura, and his children."

Husband—what the hell? Alexis was married to someone other than her supposed girlfriend? Cass pocketed her phone and headed down Old Main's central stairway, trying to figure out how these three "distinguished" academics were involved. Could they really be in a polyamorous relationship? Stranger things had happened, but at the moment, she couldn't think of any. Maybe Alexis had left her husband for Eva recently, and her changed circumstances hadn't yet filtered onto her university profile. Or maybe they were having a secret affair. But people in secret affairs didn't usually go out in public together, and they certainly didn't announce their relationship to random strangers. Especially not to random strangers who claimed to possibly know them.

Another, far more embarrassing explanation occurred to her: Could Eva have pretended to have a girlfriend to get out of talking to her? Straight women did that kind of thing all the time, according to popular culture. If that was really what had happened that night…

Cass pushed the ground floor door open and practically ran

across campus to the Humanities Building, trying to put as much distance as possible between herself and the attractive professor who may or may not have made up a fake relationship to escape a conversation with her. Her ego had suffered a multitude of blows in the past few years, but this mess? This felt extreme even for her.

But even as she went about the rest of her work that morning—helping the English department untangle their permissions issues and attending an IT department meeting on Drupal security updates—thoughts of Eva and their encounter at the Thistledown kept popping into Cass's mind at odd moments. Like the way Eva had all but laughed at her parade of seemingly corny pick-up lines when that wasn't the impression Cass had intended to give at all. Really, was it her fault that cheesy straight dudes often pretended to know women in order to justify chatting them up? Then again, there was no denying that she had approached Eva because she didn't want to spend the rest of her life—or at least the next few months—wondering who the attractive, familiar-looking woman at the bar was. No denying, either, that she had been inordinately disappointed to learn Eva already had a girlfriend.

But was Alexis actually her girlfriend? If only Cass had simply told Eva that she was a grad student from the start, they could have avoided this drama. But she hadn't been thinking clearly that night, thanks to the number of beers she had consumed while trying to come up with a graceful way to dodge Amy, one of her closest friends in the Bay Area. Or former friend, possibly. Amy hadn't texted her back or otherwise responded to her overtures since flying back to California the day after she'd told Cass she wanted more than occasional benefits from their friendship. Cass had hated hurting Amy, but she didn't feel the same way. Now Eva, on the other hand...

Damn it.

Even exercise couldn't drive the pesky thoughts away entirely. She was working out on the ergometer before rugby practice that afternoon when she suddenly recalled the moment when Eva had crossed her legs and gazed up at her from beneath her lashes in a way that no straight woman would be caught doing in a lesbian bar. Eva had been flirting with her, Cass was almost certain. What did that mean, and why did Cass's brain suddenly seem so irritatingly intrigued by the fact that Eva might, in fact, be single?

Whatever, Cass grumbled inwardly as she laced up her turf shoes and headed out to the practice fields near the stadium. She had better things to think about than her currently pathetic romantic life. Like school, which was set to start in less than 24 hours. Hopefully the summer off hadn't made her forget all of her time-management skills. Her first month of classes the previous fall had not gone well. Not only had she been away from academics for nearly a decade, but the quarter system at Edmonds had taken some getting used to after attending college in the semester-centric Northeast. Without Matthew and Maya to keep her fed and caffeinated, she suspected she might have flunked out and returned to Oakland even more bruised and battered than when she'd left. But she'd doubled down and eventually remembered how to deal with academic pressure and expectations well enough to pass her first two classes. One B in grad school wouldn't kill her, she'd decided, even if her brother acted like she'd committed a heinous crime.

Once she'd made it through that first hellish quarter, the rest of the year had gone more smoothly. She'd resurrected some of her old dyslexia-busting study techniques from undergrad and had developed new strategies that took advantage of updated technology. One of the most amazing things to happen since she'd left Vassar was the development of special fonts for dyslexics that helped keep letters and words from spinning and rotating. Loading the fonts into her Kindle and word processing programs and adding the extension to Chrome had saved her hours upon hours of slower-paced reading, writing, and researching. Still, not all course texts were available on Kindle, and after a summer without homework, she would have to readjust all over again to the challenge of balancing coaching, her assistantship, and her classes.

For now, the rugby team deserved her full attention. As the starting hooker flubbed the second line-out in a row, Cass exchanged a look with Mike, the head coach. He nodded, and she clapped her hands to stop the drill. Time to earn her coaching stipend. Their opening match was a little over a week away, and it would be nice not to lose by thirty points like they had their final preseason scrimmage.

Fingers crossed.

***

Matthew poked the fire with a stick, scattering the hot coals. In early October, the days were still mostly warm but the nights had grown cooler. Soon the leaves on the few deciduous trees in the area would experience a brief, colorful death before being swept away almost immediately by the Pacific Northwest's autumnal winds.

Cass leaned back in her Adirondack chair, beer bottle in one hand and e-reader in the other. Thank god for e-book versions of textbooks. She could highlight and take notes so much more easily on her tablet, and also the content was *searchable*. That fact alone had been enough for her to chuck her physical textbooks and never look back.

Studying beside her brother's backyard fire pit took her back to their frequent childhood sojourns at the Nelson family cabin in the Catskills. Their mom's family was more low-key than the Trane side of the clan. Retired Hudson Valley school teachers, their grandparents had approached learning as something you did wherever you were, which made it immensely more fun for Cass. Even now, decades later, the smell of wood smoke still stimulated her brain, she felt certain.

"So, how are your classes shaping up, Cass?" Maya asked, her feet up on one of the rock ledges the three of them had built around the fire pit a few months earlier.

"Not bad." Cass pushed her hair off her forehead. She needed a haircut. Freaking short hair and its incessant maintenance requirements. She wished long hair didn't feel like dressing in drag.

"Not bad?" Matthew repeated, his attention refocusing on her. "Or not good?"

Cass managed not to roll her eyes. "Not bad, I said."

"Huh." He reached for a folder of papers on the log bench between them, his eyebrows lowered.

"They're fine," she said, somehow remaining calm even though he was telegraphing his thoughts practically in all caps. "Don't worry, Mattie. I got through Vassar, didn't I? And no one there ever knew I was lexiconic."

That was the code word they'd agreed on as kids to prevent other people from discovering that she, the child of Julia and

Theodore Trane, had a learning disability.

"Yeah, well, you've killed immeasurable numbers of brain cells since then, haven't you?" he countered.

It was true, she'd suffered more than one concussion in her decade of playing club, semi-pro, and professional rugby. "Maybe, but it was worth it. Rugby is the best sport on the planet."

"I think I've heard that before. But I meant from all the drinking."

Also true. At Vassar they'd made a point of partying into the wee hours with their weekend opponents. Later, when she'd played professionally, the teams always went out together afterward, heat of the match forgotten, to celebrate the sport they all loved and were lucky enough to get paid to play however briefly.

"Brain cells are overrated," she said. "I'm good, Matthew. Really."

"I still don't understand why you have to be so secretive. Dyslexia is nothing to be ashamed of. I have plenty of students who've taken advantage of the university's disability resources. I mean, that's what they're there for."

The word "disability" had always bothered Cass. Her mind wasn't worse off than anyone else's. It simply worked differently in a world designed for normative-functioning brains. She was fortunate that her parents had noticed her struggle with letters and words when she was still in early elementary school, and had gotten her the help she needed at a critical time in her intellectual development. That was what had allowed her to successfully navigate junior high and high school, the reason she had managed to earn her way into a school like Vassar and, later, to build a career in the technology sector. Not everyone in her situation received the level of support that she had, she knew. Maybe that was part of the reason she didn't feel comfortable asking for help now.

But mostly, she suspected, at some level she had never forgotten her parents' initial disappointment when she'd failed to read as early as Matthew had. Twins offered a built-in control baby—if one sibling failed to thrive in any area, the other child's benchmarks were readily observable. While Matthew had been traditionally book-smart, he was physically uncoordinated as a child. Cass, meanwhile, learned to read late but was always picked first for every team. As they'd grown older and more comfortable in their differences, they'd joked that together they made the perfect child. At some level, though, Cass knew that they both felt their individual failures keenly.

"We expect a lot out of you two," the Professors Trane had routinely lectured, "but we know you can handle it."

Cass hadn't always been so sure of that fact herself.

"I know you're just trying to help," she said now, sending her brother a sidelong look, "but honestly, Mattie, you don't have to worry about me. I can take care of myself."

He lifted his eyebrows, inclining his head toward the detached garage where she lived in his backyard, and she felt the old anger rising. Except she wasn't a child anymore. She didn't have to deal with the whispers at school or with their parents' disappointment, never hidden quite quickly enough.

"Leave it alone, Matthew," Maya said from the other side of the fire.

Matthew stared at her. So did Cass. Maya rarely stepped between the "effing Trane twins," as she (affectionately?) referred to them.

"Yeah, Matthew," Cass said after a moment. "Tell Mom you gave it the ole college try—*again*—but I'm just too stubborn to listen." It wasn't all that far from the truth, anyway.

"Sorry." He took a swig of beer and poked at the fire again. "I know, I'm an asshole."

"You are," she agreed, because it was simply a fact. "Mom and Dad don't control you anymore, man. That was always your problem—you never individuated completely." She purposely invoked the psychology term, knowing the effect it would have on her "hard science is the only science" brother.

"Right. That's my problem." He paused, and Cass could see him trying not to rise to the bait. But that's what siblings are for—pressing buttons most people don't even know exist. "You know social sciences are pseudo-science, right? Human beings and our social groupings are too varied to derive any sort of useful data points from simple actions."

"Oh, Matthew," Cass said, her voice faux sympathetic, "I wish you could wrap your brain around the whole point of the social sciences. We're not out there trying to infer hard data from the wildly divergent experiences of dissimilar individuals. We're simply trying to examine how certain populations interact given a particular set of environmental variables."

"But what does that even mean? Seriously, Cass, people are so complex that it's meaningless to try to make suppositions about their behavior when you have no idea why someone is acting the way they are! Unless you can read minds now, in which case sign me up."

"Social scientists don't have to read minds, not when we can parse behavior."

Matthew pretended to cough. "Bullshit."

Cass pretended to cough back. "Egotist."

From name-calling, the argument progressed in a predictable manner, which Cass was tempted to point out to her data-obsessed brother. He insisted that all human experience was unique and therefore unquantifiable, and she described patterns of observable behavior that explained, for example, how classrooms were often unfair to minority groups.

"The social sciences have actually helped guide educational policy nationwide—including at Edmonds," she reminded him.

"Education? You mean the department that can't agree on best practices for more than a few years at a time?" He shook his head. "You're making my point for me."

Sometimes he could be such an arrogant straight white boy that she wanted to pummel him. So, setting aside her beer bottle and e-reader, she did. They were both laughing, though, as they wrestled in the summer-browned grass beside the fire, and Cass felt good because even a couple of months earlier her shoulder wouldn't have been able to take such rough-housing. The air was cool and the fire warm and she and Matthew were together. He could be an entitled asshole, yes, but he was her brother. They had been together more than apart over the years, and if she was honest, living in his backyard was the closest she'd felt to home since she'd graduated from college. From womb to tomb, some twins joked.

Funny she'd thought of that phrase, actually, because at one point, she shoved her brother a little too hard and his sneaker heel fell into the ashes at the edge of the fire pit.

"Oh, shit!" he said, still laughing, the scent of melting rubber mingling with the wood smoke.

Maya was around the rock pit in a flash, her eyes hard like they'd been the one time Cass had visited her in the middle of an emergency at work. She was excellent in a crisis, they'd always agreed, and this time was no different. The semi-melted shoe came off quickly, and then Maya stepped back, shaking her head.

"You two," she said, her voice a mix of affection and exasperation. "I swear to god, you are such children."

Apparently assured they were both unharmed, she returned to her camp chair where she sat gazing across the flames with a smile Cass wasn't sure she'd ever seen, hand on her belly, eyes on Matthew far more gentle than Cass was used to. *You're such children*, echoed in Cass's mind, and she blinked as the puzzle pieces clicked into place. That was why Maya had seemed so tired lately, why she'd looked so pale, why Matthew seemed almost to be walking on eggshells around her.

"Holy shit, you guys!" Cass shouted, rocketing to her feet. "Are you kidding me?"

Maya stared at her, beatific smile frozen. "Sorry, what?"

"The baby," Cass said impatiently, rounding the fire to kneel down and place her hand over Maya's. "How long have you known? When is it due? Oh my god, have you told Mom and Dad yet?"

Maya glanced at Matthew, who only laughed. "Don't look at me. I told you twin telepathy was an actual thing."

She was right, then. She was going to be an aunt. *Aunt Cassidy.* She liked the sound of it more than she would have expected.

"I'm only eight weeks along," Maya told her, "and we weren't planning to tell anyone until after the first trimester. *Capiche*, Cassidy Anne?"

Maya only invoked middle names when she was super serious. Cass nodded, aiming for solemn. "*Capiche*. Your secret is safe with me."

"Better be," Matthew said, but he was grinning as he came around the fire to pull her into his arms.

"You guys! This is so exciting!" she all but squealed against her brother's hair, his stubble rubbing against her cheek.

"I know!" he agreed, arms tightening for a moment almost painfully.

"Wait." She pulled back and glanced between them. "You're not having twins, are you?"

"No," Maya said vehemently. "Thank god. I mean, no offense."

"None taken," the Trane twins said in unison, and laughed.

Twin parenting was not for the faint of heart, their parents had always said. Privately, Cass believed that any foray into parenting required nerves of steel, but then she hadn't spent much time around babies. As a child when she'd pictured her future, she'd imagined herself living in a cabin in the woods on her own, far from other human beings. But as she'd grown up, she'd realized that being a genderqueer lesbian didn't necessarily mean a lifetime sentence of solitude. With reproductive technology and recent legal advances, she could aspire to the bourgeois ideals of marriage and parenthood as much as any straight person. But was she mature enough, unselfish enough, wise enough to raise a kid? She watched her brother lean down and kiss his wife, both of their hands pressed over the gentle swell of her belly. If they could do it, she probably could, too.

As she lay in bed that night ignoring her homework to read instead about her future niece or nephew's current development— at eight weeks, the average fetus is about the size of a kidney bean, almost an inch long and nearly an eighth of an ounce—she tried to imagine what the child would look like, who s/he would take after. Would they be smart and strong or nerdy and bookish, or all four qualities at once? Was nature or nurture more of an impact on a growing human being? Cass hoped she would be the cool aunt, the one her niece or nephew turned to when their parents were behaving unreasonably. But for that to be the case, wouldn't she have to be around her brother's kid more than once or twice a year? Maya had told her the projected due date was the middle of May. If Cass stuck to her original plan, she would be gone long before the baby arrived.

Maybe she should stay for the spring quarter, she thought for the second time in as many weeks as she traced the image of the bean-sized fetus on her tablet screen. Mike had let her know she had a job as his assistant for as long as she wanted, and Steve already had the funding earmarked to extend her graduate assistantship. Matthew and Maya were useless when it came to cooking, so if she left, they would probably subsist on pasta and take-out, which couldn't be good for a nursing mom. Besides, it might be fun to be in Edmonds in the spring with no academic requirements other than completing her thesis. Trying to write and revise fifty pages of academic text would probably present a challenge if she did return early to California and life among her friends, most of whom would rather compare favorite cocktail recipes and summer music festival plans than debate methods for combatting the high rate of homelessness among queer youth. Plus, if she did stay, maybe she and Eva—

Resolutely, she cut off the thought. Eva either had a girlfriend or had lied about having a girlfriend. Whichever the case might be, Cass would do better to keep her distance.

She pushed any potential lying liars from her mind and clicked through assorted BabyCenter.com pages. From the stories Maya routinely brought home from the hospital, Cass knew that pregnancy and childbirth weren't easy. And what about after the baby was born? The Professors Trane certainly wouldn't be dropping everything to become doting grandparents, and Maya's mom, who was only 53, didn't have the means or desire to retire early from her work as a speech therapist in Southern California. Maya's younger sisters were still in LA, too, working their way through school just as Maya had done. Cass was the only family member who didn't have an immediate job, lease, or mortgage commitment looming on the horizon.

Could she really go back to the Bay Area and resume her hipster techie lifestyle while Matthew and Maya raised an actual human being without family support? There was nothing to say she couldn't stay and help them through the first difficult bit. San Francisco wasn't going anywhere—except possibly into the Pacific Ocean, worst case doomsday scenario. Once the baby was older, she could always go back to California then, assuming it still existed.

Either way, she didn't have to decide right now, Cass told herself as she started a video that showed the development of a baby from conception through week nine. Growing an actual human being took a while. Besides, for all she knew, Matthew and

Maya might want to be on their own for the beginning of their parenthood adventure.

"A sesame seed?" she said aloud a moment later, shaking her head at her tablet.

What was it with comparing fetuses to food? It felt like some sort of creepy, cultural throwback to the Grimm brothers, the German siblings who had authored the least appropriate children's stories ever. She would bet there was a doctoral thesis somewhere in the academic ether that analyzed just such a connection. As soon as the video ended—wait, now the baby was being compared to a *grape?*—she would totally have to look for it.

***

Cass wasn't entirely sure when Eva had arrived at the stadium. One moment Maya and Matthew had been cheering by themselves in a half-empty row, and the next Eva was there beside Maya looking sporty in a baseball cap and Edmonds U hoodie, smiling and nodding as Cass's sister-in-law gestured toward the playing field.

"Get on the Trane!" Matthew called, grinning down at her from the stands.

She grinned back, and then felt her breath catch ridiculously as Eva's gaze appeared to follow Matthew's and landed squarely on her. They stared at each other, separated by fifteen rows and a smattering of fans, and then Eva smiled slightly and offered a hesitant wave. Cass nodded and turned back to the field, barely noticing the turnover the visiting team forced right in front of her. Eva had actually come to their match. That was… unexpected.

With difficulty, Cass managed to get her head back in the game, sharing strategies and tips with the girls who came off the pitch and patching up cuts and bruises as needed. She left the more active coaching to Mike, though she was happy to give her opinion anytime he asked. He liked to say that their real work was done at practice. On game day, it was up to the players to take what they had been taught and put it into play.

Despite losing a talented group of seniors the previous year, the current Edmonds team still had a handful of players who were quite strong. Brittany, a former soccer player, was a speedy back capable of juking her defenders so hard they fell over. Taffy, their forwards captain, wouldn't have been out of place on a college football field. She didn't need a helmet or pads, though. She simply put on her fiercest game face and bowled over anyone who got in her way. Still, without fifteen solid players on the pitch, the team could only hope to do so well.

Portland U, fortunately, was in the same position. The lead changed no fewer than six times over the course of the afternoon, an emotional roller coaster that Cass and Mike tried to propel their players through. But with Edmonds down by two with three minutes to go, a costly turnover meant that Portland U was poised for victory.

"Let's go, Golden Eagles! The game isn't over until the final whistle blows!" Mike exhorted from the sideline.

As his words hung in the air, Cass watched the tired players straighten their shoulders, chins lifting in renewed determination. She exchanged a look with Mike. Maybe they could do this, after all.

"Play until the final whistle!" Jaelin, their best fly-half, shouted as Edmonds set up to defend.

Portland drove down, advancing steadily—until, with less than a minute to go and only ten feet from the Edmonds defensive end, Taffy ripped the ball out of a Portland back's arms. Like an unexpectedly well-oiled machine, the line shuttled the ball across the field to Brittany, who took off running down the edge of the pitch, eyes fixed determinedly on the try line as she eluded one would-be tackler after another. And then she was leaping ballet-style over the last desperate defender and slamming the ball down onto the grass for five points.

"Hell yeah!" Mike shouted, clapping Cass on the back.

Cass high-fived him, her grin matching his. Jaelin's conversion kick just barely found its mark for another two points, and then all Cass could do was hold her breath for the final thirty seconds of the match as Portland tried to move up the field and Edmonds did everything they could to stop them.

At last the final whistle sounded. Edmonds had won their home opener for the first time in club history. Cass and Mike both laughed as the reserves poured out onto the field and the team lifted Brittany onto their shoulders. Taffy was surrounded by cheering teammates, too, but no one tried to lift her. Rugby players might be fearless, but they weren't stupid.

The post-game ritual singing of the Edmonds Women's Rugby Club song, written by a former scrum half who'd majored in theater, was rowdier than Cass had ever heard it. Afterward, she stood behind Mike while he gave his congratulatory speech. Sunglasses hid her wandering eyes as she surveyed the pitch and the stadium rows, assuring herself she wasn't looking for a particular person. But—there. Eva was still seated with Matthew and Maya behind the home bench, chatting amiably from the look of things.

After the team talk, Cass usually stuck around to chat with the players and any family members who might make their way down to the field. Today, though, she only patted Mike on the shoulder and high-fived a few of the players before heading for the stands. She could feel Eva's eyes on her as she climbed the stairs to their section, but that totally wasn't why she jogged up the last few steps. She was simply excited about the big home win.

"Hey, guys!" she said, pushing her sunglasses to the top of her head as she reached the waiting trio.

"Hey, loser." Matthew leaned over to high-five her.

"For once, that's factually incorrect," she said as she cracked his hand. Maybe a little too heartily, she realized as he winced in actual pain. She started to lean past him to high-five Maya, but then she paused, eyes uncertain on Maya's midsection. Would an overly exuberant greeting be bad for the baby?

Maya rolled her eyes and reached out to clap her on the shoulder. "Congrats on the win, Cass," she said, eying her meaningfully.

Whoops. It hadn't even been twenty-four hours and Cass was already slipping up in front of one of Matthew's fellow professors.

The conversation paused as Cass and Eva eyed one another. Then Eva smiled and waved again like she had earlier. "Hey. Congratulations on the win."

"Thanks," Cass said, eyeing her quizzically. "You came. I mean, thanks for coming. I wasn't sure..." She trailed off. What was it about Eva DeMarco that made her brain occasionally fail at stringing simple sentences together?

"I wasn't doing anything," Eva said, "and it's so nice out I thought I would take you up on your invitation. Like you said, it's important to show up for women's athletics."

The words sounded almost rehearsed. The idea that Eva might be nervous, too, settled some of the butterflies flitting around Cass's mid-section. "Well, I'm glad you made it," she said, her smile more natural.

Before another uncomfortable silence could overtake them, Maya grasped Matthew's hand and pulled him toward the aisle of the fast-emptying stands. "Come on, honey. We have that errand to run, remember? See you later, Eva, Cass."

"Bye," Cass said, giving a half-wave like Eva's. Perfect. Awkwardness was apparently contagious.

Matthew muttered a protest even as he let himself be dragged away. He'd been whipped long before he'd gotten his wife pregnant; the presence of their growing child was only icing on Maya's cake of dominance.

"Do you have to get back to the team?" Eva asked, gesturing toward the field where a cooler had magically appeared and bottles of beer were being handed out. But not to underage drinkers, of course.

"No, actually," Cass said, glancing back at Eva.

"Oh. Well, cool."

Was it? Cass's smile slipped slightly as she recalled that Eva's supposed girlfriend was, in fact, already married. "No Alexis today?" she asked, glancing over Eva's shoulder at the view of Puget Sound and the Olympic Mountains visible in the distance.

"No. Actually," Eva said, "I was wondering if I could talk to you about that."

Cass's gaze snapped back to the woman before her. Eva was chewing on her lower lip, and Cass blinked a few times. "Like, right now?"

"Yeah, unless you have plans?"

"Nope. No plans." Cass nodded toward the parking lot just north of the stands. "I'm parked over there. Or... we could go for a walk in the arboretum, if you wanted?"

The Edmonds Arboretum bordered the southern and eastern edges of campus, offering trails and an old wooden tower at its highest point that looked out over the water and the large, private estates that the university counted as neighbors. It was one of

Cass's favorite places to take a break from campus life during a busy weekday.

Eva nodded. "The arboretum is always nice."

They were quiet as they left the stadium and headed along the walkway toward the forested trails, but it wasn't exactly uncomfortable. Cass kept stealing glances at Eva, reassuring herself that yes, this was happening. Taking a walk with Eva DeMarco might not have been where she'd seen her afternoon going, but it wasn't entirely unwelcome.

"So anyway," Eva said as they crunched onto the gravel trail that wound gently upward beneath towering evergreens, "about Alexis. I have a confession to make."

The phrase jogged Cass's memory. She was pretty sure Eva had said a similar thing at the potluck right before Jace had interrupted them. "Okay."

Eva lifted her hand and fiddled with the brim of her baseball cap. "The night we met, I, well, I implied that she and I were more than friends when, in fact, we're not."

Direct and to the point, Cass noted. "Okay," she repeated, keeping her gaze fixed on the trail ahead. The main route up the heavily forested hillside had been a paved road at one time, but was now mostly dirt and gravel with the occasional crumbling chunk of concrete under foot.

Beside her, Eva released an audible breath. "You don't seem very surprised."

Cass hesitated. "I may have read Alexis's U-Dub profile after the cupcake incident."

"The cupcake incident?" Eva echoed, laughing softly.

"Not incident. Sorry. That's not what I meant."

Eva touched her arm and then quickly took her hand away. "It's fine. I'm the one who should apologize. I meant to tell you sooner, but I never seemed to get the chance."

That seemed unlikely. Still, Cass didn't call her out on the flimsy excuse. "Don't worry about it. You couldn't have known when we met that you would ever see me again."

Eva blinked. "No, I guess not."

"Anyway, thanks for telling me," Cass added.

"Of course. So," Eva said, her voice brightening, "Maya said you used to play professional rugby down in California."

"Oh, yeah. I did." Cass chewed her lip as she realized that at least some of the gesticulating she'd observed from field level had probably been about her. "Women's clubs don't pay a lot, though, so it was more of a hobby than a profession. But it was great. I was really lucky to get to do something I loved for so long."

"Why did you stop playing?"

Cass flashed back to the moment the huge woman on the San Diego team had picked her up and slammed her into the ground. She was pretty sure she would never forget the snapping sensation in her right shoulder, or the scream that tore itself out of her body without her foreknowledge or, more importantly, permission. Could have been worse, though. The dolt could have slammed her down on her head instead.

"Torn rotator cuff. Kind of hard to do much on the rugby pitch without a functional shoulder."

"Ah." Eva tucked her hands into her hoodie pockets. "Sorry. That must have been painful."

"It was. It's better now." She paused, and then a question unexpectedly forced its way out of her percolating brain: "So why did you want me to think you and Alexis were a couple, anyway?"

Eva ducked her head. "It's embarrassing," she admitted.

She was small and sheepish and lovely in her baseball cap and oversized hoodie, and Cass wanted to tell her it was okay, she didn't have to explain if she didn't want to. But then she remembered that the woman beside her was a professor with all the power that a faculty member possessed, whereas Cass was only a grad student and part-time staff member with the lack of power that attended both positions.

"Why is it embarrassing?" she asked.

"Well, I sort of panicked," Eva said, still not looking at her. "I'd been drinking, and I basically accused you of trying to use a pick-up line when you already had a girlfriend. Not my proudest moment."

"A girlfriend?" Cass echoed. And then she remembered: *Amy.* "But I don't. I'm not actually seeing anyone."

Eva squinted at her. "Really?"

"Really. The woman I was with that night is just a friend from California. I mean, she can be a bit..." She trailed off, not wanting to disparage her friend who couldn't help how she felt any more than Cass could change how she felt. "But we're not together."

Eva smiled self-deprecatingly, her dark eyes amused again. "Great. One more thing I got wrong. Is there any way we could just, I don't know, start over and pretend that night never happened?"

"Of course. My lips are sealed," Cass said, twisting her fingers cheesily in front of her mouth.

Eva's eyes followed the movement and lingered on her lips, and Cass's step faltered. There it was again. Eva was definitely flirting with her. But a queer, presumably single Eva DeMarco was apparently too much for Cass's brain to process because she suddenly found herself spinning around in an abrupt about-face toward campus.

"We should probably head back," she said belatedly.

"Okay," Eva said after a moment, her tone unreadable, and fell into step beside her.

"It's just that I have a lot of reading to get through before Monday," Cass added.

Eva didn't call her out on her weak excuse. "Right," she said instead. "I remember what grad school was like, and I wasn't coaching a sport on the side."

The conversation drifted to safer areas as they compared and contrasted graduate school experiences. When Cass asked how she had liked living in Manhattan, Eva told her she had enjoyed it at the time, her head tilting slightly.

"You and Matthew are from Westchester, aren't you?"

"Barely," Cass said. "Bronxville might as well be the sixth borough."

The county that bordered the northern boundary of New York City, Westchester boasted some of the wealthiest per capita neighborhoods in the country. Bronxville, the small "village" Cass's parents had relocated to from the Upper West Side shortly after she and Matthew were born, was considerably less fancy than other northern suburbs. She and her brother had grown up in a three-bedroom colonial on a small lot near the village center—a far cry from the mansions with in-house theater, gym, and forested acreage that half their classmates called home. Their parents were academics with nonfiction book deals, not CEOs with exorbitant annual bonuses. And yet, Cass knew from her post-Westchester travels that they had grown up more privileged than most of the rest of the world. Combined.

"I took the train through there, but I never stopped," Eva told her.

If only Cass had a nickel for every time someone said that to her.... At a population of just under 7,000, Bronxville wasn't much of a draw. Except for Sarah Lawrence, the small private liberal arts college where their mom still taught.

"What about you? Your profile said you're from somewhere out east too, didn't it?" she asked, as if she hadn't Google Earthed Eva's hometown.

"Northeast Pennsylvania. Scranton, actually," Eva admitted, and appeared to brace for something unpleasant. When Cass only smiled quizzically, she added, "Aren't you going to ask?"

"You mean about the show?" Eva's hometown had been made famous by the sit-com *The Office,* but according to Google, the show had taken significant liberties with the real city of Scranton. "I mean, I can if you want me to."

"Please don't," Eva said quickly, her scrunched-up face more adorable than it really should be.

Cass laughed, and then her smile faded as she realized how quickly they were approaching campus. Why had she panicked and bolted the second Eva gave her The Look? Even if they were both single and found each other attractive, that didn't mean they would end up like the couple she'd surprised one afternoon making out passionately on the steps to the arboretum tower. Just for a moment, Cass pictured Eva leaning against the rough-hewn wall looking up at her, lower lip caught between her teeth.... And, no. She shook the image away. It was definitely not okay to think about a faculty member like that, especially not when the woman in question was walking beside her, their arms brushing occasionally despite the noticeable width of the path.

Their pace slowed as they approached the parking lot where Cass's Jeep waited, top and sides open to the warm day.

"Nice ride," Eva said.

"Thanks. Do you need a lift home?"

"No, I have my bike. But thanks."

"Do you live near campus, then?" Cass asked, merely to be polite. It wasn't like she was fishing for personal information.

"My house is in the Bowl, only a few blocks from Matthew and Maya's." Eva backed away, offering her contagious half-wave one last time. "Thanks for the walk, and good luck with your homework, Cass. I'm sure I'll see you around."

"Right. See you, Eva."

Cass lingered for a moment and watched her go. A few blocks meant that Cass had probably run by Eva's house, possibly more than once. Had they passed on the street without even realizing it? Was that why Eva had seemed so familiar at the Thistledown? Before Eva could catch her staring all stalkerishly after her, Cass hopped into her Jeep and headed toward home, where she definitely, absolutely, in no uncertain terms was *not* going to corner Maya and demand the details of her conversation with Eva at the stadium. Or the details of her street address.

"Matthew says he told you to stay away from Eva DeMarco," a voice intoned as Cass walked up the driveway.

"Jesus," she said, shaking her head as she reached her sister-in-law. "I swear, you're like a freaking cat."

"It's *feline*," Maya supplied, pushing off the back steps where she'd been waiting. "And sadly, not for much longer. But stick to the subject, Baby B. What's going on between you and Eva?"

"Nothing," Cass said as she made her way to the studio behind the main house.

Maya followed her inside uninvited. "I'm gonna have to call bullshit on that one, little sis."

Cass set her keys and phone on the end table near the door and forced herself not to rise to the implied taunt. First of all, she was half a foot taller than Maya. Second of all, her sister-in-law was only 11 days older... But Cass didn't have to take the bait, so she didn't. Thank you, tai chi. The practice, which her instructor called meditation in motion, had helped her regain the use of her shoulder post-surgery faster than any of her doctors had expected. It had also given her something she had never before possessed:

patience. Or, at least, more patience than she had been born with, which might not be saying all that much.

"Whatever you say," she said, and grabbed a cold Gatorade from the fridge. "Do you want anything?"

Maya held up her water bottle with a "Duh" expression. Pregnancy hormones apparently did not encourage a matching level of serenity. Cass huffed under her breath as she motioned her guest to the L-shaped couch that occupied much of the apartment's main room. Like the other furniture in the converted garage, the couch had been a Craigslist find that had seen better days. But it was absurdly comfortable, and Cass had found a cover for it on Amazon.

"Start at the beginning," Maya ordered, her lack of patience once again showing.

"I'm really not sure—"

"Matthew already told me about the Thistledown."

Jackass. But when had he ever kept anything from Maya? Cass wasn't very good at hiding things from her, either, which was why it only took Maya ten seconds more of staring her down before Cass gave in and launched into a rambling account of her various interactions with Eva. As she spoke, she realized that it was actually kind of nice to have someone to talk to. She and Matthew talked, but it wasn't the same. Guys didn't do the emotional sharing thing as much, not even good guys like her twin.

When Cass finished, Maya took a swig of water and leaned back on the couch, rubbing the back of her neck. Cass knew her muscle pain would only increase as her body stretched to accommodate the baby, but she bit back a comment about tai chi being good for sore muscles. Matthew and Maya, or Eminem as she sometimes referred to them jointly (especially when her white boy brother tried to rap), had already accused her of egregious proselytizing about her new-found favorite exercise regimen. If they would only try it, she was sure they would fall in love with it too… said every cult member ever throughout human history.

Maya was quiet long enough that Cass felt a gentle push was in order. "So? Any words of wisdom to spare, big sis?"

Her sister-in-law flicked her shoulder, hard.

"Ow!"

"Oh, sorry. That was actually harder than I meant. Hormones."

Cass rubbed her shoulder. "You're totally going to blame hormones for everything for the next seven months, aren't you?"

"Try the next few years." She squinted slightly. "You said before you didn't want to get involved in a relationship while you were here. Is that still the case?"

The "of course" Cass expected to spring to her lips didn't. She thought she knew why, though. For one thing, her timeline to return to California was currently in flux. For another, casual dating took more way more energy than she'd anticipated. Before her California life imploded and Alyssa, her ex, decided to go back to *her* ex, Cass had liked being part of a couple. She'd liked having someone to explore the city with, someone to share meals with, someone she could fall asleep beside more nights than not. Most of all, she'd liked having someone she felt like herself with.

"I don't know," she admitted. "It's possible I might be open to something more serious. Not with Eva," she added. "I just mean if someone came along who was right."

"Well, that's new," Maya said, eyebrows disappearing under her bangs. For once she didn't have her long hair pulled up in a bun, and without make-up, she looked even younger than usual. She was always being mistaken for an undergrad, which she blamed on racism. White people had no idea what to do with Latinx people, other than question their right to be citizens. "Out of curiosity, why not Eva?"

"For so many very good reasons."

"Like, for example?"

Cass eyed her sister-in-law. "I thought you were here to jump on the 'stay away from Eva' bandwagon."

"I don't believe in telling other people what to do. Or, at least, not when it comes to romantic relationships," she amended as Cass snorted. "What I will say is that Eva has been through a lot and might not be in the best place emotionally speaking."

Cass frowned. "Are you referring to the fact that her husband left her for her friend?"

"He didn't," Maya said. "They were all friends, but Ben and Tina didn't get involved until after the marriage ended. From what

I've heard, Eva gave them her blessing. Otherwise, they wouldn't be together."

That was significantly more mature than what Cass was used to after spending her twenties in the San Francisco dating scene. "Then what *are* you talking about?"

"It's not my story to share. But I can tell you, mainly so that you know to tread carefully, that Ben and Eva had some issues around fertility and reproduction."

"Like a miscarriage?"

"What part of 'it's not my story' do you not get?" Maya asked. "Seriously, it's like you and your brother don't even listen."

Cass supposed it really was hormones that propelled her sister-in-law off the couch. That, or Matthew had recently tuned Maya out at his peril.

"Okay," she said, clutching her Gatorade to her chest as she watched Maya stomp toward the door. "Good talk, really."

Maya paused, visibly inhaling and exhaling. "Sorry," she said after a moment, gazing sheepishly over her shoulder. "My emotions seem to be all over the place right now."

"It's okay," Cass said. And then her mouth decided to take her life in its non-existent hands. "I'm used to your fiery Latina temper."

At the old joke, Maya's eyes narrowed, but her smile remained in place. "*Gringa.*"

"Now that's just a low blow."

Maya rolled her eyes and Cass watched her leave, relieved that her good-natured friend was still somewhere inside the woman whose body chemistry was changing to accommodate the life growing inside her. Pregnancy was not easy by any means, and yet so many women did it. Including Eva DeMarco? If so, it must not have ended well. Otherwise Ben would have said something. He would be the kind of dad who bragged about his kid any chance he got.

But that wasn't any of her business, as Maya had oh-so-gently reminded her.

Cass chugged her Gatorade and headed upstairs to change. She and Matthew had renovated the studio, including the attic, her first summer in Edmonds. Or, he had renovated it while she had mostly kept him company, feeling useless in the shoulder sling she'd had to wear for longer than seemed reasonable. She hadn't been able to drive—or, more importantly, exercise—for six weeks after surgery, so operating power tools had been out of the question. Still, she'd gotten fairly good at painting with her left hand, though in certain lighting she could see where her roller strokes had gone awry.

The attic had turned out better than she would have expected, light and airy and open thanks to cream-colored walls strung with fairy lights, a wall of south-facing windows, oak laminate floors, and a tongue-in-groove cedar ceiling that still carried the scent of the Western Washington woods more than a year later. She may not have nail-gunned the ceiling planks into place or attached the drywall to studs or cut the molding and window frames to fit, but she had helped measure and design and paint, all without the use of one half of her upper body. As a plus, she and Matthew had spent more quality time together than they had since they'd left for separate colleges more than a decade earlier.

Braless at last and clad in comfy sweats, Cass jogged back downstairs and headed out onto the studio's small deck, one corner of which was hidden from the main house by a pair of Western Red Cedars that had grown nearly together over the decades. There was still a little bit of sun to be had; she might as well enjoy the day and do some reading. She would have to finalize her thesis plan later in the quarter, so she should probably use her time wisely now before the academic rush picked up.

An image of Eva smiling at her in the arboretum, dappled sunlight reflecting from the Nike swoosh on her cap, teased Cass's memory as she settled on the chaise lounge with her Kindle and laptop, but she pushed it away. No time for daydreaming, she told herself, and waited for Chrome to load.

CHAPTER FIVE

Eva stared at the agenda blinking at her from her computer screen. The College of Arts and Sciences fall quarterly meeting had a special guest this afternoon: Tech Committee Grad Student Member Cassidy Trane would be speaking to them about how to get the most out of the new content management systems the university had rolled out over the past six months.

In the weeks since the rugby match, Eva had seen Cass only in passing. There were infrequent encounters on the stairs of Old Main; occasions when she'd glimpsed Cass in the distance on campus; and, particularly memorable, the time Cass had been in the dean's suite chatting with Steve's assistant when Eva left his office. She hadn't been expecting to see Cass, and when she'd looked up to discover the younger woman's full-wattage smile directed at her, she had actually stumbled slightly and dropped the pile of books she was carrying. That wasn't embarrassing, nor was the way Cass's smile had turned knowing for a second before she knelt down to help Eva with her books. Not embarrassing at all.

Now they would be in the same room for at least an hour while Cass reported on the recent university-wide tech developments—changes that, incidentally, faculty members of the College of Arts and Sciences had vehemently resisted. On a private campus like Edmonds University, blessed with a sizable endowment, new buildings were constantly being built and old buildings rehabbed or expanded. University leadership rarely stayed the same for more than a decade, either. Older professors retired and younger ones were hired not exactly routinely, but often enough that the faculty culture was regularly refreshed. IT changes, however, fell in a whole different category. Computer systems were tools, and once an academic found a tool that helped them accomplish their teaching or research goals more efficiently, they were loath to part with it.

As the apparent face of the newest Edmonds IT trend, Cass was going to have her work cut out for her at this meeting. Arts and Sciences faculty members were not known for their shy, retiring natures, particularly not the sizable contingent of older, straight, white men. Eva could only imagine how someone like Lincoln Anderson, a longtime History Department "rock star" who was known both for his expertise on the Civil War and for a well-publicized bout with plagiarism and lying—"How the hell didn't that get him fired?" Ben used to fume—would respond to Cass daring to tell him how to run his "personal" (i.e., university-funded) website.

Eva wondered briefly if Tina was a willing audience to Ben's periodic rants about Linc, and imagined her former friend probably was. Current friend? They were still friendly, anyway, which was good since they all worked together. In fact, Ben and Tina would likely be at the meeting today, thereby marking the first time the three of them had made a public appearance together since the reconfiguration of their relationship triad. Though Tina had attended the potluck the previous month, Ben had stayed away as a gesture of reconciliation. Today's meeting, on the other hand, was required for all College of Arts and Sciences faculty and staff.

It would be fine, Eva assured herself as she skimmed the rest of the agenda. They were adults, and Eva didn't begrudge Tina and Ben the happiness they'd found in each other. She might be envious that Ben had managed to shuck off his grief and move on so quickly, but she didn't blame him for the end of their marriage. Once her inability to carry a baby to term had been confirmed by a second and third opinion, her desire to divorce Ben had only intensified. They weren't right for each other anymore, a fact that had become especially clear one morning shortly after they lost Isabella, their second child. At 21 weeks, their tiny, perfect daughter had been far enough along to have a name, unlike the baby that Eva had lost a year and a half earlier at only ten weeks.

"You have to snap out of this," Ben had announced after Eva had slept in nearly to noon again. He'd been standing over her, lamplight a halo in his brown, curly hair, his features twisted with what looked almost like disdain. "You're not the only one who lost her, Eva. But I'm still getting up every day, still eating right, still exercising. When's the last time you went for a run or even took a shower?"

In hindsight, she could see that he hadn't been wrong. At the time, though, his exasperation with her grief had felt like the final straw. She'd asked him to leave later that same day, and after a brief, half-hearted argument, he'd packed his things and checked into a hotel near the freeway. But while finally separating from him had been a relief, it had done nothing to quiet Eva's self-recriminations. Ben had lost their daughter too, yes. But *she* was the one whose body had literally rejected both of their babies. She was the one who had failed to protect them and give them even a chance at life.

"Hey, are you going to the meeting?"

Eva blinked away the memories as she glanced toward her open door. Scott Karoly was leaning in, his bald patch shiny in the fluorescent lights from the hallway, his pale face arranged in its usual smile.

"Right," she said. "The meeting. Give me a sec?"

"Of course. Take your time."

She could hear him in the hall chatting with other fourth floor denizens while she logged off and shrugged into a wool cardigan. On her way out she grabbed a notebook, pen, and mint from her desk, telling herself her sudden desire for fresh breath had nothing to do with the featured speaker at today's meeting.

"Eva," a chorus of voices greeted her, and she smiled as she locked her door behind her.

"Everyone," she said, and fell into step beside Scott, who specialized in Russian and Soviet culture, and Elaine Chen, who studied Asian American adolescents.

Peter Moore, a specialist on issues of validity in social science research, had crashed his mountain bike on Tiger Mountain the weekend before and was still moving a bit gingerly, so the group took the elevator to the ground floor. As the car creaked downward, the conversation focused on the meeting ahead and their collective concern for Cass, "the very nice GA" who had helped each member of the group more than once with various computer issues. Except Peter, who had long viewed himself as the department techie and who, Eva noted, appeared slightly miffed that his unofficial role had been usurped by an official university employee.

"Honestly," Gwen Sanders, their department chair and resident National Book Award finalist, said, "I wouldn't be surprised if Linc Anderson or one of his cronies tried to take a shot at Cassidy today, since they can't exactly go off on the head of University Computing, can they?"

"I was thinking the same thing," Eva agreed, and then raised her eyebrows as her colleagues regarded her in seeming surprise. She supposed she did tend to be a bit on the quiet side. She'd been sure when she left grad school that she would finally overcome her lingering case of impostor syndrome. Sadly, that was not the case. Being a spousal hire had only increased her sense of insecurity, if anything.

On the ground floor, they bypassed the main entrance's dramatic stone stairway and headed instead for the accessible side entrance that opened onto a brick courtyard. There, they followed the pathway past rose bushes beginning to brown and shrivel, bricks underfoot rippling from wayward tree roots. The weather was still mild more often than not, but temperatures were noticeably cooler now. With Halloween only a week away, the fall rainy season wouldn't be far off.

As they neared the Academic Quad, the conversation turned to gossip—who had won what grant, whose divorce was almost final, whose children had started at which university—and though Elaine cast her a slightly worried glance when Tina's art therapy initiative came up, Eva only lifted her chin and smiled determinedly. She seriously couldn't wait until some other faculty members immolated themselves on the pyre of university gossip. Only then would their supposed love triangle finally fall off the Edmonds U radar.

The walk didn't take long. The only places on campus where all 16 departments of the College of Arts and Sciences could assemble were Bannister Hall, where opening convocation and assorted choral concerts took place, and the Langford Student Center. Today's meeting was at the student center, just across the Academic Quad from Old Main. The LSC was one of those buildings at Edmonds that Eva thought looked like it had gone through a mid-life crisis. The older side was polychrome brick facades and creeping ivy vines while the newer addition resembled half of a metal and glass pyramid, as if its designers had intended it to be an homage to the Louvre.

The newer half, Eva had to admit, was full of light and whimsy, with modern sculpture pieces, spiral staircases, and secret balconies galore. The older portion of the LSC meanwhile was angular and stern, the wide wooden stairway built, rumor had it, at a purposely awkward angle to prevent erstwhile students from running up or down the stairs. Today's faculty meeting would be in the original portion of the student center, in the high-ceilinged multi-purpose room where student clubs held fundraisers and University Career Services held their quarterly career fairs. The acoustics were difficult for individual speakers, with lone voices being swallowed up and multiple voices creating a cacophony. Just another challenge Cass would face this afternoon.

They were nearly across the quad when Eva glimpsed Ben and Tina entering the LSC, joined by colleagues from each of their departments. So they were here. Fantastic. Just to make matters even more interesting, the student Eva couldn't stop thinking inappropriately about would also be there to talk about the technology that the Edmonds Faculty Senate had deemed in a recent email the "result of unnecessary trend-following by short-sighted administrators."

What could possibly go wrong?

"There she is," Gwen said, her gaze on a picnic table outside the student center.

Cass occupied one of the benches, her shoulders hunched as she stared down at a sheaf of stapled papers. She glanced up when the Sociology Department entourage paused beside her picnic table, and offered a half-smile, half-grimace. "Hi, guys."

"Good luck today, Cassidy," Gwen said. "We'll be rooting for you."

Cass's expression turned wry. "Somehow I think I might need the support."

At least she knew what she was walking into.

As her colleagues headed into the student center, Eva lingered, aware of Scott and Elaine glancing back at her curiously before disappearing inside. "Hey, you."

"Hey, yourself." Cass gazed up at her, squinting slightly. By this time of the afternoon, the sun had already ducked behind the student center. But the blue sky and puffy clouds overhead were still shot through with light that made Cass's blue eyes almost seem to blaze from within.

Jesus, Eva thought, shifting from one foot to the other as she nodded hello to a group of biology professors on their way into the building. Now she was mentally composing bad poetry about her illicit crush. Perfect.

"Are you nervous?" she asked Cass, trying to stay on topic.

Cass passed a hand over her hair, which looked shorter than the last time Eva had seen her. "A little. It helps, though, that I've already given this presentation a few times."

"You have?"

"Yep." She ticked off a list on her fingertips: "The Business School, Engineering, Education, Nursing, and the Graduate School."

Eva hummed. "So basically everyone on campus except Arts and Sciences."

"Pretty much," she agreed, the tension lines around her eyes easing as she smiled up at Eva. "It's nice to see you. It's been a while."

"I know," Eva said, noticing for the first time the tawny rings around Cass's pupils. She'd never been quite this close to her, had she? "I, um, I'd almost forgotten how crazy fall quarter can be. How are your classes going? And rugby?"

"Good. Also both very busy, but good. What about you?"

"Things are going well," she said, rolling her pen between her thumb and forefinger. "It's nice to be back on campus. I'd almost forgotten how much I love teaching." She stopped then, because talking about what she loved with Cass felt too intimate.

"I'm glad you're doing well." Cass paused, looking like she might say something else, but then she only tapped her papers. "Anyway, I guess I should finish reviewing my notes. See you in there?"

"Absolutely," Eva said. "Good luck. Or, as the science geeks among us would say, think like a proton and—"

"—stay positive," Cass finished with her. Her smile widened again, and Eva wanted to smooth a fingertip over her dimple to see what the indentation felt like… And, right. Time to go.

"Good luck," she repeated, backing away.

"Thanks," Cass said, and gave a slight wave that Eva returned before turning and heading inside.

If Alexis were here, she would be shaking her head at Eva's awkwardness right now, and well-deservedly so. Smoothness with the ladies was apparently still not a quality Eva possessed. Cass, on the other hand, seemed to have confidence to spare. If Eva hadn't already known she was nervous, she would never have been able to tell as the dean called the meeting to order ten minutes later and, after going over the spring meeting's minutes and obtaining college approval to enter them into the record, introduced their guest speaker.

"As you all know," Steve said, gazing around the room while Cass busied herself on the computer projector at the podium, "University Computing launched an initiative last year intended to create a more uniform online presence across the university as well as provide more robust teaching tools. Part of the initiative involved bringing college and department websites onto the university-wide content management system, Drupal. The College of Arts and Sciences was lucky enough to have a new sociology Master's candidate join the department last year, Cassidy Trane."

He gestured toward Cass, who looked up from her keyboard to smile at the crowd.

"Most of you already know Cassidy," Steve continued, "our resident grad assistant. What you may not know is that she worked for half a dozen years in the Bay Area tech industry. She also serves on the University Tech Committee and has been a key figure in the Drupal and Canvas systems roll-out. In fact, she worked full-time this summer for University Computing, which is why she's here today to speak with us. With that, Cass, the floor is yours."

"Thanks, Steve," Cass said, her voice carrying effortlessly through the high-ceilinged room. "So. I'm here today because University Computing has tasked me with explaining their ongoing initiative to faculty and staff groups across campus. I'm not sure if they picked me because of my background in tech or because I'm a grad student and therefore easy cannon fodder," she paused as a low laugh rolled across the room, "but either way, it's gone better than expected. At least, so far." She gazed squarely out at the room. "Arts and Sciences, while first alphabetically, is the last college on my list, so I hope you'll keep the streak going."

As reluctant smiles bloomed around her, Eva relaxed in her uncomfortable wooden chair that was probably older than the building itself. Cass was doing better than Eva had anticipated. She'd thought Cass might be nervous and awkward, and had been prepared to cringe inwardly on her behalf as she stumbled through her presentation. But the ease with which Cass addressed the crowd, the intelligent way she read the room, was an indicator of a competence and poise that Eva could only admire.

"As Steve mentioned and as I know you are all aware, University Computing launched the implementation of a consistent web interface last year. The goal of this project is to assist both prospective and existing students—and faculty and staff—in navigating through what has grown to be a complex network of college and department sites. There's been some understandable pushback, so University Computing thought it might be helpful to provide some background to the decision."

She clicked the mouse, and the image on the screen behind her changed to a list of statistics labeled "Google Analytics."

"First of all, the decision to standardize the Edmonds.edu web interface wasn't made lightly. As you can see on the screen, years of web analytics revealed that users were having a hard time finding their way through the maze of non-uniform pages on the Edmonds website. Since one of the primary functions of a university website is to act as a virtual brochure for prospective students—"

A voice interrupted suddenly, and all heads swiveled to the front of the room to see who it was. Of course: Lincoln Anderson, arms folded across his chest, holding court from the second row.

"I'm sorry," he was saying in his usual snide, belligerent tone, eyes wandering across the room as if to dare anyone to disagree, "but I'm going to have to stop you right there. One of the primary functions of a university website is, in fact, to showcase the work of its faculty, the life blood of any institution of higher education."

And here we go, Eva thought: yet another existential campus debate over who was more important, the faculty or the students.

Or, you know, the staff without whom the place wouldn't run.

Cass recovered quickly from what Eva imagined was amazement at being interrupted by a member of the audience. Actually, as a female grad student, she might be used to having her ideas undercut.

"Faculty members have their own individual web pages to highlight their research and publications," she said, her voice even. "Data shows that the main audience for any university website is overwhelmingly prospective students and their fam—"

"What I'm talking about cannot be explained away by so-called data," Linc interrupted again, his tone indicating his estimation of Cass's source material if not her native intelligence. "Faculty members are the reason this university is on the map, the reason Edmonds consistently attracts the best and brightest—"

"Actually," Cass interrupted, "most first-year undergraduate students say they don't know what they want to study, so in fact—"

"*Excuse me*, young lady," Linc interjected, his voice booming. "I'm not sure you know who you're talking to!"

A new voice entered the fray, as hot and bothered as Cass was cool and dismissive. "Are you serious, Anderson?" Matthew Trane demanded, spots of color flaming on his cheeks. He appeared about to launch into an angry tirade of his own when yet another person inserted himself into the conversation.

Eva shut her eyes briefly as her ex-husband said, his voice amused and almost mocking, "I believe what Dr. Trane is trying to say is that it would be hard not to know who you are, Linc, given your media profile a few years ago."

The crowd tittered at Ben's thinly veiled reference to the newspaper articles and talk show segments that had focused on Lincoln Anderson's fall from respected academic to disputed scholar. After being coerced into making a formal, public apology for the "mistakes" contained in one of his uber-popular creative nonfiction books about the Civil War, Linc had lost his endowed chair and been suspended without pay for a year. And yet, he'd kept his office and all of his other faculty benefits while on leave. He hadn't even lost his publisher. Probably they were of the opinion that no publicity was bad publicity.

"All right," Steve said, turning around in his front row seat to regard the rest of the room. "That's enough, friends. Please grant Cassidy the same respect you ask of your students and hold your questions and comments to the end of her presentation. I guarantee that if you give her your attention, you will get more out of this meeting than you put into it."

He faced forward again and nodded at Cass, who nodded back. Then she resumed her talk, the only sign of duress pink spots on her cheeks that were rather less angry than those—Eva checked—still coloring her brother's visage. But her voice was calm as she explained higher education benchmarks, web literacy rates among Millennials and Generation Z, and acceptable visitor attrition rates. Because Edmonds.edu had been losing online visitors in recent years at a higher rate than the reported industry average, University Computing had put together a task force to determine how best the university website could serve its varying constituents. The result: a rebranding campaign with a focus on responsive design and inter-college collaboration. Each college now utilized a standard design template with consistent menu options, and the university would soon be rolling out WordPress blogs for any interested college or department.

"In fact," she added, cutting her eyes at Lincoln, "the blogs will work in tandem with University Communications to offer a forum to promote both faculty *and* student achievements as we move forward with the next stage of the initiative." She appeared to hold Lincoln's stare for a long moment before clicking on to the next slide.

Damn, Eva thought as a summary of key points appeared on the projector screen couched in language that even she understood. Cass was really smart. As in, genuinely bright. She hid it well, with her distinctly urban sense of style and the tribal tattoos on display on her forearms as she manipulated the projector and flipped between her PowerPoint and the recently revamped university website. But even Linc Anderson would have to concede that Cass knew her material. No wonder Steve was her biggest fan. Maybe University Computing would offer her a permanent job when she finished her Master's, and she would settle down in the Northwest and...

Eva closed her eyes again, this time at her own absurdity.

The presentation wasn't short, but it was, as Steve had

promised, enlightening. As Cass continued explaining the many facets of the rebranding initiative, Eva could almost feel the shift in the room from recalcitrant individual faculty members to a more supportive academic community of the sort they were always exhorting their students to strive for. Except Linc. While he sat with his arms still folded across his chest, Cass worked the room, eliciting laughter and thoughtful questions at a rate that Eva would have sworn was impossible given this generally irascible crowd. Cass couldn't have missed Linc's glowering presence, but if she did notice his petulance, she never let on. She simply continued her engaging presentation like the gifted instructor she apparently was.

Great, Eva thought, rubbing her neck. Just one more endearing quality because there weren't, apparently, already enough.

When Cass had finally answered the last question, Steve called for announcements, and then the meeting was over. But it didn't break up immediately. Eva watched as several of her colleagues approached Cass at the podium, where she was in the process of shutting down her files and logging out. Just as Ben neared the front of the room, Tina lagging behind with a fellow Psychology professor, Cass glanced up and gazed at Eva, smiling and tilting her head a little as if to say, "So, what did you think?" Then Ben stepped into her line of vision, and Eva saw the way Cass's smile deepened and became almost teasing as she turned to him.

Of course Cass would know Ben. Not only was she Matthew's sister, but Cass and Ben were both on the University Tech Committee. The faculty union had yet to successfully negotiate a certain amount of service out of the Edmonds professorial contract (though not for lack of trying), and Ben had been enthusiastic when a spot on the Tech Committee opened up their second year at Edmonds. Apparently one could still make important decisions about university computing resources even if one didn't know how to find the power button on a Mac.

Eva hesitated, her flight instinct rising as she watched her ex-husband talk to the only person since their split that she had daydreamed about kissing. Before she could make her escape, Gwen leaned in and said, her dark eyes sparkling, "Well, that was more fun than I expected. Matthew Trane is Cassidy's brother, isn't he?"

"Actually," Eva said, "he's her twin."

"No! Really?" When Eva nodded, her department chair snorted. "No wonder. I thought he was going to get up and tackle Linc at one point until your... until Ben intervened. Am I to suppose that Professor Miller and the Trane twins are friendly?" she added, nodding to the podium where Matthew had joined the small group clustered about his sister.

"Ben's on the Tech Committee with Cass, and I think he's reached out to Matthew. You know how he is about mentoring younger faculty." She glanced at her ex-husband semi-fondly. He might be overdramatic at times, but his passion combined with a creative approach to the world and an innate goodness translated into someone she was still glad to have in her life, even peripherally.

"Ben has always been great at bridging the gap for those in less fortunate positions," Gwen agreed. Her gaze was shrewd but kind as she eyed Eva. "How are you handling being back in the deep end? This is your first all-college meeting in quite a while, isn't it?"

"Yes," Eva admitted. "And though I did feel bad for Cass at times, I have to say that it was nice not to be on the hot seat."

"I'll bet," Gwen said, laughing quietly. "I'm glad you're back, Eva. The old cliché about time and healing exists for a reason, but if you need anything, you know where my office is."

She wasn't merely spouting platitudes, Eva knew. Gwen was always consummately professional, probably because as an African American woman at the top of her field, she'd always had to be. But her eyes and voice were warm as she reached out and squeezed Eva's hand. As department chair, she knew more than most people about the terms of Eva's leave. Like Steve, she'd been unfailingly supportive when Eva had asked for additional time off, assuring her that her job would be waiting whenever she decided she was ready to come back.

"Thank you, Gwen," Eva said softly, blinking back the familiar sting of tears. "I appreciate the offer."

"Even if you don't take me up on it?"

She shrugged, smiling. "Alexis blames my antisocial tendencies on my East Coast upbringing."

"That sounds like Alexis Hammond," Gwen said. "Looks like the crowd's thinning out. I'm going to go commend Cass on her composure in the face of that man's schoolyard bullying. Care to join me?"

Eva glanced again at the red exit sign on the opposite side of the room. But in truth, she realized, she wanted to talk to Cass more than she wanted to avoid Ben and Tina, both of whom were still chatting with Matthew near the podium.

"Why not," she said, and followed Gwen past the rows of empty chairs.

Besides, maybe she would get lucky and they wouldn't notice her.

Matthew saw her first. The look on his face quickly alerted the other two, and soon Eva's ex-husband and his girlfriend, Eva's former best friend—on campus, not in the world or even in Seattle, as Alexis was always quick to point out—were silently watching her approach. Exactly the audience she was hoping for when she congratulated Cass for holding her own against Linc.

When they reached her, Cass was chatting with a man Eva recognized from Chemistry. Or rather she was listening, her polite smile frozen in place, as he lectured her in a patronizing tone that made Eva's palms itch. Gwen glanced sideways at Eva, one eyebrow lifted, before practically elbowing the Chemistry guy aside to give Cass a hug.

"Nice job up there, even with all the heckling," Gwen told Cass. "I am more than proud to call you one of ours."

"Thanks, Gwen," Cass said, her smile more genuine now. "My brother told me to expect fireworks, but I have to say I didn't expect him to be starring in the show." Her gaze flicked past Gwen to Eva. "So? What did you think?"

"Very impressive," Eva said, aware of Ben's eyes on her from a few paces away. She steeled herself, willing away any sign of nerves. "No wonder Steve brags about you all the time. I don't think many of us realized what a rock star you are."

Cass glanced down and fiddled with her notes. "I wouldn't say *rock star*. I just know more about technology than the average academic."

"Which isn't all that unusual," Gwen said. "I think Eva is

referring more to your unflappability, Miss Cool-as-a-Cucumber Trane. Lincoln Anderson isn't easy, and you handled yourself with aplomb. Well done, *young lady.*" She winked, presumably to let Cass know she was invoking Linc's epithet ironically.

"Thanks," Cass said, her cheeks taking on that lovely pink hue that made Eva want to brush her fingers across—

"Anyway," Eva said, and then lowered her voice as she realized how loud she was being. "I have to get back to the office, but I just wanted to say congratulations. You should be proud of yourself, Cass."

"Thanks, Eva." Cass smiled directly at her, blue eyes even warmer now.

For a moment, the room quieted around them and Eva smiled back, entranced as ever by Cass's magnetism. But then her flight instinct twitched again as she realized that Cass's smile was probably a tad intimate for a crowd of colleagues that included Eva's department chair, ex-husband, and former best friend.

"Of course," she said, breaking eye contact. "Well done, again."

And then with a touch to Gwen's shoulder and a polite nod to Ben, Tina, and Matthew Trane, she turned and made herself walk away, even though she wanted nothing more than to continue basking in the glow of Cass's presence like the rest of the small crowd gathered around her.

"Eva!" she heard before she'd gone more than a few paces.

Damn it. She'd been so close to a clean escape.... She turned back. "Hey, Tina."

"Are you going back across the quad?"

"I am," she had to admit, and then immediately wished she'd invented an errand on any other part of campus.

"Mind if I join you?"

Actually, she wanted to walk back to Old Main alone and daydream about Cass's tattoos and the cool steel in her voice as she shot down Lincoln Anderson, a tyrant known for bragging about his ability to reduce graduate students of history—female graduate students, in particular—to tears.

"Of course not," she said.

"Great."

Great.

"I think Ben and Matthew are conspiring against Linc," Tina said as she and Eva approached the exit. Her soft southern twang held the hint of humor that had initially drawn Eva to her when they'd met all those years ago at a new faculty member function, and Eva felt a surge of unexpected affection for her longtime friend.

"More power to them." She blinked in the sudden brightness as they left the fluorescent lighting of the multi-purpose room and stepped out onto the quad. "Matthew was lucky Ben jumped in like that, though. He doesn't have tenure yet, does he?"

"Not yet. But I'm sure like with you it's just a matter of time."

Tina sounded confident, and Eva felt a wave of envy laced with the old exhaustion sweep over her. She used to sound like that, back before her world upended and she found herself holding her baby girl, so small and delicate, as she breathed what would be her first and last breaths.

"How is it being back?" Tina asked. "I thought I would run into you more."

It wasn't an accusation, but Eva could feel her defenses rise and forced her voice to remain even as she offered the words that had become almost automatic since the start of the quarter: "It's really good. I think maybe I stayed away too long."

"And your mother?" Tina asked as they started along the paved walkway that neatly bisected the grassy expanse. "Is she doing all right at Shady Grove?"

"She is. I'm not sure the staff knew what they were getting into when they approved her application, but it seems to be working out."

"How's her health?"

"It's okay. Her vision's getting worse, and she's irritated because her doctor says she has to give up golf. But for someone her age she's actually in good shape."

"She isn't still driving, is she?"

"Oh, god, no. She was never much of a driver, and anyway, the home has shuttles. She loves going to the Seattle Outlets." She shook her head, laughing a little as she remembered how her mother used to drag her to the outlet mall two towns away when she was younger. Some things, at least, never changed.

"What about you?" Tina asked. "How is it for you to have her living here?"

"Fine." She nodded at a pair of students from her research methods class approaching from the opposite direction.

"Hi, Dr. DeMarco," one girl said, smile bright.

"Hi, Keira. Hi, Nico." And really, had Eva ever been that young? Or maybe it was just the girl's easy cheerfulness that seemed so foreign.

To be honest, she had been more than a little nervous about moving her mother to Edmonds. They'd never been close, and Eva had only visited home a few times a year since leaving Pennsylvania for college. That summer, though, a few months into the new living arrangement, she'd realized that it was actually nice to have her mother living nearby. It was a good thing to have someone around who had known and loved her long before grad school, before her marriage to Ben, before Isabella. But Eva didn't tell Tina that. A year and a half ago, Tina would have known every detail surrounding her mother's move. Now their friendship had shifted, and Eva doubted they would ever be that close again.

"How's your family?" she asked Tina, and was relieved when the conversation moved on to the less personally fraught topic of the increasing polarization of red and blue states.

Soon they were pausing in the courtyard between Old Main and Bass Hall, the recently renovated headquarters of Psychology, Human Services, and the School of Education.

"Thanks for the walk," Tina said, reaching out to trail her fingertips over one of the brown rose bushes at the edge of the courtyard.

"Of course." Eva glanced up at her building and then back at Tina. "Would you want to maybe grab coffee next week? I mean, if you have time."

Tina was already nodding. "I would love to." She hesitated uncharacteristically. "I know it can't ever be the same as it was, but I've really missed you, Eva."

"I've missed you, too." Before she could second-guess the impulse, Eva lurched forward and hugged her former friend.

"Alexis has been working on you, hasn't she?" Tina said,

smiling as Eva stepped away.

"She's trying, anyway."

"Well, tell her I said hello. I'll email you about coffee, okay?"

"Sounds good," Eva said. "Tell Ben I said hi and he's welcome to borrow Harvey anytime. I know it's been a while."

Tina nodded slowly, her eyes on Eva's. "I'll tell him. See you, Eva."

"See you, Tina."

And then they were separating, each heading back to her own building. Eva took the stairs to the fourth floor of Old Main quickly, her steps lighter than they'd been in days, maybe weeks, despite the afternoon's drama. Or possibly because of it. *Fireworks*, Cass had said, and Eva couldn't help but agree.

In her office, she shed her cardigan and woke up her computer. As the screen flickered to life, she touched the photo on her desk that had replaced her old favorite of Ben and Harvey. Her mother and father smiled out from the frame in a shot that had been taken on a New York dinner cruise not long before her dad had died. The stroke had been so sudden that Eva sometimes still felt what she had described to her therapist as "emotional vertigo" when she remembered he was gone. She'd gotten the call about her dad only a few weeks after she and Ben had lost the first baby, which was probably why she hadn't insisted her mother move closer right away. She'd been too busy trying to start a family of her own to worry about her mother as much as she should have. It had taken a bad fall, complete with broken bones and a second-degree concussion, for her mom to agree to make the move to Washington.

Just because taking her mother out of Scranton was the right thing to do didn't mean the transition had been easy for either of them. But now, eight months later, Eva's mom appeared to have settled in. She had joined the elder community at the facility near the hospital, and sometimes when Eva dropped by, her mother was too busy playing mah-jongg or watching old movies with her new friends for more than a short visit with her daughter. They both still had their own separate lives, just as they always had. It was just that those lives intersected more now than they had in close to two decades.

The all-college meeting agenda was still up on her screen, and

Eva read one of the bulleted items aloud softly: "Tech Committee Grad Student Member Cassidy Trane."

Cass, she thought, the words on her computer screen melting and running together as she gave in to the daydream, a soft smile on her lips. But then she remembered how Cass had looked at her in front of their assembled colleagues, all open and sweet in front of Eva's chair and anyone else who happened to be present— including members of the college Tenure and Promotion Committee?—and she closed the agenda. She wasn't like the former business school faculty member who had launched a successful textiles venture on Etsy, or the ex-engineering professor who was now making six figures working for Tesla. If she joined the ex-professor ranks, her pool of potential careers would be limited. Somehow she doubted a *Chronicle of Higher Education* reporter would be banging down her door to hear how she had started a romantic fiction reader's blog that had acquired a whopping forty-two followers in its first six months. And being an adjunct instructor, working for minimal pay without benefits or job security? No thanks.

Resolutely, she pushed images of Cass's blue eyes and pink cheeks away and pulled up her lesson plan for the following day. Because you could never be too prepared for class, in her humble opinion.

CHAPTER SIX

Cass slammed her palm down on her desk hard enough to make her two officemates jump.

"Jesus, Trane," Zach Abbot said, pushing up the brim of his Seattle Seahawks snapback. A former religious zealot raised by fundamentalist (or *mental*, as he now liked to call them) parents, he seemed to use any excuse to take the Lord's name in vain.

"Sorry," she muttered, glaring at her laptop screen.

Normally, she didn't hang out in their shared grad office in the middle of the day because it was too difficult to concentrate, what with the cramped room, extra bodies, and classmates who dropped by to chat. But she had just finished class and had rugby practice in a little while, and it would take too long to ride her bike home and back. Ditto for packing up and finding a quiet space in the library. She'd figured she might at least get her email under control and, if she was lucky, make headway on her outline for her Race and Social Justice midterm paper due the following week. A paper she had intended to spend tomorrow working on, which plan was now in jeopardy thanks to the email she'd just received from the dean asking if she could meet with him the following morning. A *Friday* morning. Had Steve forgotten he'd agreed to no assistantship work on Fridays?

Her first semester at Vassar, Cass's classes had met Monday through Thursday, and she'd soon discovered she could use Fridays to get ahead on her homework and still have a life (i.e., play rugby and basketball) on weekends. From there on out, she'd planned her classes not only around her major requirements but also around the days they met. That was how she'd kept up with the substantial amounts of reading and writing in her sociology courses. Early on, her parents had tried to convince her to study math or the physical sciences, but sociology felt like common sense. As long as she kept her Fridays free for reading and studying, the work load was manageable. After a childhood marked by individualized education programs and administrators checking in to make sure she was keeping up with her studies, Cass had found that managing her higher education experience on her own wasn't only freeing, it was empowering.

Fortunately, graduate courses at Edmonds were slotted for Monday through Thursday, so her "Fridays are for Reading" policy had remained intact. This quarter, her Race and Social Justice seminar met Monday and Wednesday mornings, while her Gender and Sexuality seminar only met on Wednesday nights. That meant she could get most of her ten hours of grad assistant work done on Tuesday and Thursday mornings. *Not* on Fridays, as Steve had agreed when he hired her.

She started to type a reply along the lines of "My Friday policy deviates for no one" but realized that such a message would be both politically inexpedient and a violation of her rule against sending emails while irritated. Instead, she snapped her laptop shut, packed up her belongings, and said goodbye to her officemates. Then she rode her bike across campus to College Hall and jogged up the two flights of stairs to the College of Arts and Sciences dean's suite.

"Hey, Miranda," she said, smiling her most charming smile at the dean's assistant, a dour older woman who had never once smiled back.

"He's in a meeting, Cassidy," Miranda replied without looking up from her computer screen.

"That's fine. He emailed me, so I wanted to be sure to respond before I left for the day."

Miranda's brow furrowed. "Did he ask to meet with you?"

"Well, tomorrow, not today," Cass admitted. As Miranda gave her an even more irked look than usual, she added, "I can't make it tomorrow, so I thought I would try my luck now."

Before Miranda could respond, the door to the dean's inner sanctuary opened. "I'll take that under consideration," Steve was saying in what Cass deemed an exaggeratedly even voice as he escorted none other than Lincoln Anderson, terror of the History Department, from his office.

"I'll look forward to hearing back from you." Linc's eyes fell on Cass, and he seemed to pause before glancing back at Steve. "I trust that we'll talk again soon?"

"Uh-huh," Steve said noncommittally as his gaze fell on Cass leaning against the wall across from Miranda's desk. "Looks like I'm needed. Do say hello to Nancy for me, Linc."

Nancy was the new, much younger wife, wasn't she? Cass had heard that Linc's first wife had left him—and taken their teenage children with her—when the scandal over his book broke out, and now he was remarried and had started a second family. Cass couldn't imagine anyone wanting to marry him even before he'd been publicly humiliated, but there was no accounting for the tastes of some people.

"Will do," Linc said, but his gaze was on Cass as he headed toward the hallway.

They had to pass, and Cass pushed away from the wall so that she was directly in his path. He blustered toward her as if he had no intention of giving way, but at the last moment, he stepped around her. Good thing, too. Unlike him, she had no cause to lie about her high school and college athletic exploits.

"Cassidy," Steve said warningly as Linc retreated out of earshot.

"What?" she asked, flashing her dimple in an innocent smile.

He only shook his head and waved her toward his office. "Come in. I'm glad you're here, actually."

Cass grinned over her shoulder at Miranda, who she was pretty sure came the closest she ever had to smiling in her presence, and followed Steve into his wide corner office that looked out over the stadium and nearby practice fields.

"What did *he* want?" she asked, nodding in the direction Linc Anderson had skedaddled.

Steve closed the door and sat down at the small conference table near his whiteboard. He waited until Cass had taken her usual seat across from him to say, "Your head on a silver platter."

She'd already tipped her chair back on two feet, but now she let it fall to the floor with a thud. "What?"

"Linc is of the opinion that your assistantship should be terminated for the way you challenged his authority at the all-college meeting."

"The way I—are you joking?" The idea was so preposterous that Cass couldn't help her snort of derision.

"I'm not joking, Cass. This is exactly what I meant when I said you needed to be careful. Linc holds a lot of sway on this campus. If I didn't have your back..." He trailed off, tapping a pen against the table's surface.

After a decade away from the infighting of academia, Cass had forgotten how dangerous a scorned political opponent could be. Apparently she'd spent too many years in the tech industry, where teamwork and collaboration brought professional success—and, commensurately, end-of-year bonuses. "You do have my back, though, don't you?"

He frowned. "Do you really need to ask?"

And no, she probably didn't. A Montana native who had grown up on a ranch, Steve was more forthright than the average university administrator, a trait Cass deeply appreciated. "God, I can't believe what an asshole Linc Anderson is—if you'll excuse the language," she added more as a formality than out of any real concern.

It was Steve's turn to snort. "No comment, but only because my position requires it."

"Is that why you asked me to meet with you tomorrow? Because of Linc?"

"No, him showing up was just an unlucky coincidence. Or maybe it wasn't. Have you checked the *Around the Sound* feed today?"

"Not yet." She'd been too busy helping the Music Department with their Drupal settings to spend much time on the university news site.

The dean turned his laptop around to face her. "Have a look."

Cass's breath hitched at the sight of Eva DeMarco smiling out at her from the screen. Jesus, what was Steve trying to do to her? She'd only just managed to stop thinking about the moment she and Eva had shared after the previous week's all-college meeting. Unlike her blurry department profile picture, this photo was a close-up of Eva looking professional and lovely and the tiniest bit gay in a blue button-up and khakis. Beside her on the loveseat in her office in Old Main sat Alexis Hammond, similarly put together in a red turtleneck sweater and matching lipstick.

For a moment, Cass stared at the photo, but then she remembered where she was and turned her attention to the headline, hoping her brain would behave: "Edmonds Professor's Research Profiled in the *New York Times*." Nothing like national attention—the positive kind, anyway—to make University Communications forget the "assistant" in your title.

"Between you and me," Steve said, "I'm pretty sure this article had more than a little to do with Linc's sudden urge to pick a fight. Go ahead. Follow the link."

He was going to make her read in front of him? Crap. But she couldn't exactly say no to her boss. Well, not unless he asked her to work on a Friday. She took a calming breath and clicked the link to the *New York Times*, trying to keep her expression neutral. What were the odds he had the OpenDyslexic font extension on his laptop? Not like she could ask him.

When the page had loaded, she read the text slowly, relying on contextual clues as the letters did their usual attempt at spontaneous movement. The article offered a look at Eva and Alexis's paper "Trashed: Stereotypes and Stigmatization in Romancelandia," which had been published in the latest volume of *Gender and Society*. Apparently Eva and Alexis had attended the previous year's Romance Writers of America (RWA) national convention, where they had interviewed dozens of romance writers. One of the patterns that emerged was the response authors experienced when they revealed they wrote romantic fiction. The most common reaction was open derision or some form of the question, "I bet you have to do a lot of research for those sex scenes, am I right?" As a result, many of the authors interviewed had expressed a chronic reluctance to admit to being romance writers.

After the RWA convention, the article went on, Eva and Alexis had conducted a survey of writing about genre fiction. Unsurprisingly, they found that while mystery, science fiction, and fantasy also have specific conventions and restrictions their authors are expected to adhere to, the genres are afforded considerably more respect than romantic fiction. Romance novels, Eva and Alexis pointed out, are generally written by women, published by women, and read by women. The bestselling authors in the more highly regarded genres of mystery, science fiction, and fantasy, on the other hand, are predominantly male.

"And yet," the *NYT* writer added, "as DeMarco and Hammond note in their paper, romance novels gross upwards of a billion dollars a year—more than mystery, sci-fi, and fantasy *combined*. As bestselling author Toni Donovan told the research duo, 'Romance pays the bills for the entire publishing industry.'"

Cass glanced up from the screen. "A billion dollars? I had no idea."

"I didn't, either," Steve told her, folding his arms across his chest. "When Eva first approached me about her new research direction, I have to admit I didn't respond well. But she stuck to her guns and pointed out the stigmatization of women's fiction in general—and my cultural conditioning in particular. She was kinder than she needed to be about it, really."

That didn't surprise Cass. So far in her interactions with Eva, the other woman seemed to care about ideas and concepts more than she needed to be right, which was a welcome change from the Trane approach to the dissemination of facts.

"This is interesting and all," she said, hoping Steve wouldn't pick up on just how interesting she found Eva DeMarco, "but why did you want to talk to me about it?"

He leaned forward again, hands on the table. "Your last Drupal meeting was about the new Wordpress blog plug-in, right?"

"Riiight," Cass admitted, drawing the word out as her mind skipped ahead.

"And you've already tested the code on the Arts and Sciences website, correct?"

"Correct." That was the problem with University Computing knowing her techie background. She was always their first pick for the early roll-out of new features. "You want me to profile Eva DeMarco for the Arts and Sciences blog, don't you?"

Steve nodded. "I think it's the perfect opportunity to highlight the work our younger faculty are doing, especially work that falls outside the usual research norms."

"Research norms like the Civil War, for example?" Cass asked, one corner of her mouth lifting.

Steve didn't quite smile back. "Maybe."

At that, Cass shook her head, laughing. "You know Linc is going to be totally pissed when he sees the blog post, don't you?"

Steve shrugged. "I'm more concerned about reaching our website's main audience, which I've been told is prospective students and their families. And since the data shows that prospective students are more interested in pop culture than American history...."

"Even here," she said, "half the students probably have no idea what the Battle of Fort Sumter was."

"Or the Siege of Vicksburg, or even Bull Run. And don't get me started on World War Two," Steve added.

The conversation detoured briefly to a recent report that more than 60 percent of Millennials surveyed didn't know what Auschwitz was, while another 40 percent believed that 2 million or fewer Jews had died in the Holocaust. Even more troubling was the 22 percent of Millennials who said they either hadn't heard of the Holocaust or weren't sure if they'd heard of it.

The Holocaust, only the worst case of genocide in recorded history.

"Seriously," Cass said, "what are they teaching kids these days?"

"Said Aristotle twenty-five hundred years ago."

"The difference is, he was blaming the younger generation while I'm blaming yours."

"Oh, really? Just for that, I'm going to expect Eva's profile to be online by the end of next week." As Cass stared at him, he held her gaze. Then his eyes crinkled at the corners. "I had you, didn't I?"

"It's not like I would have agreed," she said, mildly miffed that she had almost fallen for his bluff.

"Do you think you'll have time to work on it after midterms, though?" he asked.

Not if she wanted to get any other GA work done. She pulled her phone from her messenger bag and checked her Google calendar. Once she turned in her midterm papers, there would only be a few weeks of classes left before finals. The profile would take her some time to compile and even more time to write. Plus, she would have to interview Eva, possibly more than once, and give her a chance to review the final draft. After all, this would be the first official blog profile on campus. Cass wanted to do it right.

"It would probably end up being rushed if I tried to finish it before the end of the quarter," she told Steve. "Also, um, I'm not sure if I'm the best person for the job. I'm not the PR writer type. I'm not the writer type at all, really."

Steve's eyes narrowed, almost like he knew what she was getting at, and she froze. Had she given herself away somehow?

"I've read some of your writing, Cass," he said, "and I have to respectfully disagree. Winter break is fine. Are you still planning to pick up extra hours in December?"

"If that works."

He nodded. "It does. I'll email Eva and let her know about our conversation. Can she expect you to get in touch in the next week or so?"

"Absolutely," Cass agreed, unable to stop the flutter in her stomach at the idea of working with Eva over break when campus was nearly empty. Or maybe they wouldn't meet on campus at all. Maybe Eva would invite her to her house to discuss her research over dinner and—

"This is going to be great," Steve said, smiling as he escorted her out. "You'll see."

"Sure thing, boss," she said, smiling back at his contagious enthusiasm. Only really, she thought as she jogged down the stairs and headed out into the cool fall afternoon, his reason for being excited about the college's first blog post was probably very different from hers.

***

Despite her promise to Steve, Cass didn't get in touch with Eva that week. She meant to, and even tried to draft the email a couple of times. But then she would worry that she sounded either too familiar or too formal, and she would delete the draft and find something else to think about. With midterms kicking her butt and the end of the rugby season fast approaching, it wasn't difficult to refocus her attention. The same day she handed in her second and last midterm paper, she boarded a charter bus for Portland, where the rugby team was slated to compete in the final conference tournament of the fall season. The weather cooperated and the team played well enough to reach the semi-finals for the first time ever, and Cass had to admit it was nice to be away from the university's pressure-cooker atmosphere. The only drawback was the ride home on Sunday evening. What should have been a three and a half hour trip back to Edmonds turned into six hours, thanks to two separate accidents on I-5. The extra time on the bus may have given her a head start on the week's reading, but by the time she drove home from the gym that night, Cass was more than ready for downtime that didn't include moving vehicles.

Back at Matthew and Maya's, she unlocked the door to her studio and pushed it open, sighing as the familiar scent of cedar and vanilla greeted her. She closed the door behind her and then paused, wondering why the scent of candles was mixed with... was that pizza grease? Had she left a box in the recycling bin under the—

"Hey!" A head suddenly popped up over the edge of the nearby couch.

"Jesus *fuck*!" Cass screeched, dropping her bags.

Her brother guffawed from his position on the couch. "Man, I should have recorded that! I forgot what you sound like when you're scared shitless."

When they were kids, they used to take turns sneaking up on each other, much to their parents' dismay.

"Shut up," she said now, tossing her keys onto the side table near the door. "What are you doing here, Matthew? You know the house rules: You can't be here if I'm not."

"Apparently that's not true, because here we are."

"God, you're such an entitled white boy. I'm definitely taking away your key this time."

"You can't," he said. "I'm your landlord. In fact, from now on I think you should call me Lord Matthew."

"As if." Cass dragged her bags to the foot of the attic stairs. "You know, I'm getting sick of how you *lord* your home ownership over me." She paused. "Did you see what I did there?"

"Yes, Cassidy, I saw what you did there." He nudged a white

cardboard box on the coffee table with one socked foot. "Got you some pizza. Or, I got myself pizza, but there's a couple slices left for you. Figured you cook for us enough, I should probably return the favor once in a while."

She grabbed her water bottle from her messenger bag and dropped down on the couch next to her brother, reaching eagerly for the box. A couple slices turned out to be three pieces of a veggie pie that she eagerly helped herself to. Her bus snacks had run out somewhere around Olympia.

"Why are you hiding out here, anyway?" she asked around a mouthful of olives and fresh garlic.

"Ugh," her brother groaned. "Maya kicked me out."

"Dude! What did you do?"

"Nothing! I swear, it's her hormones. Turns out the stereotypes about pregnant women are spot on."

Cass eyed her brother. "You had to have done something." Maya was nothing if not logical. Even if her hormones did make her pregnant-lady-crazy, she wouldn't get mad for no reason. Would she?

"All I did was mention that I might be interested in checking out the Unitarian church sometime."

Well, that explained it. Raised in an extended Catholic family, Maya detested organized religion and believed that everyone else should, too. Cass was happy to oblige. "Did you tell her they have a co-minister who's a Wiccan priestess?"

"She didn't give me the chance! Seriously, I hope our marriage survives this baby."

"So do I," Cass agreed, frowning slightly.

She couldn't imagine her brother and Maya splitting up. They had met sophomore year of college and gotten married a month after they graduated. Married housing at UC Davis, where Matthew had done his PhD, was only available to actual married couples, though Matthew claimed that wasn't the reason he'd proposed. While their parents seemed skeptical, Cass believed him. She was fairly certain that Maya had done the proposing, anyway.

As Cass finished off the pizza, Matthew turned the TV on and resumed a paused game of *Legend of Zelda*. Inwardly, she had to admire his commitment to scaring her when she'd walked in.

Outwardly, she stole the controller and killed his character so that they could restart the game in multi-player mode.

"Do you want to sleep on the couch or the futon?" she asked him a little while later, eyes narrowed at the screen, tongue peeking out of the corner of her mouth.

"Neither. I should go home and apologize, even though I'm not sure what I'm apologizing for. But Ben says you can either be right or you can be married." As Cass cast him a skeptical look, he added, "Obviously, he didn't make the right choice himself."

"Obviously," she grunted.

No one could know what went on inside anyone else's relationship, but Cass had a hard time understanding how Ben Miller, an average looking white guy who specialized in African colonial history, could have walked away from Eva DeMarco. Maya had said Ben and Tina didn't get together until later, but Jace had told Cass that they'd been pretty close even before the divorce. Ben's poor judgment on the marital front wasn't why she was currently avoiding him, though. Well, maybe a little. But mostly she was pissed at the knight-in-shining-armor routine he'd pulled a few weeks earlier. She knew that Ben had taken on Linc Anderson at the Arts and Sciences meeting more on her brother's behalf than hers, but she could handle Linc on her own. She had, in fact, been handling him before her brother and Ben jumped in.

Boys.

"Speaking of Ben and marriage," Matthew said, moving the controller—and his head—from side to side, "Eva asked about you the other day."

Cass nearly choked on air but masked it with a cough. "She did?" she said as casually as she could manage, resisting the urge to demand all of the details at once.

"Yeah. You're not—I mean, you're, like, keeping your distance, right?"

Cass thought of the email she had yet to send. "You could say that." She wasn't sure why she hadn't told Matthew or Maya about the blog post Steve had assigned. She only knew she wanted to keep it to herself for now. "Did you tell me to stay away from her because of Ben?" she added, pretending to concentrate on upgrading her sword onscreen.

"No, that's totally not it." He sounded mildly offended, so she knew he was telling the truth.

"Then was it because of their fertility issues?"

Out of the corner of her eye she saw his head whip toward her. "How do you know about that?"

"Don't you wish you knew?"

"This isn't a joke, Cass," her brother said, his voice serious like it got whenever he waxed poetic over the awesomeness of the universe. "You don't realize how thin the line is between life and death until you watch a child growing inside your wife's body. I can't even imagine what it must be like to be Maya right now, knowing what she sees at work on a daily basis."

Neither could Cass, to be honest.

He expelled a noisy breath and stood up, and she paused the game to look up at him. He was staring out the window toward the main house, where a light shone upstairs in the master bedroom.

"Time to go home?" she asked.

"Yeah," he agreed. "Time to go home."

"You up for a run in the morning?" They had gotten in the habit of running together through the arboretum three or four times a week.

"Wouldn't miss it. Later, Crater."

"After a while, Anglophile."

He slapped her shoulder, but gently, and headed for the door.

"Leave your key," she ordered in her best coaching voice.

"Nice try," he replied, jangling his key ring as he let himself out.

She turned back to the game, fingers hovering over the resume button. Then, in an act of willpower, she shut off the television and cleaned up the pizza mess. It wasn't even ten, but she was tired. In a good way, though. Underneath the travel fatigue, she felt recharged, ready to take on the remainder of the quarter. Which was good—only two and a half weeks until Thanksgiving. After that, the quarter would almost be over.

She locked the studio door and carried her bags upstairs, where she dropped face first onto the queen bed one of the neighbors had sold her shortly after she'd moved in. Her brother's old futon had been thin and lumpy even when Cass's shoulder wasn't plaguing her. After surgery, she probably wouldn't have slept at all if not for the new-to-her mattress. There had been a time after college when she had couch-surfed her way across the US and several foreign countries, playing semi-pro rugby and picking up whatever side jobs she could. But eventually she'd built a more settled life in San Francisco, where she grew accustomed to apartments stocked with higher end furniture. She'd left most of that furniture in a storage unit in Oakland, a decision she had grown to regret. Once you'd lived like an adult, it was hard to go back to the student lifestyle.

Before she could become too sleepy, she rolled onto her side and pulled her Kindle out of her overnight bag, tugging her green and blue tartan blanket up to her chest. Only a few months ago, she wouldn't have been able to lean on her right side like this. She would have had to lie rigidly on her back, careful to distribute her weight evenly. For months before and after surgery, she had lived with pain so intense that she would randomly emit pathetic, wounded animal sounds. Now it was as if The Year of Terrible Pain had happened to someone else. Her brain appeared to have erased any evidence of her injury, despite the tiny incision scars that she had covered up with a new tattoo—an inscribed half-sleeve of medieval armor that wouldn't have looked amiss on Wonder Woman or one of her Amazonian sisters.

When she'd commented to Maya recently on the phenomenon of forgotten pain, her sister-in-law had laughed.

"One of the nervous system's better tricks. Ingenious, really, from an evolutionary standpoint. Otherwise, women would never have more than one child and the human race would go extinct."

When Cass considered the possibility of pushing something the size of a watermelon out of an opening one-sixth its size, she had to swallow back a wave of unease. She understood that the female body was equipped to bear life, but the idea of growing a child inside her body and then pushing it out into the world was a bit too close to *Aliens* for her taste, only without the exploding chest cavity. If you were lucky—Maya had come home with some pretty gruesome tales from the birth front.

An image of Eva popped into Cass's mind, as had been happening lately whenever she wasn't concentrating on not allowing it to do so. Had Eva starred in one of the seemingly anonymous stories Maya had brought home at the end of a long shift? There were so many ways a pregnancy could end, more than Cass had ever suspected before her brother had married an obstetrics nurse. The tragic tales only reinforced her own uncertainty about having a baby.

For all their outward radicalness, her friends in San Francisco were mostly the type of queer and not-queer women and men who wanted the traditional, stereotyped American dream: one spouse, a house with a fenced yard, and two point five gender non-specific children. Even as they spent most Friday and Saturday nights out trying new sushi spots and drinking microbrews at their favorite hipster bars, they debated whether to raise kids in the city or suburbs; what minivan-like car they could be prevailed upon to drive (though not an actual minivan!); the best gender-neutral names; and whether to use an anonymous or known donor. Cass circled around the edges of these conversations, dipping her toe in occasionally but never fully leaping in.

It wasn't that she didn't like kids, as her friends sometimes teased her. She had babysat for neighbor families throughout high school and had watched professors' kids in college for extra spending money. She liked kids, sometimes more than her peers. Children didn't try to impress you with perfectly ironic pronouncements. They weren't pretending to be someone they thought they should be, and Cass appreciated that. She'd occasionally even allowed herself to indulge in a variation on her friends' daydreams: a comfy home with a crossover SUV in the driveway and a smiling wife making homemade pizza in the kitchen while Cass played with their two point five children.

Her doubts about becoming a parent were rooted in other issues. For one, she'd never seen herself as the type of person who would bear children. Not only that, but if she did have kids, how would they see her? A non-binary lesbian wasn't exactly the kind of parent most kids would pick. Would they resent her difference when they grew old enough to recognize it? Would teachers and school administrators—not to mention other kids—treat her children badly because *she* failed to live up to cultural norms? Throw in the dyslexia, and her anxieties over parenting became a clamor. One day her children would realize they read better than their queer, gender nonconforming mother, and really, did she want to put herself through that?

And yet, rugby carried a firm ethos, the gist of which was that you didn't let fear stop you from accomplishing what you wanted. You pushed through fear and pain and doubt, and you did so out of a desire to be the best you not only for yourself but for whomever else you counted as a member of your team, both on and off the field. When you committed to something or someone, you gave no less than a hundred percent. Always.

She rolled onto her back and scooted up the bed to her pile of pillows, settling her Kindle on her lap. No more babies on the brain—or at least, no more thinking about her own future babies. Though Maya still wasn't showing, it wouldn't be long now. The plan was to fly to California at Christmas to tell her mom and sisters in person. Then Cass and Matthew's parents would fly into Seattle at New Year's for the second round of family announcements.

But that was weeks away. For now, Cass should stop worrying about the future and concentrate on the path directly in front of her: finishing the quarter strong. Everything else could wait.

Pushing away her sleepiness, she snuggled further under her fleece blanket and hummed Mozart's *Eine Kleine Nachtmusik* as she dug into a PDF article about the erasure of queer and trans people of color from the climate movement.

***

Even though she had rehearsed the encounter in her head multiple times, she still wasn't prepared the following morning when she pulled open the door to Old Main and came face to face with Eva DeMarco.

"Cass!" Eva said, her eyes wide. "Um, hi."

"Hi, yourself." She almost asked Eva what she was doing there, but (thankfully, because DUH) said instead, "I'm glad I ran into you, actually."

"You are?" Eva's eyebrows rose.

People were streaming past them through the other door, so Cass stepped aside and allowed Eva to exit the building. "I was going to get in touch with you today," she explained as they paced toward the brick patio edged by rose bushes recently cut back for winter. "Did Steve email you about meeting with me?"

"You mean about the blog thingie?" Eva asked, fiddling with a lock of dark brown hair that had come loose from her otherwise neat bun.

"Exactly. I won't be working on the post until break, but in the meantime, I was thinking maybe you and I could grab coffee. You know, to talk about a plan," Cass said, sticking to the script she'd practiced in the shower that morning.

"Coffee?" Eva frowned slightly, her eyes darting around the courtyard.

Cass tried to pretend she didn't feel a pang of hurt at Eva's coolness. This was why email was a far superior mode of communication. "It's fine if you don't have time. I could just stop by your office hours at some point, if that would be better."

"No." Eva finally made eye contact. "Coffee would be fine. I mean, I like coffee, and Steve wants us to talk, so."

"So...?" Cass felt her forehead crinkle as she tried to interpret Eva's mixed messages. A few weeks earlier they'd run into each other in the dean's suite, and when she'd smiled at Eva, the other woman had promptly dropped her books. Which was adorable and all, but Cass was used to the casual indifference of the San Francisco queer scene where unless you were someone's best friend or ex, you were basically invisible. This hot and cold act Eva had going was more difficult to parse.

"So, okay," Eva clarified. She checked the thin silver watch on her wrist—*did people still wear non-digital watches?*—and glanced up. "I have a little time now. Would you want to...?" She gestured vaguely toward the quad.

Cass followed the direction she'd indicated. Ed U Brew, the campus's most popular coffee shop, was tucked into a corner of Bass Hall. Like the rest of the building, the shop had been renovated, and was now even more of a draw than its excellent coffee and homemade pastries had originally made it.

"Um," Cass said articulately. "You mean right now?"

"It's okay if you can't," Eva said, looking away again. "You can just email me later if you want."

"No," Cass said. "I have time." She didn't really, but Gwen would probably be in her office for a little while even after her official office hours ended.

The tightness around Eva's eyes eased, and she smiled as she held out her arm in an oddly gallant move. "In that case, after you."

Yep. Totally adorkable.

A moment later, they were walking across a corner of the Academic Quad. Cass matched her pace to Eva's and tried to ignore the voice in her head that insisted on remarking repeatedly that she and Eva were going to coffee. Together. Like a date. *But not a date*, Cass reminded the stupidly romantic, deluded part of her brain, because they were colleagues working on a project assigned by their mutual boss. It was work coffee to keep their minds sharp while they discussed the parameters of the project in question, that was all.

Still, it was hard not to notice the look two girls with shaved hair and multiple piercings gave them on their way across the quad: knowing and excited at once, elbowing each other as if they had discussed Professor DeMarco's gaydar score, and this sighting of Eva with an obvious lesbian was confirmation of her potential queerness. She stole a glance at Eva, only to find her staring conspicuously at the path in front of them, cheeks tinged pink. Had she noticed the girls, too? Then again, they were hard to miss.

"Anyway," Cass said, "how's your quarter going? Still good to be back?"

Eva nodded. "Still good. What about you? You must not have too many quarters left on campus."

"Nope. Not too many."

"Have you started the research component of your thesis yet?"

"Not yet. I haven't had the time. I'm hoping to use winter quarter for research and do the actual writing in the spring."

"Will you stay here to write or go back to California?"

Cass looked at her quickly. How did she know—?

"Maya told me at the rugby match that you're moving back to the Bay Area 'as soon as humanly possible,' I think she said."

So much for not telling other people what to do. Announcing to Eva that Cass was only in Edmonds for a few more months seemed a lot like warning her away. "I actually haven't decided what my plans are yet, but writing off-campus is a definite possibility."

Eva looked at her and then away, her gaze appearing to settle on Bass Hall's new brick facade, tidy and uniform in color and pattern especially when compared to the building's older, ivy-colored wings.

As they entered the double doors closest to the Ed U Brew order counter, Cass asked, "Are you getting anything?"

"Of course." Eva sounded almost offended, as if the thought of not buying coffee at ten AM on the Monday after midterms was absurd.

Cass hid a smile. She still remembered how Eva had waited to see which cupcake she would choose, tensing as her hand hovered above the salted caramel and only relaxing when she'd settled on the red velvet. Apparently when it came to food and drink, the good professor wasn't quite as mild-mannered as she seemed.

They ordered drip coffee and doctored it with cream and sugar, though Cass chose dark roast and Eva selected blonde. On the tip of Cass's tongue was a flirty question about Eva's affinity for blondes, but once again she caught herself in time. Work coffee meant no flirting allowed, even if Eva was especially adorable when she was flustered.

An atrium bordering the coffee shop offered seating, and they found an empty bar table off to one side. Cass led the way between the tables and booths alight in morning sun, coffee held carefully before her. She claimed one of the high-backed stools and stripped out of her ski jacket while Eva hung her wool pea coat and vintage rucksack-style backpack from the back of her stool. Then they both placed their phones on the table beside their coffee cups and finally took a seat.

"So," Cass said, entwining her twitchy fingertips in her lap. Eva's cowl-necked sweater looked incredibly soft, and Cass had to actively tamp down on the urge to reach out and test the texture.

"So how did you end up in California?" Eva asked, curling both hands around her coffee cup's protective sleeve. "San Francisco is pretty far from New York."

"About as far away as I could get and still be in the US." Cass softened the statement with a half-smile. "I had friends there, actually, and the local women's club was looking for players right when I needed a new team."

"When did you start playing rugby? High school or college?"

"College." For the next few minutes, Cass found herself sharing the story of her post-college life: how she'd graduated with a degree in sociology and no clue what to do next, and one of her former teammates had invited her to Portugal to play semi-pro rugby. How that experience had led to other clubs in Spain and France, and then somehow she'd been out of college—and out of the country—for three years already and she still didn't have a long-term plan.

"I loved Europe, and I met so many great people and got to travel to so many incredible places, but I was homesick for the US," she admitted. "So when another old teammate told me about the Berkeley All Blues, I figured the Bay Area could be my next adventure."

"And how did you end up in the tech industry?" Eva sipped her coffee but kept her gaze trained on Cass, open and inquisitive.

"By accident. I signed up with my friend's temp agency, and the third assignment they sent me to was at Avicom, a mid-sized social media company. I was only supposed to be there for a week answering phones, but the head of HR had gone to Bryn Mawr. She looked at my résumé and offered me a position running the corporate library, which led to intranet development, which eventually led to working on the company-wide content management system."

"Drupal?" Eva guessed.

"Right. Drupal. Then Avicom's IPO tanked, and I and many other people found ourselves unemployed."

"Ouch." Eva wrinkled her nose in sympathy.

"A month later I tore my rotator cuff and had to quit rugby, so..."

"Grad school." Eva nodded. "Why not?"

"Exactly." Cass gazed at her across the small table. "What about you? How did you end up at Edmonds?"

Eva looked down, clasping her cup in both hands again. "Easy. It was the first place that offered tenure-track positions to both Ben and me." She glanced up, her expression contemplative. "You did know I used to be married to Ben Miller, didn't you?"

"Yeah, I heard. Only recently, though," Cass added. She didn't want Eva thinking she'd known about Ben when she'd first approached her at the Thistledown. "I'm not exactly up on Arts and Sciences gossip. Now, if you want to know what's going on behind the scenes in the PE department, I'm totally your woman."

Eva smiled at her, dark eyes warm in the sunlight spilling in through a nearby wall of windows. She was lovely, and yet there was an air of sadness in the curve of her shoulders, in the almost wistful twist of her mouth. And once again, Cass couldn't help but wonder how it was that Ben could ever in a million years have walked away from her. What had happened to their marriage? How did Eva feel about Ben moving in with Tina so soon after their split? And, most importantly, did Eva feel the flicker of attraction between them, too?

Before she could cross a line and ask any of the questions swirling around inside her brain, she noticed Eva's eyes settle on a point over her shoulder, saw her mouth tighten, heard her slowly inhaled breath. Cass followed her gaze. Speak of the devil. Ben and Tina were walking toward them, Ed U Brew to-go cups in hand.

"Hello Eva, Cassidy," Tina said, pausing beside their table while Ben skulked behind her.

"Hi, Tina." Eva's voice was kind but perhaps a touch resigned. "Ben."

"Eva." He nodded at her and focused on Cass, his gaze narrowing. "What's up, Cass?"

"Not much." She regarded him evenly, refusing to feel uncomfortable. It wasn't like he could tell that she had a crush on his ex-wife.

"I didn't know you two were friends," he said, his tone more than a little accusatory.

Oh. Well, maybe he *could* tell. She resisted the urge to announce that they were only work colleagues and looked to Eva, who only raised an eyebrow at her and sipped her coffee.

It was Tina who gave Ben the look that said he was being an asshole; Tina who said, her voice almost scoffing, "Why wouldn't they be? They're in the same department."

"No, I know." At least he had the grace to look abashed. "Cass, catch up with you at the Tech Committee meeting tomorrow?"

"Yep," she said, popping the "p" with unnecessary vigor.

Although, at the moment, she was thinking she might forego her usual spot beside him to sit with Sara from the student center instead.

"Anyway, it was nice to see you," Tina said. "Enjoy your coffee."

"Thanks," Eva said. "You too."

Cass contented herself with a nod. And then, thankfully, Tina all but dragged Ben away, her voice low and sibilant as she murmured unintelligibly to him.

They were quiet for a moment, and then Eva said, looking tired, "Sorry about that."

"Why are you sorry?"

"Did you miss the awkward weirdness that just happened?"

"It wasn't that bad." As Eva stared at her, that lone eyebrow once again lifted, Cass conceded, "Fine. It was a little weird."

"Divorce has a way of doing that even to perfectly reasonable people."

Her earlier questions came back, but Cass pushed them away. She had practically shared her entire life story and still knew very little about the woman currently watching her from across the table, so she said, "Okay, my turn. Why sociology?"

Eva leaned back in her chair, smiling slightly. "Why not sociology?"

"Come on," Cass pressed. "You don't get a PhD on *why not*."

"And yet it's good enough for a Master's?"

"A Master's only takes two years and is noticeably lacking in doctoral-level hazing."

"True." Eva swallowed the rest of her coffee, and for a moment Cass thought she was going to dodge the question. But then she pushed up her square black glasses and said almost shyly, "Because of Marxism, actually."

Cass tilted her head. "Care to elaborate on that?"

"My sophomore year of college—"

"At Cornell."

"Right. Fall semester, I took the Sociology of Education, and we read a Marxist critique that described the 'hidden curriculum' in the public education system."

"Bowles and Gintis," Cass said, trying not to preen too much as Eva gazed up at her, smile appreciative.

"Exactly. I felt like a blindfold had been stripped away, and all of a sudden I could see this system I'd been a part of my entire life and never once thought to question." She shook her head, tracing an invisible pattern on the table with her fingertip. "The average Westerner spends the majority of her pre-higher education life—"

"—assuming she goes to college," Cass put in.

"The majority of her *childhood*," Eva amended, "in a public school classroom. The system is indoctrinating her into the labor market, or so the argument goes, preparing her to spend the majority of her adult life working. This is why public schools don't promote creativity or independent thinking, why they reward behavior typically associated with 'good workers'—dependability, consistency, obedience, punctuality."

Cass nodded. "The reproduction of the social relations of production."

"Right. Correspondence theory." Eva regarded her across the table. "Have you read Bowles and Gintis, or have you just heard about their work?"

"I've read excerpts. One of my professors at Vassar was a closet Marxist."

Eva laughed, the sound short and surprised.

"Does that term apply to you, too?" Cass asked, teasing. "I can't imagine there are as many radicals on the faculty at Cornell as there are at NYU."

Eva's smile turned rueful. "I'm the first member of my family to go to college, so as you can imagine, I was in the closet about more than just my philosophical tendencies."

Cass blinked, wondering how much she should read into the subtext of their conversation. Should she take this opening to ask Eva what she had been doing that night at the Thistledown? Were they at that point yet?

As Cass hesitated, Eva glanced at her watch and said, "I hate to say it, but I have class this afternoon and I don't have a lesson plan yet. What exactly has Steve put you up to?"

The business portion of their coffee date—*meeting*—only took a few minutes. Cass explained the plan to get the profile done during winter break, and Eva agreed that would work on her end. She didn't have any travel plans this winter, she said, mostly because she needed to finish up her Tenure and Promotion portfolio. Working through the holiday break wouldn't be much fun, but the packet was due in January. Besides, she and Alexis were scheduled to speak at a conference over spring break, so there was a vacation of sorts in the near future to look forward to.

"Which conference?" Cass asked.

"The annual meeting of the Cultural Studies Association," Eva told her, and then bit her lip in that way that wasn't distracting at all. "It's in San Francisco this year."

"March isn't the best time of year to visit the Bay Area," Cass said, "but I'm sure you'll have a good time anyway."

"With Alexis along for the ride, that seems likely." Eva smiled at her across the table, eyes warm and just that tiny bit shy again. "I really enjoyed this, Cass. I'm glad we ran into each other."

"Me, too." She hesitated. "Maybe we can grab lunch next time. I mean, when we're working on the profile, of course."

"Of course." Eva's smile turned noncommittal and she rose, pulling on her coat and slinging her bag over one shoulder. "You'll email me about getting together in a few weeks?"

"I was thinking it might be easier if I text you." Cass held her breath, fists hidden inside the fleece-lined pockets of her ski jacket. Had she really asked Eva for her number at the end of the work date they had spent talking mostly about non-work-related things?

"Um, sure." Eva fumbled with her phone. "What's your number?"

Cass gave it to her, trying to quell the stupid surges of excitement shocking her brain. They were exchanging numbers so that they could work together on Steve's blog project. That was all.

"There. I just sent you a text. I think. For a Millennial, I'm a bit of a bust when it comes to technology," Eva admitted, holding up her iPhone. "This is actually my first smart phone."

The text alert on Cass's phone sounded, but she resisted the urge to immediately read what Eva had written. "Looks like you've got it figured out."

"Definitely an illusion," Eva said, and laughed a little, her eyes still on Cass's.

Cass smiled back, and they held eye contact for a long moment. Work date. Riiight.

They collected their things and walked outside, lingering in the sunlight filtering through the nearly barren deciduous trees that lined the paths across the quad. The angle of the light overhead had shifted significantly during the brief time they'd spent in the atrium. The shortest day of the year was only a handful of weeks away now.

"I'm headed to the library," Eva said, tilting her head in one direction. "You?"

"Gwen's office hours." She nodded in the opposite direction, toward Old Main. "She's my thesis adviser."

"Right, then." Eva backed away. "See you soon, Cass."

"Text you soon," she replied, smiling goofily, and then cursed her cheesiness as Eva's lips pursed and her eyes lit up in a gentle *I'm-totally-not-laughing-at-you-but-really-I-am* way.

"I'll look forward to it." And then Eva turned and started across the quad, hands in her coat pockets, straps on her rucksack swinging lightly with each step she took.

Cass managed to wait until she reached Old Main to check her phone. When she did, her heart melted a little and she smiled so widely it hurt her cheeks.

"Hi, Cass!" Eva had written. "Thanks for the coffee date."

Coffee date. At least she wasn't the only one calling it that.

In the next moment, her smile slipped as she realized that the end of the quarter—and thus their excuse for spending more time together—was still weeks away. Not that that would stop her from "perseverating," as her mother used to call it, about Eva. Even when their interactions were brief, it took her days to stop thinking about Eva, to cease looking for her on campus, to keep herself from dreaming up excuses to visit the fourth floor of Old Main. This project would only make it more difficult for her to keep her distance, as this morning had ably demonstrated. But really, was avoiding Eva even necessary anymore? Or, for that matter, possible? After all, Steve had basically ordered Cass to get to know her better.

Although technically, she supposed, he'd only asked her to write about Eva's research. There was a difference, at least in theory. In practice, not so much.

She pocketed her phone and jogged up the stairs toward the Sociology Department's cramped wing on the fourth floor. Hopefully Gwen would be there, and hopefully Cass would be able to focus her wandering mind on research questions, literature lists, and datasets. Her thesis wasn't about to write itself. Now if she could only manage not to somehow find an excuse to work Eva's research into the conversation....

Yep, she thought as she neared Gwen's office, relieved to find the door open and the light still on. That was definitely a good goal to keep in mind.

She paused in the hallway for a moment, shaking her head at her own ridiculousness. She couldn't let her crush on Eva DeMarco spin out of control. But at the same time, she could hear Maya's voice in her head: "Why not Eva?"

She was starting to think that maybe that was a good question.

"Is that you out there, Cassidy?" Gwen chose that moment to call out.

"Yes," Cass said, and pasted a smile on her face as she headed into the older woman's office. "Sorry I'm late. I ran into Eva DeMarco and we started talking about her research."

From behind her desk, Gwen gave her an enigmatic smile. "I'm sure you did. Well, you're here now. Have a seat and let's see what you've been up to."

Cass reached into her bag for her notes, scolding herself for her lack of impulse control. There would be plenty of time later to think about Eva. Because Cass was under no illusions at this point. Eva DeMarco would definitely be starring in her daydreams for the foreseeable future.

CHAPTER SEVEN

Eva lifted her delicate porcelain tea cup, but she could still feel the weight of her mother's stare. She lowered her cup and frowned across the crisp white tablecloth. "What?"

"That's exactly what I was about to ask you."

Eva tried not to fidget under her mother's narrow-eyed gaze. Where was the waitress, anyway? They had been done eating for at least ten minutes and had only seen their server from a distance. But the freshly-made scones and quiche had been as delicious as ever, and the restaurant's dining room was full as it nearly always was during their weekly breakfast dates. Her mother loved the traditional ambience of the tea room operated out of a Victorian mansion just up the hill from the ferry terminal, so Eva swallowed her complaints over the customer service and brought her mom to the Secret Garden Tea Room every Saturday morning.

"I don't know what you mean," she said, forcing herself to stare straight into her mother's light brown eyes. There was no outward sign of the macular degeneration that Eva knew was steadily weakening her mother's eyesight, creating a blurry spot in her central vision field while leaving items in her periphery comparatively clear.

Her mother focused on a spot over Eva's shoulder, no doubt in order to see her better. "Eva Marie DeMarco, don't lie to me. We said we would be honest with each other, remember?"

As if she could forget. After The Fall, as they referred to her mother's accident, they had each discovered certain truths about the other. Eva had learned that her mother had been keeping a wide range of health problems to herself, and her mother had learned that Eva and Ben were in the process of getting a divorce. No more lies, they'd agreed. Not even to protect each other.

In theory, that was all well and good. But the topic that was weighing on Eva currently, the one that had made her check her watch and fiddle with her hair so much that even her half-blind mother had noticed, was not an easy subject to discuss with her mother.

"It's nothing, really," she said, glancing down at her mostly empty plate. "Just school. I'd forgotten how stressful fall quarter can be."

That much was true. She was already looking forward to the comparably quiet winter quarter, and she'd only turned her fall grades in the night before.

Her mother was quiet, and when she spoke again, her voice was hesitant. "Is it Ben? Are the two of you having problems working together?"

"No," Eva said, and then she paused. Or were they? He *had* behaved like an ass the day he saw her with Cass at the coffee shop. Cass, who she would be meeting for lunch a couple of hours from now. A working lunch date, they'd called it, but Eva wasn't even bothering to pretend to herself that work would be the primary focus. At least, not for her.

"No, but...?" her mother pressed.

Well, Eva thought grimly, so be it. "But there's a girl."

Her mother's jaw dropped momentarily. "Ben is dating someone else? I thought he and Tina were living together."

"No, not for Ben. I meant for me. There's a woman at work I'm interested in." Saying the words out loud did nothing to diffuse the nervous energy bubbling inside her gut. As her mother leaned away from the table, lips pursed in obvious disapproval, Eva's anxiety only intensified. "You see? This is why I didn't want to tell you." She glanced around again for their elusive server. Where was she?

"I'm sorry," her mother said after a moment, and reached for her hand. "I was surprised, that's all. Please tell me about... her. I want to know about your life, Eva. Please don't shut me out again."

Sandy DeMarco was not a woman who normally implored

others. She was someone who told people what to do, confident that her wishes would be met by those around her. That was what had made her such a good office manager at the Ford dealership where Eva's father had worked. She had run the front office and he had run the service department for three and a half decades before the 2007 recession had sent them both into early retirement.

Eva left her hand in her mother's grasp, though the contact felt almost too intimate. They didn't often hug or hold hands in their family. "What do you mean, again?"

Her mother sighed. "You went off to college and you never looked back, Eva. Which I understood, of course, but your father and I... well, we often wished we were closer to you."

"You did?" Eva shook her head, her anxiety morphing into guilt. "I didn't know that."

"I never told you."

"No. I guess you didn't."

Their harried server finally arrived, and Eva pulled her hand away to reach for her credit card.

"Let me?" her mother asked, gaze hopeful.

She hesitated and then nodded. "Okay. Thanks, Mom."

"You're welcome."

Outside a few minutes later, rain sputtered from low gray skies, and Eva pulled up the hood on her jacket as she helped her mother get situated in the Subaru's passenger seat. The ride back to Shady Grove was quick, the sound of the radio filling the space between them. Eva was pulling her car into the driveway of the assisted living facility when her mother touched her arm.

"Come in with me?"

That unfamiliar entreating tone was back, and all Eva could do was nod and park in a visitor's spot. She saw her mom at least a couple of times a week, but it still felt like it was never quite enough.

The parking lot was a short walk from her mother's single-story unit that sat in a cluster of similar homes behind the main nursing facility. Eva followed her mother up the paved walk and into the spacious duplex, pausing to assess the interior. Sparkling, just as the cleaning company had promised. Every Saturday while Eva took her mother out to breakfast, someone came to clean the unit top to bottom. Shady Grove offered "simple housekeeping" as an included monthly service, but Eva had learned that her mother's reduced vision meant she required more assistance when it came to taking care of her physical space.

"So," her mother said, leading her to the couch in the living room and patting the cushion beside her, "you were saying something about a girl."

Eva settled next to her mother, hands in her lap. "Oh. Um, yes. But she's a student, so I don't think—"

"A student?" her mother interrupted. "Eva, how young is this person?"

"Thirty-one. She's a graduate student, not an undergrad."

Her mother's alarm faded. A different gender she could (sort of, almost) accept, but apparently she drew the line at a younger woman. "Your father and I were five years apart too, and it was never an issue. What's the problem?"

"Who says there's a problem?" Eva deflected. As her mother tilted her head sideways and once again fixed her gaze over Eva's shoulder, she relented. "I'm not supposed to date a student, not even a graduate student."

Her mother frowned. "Are you her teacher?"

"No."

"Does she work for you?"

"No, she works for the dean's office."

"Then it isn't really a conflict of interest, is it?"

Eva rolled her shoulders, trying to ease some of the tension that had built up over the quarter. "Maybe not, but it's still frowned upon, especially within the same department. Anyway, she's going back to California after she finishes her degree."

"Ah." Her mother's brow smoothed out as much as it ever did. She used to complain about her wrinkles, but lately she seemed to have grown more comfortable with her aging self. Maybe going blind in this case was a mixed blessing. "Is the work part of it really what's bothering you?"

"Yes," Eva said. "I'm afraid that if I get involved with her, I won't get tenure. And then I'll have to find another job in a different city or even state, and I'm not ready for that. I like it here. I can't imagine living anywhere else."

"Uh-huh," her mother said, condescension obvious in the line of her mouth and the tilt of one eyebrow.

Growing up, Eva had been stuck with her mother's passive aggression, but as an adult she could simply walk away. She glanced at her watch. Still some time to kill before she met Cass. She could always take Harvey for a quick run....

"Honey." Her mother placed a hand on Eva's shoulder and squeezed, grip surprisingly strong. Physical therapy twice a week must be working. "I know that your father and I weren't the best parents for you." Automatically Eva started to protest—on principle, not because what her mother said was wrong—but her mother waved away her objections. "We weren't the best fit for you, and there is no shame in admitting that. Children come into this world who they are, and as older parents, your father and I were already stuck in our ways. Neither of us came from families that valued education, so, as I think you know, we struggled with raising a gifted child. But here you are, and here I am, and I would like to try to be the mother you deserve even if it's a little late for all of that. And so I will tell you this, my dear: Don't let fear of what *might* be keep you from what *could* be."

Eva blinked at her mother. The speech seemed so unlike her, but then again, did Eva truly know her mother? Had she ever really known her father? She'd left home at the age of 17 and, as her mother had said, stayed away. The past year had been the most time she'd spent with her mom in the nearly two decades since high school, and even then half the time had been spent in navigating health crises and other "life events," as she and Ben had always referred to any major challenge they'd faced.

Her mom squeezed her shoulder once more before rising from the couch. "I have some chocolate chip cookies for you in the kitchen. Bella Burke, the lady in unit number four, helped me, so this time all the ingredients should be there."

The sudden switch from philosophy to baking was a bit disorienting, but so was this entire conversation. Eva rose and followed her mother into the tiny kitchen at one end of the living space. Hopefully this time she hadn't mistaken flour for sugar. One could hope.

***

Eva saw Cass first, standing on the sidewalk under a red

awning outside Angelina's Fish and Chips, an Edmonds institution. She nearly stumbled but quickly righted herself and crossed the street, nervousness from earlier now tinged with a kind of excitement she didn't remember feeling with Ben. He'd started out as a friend of a friend she would see around the city occasionally, amiable and nerdy and cute, and she honestly hadn't thought of him in a romantic way until he'd asked her out. She'd said no at first. They were in different PhD programs at different New York institutions—his Columbia pedigree was a bit fancier than her NYU degree—but things could still get awkward in their group of friends if it didn't work out. Not only that, but securing a tenure-track position was difficult enough without having to find two. Ben had been persistent, though, and eventually she'd fallen for his passion and his intelligence, qualities that had never wavered over the course of their relationship.

But this spark of energy she could feel bouncing back and forth between her and Cass, this was different. It had been there from the first moment they'd met—at least on her side. She imagined that while Cass probably made more than her fair share of women feel an immediate flash of attraction, that didn't mean she always felt it in return. She seemed to feel it now, though, Eva was fairly certain. Or maybe that was just wishful thinking.

As she neared, Cass looked up from her phone and smiled, her dimple as adorable as ever, her hair sweeping back in its trendy style, and Eva couldn't decide which would be worse: if Cass felt the same way or if she didn't.

"Hi," Cass said, tucking her phone into the pocket of her navy blue jacket. "You made it."

"Sorry I'm late," Eva said. "I was with my mother earlier and lost track of time."

No way was she about to admit that her tardiness was due to an inability to decide on an outfit for their work date. Her favorite sweater had smelled like food from breakfast, so after trying on at least six different tops while Harvey snuggled in her covers and watched, a slightly confused look on his wrinkled face, she'd finally settled on a dark green fleece pullover that she'd bought in the kids' section of REI. Sometimes it was good to be small.

"Your mother?" Cass repeated. "Is she visiting?"

"No, she lives here." As Cass's face registered surprise, Eva remembered that they didn't know each other very well at all. "That's why I was on leave for part of last year. She's got some health issues and had a major fall, so I moved her out here to be closer."

"I'm sorry. That's rough."

"Rougher on her than on me, but she's tough. The Pennsylvania Dutch are a stoic lot." Eva said this casually, as if she hadn't spent the past year and a half in therapy trying to unlearn her culturally-instilled stoicism so that she might one day be able to feel her own feelings. "Should we go inside?"

"Sounds good," Cass said, and let her hand rest for a moment on the small of Eva's back as she held the restaurant door open for her.

Eva paused, the heat from Cass's body making her sway closer. "Thanks," she said, and then made herself join the line at the counter.

"So." Cass's head tilted as they waited for their turn to order. "Your name doesn't sound very Dutch."

"It's Italian. My father moved to Scranton from New York when he was in his twenties. I grew up around my mother's family, the Vandenbergs, with regular pilgrimages to Brooklyn to visit my dad's side."

Visiting the city had felt almost like a religious experience when she was a kid, with the foreign sights and sounds and, later, the museums. Plus, there was her father's extended family making her feel like part of something special whenever they stayed there.

"Is that why you picked NYU for grad school?"

"Mainly. But visiting New York is very different from living there, as I learned."

Cass nodded. "You said your mom's here in Edmonds. What about your father?"

"He died a few years ago." The words still felt foreign as they passed her lips, her mind still shocked by the reality of losing her dad even after all this time. She sometimes wondered if she would ever fully accept it.

"Wow. I'm sorry," Cass said, her voice soft.

"Thanks," Eva said, her eyes on Cass's, dark blue inside the dimly lit restaurant. But before she could give in to Cass's gravity and drift closer again, it was their turn to order.

They ordered separately, each choosing one of the halibut and chips meals. Once they had paid, they carried their fish-shaped table markers—a tribal salmon painted in magenta and black swirls—to a booth in the far corner. The walls were decorated in the same Northwest tribal style, while the booths and tables were fashioned from solid wood stained a dark red, and Eva wondered as she often did what local natives thought of their art being used by white business owners to sell their products. She thought she could probably guess.

While Cass placed the markers on the table, Eva slid into the booth. As she folded her coat and placed her handbag on top of it, she glanced around the room, checking for familiar faces. She and Cass were here at Steve's behest (mostly), but even so, she knew the gossips would pounce if they were seen out together. Maybe they should have just met at her office. What was it about Cass that made her throw discretion to the wind?

But she knew the answer to that question, too.

"Are you okay?" Cass was watching her from the other side of the booth.

"Fine," Eva said, and toyed with the hem of her fleece pullover. "So, uh, I guess winter is finally here, huh."

Cass sipped her ginger beer. "Right. Definitely."

The silence lengthened, and Eva tried not to squirm. The weather, really?

"How long have you lived in Edmonds?" Cass asked.

"Seven and a half years." She started to say that they had finished their coursework, packed up the Subaru, and moved west in a matter of weeks, but she found she didn't want to talk about Ben. She had already spoken of him enough to Cass. "I moved here sight unseen."

"Seriously?"

She shrugged. "It's the West Coast. I figured it couldn't be that bad. Plus, you know, at least it wasn't Topeka."

"Hey, now, Kansas is a nice place." Cass paused. "I mean, probably."

"You don't actually believe that, do you?"

"Not in the least."

Eva sipped from her can of Limonata, pursing her lips momentarily at the sweet/sour taste. "You mentioned Gwen is your thesis adviser. I assume by this point you've chosen your research problem?"

"Yes," Cass agreed, and seemed to perk up. "I'm using break to complete my literature review. Then I'll start the research portion during winter quarter."

"Can I ask what your topic is?"

She nodded, eyes bright. "I'm researching the impact of an LGBTQIA-centered writing workshop on queer homeless youth in Seattle. Basically, I'll meet with them a couple of hours a week for eight weeks and teach them how to empower themselves by reframing their own narratives. There isn't a lot of relevant data out there to draw on, so I'll be using a series of surveys to assess the program's impact."

Eva was impressed. Definitely a worthy Serious Research Interest with the potential to positively affect its subjects.

They spent the next few minutes discussing methodology, hypotheses, and Cass's previous work with an Oakland LGBTQIA youth project that had produced the curriculum she would be using with the Seattle youth group. The premise underlying the writing program was that marginalized groups go through the world as basically invisible, their voices silenced. Autobiographical writing, on the other hand, provides marginalized people the opportunity to express themselves and to combat damaging stereotypes by sharing their stories.

"It's not a complex curriculum," Cass said, "but it's really effective. Or it was for the kids I knew in California, anyway. Their self-esteem grew so much in such a short time."

"Have you already met with the youth in Seattle?" Eva asked.

"Yeah, I've been volunteering with the resource center on and off since I got here. There are more queer homeless kids than you might think. Even though queer youth only account for like ten percent of the American young adult population, they make up around forty percent of homeless youth."

"Forty percent?" Eva echoed. She'd had no idea the statistics were so high. She could honestly say she hadn't spent much time thinking about homeless youth, queer or otherwise.

Cass nodded. "These kids are so freaking resilient, especially given what some of them have faced at the hands of their families."

"I can only imagine."

She'd always felt fortunate that her parents hadn't disowned her when, during her sophomore year of college, she'd told them she was interested in both men and women. Her mother had been resistant in the beginning, her dad even more so. But then they'd met Robin, Eva's first girlfriend, and they'd adored her. Sometimes Eva thought Robin was the reason her parents had grown to accept who she was.

"Can I ask you something?" Cass started, but then their server appeared with a tray of food, and conversation paused while they arranged their plates and traded condiments.

Eva waited until their server had walked away to say, her heart beating faster, "You had a question, I think."

"Right." Cass concentrated on dipping a french fry in ketchup. "I guess I was wondering what you were doing at the Thistledown that night. Were you and Alexis there for some kind of research project?"

A research project? Eva stifled a nervous giggle at the question because, in fact, her visit to a lesbian bar a year after divorcing her husband could certainly be described as a form of research. "Um, no. It wasn't for anything we're working on." She paused. Could she really tell Cass that she was queer? Coming out to her would change the dynamic of their working lunch, wouldn't it?

"Sorry if that was too personal," Cass said, swallowing a large bite of fish. "You don't owe me or anyone else an explanation."

Maybe not, but she owed herself the dignity of telling the truth, didn't she? Not once in her life had she lied about who she was to someone in her life. Strangers, yes, because safety was a realistic concern for all women, queer or not. But not telling Cass wouldn't impact her safety. It would only impact her self-respect.

Besides, if she were honest, she wanted Cass to know who she was.

"It's okay," she said, smiling at Cass across the table. "I've been out since college. I'm bisexual, actually. Alexis and I stopped at the Thistledown for a drink because she thought it was time I get back out there."

And, crap, why had she admitted that last part? Telling a student she was bi was one thing, but basically admitting that her best friend thought she needed to get laid was something else entirely. Cass was smiling back at her, though, open and accepting, which was a relief. Coming out as bi didn't always go well, in her experience.

"Thanks for telling me," Cass said. "I know it isn't always easy to be yourself in the world."

"From personal experience?" Eva hazarded. "Sorry," she added as Cass's smile slipped.

"No, it's okay." Cass looked down at her fish and chips platter. She'd selected four pieces of halibut and extra fries and had already winnowed her meal in half. The girl—woman, Eva corrected herself—could eat. "You're not wrong. Being gay and gender nonconforming isn't the easiest road. But I've been lucky enough to find people who accept me for who I am and not who they wish I would be."

"The West Coast is more progressive," Eva commented. "That's one of the things I love about living out here."

Cass swallowed another bite of fish. "Would you ever go back to the East Coast?"

"God, no," she said, and popped a fry in her mouth. "What about you?"

"Nope. Not a chance."

Eva knew a little about Cass and Matthew's parents, mostly from university gossip. She always assumed that people like them—well-known scholars employed by venerable institutions back east—would be liberal, even though she'd met enough conservative academics to know better. Were the Professors Trane the type who were comfortable with queer people as long as those people weren't their children? Or was there something else beneath the tightness in Cass's voice?

"It's nice that your brother lives here, too," Eva offered.

Cass glanced up at her, her lips quirking. "Yeah. He's a jackass, but I love him. Do you have any siblings?"

"Nope, it's just me."

"Ah." Cass didn't say she was sorry this time, but she didn't have to.

Eva bit into her second piece of halibut and moved on to tamer subjects: the Trane family's holiday plans. Cass and Matthew's parents would be in London at the end of the month, she learned, so the Trane twins would be celebrating Christmas in Southern California with Maya's family.

"That'll be nice," Eva said a bit enviously. The winter rains had only started a few weeks earlier, and already she was tired of the seasonal cold and darkness.

"Yeah, Maya's family is fun. They're going to totally lose it when—" She stopped suddenly and reached for her glass of water, her face slightly stricken.

"Are you okay?" Eva asked, frowning.

Cass nodded and wiped her mouth with her napkin. "Sorry, I thought I swallowed a bone. Anyway, Maya's younger sisters are a lot of fun, so it should be a good time. And then our parents are coming here for New Year's, so you know, there's that to look forward to."

Eva detected more than a little sarcasm. "Is that not a good thing?"

Cass shrugged. "Have to wait and see."

Evidently she didn't want to talk about her parents, and in theory they weren't here to talk about families, anyway. Eva was trying to think of a safer subject when she heard a voice say, "Cass?"

Matthew Trane stopped beside their table glancing between them, his brow furrowed in a way that seemed more thunderstruck than was really necessary. Except then Eva remembered that other than Alexis, Cass's brother was the only other person who knew how they had met. And yeah, she could see how this looked.

Cass stared up at her brother. "What are you doing here, Matthew?"

"I could ask you the same thing," he said, his gaze flicking back to Eva. He nodded at her. "Hey, Eva."

"Hey, Matthew." She sipped her Limonata, working hard not to let the sourness affect her expression. Why exactly was it that he was behaving like Ben had the day he'd run into her and Cass at the coffee shop? Was he somehow running interference on behalf of her ex-spouse now, or did Matthew have his own reasons for disapproving of their friendship?

"Are you okay?" Cass asked. "Is Maya—" her gaze flicked to Eva briefly—"in the mood for fish and chips, or something?"

"Or something," he said, and made a face the meaning of which Eva couldn't quite grasp.

"Got it," Cass said. "I would say you should join us, but we're actually sort of busy."

"Busy?" he repeated.

"Cass and I are discussing a project Steve has us working on over break," Eva explained.

"What kind of project?"

"A profile of Eva's research for the new Arts and Sciences blog." Cass's voice turned teasing. "You know, because she's a hot shot social scientist who was recently profiled in the *New York Times*."

Eva wadded up her napkin and placed it in the center of her empty plate. "I'm hardly a hot shot. I'm not even tenured."

"Tenure does not the department star make," Matthew said, his voice matching his sister's. "Congrats, though, Eva. Your research is garnering some good attention lately. You're on a panel at the Cultural Studies conference in the spring, aren't you?" As she glanced up at him, surprised, he added, "I'm pretty sure most people on campus read the *Times* piece. Even Linc Anderson, probably."

Cass snickered. "I doubt that jackass reads anything that isn't about him."

Privately, Eva agreed. Publicly, she changed the subject because you never knew who might be nearby. "The funny thing is, I thought studying romantic fiction might get me chucked out of the academy."

"Nah." Cass smiled at her across the table. "They'd be stupid to let you go. Besides, pop culture, as I'm sure you both know, scores well with prospective students."

"I think I might've heard that somewhere," Eva said, smiling back. And yes, she was flirting with Cass in front of a colleague, but it was only Matthew, after all.

"Well," he said, "I guess I should leave you to it. Good luck with the blog post."

"Thanks," Eva said. "It's right up your alley, Matthew. You know, all about stigmatization and cultural biases and romance novel tropes."

He practically recoiled. "Right. Uh-huh. Totally up my alley. And on that note… Cass, see you at home later?"

"You got it. Hang in there, okay?"

"I'll try." Matthew waved and retreated.

Eva waited until he was out of earshot to ask, "Are he and Maya okay?"

"What? Oh, yeah, they're fine. Maya's just all keyed up about Christmas. She hasn't been to California at the holidays in a couple of years, and, um, well, I guess their extended family can get pretty intense. I'm a little leery of the whole group thing, actually."

"You are? Why?"

"Catholics and queers do not typically mix well," she said, her smile rueful. "But anyway, I guess we should probably get some work done while we're here. What do you think?"

"I think you're right." And if talking about the blog post would prolong their time together, that was just a side benefit.

"Do you mind if I record our conversation?" Cass fiddled with her phone and set it between them, her finger hovering over the red record button.

"Sure. That's fine."

"Okay," Cass said, and smiled at her as she pressed the button. "Let's talk romance novels."

This interview was significantly different from the one with the *Times* writer, and not only because Alexis was absent. Cass was just as sharp as the other interviewer, but her questions were better researched and significantly more academic. Her humor was more evident, too, as they discussed the realities that romance writers and their fans faced, and her interest seemed more genuine as Eva tried to describe the pro-woman environment at the Romance Writers of America convention she and Alexis had attended.

"There were these bestselling authors making millions of dollars a year, and they were so kind and so gracious to the women who came to see them. And talk about encouraging—the awards speeches were all about working hard and persevering and how if they could do it, other women could too."

"Is that not typical of other types of writers?" Cass asked.

"For some, it probably is," Eva conceded. "But Alexis and I have gone to a few other smaller conventions for sci-fi and fantasy and for mystery and crime writing, and the award winners were mostly men who talked mainly about themselves and what they had done to deserve the award. There was actually a female crime writer at RWA receiving an award for her first romantic suspense series, and her speech was like those of the men we'd seen at the other conferences. So, yes, I think the supportive, collective model at RWA is unique compared to the rest of the industry."

"All-women's spaces are really different," Cass commented. "Even though Vassar is co-ed now, we still played the other Seven Sisters schools in sports, so I spent some time on those campuses. Smith and Mount Holyoke were these cool, amazing pockets of sisterhood. I almost transferred, but I loved Vassar too much. Even if there were—" she made an exaggerated face—"boys."

"I know what you mean," Eva said, laughing. "If I had it to do over again, I'd probably pick a women's college."

"Not Wellesley, though. That's the only women's college I've been to where another player called me a dyke on the basketball court." Cass shook her head. "It was fairly routine to get heckled at the co-ed schools, but when the girl there did it I was like, where do you think you go?"

"You played basketball in college?"

"Yeah, I did. We weren't very good, but it was a lot of fun."

That made sense. After all, Cass was tall and athletic with just the right amount of muscle, not too lean and not too bulky, with an ass that—Eva caught herself. Unprofessional thoughts. Highly unprofessional, even. She should be focusing on the interview, not picturing Cass in small shorts and a sports bra, wiping away a sheen of sweat from her neck....

And yet she couldn't quite tame her errant thoughts enough to keep from saying, "I've always wanted to check out a Seattle Storm game."

"You've never been?" Cass huffed in mock disapproval. "If I'm here next summer, we're definitely rectifying that."

If she was here next summer—did that mean she might not move back to California at all after she finished her program, or

123

just not right away? Not that it mattered to Eva what she decided to do.

"Anyway," Cass said, and turned off her phone's voice recorder. "I think that should do it."

"Probably just as well," Eva said, glancing toward the back of the restaurant. "I think the busboy was giving us the side-eye."

"I saw that too," Cass said, smiling. She rose and slung her messenger bag across her broad shoulders, stretching her neck from side to side.

"You okay?" Eva asked, rising and pulling on her jacket.

"Just sore from lifting. Today was an arms day."

"Do you work out on campus?"

"Yeah. The gym is one of the things Matthew used to lure me here. It's amazing. I did all my rehab there."

"Have you ever tried the rock wall?" Eva asked.

"Ah, no. Heights and I do not get along."

They started toward the door together, still chatting, and even though their "working lunch" had lasted more than an hour and a half, Eva found she wasn't ready to say goodbye yet. Maybe Cass felt the same because when they stepped outside into the cold, rainy afternoon, she paused under the awning and asked, "Do you have plans?"

"Not until later." As Cass's eyes flickered, Eva clarified: "I go to Alexis and Tosh's house every other Saturday for pizza and movies with the kids."

"Ah."

"What about you? Headed to the Thistledown?" Eva asked, and then cringed inwardly at the ridiculous question.

"Why, are you interested in going back?" Cass asked, half-smiling. As Eva sputtered uselessly, she added, "Just kidding. Unless you did want to go back sometime, and then I'm not."

"I think children's movies are more my scene," Eva said, and then froze as the images suddenly began to sweep over her entirely unbidden: Isabella, her tiny body barely larger than Ben's hand, her skin dark and almost translucent, her chest struggling to rise and fall for the minute and a half she'd lived. Eva blinked, trying to slow the avalanche of images. This happened sometimes. She would say something seemingly innocuous and all at once the memories would cascade down, a deluge she couldn't stop or evade.

Cass's eyes changed, and she stepped closer in the reddish light beneath the awning, one hand extended. "Eva?" she asked, her voice low.

But Eva turned away, ducking her head and closing her eyes. With supreme will, she regulated her breathing and chanted her mantra inside her head while focusing on her breath: "May I be free from suffering; may I be well; may I be at peace; may I be joyful." She usually had a hard time channeling that last one, but today as the river of images slowly ebbed, she remembered how it had felt to sit inside the warm restaurant in the booth with Cass, talking and laughing, insulated from the winter rain and the rest of the cloud-shadowed world.

The third time through the mantra, she held an image of Isabella in her mind and changed the words: "May you be free from suffering; may you be well; may you be at peace; may you be joyful." At last, with her brain thankfully quieted, she took a breath and turned back to Cass who was standing with her hands in her pockets, brow furrowed just as Matthew's had been earlier.

"I'm sorry," Eva said, her throat still tight. "That happens sometimes."

"Are you okay?" Cass asked.

"Not really," Eva confessed. "But I'm getting there." She hesitated. Isabella wasn't something to be ashamed of; she wasn't someone Eva ever wanted to hide. Cass, she could tell, was a good person. If they were going to move forward with whatever this thing was between them, Cass deserved to know what she was getting into.

Assuming Maya hadn't already told her.

"I lost a baby," she said, and then as Cass straightened up, eyes widening, Eva wished she had asked if it was all right to share her story.

"I'm so sorry," Cass said, and this time the hand she lifted made contact. She held Eva's palm against hers, warm and strong and solid, and waited, her eyes on Eva's.

"I lost two, actually, but the first one was still in the first trimester. Isabella, though, she was twenty-one weeks when I went into labor. A few more weeks and she might have—" She stopped and looked down at Cass's larger hand clasped around hers. That was something she and Gayle, her therapist, were still working on together: not spiraling away into the might-have-beens but sitting with the difficult realities instead. "Sometimes the memories of the day she was born just sort of, I don't know, overwhelm me."

"That's understandable," Cass said, her voice as comforting as her touch. "Can I do anything to help?"

Eva liked that she offered support without making it about herself. Ben used to ask what he had done wrong, why she was shutting him out, how she could be so cold to him when it wasn't his fault, was it? Then he would hurry to add that it wasn't anyone's fault, but the unspoken words built a wedge between them, driving them farther and farther apart. Cass, on the other hand, seemed to understand that Eva's pain was her own and had nothing to do with her.

"Yes," she said, and released a long breath. "You're already doing it."

They stood quietly together for another minute until Eva remembered where they were: a sidewalk in downtown Edmonds less than a mile from the university. It would be a miracle if they didn't run into someone else they knew here, only half a block from Main Street. She tugged on Cass's hand and pulled her away from the restaurant toward another awning two doors down. As they passed into open air, the rain felt cool and gentle on her skin. Washington rain was soft and sweet, so unlike the driving torrents she'd grown up with back east.

Still, it was nice to duck into the Edmonds Bookshop, where she reluctantly released Cass's hand and busied herself wiping the traces of rain from her glasses. When she put them back on, she could see Cass gazing around the store, her lips twitching slightly.

"Is this okay?" Eva asked.

Cass hesitated, and for a moment Eva thought she might say it wasn't. But then she held out her arm. "It's perfect. I've actually never been inside. Want to show me around?"

A grad student who had never been inside the local independent bookstore? But Eva didn't question it. She simply slipped her arm through Cass's and leaned into her heat. "I'd love to."

And for a while, Eva thought it might be nice to simply exist with Cass in this warm, dry place that smelled of books and coffee—two of her very favorite things in life.

CHAPTER EIGHT

Cass couldn't breathe. There was literally no oxygen entering her lungs, which did not bode well for her ability to survive the perilous situation she'd gotten herself into. She clung to the rough stone surface, eyes closed against the precipitous drop grasping at her. How had she gotten to this moment, with sweat in her eyes and chalk on her hands and Eva standing below her calling up useful tips about where to position her fingers and toes?

Eva, of course, was the reason. She had seemed so hopeful and Cass hadn't wanted to hurt her feelings. She also hadn't wanted Eva to know how deep her fear of heights ran, so instead of making up an excuse, she'd agreed to meet her at the university this morning for a rock-climbing lesson. And yet now that she was actually 15 feet up the Edmonds U climbing wall, she could see where her decision-making had gone wrong. She should have said no and blamed her shoulder—except that would have been a lie, and Cass didn't want to start lying to Eva, especially not after how their lunch date had played out the previous afternoon.

Their working lunch had turned into a leisurely stroll through the shops of downtown Edmonds (between rain bursts), with an eventual stop for smoothies at Emerald City, Cass's favorite Edmonds establishment. After their earlier emotional exchange, the conversation had skewed significantly lighter, except when they told each other their coming out stories. Eva's parents hadn't responded well, but they hadn't responded terribly, either, for which she said she was grateful. Cass's story was similar. At first her parents had simply ignored her unsubtle hints midway through her junior year of high school. But then she brought her first girlfriend home, and they had no choice but to deal with her identity. Unfortunately, their preferred approach was to accuse her of acting out for attention-seeking purposes.

The memory still made her fists curl, which was exactly what had happened as she and Eva sat in the window at Emerald City. Then Eva had reached for her hand, and Cass had opened her fist so that their fingers could intertwine, and the anger had drained away almost instantaneously. Eva's touch was a bit magical, she'd decided as they smiled at each other over the top of their smoothies.

There had been more hand holding after that, with little apparent regard for who might be in the vicinity. They had actually been holding hands when Eva invited her rock-climbing. Cass wasn't sure which had clouded her mind and compelled her into a Very Poor Decision more: Eva's palm pressed against hers or the vision of Eva in a tank top, shorts, and (*gulp*) climbing harness.

Now Cass opened her eyes and looked down, nearly swaying as she took in the distance between her precarious perch and the floor mat. Her eyes met Eva's. Instead of ridicule or amusement, though, she saw only patience and reassurance.

"You're doing great!" Eva called. "I can't believe this is your first time climbing!"

First and last, most likely. "Thanks," she called back, glad her voice didn't shake. "So, hypothetically, how would one descend from this point?"

Rappelling backward down a steep rock face was not nearly as terrifying as she would have expected. It was still frightening, possibly exceedingly so, but Eva knew what she was doing and the whole experience only lasted a few moments. Then Cass was touching down and heaving a sigh of relief. When she had extricated herself from the rope, she knelt down and kissed the floor mat.

"I'm so sorry," she murmured, caressing the mat lightly. "I will never leave you again, I promise."

"Hey, now," Eva said, laughing. "I thought *I* was your date!"

Cass glanced up at her, eyebrows raised. "Date?"

"Oh. Um, like, a friend date, I mean," Eva amended.

"Right," Cass said, and smiled slowly because not only was she no longer in danger of falling to her death but Eva was now gazing down at her shyly, her face suffused with what Cass thought might be the same hope currently taking root inside her chest. "Help me up?"

"Of course." Eva extended a hand, and Cass watched the ripple of smooth muscle under her olive skin.

Maybe nearly falling to her death in front of the exactly two undergrads in the gym was worth it, after all.

Overcoming her fear of heights however temporarily seemed to have emboldened her. At least, that was the only reason Cass could find to explain why her mouth opened and the following words emerged: "My shoulder's a little sore. What do you think about a visit to the steam room?"

Eva blinked several times—she wasn't wearing glasses today, and her eyelashes seemed even longer than Cass had remembered—and then touched her tongue to her lips. "I think that sounds lovely."

Cass led the way to the locker room in a haze of anticipation and nerves. She had shaved and waxed all the right places this morning, just in case, but still. Hanging around the very public rock wall with a half-naked Eva had tested her resolve enough as it was. Now they would be completely naked under a towel (at least, in her case—*oh god, what if Eva was a free, naked spirit kind of person?*) in a small room, possibly by themselves. What had she been thinking?

Five minutes later, Cass knew exactly what she had been thinking. She was a genius, she realized, as the door opened and in walked Eva, one of the gym's white cotton towels wrapped primly around her body. But the towel didn't hide Eva's shoulders, or the arc of her neck, or the wisps of dark hair from her messy bun curling about her face in the locker room's humidity. It didn't hide her strong calves or the glimpse of upper thigh when she turned to close the door, and it couldn't mask the curve of her hip or the swell of her breasts as she approached Cass and took a seat on the same bench almost within arm's reach.

Definitely a genius, because here they were alone together in the women's steam room, the heat rising between them.

"Hey," Eva said, smiling at Cass.

"Hey," Cass said, clearing her throat as her voice did its best impression of a 13-year-old boy.

"I always forget how hot it is in here," Eva said, leaning back and closing her eyes.

Cass's breath caught as she watched Eva tilt her head back, the lines of her neck revealed intimately. She could see Eva's pulse thudding in the hollow of her throat, the thin, delicate structure of her collarbone, the tiny drops of moisture collecting on her skin. What would it be like to kiss her there, to dip her tongue into a salt-tinged indentation, to suck on the skin just below Eva's small, perfect ear....

Eva's eyes opened. "So I was wondering..." she started, her voice teasing. But then her gaze caught Cass's and she stopped, playfulness appearing to recede as her velvet-brown eyes darkened.

"You were wondering," Cass echoed, voice husky now as she felt herself shifting forward, drawn to Eva's warmth. At this angle Eva looked almost like a different person, all full lips and high cheekbones, and Cass could easily imagine bridging the faint distance that remained and pressing their mouths together. Her eyes flicked downward and she heard Eva's breath catch, and then it was like their minds were synchronized as they moved forward the last few inches and...

Voices sounded at the door, disturbing the quiet of the room. As the handle turned and the hinges screeched, Cass scooted back, putting space between her and Eva. She leaned against the concrete ledge behind her and closed her eyes, but not before she saw Eva rearranging her towel. Had it slipped when they broke apart, revealing even more of her luscious body? Cass hummed inside her head, trying to calm her insistent libido. They had come so close to kissing.... She clamped down on the thought and dredged up one of her most embarrassing memories: the day she was playing softball and tore her pants on a slide, affording both teams and a sizable portion of the fans a clear view of her white cotton underwear. She'd been thirteen, and even now, nearly two decades later, the memory could stave off many a strong emotion.

Two thirty-something women entered the room and stopped short at the sight of Cass and Eva before slowly making their way into the room. Had they seen how close she and Eva were, or had they simply mistaken Cass's short hair and lean upper body for those of a man?

"Hello, Eva," the taller woman said. She was willowy and elegant, or maybe just haughty. It was hard to tell through the room's steamy glow.

Cass glanced at Eva, noting the way her shoulders tightened. Her voice was as smooth as ever, though, as she replied, "Hello, Nancy."

Nancy. Wait, that was why she looked familiar! Nancy Anderson, Linc's second wife and the mother of his young daughter. If she was here, then who was watching the kid? Somehow Cass had a hard time imagining Linc Anderson crawling around on the floor with a toddler, but who knew. Maybe he was a crappy person but a good dad.

Nah.

"I heard you were back on campus. How are you doing?" Nancy asked as she took a seat on Eva's other side, her voice so saccharine it made Cass's teeth itch. Apparently she knew about Eva's miscarriage, even if Cass hadn't.

Nancy's companion hesitated, her gaze on Cass—or rather, on her tattoos—before selecting a bench behind Nancy. Cass resisted the urge to roll her eyes. They reminded her of girls from high school, with Nancy the leader and her friend the follower. But where did Eva fit in?

"I'm fine," Eva said, and offered a smile that looked forced. "And you? How's Maisie?"

Cass winced. Maisie, Linc's daughter, had to be fairly close in age to the child Eva had lost.

Nancy smiled, her eyes bright. "She's wonderful. Talking up a storm, though none of it makes much sense yet. I wanted her to call me 'Mama,' but she decided on her own that I'm 'Mommy,' so what can you do?"

Did this woman not understand how painful it must be for Eva to listen to details like that, or did she simply not care? Cass leaned forward and caught Nancy's eye. "Hey. Aren't you Linc Anderson's wife?"

"I am. And you are?" Her smile vanished, replaced by her friend's guarded squint.

"Cassidy Trane. I'm the Arts and Sciences grad assistant. I'm on the University Tech Committee, too, and I have to say, your husband has been quite vocal about the direction he believes University Computing should take."

Beside her, she heard Eva's low, soft chuckle. Mission accomplished.

Nancy tossed her dyed blonde ponytail. "Vocal—that sounds like Linc, doesn't it, Joanna?"

Her friend laughed. "Totally."

Linc had to have told his wife about the showdown in October, didn't he? But if he had, Nancy Anderson didn't seem to think her husband's position was worth defending. That was one of the things about straight women that often took Cass aback: They didn't always seem to respect—or even like—their male spouses. At Vassar, her friends who dated guys used to sit around their dorm rooms drinking cocktails and making fun of their boyfriends. They would joke about the guys' clothes, bodies, intellect, and even families, mostly from a place of gentle disparagement. But as Cass had grown older, she'd noticed the derision turned harsher. The straight women she'd worked with at Avicom had often bemoaned their husbands' lack of initiative both at home and at work, their inability to cope with basic parenting tasks, their tendency to cave at the slightest pressure from their own mothers. Cass had met many of these men and had struggled to recognize them in their wives' rants. But maybe that was simply the way of the straight world. Even Cass sometimes thought that maybe men really were from Mars.

Had Eva and Ben succumbed to stereotypes? Was that why their marriage had broken up? Or had they simply been unable to overcome the tragedy of losing not one but two babies?

Beside her, Eva stirred, her cheeks even more flushed. "I think I'm done," she said, directing her words to Cass. "What about you?"

"Same," she agreed.

"Nice seeing you, Nancy," Eva said politely as she rose and headed for the door.

"You, too," Nancy said, the faux concern back in her voice.

Even before the door closed, Cass heard it: whispering that contained both her and Eva's names. Just for a moment she paused, remembering Steve's warning. Linc Anderson had powerful friends at Edmonds. Had Cass just jeopardized Eva's standing on campus? But no, that was ridiculous. Still...

"So," Eva said as they walked back toward the shower area.

"So. Meet you outside?"

"Sure," Eva said. She smiled and offered up her trademark wave, and then she ducked down one row of lockers while Cass headed for another at the opposite end of the locker room. They might be friends, but they were definitely not the kind of friends who showered in public together. Or in private, for that matter. Which of course had Cass thinking highly inappropriate thoughts in a private shower stall as she quickly washed the sweat away and toweled off. Judging from the way Eva had leaned into their near-kiss, though, maybe the thoughts weren't completely inappropriate. Or unrequited.

Softball slide, underwear, crowd, she reminded herself. And yep, well done, horrible memory. She could face Eva without combusting. She hoped.

Eva was leaning against a concrete pillar when Cass emerged from the locker room into the rec center lounge. She glanced up from the phone, and the way her face lit up had Cass smiling back in a super-cheesy grin. But whatever. She liked Eva DeMarco and she didn't care who knew it.

"So," she said, drifting to a stop a few feet away. "I'm starving. Do you have to work on your tenure stuff this afternoon, or do you have time for brunch?"

"I should get some work done," Eva admitted. "But there's no reason we can't do both. You have to finish your lit review, don't you?"

Cass nodded.

"Well," Eva said, stepping closer and toying with the tassel on Cass's hoodie, "why don't you go home and get your work and meet me at my house? I think I have the fixings for an omelet, assuming you do eggs and dairy?"

This had been Cass's fantasy, hadn't it? She had daydreamed about Eva inviting her over to her house to work on the profile. But this was different. This would involve Cass reading in front of Eva, who might put two and two together and figure out that her reading abilities were less than normative. Then she remembered how Eva had turned to her after her obvious panic attack and told her the truth.

"I love eggs and dairy," she said truthfully, and touched Eva's hand. "Brunch at your house sounds perfect."

"It does? I mean, good. Great. Okay." Eva paused. "I'll just text you the address then. Sound good?"

"Sounds great," Cass said, laughing a little as Eva backed away from her and nearly collided with the concrete pillar.

Eva laughed, too, and then they were heading outside into the cold, bright late morning where the wind off the Sound whipped through the university, state, and American flags that occupied the flag posts at the southern tip of campus.

In the parking lot, they waved and climbed into their separate cars, Cass with her winterized Jeep and Eva with her ancient Subaru wagon—also more than a little gay, Cass thought. Just as Cass turned the key in the ignition, her phone buzzed. She grabbed it from her messenger bag and pulled up Eva's text. She'd written her address, followed by a smiley emoji. Cass pressed her phone to her chest, feeling all of 13 years old again. Or more like 16, since she hadn't fallen in love for the first time until well after most of her peers.

Not that she was falling in love now, because she totally wasn't.

After a moment, she sent back the same smiley emoji and put the Jeep in gear. What a day, and it wasn't even half over.

***

"How was yo   ̣te?" her brother asked, smirking at her.

"Oh, for fu ̣k's sake," Cass said, tossing her keys on the table beside the front door.

Both Matthew *and* Maya were seated on her couch this time. But instead of playing video games, Matthew was grading finals on a bamboo lapboard—Cass's bamboo lapboard—and Maya was reading *People* magazine, her self-professed guilty pleasure.

"Dude, you're still not done grading?" Cass asked. "I thought the deadline was tomorrow."

He frowned up at her. "Tomorrow is twenty-four hours away."

"They aren't due until four, so technically it's twenty-nine hours," Maya said without looking up from her magazine, which rested on her slight but growing baby bump. "And how is Ms.

DeMarco?"

"Good," Cass said, and then before she could start gushing and open herself to the ridicule of the old married couple currently squatting in her living room, she headed upstairs.

The mirror beside the dresser confirmed that she looked fine for the gym but not so much for a first visit to Eva's home, so she opened her T-shirt drawer and surveyed the contents. Or maybe she should wear a collared shirt. This *was* basically a study date, so nice attire was probably not required. If Eva didn't plan to change, Cass didn't want to dress up. Despite their near make-out session in the Edmonds U steam room, they were still only friends.

Could she text Eva to find out what she was wearing…? But even as she immediately rejected the idea in all its suggestive glory, Cass realized she'd left her phone in the outside pocket of her messenger bag. Downstairs. With her brother.

She swung down the attic stairs in one giant leap only to find Matthew holding her phone up and squinting at the screen. Had he hacked her phone, or did he somehow know her pass code?

"Give me that," she demanded, tempted to jump on top of him but leery of jostling the pregnant lady currently sharing the couch with him.

"I may have gotten you locked out," he said, giving her the guilty puppy dog look that had always worked on their gullible parents.

"Asshat!" She grabbed the phone away and hit the "Forgot PIN" button. Then she logged into her Google account, and the phone vibrated. Good to go. She slid it into her hoodie pocket and glared at her brother. "What are you doing here, anyway?"

"Paint fumes," Maya said. "Your brother decided the nursery had to be done this morning."

"You're such a procrastinator." Cass shook her head at him. "Seriously, waiting until the last minute would drive me crazy."

"Whatever. I've never once missed a deadline."

"Junior year philosophy midterm," Cass said.

"Dude, I had mono!"

"Senior honors thesis," Maya noted.

"Doesn't count. No one turns their first draft in on time."

Cass and Maya rolled their eyes in unison. The mansplaining

was real *and* annoying as all get out.

Maya tiled her head slightly and said, "So Eva, huh?"

Cass felt a small, secretive smile steal across her face. "Maybe."

"Good for you," Maya said, her own smile affectionate.

"I thought you said you would never in a trillion light years date a professor?" Matthew reminded her.

She shrugged. "Rules are made to be broken."

"No, they're not."

"Says the man who hasn't turned in his grades yet," she said, and headed back upstairs to change.

"Twenty-nine hours, Cass!"

She settled on a navy blue cotton tee with lighter blue flecks, paired with her favorite red and blue flannel shirt and her comfiest pair of skinny jeans. Smart wool socks with multi-colored reindeer finished the outfit. In the bathroom downstairs, she blew her hair dry and added a dab of product to keep it in place. Then she brushed her teeth, applied lip gloss, and examined herself in the mirror. She was ready.

"Wait, you're going out again? With who?" her brother demanded when she emerged from the tiny bathroom.

"It's with whom," she pointed out. "You would know that if you'd ever taken an English class."

The insult distracted him as she'd known it would, and he lectured her on the contents of his undergraduate transcript while Maya watched her repack her messenger bag. She needed her laptop, her Kindle, three texts that hadn't been available in e-book format, her notebook, and, of course, her binder of PDF articles. Plus her water bottle and a couple of granola bars, her study snack of choice.

"Wait a minute," Maya said. "Are you going on a study date?"

"What?" Cass asked, stalling as she pulled on her waterproof hikers.

"Oh my god, you are," her sister-in-law said, laughing. "You act like this cool jock, but you're really just as much of a nerd as your brother, aren't you?"

Cass pulled on her coat and looked at her brother, who gazed back, his shoulder lifted in mute agreement.

"Apparently," Cass said. "In fact, I'm such a nerd that I need my lapboard." She held out her hand to her brother, tapping her foot as he whined about how she was hurting his grading system and if he didn't make the deadline now, it was on her.

"Yeah, no," she said when he finally handed it over. "That's on you and your male nesting instincts. Don't wait up," she added, and grabbed her keys and ran out, laughing as their chorus of protests and questions followed her out.

Eva's house really was only a couple of blocks away. Cass made it there in under a minute and parked her Jeep on the street in front of the small, tan and white bungalow nestled between two larger homes. Probably she should have walked over, but her books were heavy and she'd needed a quick escape. Not like her brother didn't know exactly where she was headed. Hopefully he and Maya wouldn't "happen" to swing by later on a stroll around the neighborhood.

Cass checked her reflection in the mirror, fussed with her hair briefly, and then took a breath. *Study date*, she reminded herself. Not a real date. At the moment, it was hard to know what the difference might be.

The sound of a dog barking reached her as she walked up the concrete path to the front porch—Harvey, she was pretty sure his name was. Eva had multiple photos of her dog on her computer at work, and they'd chatted briefly about him while they worked on Eva's profile earlier in the quarter. Eva referred to him as her roommate, which Cass found adorable—just like everything else about her, really.

Harvey's drool, however, was less adorable, as Cass discovered when Eva opened the front door and the dog launched himself at her, whining in—she hoped—excitement.

"Sorry," Eva said, laughing, and dragged him back inside by the collar as his whole body wriggled. "Harvey, no! Come on in. He'll calm down in a second."

"He's fine," Cass said, stepping aside to let Eva close the door behind her.

While Eva lured Harvey into another room with the promise of a treat, Cass removed her coat and shoes and looked around. The front door opened onto the main living space, with a sectional couch and television to the right and a dining set and gas fireplace to the left. The narrow archway Eva had disappeared through appeared to lead to the kitchen, judging from the cabinets Cass glimpsed. She headed in that direction and leaned in the open doorway, smiling at the sight of Eva's dog sitting at her feet trembling and salivating as Eva held a treat close to his nose.

"He's mostly excited because I was gone all morning," Eva said without looking up. Then she gave the dog the treat and he ran off through another doorway. Eva shook her head, smiling, and leaned against the kitchen counter. "Hi."

"Hi."

"So, this is the house," Eva said, gesturing around her.

"I kind of guessed."

"Do you want the tour? You've already seen half of the rooms, so…"

"Sure," Cass said, smiling. "I'd love a tour."

Eva led her through the door Harvey had taken into a hallway, off of which sat a square bathroom with a claw foot tub and a granite counter that matched the kitchen; a small bedroom with pale gray walls, white Craftsman-style trim, and a queen bed that Cass tried not to look too hard at; and a second small bedroom with a twin bed where Harvey currently lay licking the dark blue comforter, a wide white dresser, and walls painted a bright, happy yellow. The baby's room, Cass realized, and followed Eva out again, Harvey at their heels.

The last stop was the mud room off the kitchen, where one door led to the fenced backyard and another to a small daylight basement that held Eva's washer and dryer, her exercise equipment, and a stack of moving boxes.

"Told you it wasn't very big," Eva said, clasping her hands together as they returned to the kitchen.

"Size isn't everything," Cass quipped, and then wished she hadn't as Eva's eyes widened. "Or so they say, ha ha. I wouldn't know myself." *Oh my god,* she told herself, *STOP TALKING.* Except she couldn't just stop after saying such a thing. Far better to change the subject. "My parents told Matthew and Maya to buy the smallest house in the nicest neighborhood. Their house is a little bigger than yours, but renting out the studio helps out with the mortgage."

Eva nodded, seeming to have recovered from Cass's off-color commentary. "They're lucky. Mortgages around here aren't cheap."

"It's not as bad as the Bay Area, but Seattle's cost of living is definitely up there."

Cass didn't ask how Eva afforded the mortgage on her own. She had queried Maya about Eva's living situation the night before, and Maya had told her that Ben came from money. His parents had helped them purchase the house, and after the divorce, he'd given it to her in the settlement. He hadn't needed money for a new down payment. Even before the divorce was final, he'd moved in with Tina, who lived in a rambler a dozen blocks up the hill from the Bowl.

"So," Eva said brightly. "Are you hungry?"

"I'm pretty much always hungry," she admitted. "High metabolism."

Eva's eyes dipped to her torso and then even lower before returning to Cass's face. "I hope you like vegetables," she said as she turned away. "Because I'm not a fan of red meat. Or pork, either."

Jesus, brain, keep out of the gutter, Cass scolded her mind. "That's fine," she said aloud. "I'm a pescetarian, so that works. Is there anything I can do to help?"

"Would you mind snapping the ends off the peas?" Eva asked, gesturing toward a strainer filled with sugar snap peas.

"No problem," Cass said, and moved past Eva to wash her hands at the sink.

While they prepped the meal, they chatted about favorite foods, and soon Eva was telling her about one of her roommates in grad school who had been in culinary school.

"The rest of us got the better end of that arrangement," she told Cass as she chopped green and red pepper slices into bite-size bits. "All we had to offer was an endless supply of coffee and the occasional stress batch of cookies, while Tanya was always begging to try out her new truffle recipe or her homemade ravioli. We were like, yes, we very much agree to be your official tasters."

"I feel like any roommate after that would have impossible expectations to live up to."

Eva shrugged and cracked an egg against the side of a ceramic bowl. "I don't know. Harvey's a much better snuggler than Tanya ever was."

Cass glanced down at the dog, who had stationed himself at Eva's feet and was avidly waiting for something edible to fall from above. "Somehow I can see that. So where did you live during grad school?"

"The East Village. Close enough to walk to class but far enough away to be quasi-affordable. Then again, four of us lived in a three-bedroom apartment only slightly larger than this house, so affordable is relative."

"Isn't everything about New York relative?"

Eva smiled at her before pouring the egg mixture into the pan heating on the stainless steel stove. "Pretty much."

A few minutes later they were seated kitty-corner at the dining table in the main room. Eva had turned on the gas fireplace, and it cast a warm glow across the room. Clouds had moved in off the water now, and the mid-day skyscape outside the bungalow's wide windows was more wintry than the morning had been. Cass found that Seattle was the opposite of the Bay Area in that regard. In San Francisco, the morning fog regularly burned off by mid-day, while in Seattle, morning sun was often short-lived.

Over veggie omelets and whole wheat toast, the conversation shifted from Manhattan apartments to the best and worst things about living in or near The City. Gay bars and queer culture were a plus while homelessness and low wages were problematic in a city where people routinely spent millions of dollars on an apartment. Eva had hated how commonplace it was for men to harass female passersby, and Cass admitted that New York was the only place she'd regularly been hassled for being queer. Also, neither appreciated the mindset that New York was The Best and Only Place to Live.

"I mean, I wouldn't live in Kansas, as I think we've already established," Cass said, "but to call the states in the middle of the country 'the flyover states' is too insulting even for my West-Coast-aligned self. Chicago is every bit as cool as New York. Maybe cooler, even, because it has Lake Michigan and the jazz scene."

"You've traveled a lot, haven't you?" Eva asked, pausing to sip her pineapple-orange juice.

"Thanks to rugby. Without it, I probably would have been to fifteen states total, mostly on the coasts. What about you?"

"I've been to thirteen states, pretty much all on the coasts."

"Well, as long as you're happy where you are," Cass said, trying to make up for her slight social faux pas.

Eva shook her head. "I don't know if I am. I've been on this track my whole life, you know? I had to do well in high school so that I could get into a good college. Then I had to do well in college in order to get into a good grad school. My PhD program was all about finding a tenure-track position, and now here I am worried that I'll misstep and end up having spent all of this time and money on a path that ends in failure."

Cass leaned away from the table, frowning. "Is that how you really feel?"

Eva shrugged. "I don't know. Maybe. Sometimes I think I should leave Edmonds and go work at one of the community colleges. At least there wouldn't be as much pressure."

"What's stopping you?"

"Honestly? I'm a horrible snob."

Cass laughed.

"No, really," Eva said earnestly, tucking a strand of hair behind her ear. She'd left it loose after the gym, and now it fell in rich brown waves around her shoulders, occasionally glinting reddish in the light. "I'm a total academic snob. I can't imagine telling people I quit a tenure-track position at a school like Edmonds because I needed a break."

"It's okay to need a break," Cass offered.

"I know. And I'm glad I took one. Really. But I should probably quit whining because I'm lucky to be where I am."

"It's not luck. You worked your butt off, you just said as much. And I think it's really common to question a dream right when you're on the brink of achieving it."

"You do?" Eva asked.

"I do. In fact, I bet there's a study out there that would confirm my theory."

Eva nodded. "I'm sure you're right. Multiple studies, in fact."

"No doubt."

As the delicious meal wound down, the conversation returned to their pre-West Coast lives. Eva had skipped a grade in early elementary, which had contributed to her sense of otherness as a child and her desire to make a life far from Eastern Pennsylvania. Cass knew all about that feeling, and for a moment, she wondered if she should mention her dyslexia. Eva had trusted her the day before with the story of her lost pregnancies, and had invited her into her home today. Could Cass return the gesture and open up about the part of her life she still regularly kept hidden?

In the end, though, she guided the conversation in a different, safer direction: "How did you like Cornell?"

"Cornell was… a culture shock, actually," Eva admitted.

"What do you mean?"

"Well, it was the first time I'd ever been around prep school kids, and they were, um, interesting."

"I think you mean assholes," Cass said.

Eva choked out a laugh and covered her mouth. "Not all of them."

"Wait. Did you just 'not all prep school kids' me?"

"I totally did."

Cass shook her head, smiling. "So the rich kid Ivy League thing wasn't really your scene."

"Not really. For me, Cornell was this amazing dream I couldn't believe I'd achieved. But for so many of those kids, it was their safety school. The classes were amazing, though, and I was lucky enough to find some really great mentors who encouraged me and opened doors for me to stay in higher ed, so it was worth it."

There she was again, chalking her academic success up to luck. But Cass didn't point it out this time. Eva was genuinely humble—an unusual trait to find in an academic, in Cass's experience, but one that was admirable.

"What about you? What was Vassar like?"

Cass almost felt bad for gushing about how much she had loved her undergrad experience, but she couldn't help it. A former women's college, Vassar had maintained its feminist, pro-women culture despite the admission of male students. Classes were small and intimate, and professors were teachers first, researchers second, unlike a lot of larger schools. The library was amazing, queer culture thriving, and though Vassar was another Eastern liberal arts school with a mostly white, middle and upper class student body, it was progressive-minded for the most part.

"Wow," Eva said when she'd finished extolling Vassar's virtues, eyebrows raised. "Sounds like you really loved where you went to school."

Cass shrugged sheepishly. "Just a little."

"I guess with academic parents, you were probably a little more familiar with what was out there."

"Probably."

Traveling to schools around New England had been second nature to Cass for as long as she could remember. Her parents were always combining academic conferences or association meetings with family vacations, so she and Matthew had been along for many an informal campus visit when they were younger. She could still remember the first time she'd seen the library at Vassar. She'd been ten, and her mom had parked her and Matthew there with instructions not to "move a muscle," but of course it was Cass she'd been talking to, so what did she expect? She wasn't about to wander the stacks the way Matthew had, reading a few pages of a book before trading it for another. No, instead she wandered the entire building, entranced by the wooden balconies and the stained glass windows. For once in a library she didn't worry about words or reading. She just absorbed the sense of being transported back in time and place to a world out of someone's imagination.

But she didn't tell Eva that. Instead she said, "What year did you graduate from undergrad?"

"Class of '03. What about you?"

"Class of '09."

Eva's head tilted. "You seem mature for your age."

"Really? Pretty sure my parents would disagree with you on that one," Cass said, and then frowned slightly as she heard how bitter she sounded.

"I'm guessing you don't get along with them."

"Let's just say I haven't quite lived up to their expectations."

"Because you're not like them?" Eva asked.

"Maybe. Probably," she agreed, folding and unfolding the cloth napkin Eva had laid beside her plate.

"I'm sorry," Eva said, and reached out to still her hands. "I've never met your parents, but if they can't see that you're amazing, then the problem is theirs."

Cass looked up at her, nonplused. "Oh. Well, thanks. I mean, you're obviously amazing too."

"Obviously," Eva said, tossing her hair.

Cass shook her head, smiling. "And here I was thinking how humble you are."

"Pssht. As if. Now come on. We should probably clear off the table if we're going to get any work done."

The kitchen clean-up didn't take long, and soon they were settling in at the dining room table, books and folders spread out before them. The next few hours passed far too quickly, just as brunch had done. Cass had to actively stop herself from watching Eva over the top of her laptop, but it was hard not to stare. She was so cute in her pale blue jeans and oversized Edmonds U sweatshirt, sitting at the table with one knee upraised while she frowned at her Macbook and chewed on the end of a Pilot pen.

At one point Eva glanced up and caught her watching. "What?"

"Nothing. Just—this is nice," Cass said.

"It is, isn't it?" Eva agreed, her voice soft.

And then Harvey snored loudly from his blanket nest on the couch, and they both cracked up.

Matthew and Maya didn't drop by, but her brother did text. "Are you ever coming home???" he asked, including a picture of himself in the new nursery surrounded by what looked like a crib that had exploded.

"Are you needed elsewhere?" Eva asked, leaning away from the table and rubbing her neck.

"I told my brother I would help him build furniture this weekend, but I seem to have been otherwise occupied."

"Furniture? Did he and Maya make an Ikea run or something?"

"Yes." They had. This particular furniture set, however, had come from Amazon's Baby Store. "Our grandfather's hobby was woodworking, so Matthew is fully capable of building any furniture item by himself."

"It's okay if you need to go," Eva said. "I know I've been hogging your company."

Cass hesitated. Was Eva tired of having her around? After all, they'd been together for most of the day. "Okay," she said at last, though she didn't really want to leave Eva's warm, bright house. But if Eva needed space, the last thing Cass wanted to do was crowd her.

She packed up her books and laptop and carried her juice glass to the sink, despite the fact Eva told her she didn't have to. Then she crossed to the couch and scratched Harvey's ears, laughing when he rolled over on his stomach and snorted happily. His chin had whiskers sprouting out of a lump of fur that looked almost like a wart, and she shook her head. This dog was ridiculously cute—just like his owner.

Hands in her hoodie pockets, Eva walked her to the door and stood by silently as she pulled on her shoes and jacket. Then she appeared to hesitate before stepping toward Cass, arms opening for a hug.

Cass moved to meet her, tugging Eva as close as she dared. This was no straight girl straight-armed hug. This was a full body contact hug between two people who had almost kissed only a few hours before. Cass turned her head slightly, inhaling the scent of Eva's shampoo—lavender, with a hint of something slightly spicier. Eva's chin was tucked into her open jacket, and Cass was pretty sure she felt her breath against her neck, soft and warm and just a little bit shallow.

"Thanks for coming over," Eva said, pulling away to look up at her.

It was dark out by now, even though it was barely five, but the firelight reflected off the windows by the door and flickered in Eva's dark eyes. This close, she wasn't cute at all. She was beautiful.

"Thanks for inviting me," Cass said, her own breath slightly hitched.

Eva's gaze dropped to her mouth, just as Cass had done earlier in the steam room, an obvious invitation to resume the moment they'd been interrupted, and Cass felt herself start to lean in. The whole day, the whole weekend, really, had been leading them to this point, hadn't it? Or maybe the whole quarter, ever since Cass had first approached her at the bar in the Thistledown, not wanting the beautiful, familiar-looking woman to disappear before she figured out how she knew her.

Just before their lips met, though, Cass pulled back. "Wait."

Eva looked up at her, blinking. "What?"

"I was wondering," Cass said, "about the whole friends thing."

Eva shifted back in Cass's arms. "What about it?"

"I guess I was wondering what you would say if I asked you out on an actual date. You know, hypothetically speaking."

Cass held her breath, almost wishing she could take the words back but not quite. Why did asking a pretty girl out never, ever get any easier? There was still that moment before she answered when your hopes were high and so were your regrets, that split second before she either smiled at you—*elation*—or looked away—*despair*.

Slowly, Eva smiled up at her. "Hypothetically speaking?"

"Yeah," Cass said, starting to smile herself.

"Well," Eva said, drawing out the suspense longer than Cass was certain her heart could withstand, "I think I would probably have to say yes."

"*Probably?*" Cass echoed, her hands tightening on Eva's sweatshirt. "You think?"

Eva shrugged. "I guess we won't know for sure unless you give it a try."

That sounded like something a teacher—or coach—would say. Cass straightened slightly and said, "Eva DeMarco, will you go out on a date with me?"

Eva gazed up at her. "Cassidy Trane, I would love to go out on a date with you."

"Awesome," Cass said, trying to rein in her relieved grin. "What about tomorrow night?"

"Oh." Eva squinted. "I told Alexis I'd have dinner with her and Tosh. What about Tuesday?"

Cass nodded quickly, as if Eva might change her mind. "That'll work. I'm actually leaving for California on Wednesday so..."

"So," Eva said, nodding, "it's a date."

"Awesome," Cass said, unable to hold her smile back any longer. "Should I pick you up here around six?"

"Sure," Eva said, a matching smile lighting up her face. "Where are you taking me?"

"You'll see," Cass said mysteriously.

It was literally a mystery because she hadn't yet figured out where she should take Eva DeMarco on their first date.

They stood grinning at each other a moment longer, and then Cass's phone buzzed again. Matthew, no doubt.

Eva leaned up and pecked her on the cheek. "Tell your brother and Maya I said hello."

"I will." Cass inhaled the scent of lavender and spice one more time and then pulled away. "Have a good Monday."

"You, too. See you soon."

Cass forced herself to pick up her things, turn around, and walk away from Eva. Maybe, if she was lucky, she wouldn't have to leave so early next time.

"Bye," Eva said, and Cass glanced back from the walkway to see her silhouetted against the living room, her face in shadows.

"Bye," Cass said. And then, marshaling her strength once again, she turned and walked the rest of the way to the street.

Holy crap. She and Eva were going on a date. Now Cass just had to figure out the perfect, romantic plan, she thought as she pulled away from the curb.

No pressure, really.

CHAPTER NINE

Forty-eight hours was plenty of time for Eva to talk herself out of going on a date with Cassidy Trane. It had been all fine and good spending time with her while most of the university's faculty and students were away on break, but breaks always ended and new quarters always began. With her tenure packet mostly complete and her committee review only a few months away, Eva couldn't afford to lose track of what mattered.

"What do you mean?" Alexis asked after dinner, when it was just the two of them curled up on the couch in Alexis and Tosh's living room, Prime Music playing classic Motown hits on speakers hidden somewhere in the room. Tosh's kids were at their mother's house this week, and Tosh had shooed the two women out of the kitchen so that he could clean up after dinner. That was their exchange—one person cooked and the other cleaned up. For the most part, Eva knew, Tosh's commitment to an egalitarian household was more than just lip service. His parents were very traditional, but Christine, his first wife, had broken him of any latent patriarchal habits, Alexis liked to say.

"What do you mean, what do I mean?" Eva said, running a finger around the top of her wine glass to see if it would make noise. "I can't really go out with her, Alexis."

"Oh my god," Alexis said, tilting her head back and staring at the ceiling. "What am I going to do with you, Eva?"

Eva merely hunched her shoulders and sipped her wine.

"Correct me if I'm wrong, but you did agree to go out on a date with her, did you not? Which means that you sort of have to go."

"Of course I don't," Eva argued. "It's not like we signed a contract."

Alexis rolled her eyes. "Oh, okay. I didn't realize there wasn't a signed agreement on the table. So tell me, then, what exactly are you going to tell her?"

"That I reassessed, and that given her standing in my department, it's not a good idea if we pursue a personal relationship." The words had sounded fine in Eva's head, but now as she trotted them out for Alexis, she realized that they weren't fine at all. They were lame. Very, very lame.

Her best friend side-eyed her, but her words, when they came were kind. "Sweetie, that's just an excuse. We both know the real reason you want to bail on her, don't we?"

Eva looked down at her legs curled beneath her. "I told you why."

"Hey." Alexis tapped her thigh. "Look at me. I was there when you started dating Ben, and I was there when he left. I know how much you wanted that relationship to work and how devastated you were when it didn't. But I also know that Cassidy Trane makes you smile more than anyone else has done in years—other than me, of course. That's something to hold onto, Eva, not run away from."

"But won't people accuse me of abusing my power, and worse, accuse her of trading sex for faculty favor?"

"You're not actually in a position of authority over her, and she's not planning a career in academics, is she? People aren't going to accuse her of sleeping her way to the top of her Master's cohort because that's not really a thing."

Eva couldn't argue with Alexis on that.

"It's only a first date, Eva," Alexis added. "There's nothing to say there has to be a second one. And even if you did decide to keep seeing her, you wouldn't have to tell anyone at Edmonds. You're under no professional obligation to report your relationship, and by keeping it quiet, you would protect both of your reputations. Assuming Cass was okay with that arrangement, of course."

Eva couldn't imagine asking Cass to keep what they were doing a secret. But then again, canceling their date was at least as awkward a prospect.

"Damn it, Lex," she said, covering her face with both hands, "what am I even doing? Everything feels so out of control."

"I know," Alexis said, and patted her thigh again. "But maybe that isn't such a bad thing."

Eva dropped her hands and slowly nodded. Maybe Alexis was right. Maybe relinquishing some of the control she'd always rigidly maintained over her life and career wasn't the worst idea ever.

That *maybe* lingered at the back of her mind the following day as she worked on her personal statement for her tenure packet. But developing a cohesive narrative of where her research, teaching, and service fit into the broader Edmonds community didn't allow her much time to dwell on Cass or on what Alexis had said. In the end, she didn't make a decision about whether or not to go on the date. She simply did nothing, which was far easier, she'd always found, than doing something.

At six PM sharp, Cass's Jeep pulled up at the curb. As Cass made her way up the walkway, Eva adjusted her navy blue slacks and crisp white button-up shirt, one boot-clad foot tapping nervously. She'd texted Cass earlier to find out what the dress code was for where they were going, but Cass's response had been fairly cryptic. "Business casual," she'd written, followed by a wink emoji. Eva had stared at her phone in exasperation because the addition of the emoji threw her. Did it mean she was supposed to dress in one of her teaching outfits, comfortable but a step up from jeans and a T-shirt? Or did it mean something even nicer? Apparently Cass didn't have any idea what it felt like to be rejoining the dating world after more than a decade away or else she would have been more communicative.

Before she could throw her phone across the room, though, she'd closed her eyes and conjured up an image of Cass in her white towel in the steam room, her tattoos on display, her blue eyes hooded as she leaned in toward Eva, closer and closer.... It would be fine, Eva told herself. It didn't really matter what she wore, anyway. What mattered was that after months of dancing around the rainbow elephant in the room, they had finally admitted to each other that there might be something between them worth exploring. That was what tonight would be: an exploration.

"Hi," Cass said when Eva opened the door and invited her in.

"You look beautiful."

"Thanks," Eva said, her nerves evaporating as she smiled up into Cass's eyes. "I'm going to assume that under your jacket, you do too."

Cass laughed. "Thanks, I think. Ready?"

"Sure." She shrugged into her coat and shouldered her purse, and then glanced down at Harvey who was jumping around them, whining. "Sorry, boy, you have to stay here."

"He doesn't, actually, if you don't want him to," Cass said. "At least, not for part one of the evening."

Their evening had more than one part? Eva suppressed a shiver that definitely arose more from fear than excitement. Dating was stressful. It probably would have been easier just to stay in a loveless marriage.

Well, maybe not.

"What exactly is part one?" she asked.

"I thought I'd make you dinner at my studio," Cass said. "We can drop Harvey back here on our way to the second part of the date, if you'd like."

A date that included Harvey? Cass was already scoring all of the points here. Except that Eva knew Cass wasn't trying to score points. She was simply treating Harvey like the important, highly neurotic family member he most definitely was.

"Did you hear that, Harve?" Eva asked, reaching for his leash on the coat tree beside the front door. "You get to come along, after all, boy."

A moment later they stepped out onto the porch, Harvey hopping excitedly between them.

"I hope you know how lucky you are, Harvey," Cass said, bending to scratch his head as Eva locked the front door. "I haven't gone on a date with a boy since Y2K."

Eva stared at her. "Are you serious?"

"Totally," Cass said, and offered her arm for the short walk to the curb.

Eva arranged Harvey on her other side and took Cass's arm. One good thing about her dog's clinginess was that he rarely pulled on the leash; he didn't want to get too far away from her. "Y2K— that means you came out when you were in, what, eighth grade?"

"Wow. I had no idea you were a math ace, too."

"Shut it," Eva said, but she was smiling as she helped Harvey into the back of the Jeep and slid into the passenger seat.

"I tried dating a boy once," Cass told her as she started the car and pulled onto the quiet street. "It didn't take."

"So you were one of those precocious queer kids, huh?"

Cass shrugged. "What can I say? Always on the cutting edge, us Trane kids."

"Right," Eva said, and shook her head. But she couldn't help smiling at Cass's exaggerated cockiness. At least, she thought it was exaggerated.

They parked in the driveway at Matthew and Maya's house, and Eva took a breath as she slid out of the car, Harvey's leash in hand. As they approached the studio behind the main house, she pushed down the memories of the last time she'd been here. Matthew and Ben had become friends shortly after the younger man had been hired, and the two couples had spent time together back in happier days, including more than one dinner party at this very house.

For a moment, she thought about who she'd been back then, younger and shinier and altogether lighter, unaware of what lay before her. If someone had told her then that one day she would be back here on a date with Matthew's twin sister, would she have believed them? Not a chance. But here she was, older and less shiny and, she hoped, more secure in herself. And definitely excited to see where the evening would lead.

"I could have walked over, you know," she commented as they approached the studio.

"It's supposed to rain. Besides, I wanted to pick you up. It makes it feel more official somehow."

Eva knew what she meant. Her conversation with Alexis came back to her, and she silently expressed her gratitude for her friend's ability to call her out on her BS. There really wasn't any good reason that she and Cass couldn't enjoy each other's company. No romantic relationship came with a guarantee. Maybe it would work out and maybe it wouldn't. For now, she was choosing to live in the moment and let what would happen, happen.

Gayle would be proud of her, assuming Eva told her about

Cass.

"It's even smaller than your house," Cass said as she unlocked the door and held it open for Eva and Harvey.

The last time Eva had seen the studio, it had still been a garage. Now the front wall had been replaced with drywall and new windows, and the cement floor had been done over with wood flooring and decorative rugs. The garage interior had been completely renovated and now included a stainless steel kitchen along the left side of the room with a sliding door that opened onto a private deck, a combined dining/living area that occupied the right half of the room, and a door to what looked like a small bathroom at the rear of the large room. Narrow stairs led up into what Eva assumed was a sleeping space, given that there was no sign of a bed downstairs.

"Wow," she said, looking around at the warm, welcoming space. "It's so much lovelier than I expected."

Cass closed the door behind them. "Can I take your coat?"

"Sure. Thanks."

As she hung their jackets on hooks near the door, she asked, "Have you been in here before?"

"Once or twice," Eva admitted, and wandered over to look at the framed art on the walls, oil paintings of Western Washington scenes—forested trails lined with cedars and firs, lakes nestled into the sides of glacier-topped mountains, Skagit Valley tulip fields with Mt. Baker in the distance. The walls themselves looked perfectly normal, though if she looked close enough she could see places where the drywall tape hadn't been completely sanded into submission. "Did you help with the remodel?"

"As much as I could with my shoulder. Any paint streaks you see are probably mine. Matthew and Maya renovated the main house right after they moved in, so they're a bit better at the home remodeling thing than I am."

Eva and Ben had worked on their house, too, replacing worn carpeting and damaged drywall one room at a time to get the interior ready for growing their family. It had been fun—until it had come time to break down the nursery. There was still an unbuilt crib somewhere in a box in the basement. She tended not to look in boxes much.

Harvey chose that moment to hop up on the couch and nestle into a neat pile of blankets, digging and spinning in an effort to create a comfortable nest.

"Harvey," Eva said, starting to move toward him. "You can't just destroy other people's houses!"

"He's fine," Cass said, catching her wrist and giving it a squeeze. Then she let go and gestured toward a bottle of red wine on the counter. "Can I get you something to drink? I also have beer and cider. We're having salmon for dinner, if that sounds okay?"

"Sounds delicious," Eva said. "And I'd love some wine." Alcohol plus something to occupy her fidgety hands sounded like an excellent plan.

Cass poured two glasses of a local Washington Pinot Noir and offered Eva one. "I'm glad you're here," she said, and clinked their glasses together lightly.

"I am too," Eva said, gazing up at her.

Their eyes caught, and Eva could feel that same pull as ever between them, the one that made her want to tug Cass closer by the collar of her blue chambray shirt, the one that made her body tingle in nearly unforgotten places as she imagined winding her arms around Cass's neck and....

"Time to cook," Cass announced. She took a sip of wine and set her glass on the counter, turning a laptop screen to face her.

"Can I help?" Eva asked.

"Nope. Everything should be ready to go in the oven. Just to confirm, no food allergies or restrictions, right?"

"Right."

"Groovy."

Eva sipped her wine and watched Cass pull two pans from the refrigerator. Inside one a slab of salmon lay atop a bed of mushrooms, garlic, and peppers, while the second held red potatoes, quartered and tossed with more garlic.

"That looks amazing," Eva said, staring at the food in surprise.

"Some jocks can actually cook," Cass said, her tone teasing.

"Sorry, I didn't mean it like that. It's just that most graduate students I've known, myself included, tend to subsist on pasta and baked potatoes, if they're lucky, ramen and Domino's if they're not."

"I've always really liked to cook, and your story about your cooking school roommate inspired me," Cass said, sliding the pan of potatoes into the pre-heated oven and setting the timer. "Tonight we'll be having truffle oil roast salmon and mushrooms with a side of roast potatoes and spinach. The recipe actually calls for mustard greens, but it's not really the season."

It wasn't really the season for wild caught salmon, either, but Eva wasn't going to complain. "Where did you find the truffle oil? Or did you already have some?"

"Matthew and Maya, actually. Our parents gave them some for Christmas last year."

Based on previous interactions, Eva didn't think that Cass's brother and sister-in-law were huge foodies. Why, then, would Cass's parents give them fancy food items, especially when Cass was the one who liked to cook? The more she learned about the Professors Trane, the less she liked them. But at least they'd made this delectable meal possible.

As Cass pulled a package of spinach from the refrigerator and began to prep a large skillet, Eva leaned against the counter and watched. Music sounded from a Bluetooth speaker near the television, some indie band like The Postal Service or Bon Iver crooning low and soft. That wasn't quite what she'd expected from Cass either, and she realized that maybe she should let go of her preconceptions and get to know the woman before her for who she was, not who she seemed to be.

"So how's your tenure packet coming?" Cass asked, not looking up from the skillet.

"Good," Eva said. "It's mostly done at this point."

"Matthew said it's due to the dean in January, and then he makes a recommendation and forwards it on to the Arts and Sciences T. and P. Committee."

"Right. The committee meets in spring quarter and reviews all the candidates for the college, and then forwards their recommendation on to the university Tenure and Promotion Committee for review in the fall. From what I've heard, the university committee basically rubber stamps the college's rec, so it's really a matter of making it past the Arts and Sciences people."

"Do you have any idea how it'll go?"

Eva shrugged and stared into her wine. "Not really. I mean, I have Gwen and Steve's support, and my teaching evaluations and external letters of rec are solid, so that's good. But the committee is its own entity."

"Do you know the people currently serving?"

"Three of them. The other two spots are still open at this point, so there's no way to predict how a vote might go." She didn't mention that the current committee was made up of at least two known hardliners, one from History and one from Poli Sci, neither of whom could be expected to look kindly upon her current research topic.

"They're still open? But the school year is half over."

"Only a third, technically. The committee doesn't meet until after spring break, so Steve has time to recruit new members." And by recruit, Eva meant threaten and cajole. "What about Matthew? Is he on track?"

"So far. Two more years and he should be where you are."

"He'll do fine. He's got a great reputation within the college, and from what I've heard, his student evaluations are solid."

Cass glanced up from the chopping board. "How do you know that?"

"The Arts and Sciences grapevine." She wasn't actually sure how she knew that, or even if it was true. Gossip on a small campus like Edmonds was endemic and traveled through wildly varied pathways. She only knew she'd heard that Matthew Trane was popular among students, which in a challenging field like physics usually meant something. Not all scientists were accomplished at teaching, no more than all social scientists or linguists or musicians were. It was just that some members of the Physics Department literally wore pocket protectors, so their social skills were often presumed to be more suspect than those of others on campus.

"Well, that's good to know."

Cass went back to mincing garlic, and Eva watched, enjoying the way Cass's focus narrowed on the work before her, eyes drifting every once in a while to the computer screen. Her lips moved as she read the online recipe from—Eva squinted—was that *Cosmopolitan* magazine? "11 Romantic Dinners Anyone Can Cook" the headline read, and Eva smiled into her wine. Aw, Cass was so cute. And funny. And hot. She liked weird fonts, though. Eva could barely read the words printed on the screen.

They chatted about their department and the college as Cass made dinner, and Eva shared campus history of the past decade that Cass didn't know. Then the conversation moved on to the holidays and their plans, and Cass said again that she was both looking forward to the trip to California and partially dreading it, too.

"Maya's mom and sisters are awesome and have only ever been kind to me," she explained as she slid the salmon in beside the potatoes and reset the oven timer. "But I guess there are some aunts and cousins who have been less than cool about queer relatives or friends, people who actually voted against gay marriage when the whole Prop Eight thing went down. I don't even know if they voted for or against Prop Eight—the wording on those measures is always so convoluted, like the people who write them purposely want to confuse voters."

"They totally do. Right after we moved here, the Washington legislature passed a gay marriage initiative, so of course there ended up being a referendum. The attorney general was a Republican, and when he wrote the referendum text, he used some phrase that was so obviously anti-gay that a judge ruled it had to be changed. Something about redefining traditional marriage, I think."

"How did the vote turn out?"

Eva smiled, remembering how she and Ben had celebrated with their friends, mostly straight progressives. "Washington became the first state in the US to vote in favor of a gay marriage measure."

"Nice," Cass said, returning her smile. "Sometimes I can't believe how much everything has changed in such a short time."

"I know. Only now it feels like things are swinging back. Like the old, straight, white men feel their power slipping away, so they keep doing these increasingly desperate things to try to maintain their hold."

"Backlash can be brutal," Cass agreed, "but I try to remind myself that it's usually a sign of progress. Have you seen any of the TED talks by that Swedish statistician, Hans something?"

"Rosling? I love that guy. I've actually used a couple of his videos in my classes."

The timer went off again, and Cass pulled the salmon out, covering it in foil to keep it hot while she sautéed the roasted potatoes with the spinach. A few minutes later she served their plates and they headed to the table, Harvey wending between their legs doing his best to trip up one or both of them. He might be neurotic, but he wasn't stupid.

Cass topped off their wine glasses and held hers up. "Thanks again for coming over tonight, Eva."

"My pleasure," Eva said, clinking their glasses together. And then to cover her blush, she took a long sip. "This looks amazing."

"I hope it lives up to the hype."

They dug in, and after the first delicious bite, Eva found herself thinking that Cassidy Trane had to have a flaw somewhere. Because a beautiful sociology major who could cook, was single, *and* appeared to dote on Harvey?

"Holy crap," she said after swallowing. "Cass, this is incredible."

"Thanks." Cass smiled down at her plate.

"I'm serious. You should work in a restaurant."

"I actually did when I first got to San Francisco. But the hours are crazy and the people—they're really great, but restaurant people like to party. Like, a lot. It got to be that my co-workers were taking bets on who was going to convince me to try 'shrooms and E and a bunch of other things, so I left. I started temping, and next thing you know I ended up at Avicom. Sometimes I wonder what I'd be doing right now if I'd stayed in restaurant work. Somehow I doubt I'd be in grad school."

"In that case," Eva said around a mouthful of truffle-flavored spinach, "I'm glad you started temping."

Geez, cheesy much? Eva asked herself. But as Cass's eyes crinkled with her smile, Eva decided she didn't care if she sounded more like Alexis than herself. There were far worse things in life.

Midway through the meal, Cass asked the question that Eva had always thought defined their generation: "Where were you on 9/11?"

They talked about their experiences briefly. Eva had been in her junior year at Cornell, and one of her cousins, a firefighter in Brooklyn, had lost dozens of friends when the towers fell. Cass had been a freshman in high school, and one of her best friends had lost his father when the plane struck the South Tower. Each had known intellectually that things like that were possible, but neither had previously witnessed casualties on such a scale, especially not in a building they had visited, on streets they had walked, in a city where they had both slept more than a few times while commercial airplanes flew harmlessly overhead.

"Sometimes I think I have PTSD from 9/11," Cass confessed. "Not because I was anywhere near Manhattan that day but because I could have been. My friend Mia's mom worked in the North Tower, and in the summer we used to visit her so that we could see the views from her office on the sixtieth floor. We were actually there only a couple of weeks earlier."

She shuddered a little, and Eva squeezed her hand briefly before letting go. 9/11 had changed her view of the world dramatically, too. Instead of a place where she went to escape Scranton and spend time with her father's family, New York became the city where the worst could—and did—happen. She almost didn't apply to NYU for grad school, but in the end she decided that was the response terrorists wanted, and she refused to give fear that much power over her life.

"We probably all have some form of PTSD from the media coverage alone," she said. "It doesn't help that the news stations replayed the worst parts over and over again."

"Totally." Cass waved her potato-encrusted fork through the air. "Is cultural PTSD a thing?"

"If only there was an online encyclopedia," Eva said, pretending to frown. "Oh, wait, there is!" She turned on her phone. "Siri, do a web search for cultural PTSD and 9/11."

With the screen tilted so that Cass could see the results too, they scrolled through the list, clicking on promising links. It took a bit of winnowing, but finally they reached a paper on psychological reactions to 9/11, deemed by the authors an example of collective trauma: a traumatic psychological effect shared by a group of people of any size, up to and including an entire society.

"I feel like this should be common sense but somehow isn't," Eva said as she digested the article's main takeaway: People should limit repeated exposure to disturbing images because watching a terrorist attack or other traumatic event on TV—live or on replay—can lead to post-traumatic stress and other negative outcomes, both physical and emotional.

Cass had already gone back to eating, and looked up at Eva rather than down at the phone. "What should be?"

"The fact that more television viewing around an event like 9/11 correlates to a higher trauma response."

"Ah." Cass nodded sagely. "Speaking of trauma responses, how do you feel about space travel?"

Eva set her phone down. "Unless we're talking about the Challenger or the Columbia, I feel like that's a non sequitur."

"No space shuttle accidents, I promise," Cass said, wiping her face with a cloth napkin and placing it beside her now empty plate. "Asking for a friend—are you cool with space exploration, or not so cool?"

"I'm cool with most things related to space." Were they going to the Pacific Science Center? But no, it was too late. An IMAX movie with 3-D spacecraft footage? If so, she was prepared to deem this the best first date of her life.

"Noted," Cass said. "One more choose your own adventure question: Dessert now, or after part two of the date?"

Eva regarded her thoughtfully. "That depends."

"On what?"

"On what kind of dessert you're offering."

"Tiramisu," Cass announced, and then smiled as Eva all but squealed. "I thought, you know, since you're Italian and all..."

"Can you seriously make tiramisu?" Eva asked.

"I can make tiramisu," Cass confirmed.

"In that case, before. And maybe after, too?" As Cass's eyebrows rose, Eva realized how that sounded and added, "I mean, maybe I could have leftovers. At my house." Cass snickered, and Eva covered her face. "Oh my god, forget it. I'm going home right now."

She felt a gentle tug on her hands and peeked out to see Cass smiling softly at her.

"I can totally send you home later with leftovers. I'll be in

California for the rest of the week, remember? Wouldn't want anything to go to waste."

The tiramisu, like everything else Cass had made, was delicious. So much so that Harvey, who was nosing around the floor by the kitchen sink, made a beeline for Eva and nosed at her leg, apparently concerned by the string of unintelligible sounds she was emitting.

Cass paused, wine glass in hand. "Does that mean you like it or…?"

"I adore it," Eva assured her. "I take it back. Forget restaurants. You definitely have to open your own bakery."

"I'll add 'baker' to my list of back-up professions," Cass promised.

She was so pretty, Eva thought, watching Cass reach down and rub Harvey's head. Pretty and sweet and tough and strong, smart and athletic *and* a good cook. Honestly, there had to be something wrong with her. She was almost too perfect to be real. Except that she was undeniably real. This studio was real, and her tattoos, and the tawny flashes of color in her otherwise blue eyes. Her lips were real, and the dimple Eva had noticed the first night they met.

"Can I ask you something?" she questioned, tiramisu melting on her tongue. When Cass nodded, she continued, "The night we met. Did you already know who I was when you came over to talk to me?"

Cass leaned back and swallowed a bite of the sweet dessert. "No. I didn't really figure it out until you said you were a teacher. I was just connecting the dots when…" She trailed off and looked down at the table, moving her fork around her plate.

"When your friend came over," Eva finished. "What was her name again?"

"Amy."

Eva touched her napkin to her lips. "I know you said you weren't together, but it definitely looked like you were more than friendly." She waited, hoping Cass would read between the lines. Because if they weren't on the same page, Eva wanted to know right now, this second, before she fell any more in love with Cass's—cooking. Right. Her amazing foodie goodness.

"Amy and I have been friends for a long time, but yeah, it was more than that. Right before I moved up here we started dating casually. You know, without a commitment in place."

"Like friends with benefits?" Eva hazarded. When Cass nodded, she felt it: the deflating as she realized that this, this right here was Cass's fatal flaw. "Is that what you're looking for now?" she made herself ask.

"With you? That depends."

"On what?"

"On what you're looking for."

They gazed across the table at each other, and Alexis's words came back to Eva: *a short and sweet affair might be just what you need.* At the time she had assured her friend that she didn't do short and sweet affairs, but that was before she had discovered that her attraction to Cass was mutual. Could she actually do casual? Other people did it all the time. As a plus, if it didn't work out, Cass was returning to California in a matter of months, so they wouldn't have to run into each other on campus forever after.

Cass was still watching her, so Eva set her fork down and said, "I like you. I'd like to spend more time with you and see where this goes."

Cass's smile was small but genuine. "So would I, Eva."

"But at the same time," she added, "if people knew we were seeing each other, it could damage both of our professional reputations."

"I looked it up, though," Cass said, frowning slightly. "There's no policy that says we can't date."

"I'm not talking about policy. I mean the gossip and rumors that come when a student and a professor get involved. While you might not be planning a career in academics, I very much am."

Cass's shoulders lowered slightly and she nodded. "I understand. Well, I guess it's good we figured this out now." She stood up and began clearing the table, her eyes focused on her hands. "I'll drive you home, okay? Unless you'd rather walk?"

"Wait." Eva rose beside her and hooked her hand around Cass's elbow. "That's not what I meant. It's just, if we do agree to try this, I would need there to be some pretty clear boundaries at school."

Cass's brow was furrowed again. "Are you saying you wouldn't want anyone to know?"

"I'm fine with the people closest to us knowing. Just, you know, not the rest of campus." Eva winced as she heard exactly how that sounded: like the formerly heterosexually married woman asking her lesbian partner to join her in her closet. But it wasn't her fault academia was so political. She didn't make the rules. She only, like everyone else, had to live with them.

"Huh." Cass resumed clearing the table. "I'll have to think about that. This conversation feels a little premature, anyway."

"It does?"

"Well, yeah. We still have to see how the rest of the date goes, don't we?" Cass said, carrying their plates to the sink.

Add general cheekiness to her list of cons. Or maybe it was another pro. The jury was still out.

***

The rest of the date was, Eva thought a little while later, going even better than the first part—if you didn't count the fact that Cass had invited her twin brother along. Eva had to admit to being a bit surprised when Matthew drove them up to campus, stopping briefly so she could drop Harvey and the leftovers at her house, and parked his Camry with its correctly coded faculty pass near the Physics and Astronomy building. The parking pass was important because even on a Tuesday night during December break, the Edmonds parking powers that be were overly officious terrors.

By the time Matthew led them through the observatory and into the empty planetarium, Eva was pretty sure she knew what part two of the date entailed. She just hadn't counted on having her date's brother along for the romantic star-gazing portion of the night. Was this a twin thing? Did Cass do this often? Did other twins do this sort of thing often?

"Right here," Cass said, stopping in the middle row and pointing to the center seats, which were roomy and comfortable, Eva discovered when she settled onto one.

Instead of sitting beside her, though, Cass moved to join Matthew at the computer station at the back of the room. Eva could hear them talking quietly, and then, as the lights dimmed even further, she heard Matthew say, "Have fun, kids. Text me when you're ready to be picked up."

The door opened and closed, and Eva heard Cass type something on the computer. A moment later, a distant light began to take shape on the darkened dome overhead while low music began, steadily climbing. Cass dropped into the seat next to her and said, "Sorry about Matthew. He's sort of necessary for all of this to work."

"It's fine," Eva said, relaxing into the seat. "It's excellent, actually."

A private planetarium show after truffles and tiramisu? She had never before experienced such a decadent, romantic first date. She hoped Cass knew she was ruining Eva for all future first dates. Probably, she thought as Cass's hand brushed against hers where it rested on her chair arm, Cass knew exactly what she was doing.

Eva turned her hand over and slipped it beneath Cass's, weaving their fingers together. Yep. Definitely ruined for future dating—even with the temporary sibling involvement.

Cass held out a flask. "More wine?"

"Sure."

Eva unscrewed the cap while Cass held the container, and they took turns sipping its contents, never once relinquishing each other's hand. Overhead the star show amped up as Neil deGrasse Tyson narrated the viewer's journey from the depths of space back to our solar system, with close-ups of the moon and Earth's surface. The wine warmed Eva's belly, as did Cass's proximity though in a significantly different way, and as the show went on Eva realized that for the first time in a long time, she had spent hours living in the moment, a hundred percent present, without even noticing.

Cass leaned in. "How can the universe not have a center?" she whispered. "My brain hurts just thinking about it."

"I don't know," Eva whispered back. She didn't know why they were whispering, either. It wasn't like they would disturb anyone else.

As Neil deGrasse Tyson described the expanding, cooling universe, Eva could feel Cass's eyes on her. She glanced sideways, intending to fake-chastise her, but then she realized how close their faces were and forgot about telling Cass to keep her eyes on the skies. Instead she found herself leaning even closer, chin tilted up, just as she had done twice before. Only this time, Cass closed the distance between them and pressed her lips to Eva's.

Light burst from the simulated night sky above them, pulsing against Eva's eyelids as she returned the faint pressure Cass's mouth offered. Cass tasted of red wine and tiramisu, her lips soft and surprisingly cool. Her body gave off waves of heat, and her smooth skin was so different from Ben's ever-present stubble—but she didn't want to think about him. She wanted to think about Cass and her lovely lips and—her laugh?

"What?" Eva asked, opening her eyes and pulling away.

"He said 'the Big Bang' just as I kissed you."

"Hey, didn't I kiss you?" Eva teased.

"How about we kissed each other," Cass suggested.

"Sounds good to me," Eva said, and leaned closer again as Neil discussed the glow of cosmic background radiation.

She didn't learn as much about the universe from the second half of the show, but she didn't mind. She was too busy exploring Cass's lips, her mouth, her tongue. She'd forgotten how different it was kissing a woman. Cass's touch was gentle but insistent, her kiss deepening as Eva tried to get closer. After a minute of fighting the chair arms between them, Cass pulled her up.

"Come here," she said, her voice raspy.

Eva was only too happy to comply. And that was how she ended up on Cass's lap, arms around Cass's neck as their kisses grew deeper and hotter. It had been so long since Eva had kissed anyone, and after a little while she realized her stamina was failing. She pulled back finally, resting her forehead against Cass's.

"Wow," she said.

"Wow," Cass agreed. "Did you see stars?"

Eva cracked up. "Totally. Did you?"

"Millions, actually."

Eva settled more comfortably against her and returned her attention to the show above them, trying to concentrate on galaxy clusters and what they meant about the size of the universe. With that many star systems, didn't there almost have to be other intelligent life somewhere out there in the deep dark of space? She'd always thought there must be. She just wasn't sure she wanted to be present at first contact.

When the show was over, Cass texted Matthew and shut down the projector. He appeared at the door not long after, fully prepared to chauffeur them home.

"Thanks, bro," Cass said as they stopped in front of Eva's house, the porch light bright against the dark night. "I'll see you back at home."

He started to say something but Cass was giving him a meaningful look, and Matthew coughed lightly. "Got it. Good night, Eva. I hope you enjoyed the show."

"I did," she said, glad the cover of night hid her blush.

Then they were walking up the front walk while Matthew's Camry pulled away, and Eva was trying to decide whether or not to invite her in "for coffee." The date had been wonderful, but she was tired and, if she was being honest, a little overwhelmed. She hadn't kissed anyone other than Ben in what felt like forever, and even though she'd enjoyed kissing Cass—like, really *really* enjoyed it—she still needed time to process everything they'd said and done.

Cass stopped beside her at the bottom of the porch steps. "I had a really great time tonight," she said as Eva fished in her purse for her keys.

"So did I," Eva admitted, glancing up at her. "Thanks for a wonderful evening."

"My pleasure. We're leaving early tomorrow for California, but maybe when we get back you and I could do this again? I mean, not exactly this because it'll be New Year's, but you know, something together, like another date?"

It was the first time Eva could remember seeing Cass stumble. Smiling, she touched her palm to Cass's warm cheek and said softly, "I would like that very much." She leaned up and kissed Cass on the lips, lingering for a moment before pulling back. "Are you sure you're okay walking home?"

Cass nodded, her smile turning rakish as she teetered back on her heels. "I'm sure."

She waited while Eva unlocked the door, and then she waved and started off down the walk to the sidewalk. "Good night."

"Good night," Eva responded, watching her for another

moment. Then she slipped into her house and locked the door behind her, laughing as Harvey danced around her, possibly peeing a little in his excitement to have her home after an hour—*a whole hour*—of being apart.

It *had* been a good night. She had a feeling that more good nights lay in the not-so-distant future.

CHAPTER TEN

Cass straightened her bow tie, smoothed down the unruly cowlick at the back of her head, and nodded at herself in the mirror. Here went nothing.

The walk to her brother and Maya's side door didn't take long. In a matter of seconds, literally, she was rapping lightly on the door before letting herself in and pacing up the handful of steps into the small, eat-in kitchen painted a warm yellow. Maya was leaning against a nearby counter with Cass's father while Matthew and their mother peered into a pot on the gas stove, and traditional holiday music sounded from a Bluetooth speaker on the table in the dining alcove that overlooked the backyard patio. Cass pushed down the sudden urge to flee and made herself say, "Hi."

The look Maya gave her was tinged with equal parts relief and desperation. "Cass," she all but exclaimed, stepping forward to take the bag of food Cass carried. "There you are." With her back to the room, she mouthed "HELP."

If only she could.

Cass smiled at her sister-in-law and started to wave at the rest of the room before dropping her arm. That was not a habit she necessarily wanted to cultivate, even if the person she'd borrowed it from was. Speak of the devil—her phone buzzed, and she checked it nervously: "On our way. See you in a few."

A smiley emoji followed, and Cass's nerves began to settle. But the temporary letup didn't last long because *holy shit*, Eva was on her way over... with her mother. They were really doing this. They were really spending New Year's Eve with their parents.

Because meeting the family after one official date wasn't a bad idea at all.

It felt like they'd been dating longer than that, mostly because they had talked every night she'd been in California. The week away had felt longer than Cass had expected, knowing that Eva was back in Edmonds working on her Tenure and Promotion packet and waiting for Cass to get back. Maya's family had been awesome as usual, and their joy when they found out about the baby had been incredible to share. Even her extended family had been much less conservative than Cass had anticipated, if you didn't count the cousin whose young son had refused to accept that she was a girl. But despite the warm weather and warm family reception, Cass had been just as glad to return to the winter rains a couple of nights earlier for one very specific reason: Eva DeMarco. Talking for hours on the phone was great and all, but it didn't come close to being in the same room.

"Was that Eva?" Maya asked now.

Cass nodded, unable to draw in enough breath to answer. Eva and her mom were coming over now to meet her parents. Why had Cass ever thought this was a good idea? Oh, right. She hadn't.

Maya patted her arm. "Why don't you and I go meet them?"

"Okay," she managed.

"But—" Matthew started. Then his eyes caught Cass's, and he stopped. "Ask her if her mom likes eggnog."

"Will do," Cass said, avoiding her own mother's gaze as she followed Maya out of the room.

A minute later they were on the sidewalk in front of the house, hands tucked into coat pockets, breath actually visible in the air before them. Pacific Northwest weather was sort of unintuitive, Cass had always thought. Clear skies meant cold air while clouds brought warmer temperature. Tonight's fireworks off the Space Needle would be visible, but the crowds would be smaller than usual.

"Jesus H. Christ, it's cold," Maya said, huddling deeper into her down parka. A week in Southern California had done nothing to improve her anti-winter sentiments. "Thank you for the timely interruption, by the way."

"Let me guess. He was talking your ear off about nanocrystals again?"

"Yep. I'm always stunned when that stereotype about scientists not having social skills holds up."

"At least Matthew isn't like that."

"Thank god."

They walked down the block in silence, the only sound between them an occasional teeth chatter, until they reached a stop sign and turned onto the next street.

"So," Maya said, her eyes peeking out at Cass from inside her faux-fur hood. "How did Eva react this morning when you told her?"

"Um," Cass said, thinking back to earlier in the day when she and Eva had gone for a run at the arboretum. "Okay, I guess. She's still coming over tonight, anyway."

In truth, Eva had turned more than a little pale as she'd stared out over the view of the Sound from the arboretum's wooden tower. "Maya?" she'd echoed. "Pregnant?"

"Yes," Cass had confirmed, trying to quell her own anxiety. If they were going to hang out, Eva needed to know the truth. "She's due in mid-May."

"Mid-May?" Cass could see Eva's mental wheels turning. "So that means she's, what, twenty weeks along?"

She winced, remembering how far along Eva had been when she'd lost her own child. "Yeah."

"Wow. That's—I mean, congratulations. You must be excited." She'd smiled, but it was so clearly forced that Cass had reached out and touched her hand where it rested on the railing. But Eva had flinched away from the contact and moved toward the tower stairs. "We should probably get going. I have to meet my mom in a little while."

And that had been that. Cass hadn't said anything else about the baby, and Eva hadn't asked.

All day she'd half-expected a call or text from Eva saying she wouldn't be able to make the dinner party tonight after all, but the hours had passed and her phone hadn't beeped, and now she and Maya were rounding the corner onto Eva's street—and there she was, walking toward them, smiling at something her mother had just said.

"Eva," Cass said, feeling her heart start its silly racing as Eva's gaze fell on her. Jesus, they had just seen each other this morning. But a few hours exercising together didn't make up for a week spent apart.

Eva was walking arm-in-arm with her mother, who, Cass was surprised to see, was even shorter than she was. Sandy DeMarco gazed between Cass and Maya and then elbowed her daughter. "Your girl is the taller one, right?" she asked in a voice Cass suspected she intended to be quiet. But sound travels farther in cold air, a fact Eva's mother didn't seem to be aware of.

Your girl. Cass liked the sound of that far more than she probably should, especially given that they hadn't defined what they were doing. Still, here they were meeting the parents, so that seemed promising. Didn't it?

"Hi, Mrs. DeMarco," she said, holding out her hand when they got near enough. "I'm Cass. It's really great to meet you."

"Well, thank you. It's nice to meet you, too," Eva's mother said, tilting her head on a slight angle as they shook hands. "And please, call me Sandy."

Cass knew the head tilt was so that she could see better. But as she offered to take the shopping bag Eva was carrying (she refused), Cass couldn't help feeling she was being examined by a curious bird. A red bird, given that Sandy DeMarco's jacket and scarf were both a slightly darker shade of scarlet.

"Oh, and this is my sister-in-law, Maya," she added.

"Lovely to meet you as well. Thank you for inviting us into your home tonight."

"Of course," Maya said. "The more the merrier."

Which was probably true. The Professors Trane usually behaved better around other people.

"How was Vancouver?" Cass asked as they started back down the sidewalk toward Matthew and Maya's house.

Eva and her mother had spent two nights in Vancouver because Sandy wanted to see everything while she still could. Plus, Eva had completed her tenure portfolio earlier that week and was planning to turn it in before classes started, so her mother had insisted they celebrate.

"It was wonderful," Sandy said. "This girl spoiled me rotten.

We had massages and mud baths, and we even had a hot tub in our room! Can you imagine?"

Cass could, but she only smiled at Eva over the top of her mother's head and said, "It sounds great. I'm surprised you guys came back at all."

"We couldn't miss out on your dinner party," Eva said, smiling back, and then nearly tripped on an uneven slab of pavement. She faced forward again, clutching her mother's arm to her chest.

Cass trained her eyes front and center, too. By now she'd realized that Eva suffered from occasional bouts of clumsiness. Better not to distract her on New Year's Eve with a house full of people waiting for them.

They chatted about Vancouver's sights and sounds as they walked, and soon they were back at Matthew and Maya's house stripping out of their winter gear.

As Cass took Eva's coat, she leaned close and murmured into her hair, "I'm glad you're here."

"So am I," Eva replied, smiling up at her.

And then the rest of Cass's family descended on them, and both of their smiles faltered. *Crap*, Cass thought. What had they been thinking? But this get-together hadn't been their idea. When Cass's mother had learned that she intended to eat dinner with them and then spend the rest of New Year's Eve with her new girlfriend type person ("We haven't made it official yet, okay?"), she'd insisted that Cass invite Eva to dinner. Eva had accepted the invitation—probably because she was too polite to refuse—and since she already had dinner plans with her own mother, the guest list had grown by two.

It would be fine, Cass told herself as Maya offered drinks all around. Not like they could back out now. But as her dad made a joke about the pregnant lady managing the drinks station, Cass almost wished they could. If Eva didn't already feel the exact same way, it was only a matter of time.

***

What had they been thinking, indeed.

Cass could detect the disapproval wafting off her mother as Sandy DeMarco explained that she and her husband had run the sales and service departments of a Ford dealership in Scranton, Pennsylvania, for more than three decades. But at least her mother only smiled thinly and nodded before turning her hawk-like gaze to Eva.

"Matthew tells us you're an assistant professor in the Sociology Department."

"That's right," Eva said, and poured two glasses of wine from the bottle Maya had passed her—one for her mother and one for herself. Turned out the DeMarco women were not fans of eggnog.

"Is that how you met my daughter?" Cass's mother asked, disapproval now emanating from every pore on her long, narrow face.

And, okay, Cass hadn't seen that one coming. "Actually, we met outside of school," she put in before Eva could answer, staring hard at her mother. "Eva and I haven't crossed paths much at the university." By which she very clearly meant, *She's not pursuing an unethical relationship and neither am I.*

Her mother's eyebrows rose, but she merely nodded and sipped her glass of eggnog. "I see. And what is your area of research?"

Eva glanced at Cass, who raised her beer bottle in what she hoped was a universal gesture of *You got this.* Then again, Eva wasn't much of a sports fan, which was probably why her brow knitted subtly before she leveled her gaze—and her chin—at Cass's mother. "Stigmatization and cultural bias."

For a moment, Cass thought Eva was going to leave it at that. Which was fine and cool and all, but really not.

"Specifically," Eva added, swirling the wine in her glass, "cultural biases toward readers and writers of popular romance fiction."

The room grew silent, and Cass caught Eva's mother tilting her head from side to side as if to view the occupants better.

"Personally," Maya said, "I like a good romance novel. With all the gloom and doom over climate change and health care, not to mention our current political reality, I'm pretty sure I wouldn't be able to get out of bed in the morning without a happy ending to look forward to every once in a while. Even if that happy ending is fictional."

"Same here," Cass said, and then instantly clocked her mistake as both of her parents turned surprised gazes on her.

"Really?" her mother enquired, almost eagerly. "Since when have you become a reader, Cassidy?"

Matthew turned away from the counter where he was arranging the garlic loaves Cass had brought to supplement the two pans of vegetarian lasagna currently in the oven. She'd baked the lasagna the night before so that it would only need to be warmed, but now she wished she had left something to keep her hands—and brain—occupied.

"Mom," her brother said, smiling brightly, "I wonder if you could help Maya set the table."

Their mother stared at him for a moment, one eyebrow raised, but then she pushed away from the counter, eggnog still in hand. "I would be happy to help Maya."

Cass could feel Eva's gaze on her as she turned to her father and said, "So, Dad, it sounds like you've had some success with your new solar concentrators."

He nodded and, as she'd known would happen, was off and running about the challenges of balancing absorption versus scattering in luminescent solar concentrators. A materials chemist, he had been an early proponent of solar energy as a means of combating climate change. After all, as he'd said time and again when she and Matthew were growing up, at some point the world would run out of fossil fuels. Where would they be if they didn't develop alternative fuel sources ahead of time?

Dead. The answer was they'd be dead, as he'd often told them while their mother shook her head, irritated with what she termed his pessimistic outlook. An energy apocalypse wasn't a guaranteed outcome, she'd liked to point out. The odds of humanity self-destructing because of energy consumption were far less than the odds of nuclear annihilation or even a global pandemic.

Fun times, growing up in the Trane household, Cass thought now, shaking her head slightly to herself. No wonder September 11 had felt legitimately like the beginning of the end.

The lasagna didn't take long to reheat and the garlic bread took even less time on broil. Soon they were carrying the food—including the salad Eva and her mother had contributed—out to the dining room, where Matthew and their dad had managed to get the leaf into the dining table with nothing worse than bruised knuckles. As the most athletic member of the family, Cass had almost offered to help. But her brother and father could be sensitive about such things, especially in front of non-family members, so she'd opted to stay in the kitchen. Like a good girl, her mind supplied mockingly, but whatever. Bowing to the patriarchy at holiday gatherings was an American tradition.

As Maya directed everyone to their proper chairs, Cass shot her a thankful look for giving her the seat between Matthew and Eva. Maya nodded subtly. This was not her first Trane family dinner party. The same couldn't be said of Eva and her mother, though, and Cass tried to enjoy Eva's closeness without worrying too much about the inevitable conversational mines waiting to be tripped.

The first topic had her guard up right off the bat: the baby. Sandy asked a few questions while Cass kept an eye on Eva, relieved to see that she didn't seem upset. Maya soon guided the conversation in a less fraught direction: namely, Edmonds U's new president, a woman who had previously been a provost at Columbia. This discussion took some time, and Cass took advantage of her parents' distraction to chat with Eva's mother, who was sitting on her daughter's other side. This was how she learned that the older woman was an avid golfer. Despite her doctor's recommendation, she intended to continue the game she loved until she was legally blind.

"I just need a spotter, you know?" she told Cass. "Just a little help finding my ball and the hole."

"And other golfers?" Eva asked. "It would probably be good to know where they are, so that you don't brain anyone."

"Oh, honey," Sandy said, patting her daughter's hand, "you worry too much. I promise I will not brain any other golfers."

Cass snickered under her breath, and then stopped as Eva cast her a withering glance. But after a moment she broke and smiled at Cass, shaking her head.

The food was delicious, everyone agreed. When Sandy learned that Cass had prepared the entire meal except for the flourless chocolate torte Maya planned to serve for dessert, she pointed at her daughter. "I knew it. This one is a keeper, Evie."

Eva's cheeks positively bloomed at that while Cass murmured

her thanks and tried to ignore her own mother's probing look. Her parents had rarely approved of anyone Cass had introduced them to, but Eva was different. She was an academic like them. Though not like them, really. Cass's father was an internationally known chemist and her mother was a brilliant mathematician known for her work on chaos theory. A sociologist who wrote about popular fiction was not, Cass was fairly certain, the type of academic they considered their equal. But she suspected that in their minds, Eva's status even as an untenured professor would be preferable to Maya's as an obstetrics nurse. Not that Cass was competing with her brother on that front. Their parents were the ones who compared them incessantly to each other, not her or Matthew.

Still, Matthew's engagement to his college girlfriend was the one major life decision he had made without consulting their parents ahead of time. Later, he'd told Cass that he hadn't asked for their approval—or for their help with planning or paying for the wedding—because he honestly didn't want to know what they thought about the match. Surprisingly, though, the professors had generally been kind to Maya. Only sometimes their efforts to let her and Matthew know they approved of their relationship came across as a bit more PC than genuine.

"Then again, better PC than racist," Maya liked to say. And yeah, Cass could see her point.

Like every other Trane family dinner before this one, the peace only lasted so long. By midway through the meal, their parents were back on familiar territory, probing Matthew about his spring quarter teaching award and his volunteer outreach work with the local chapter of the Planetary Society. They were especially impressed with his recent participation on the American Astronomical Society's Committee on the Status of Minorities in Astronomy. His commitment to equality was a hallmark of their family values, namely that education should be open to all regardless of race, gender, or ethnicity.

"Or sexual orientation, right?" Maya added, her smile bright. "And gender identity, too?"

Cass's parents exchanged a look before her mother smiled back at Maya—her professional smile, though, not her warm one. "Of course."

Cass felt a gentle touch on her thigh and took a calming

breath as she turned to meet Eva's gaze. Eva turned her hand palm up beneath the table, and Cass covered it with her own, squeezing once before reaching for her wine. She didn't want to get too drunk to drive Eva's mom home, but alcohol at this juncture felt like a necessity.

Matthew broke the ensuing silence. "Cass has been pretty busy this year, too. Did you know she was chosen as the IT department's spokesperson for the campus's new content management system? She actually gave presentations to all of the colleges and academic units on campus this fall."

"That's great, kiddo," their dad said, offering his slightly spacey smile, the one his students described in their evaluations as the classic absent-minded professor look.

"Thanks," she said, exaggerating the *s*. Because she knew that Matthew meant well, but did he have to throw the big brother pity party in front of Eva? She blew out a noisy breath and reached for her wine glass again.

The Tranes weren't the only proud parents at the table, and soon Sandy DeMarco was listing Eva's many accomplishments dating all the way back to high school. It was Cass's turn to provide a comforting hand squeeze and whisper, "Don't worry. We only have to stay until the ball drops on the East Coast."

Cass's parents smiled through the recitation of Eva's many accomplishments—which Cass enjoyed; seriously, she was a brown belt in Judo?—but they didn't waste any time in returning the spotlight to their darling boy. Topics they had apparently failed to highlight effectively included his popularity among Edmonds students, the planetarium show he was working on in partnership with the Pacific Science Center, and, of course, the robustness of his tenure review portfolio, which was in good shape even though it wasn't due for two more years.

Eva's mother looked like she was about to chime in, but Matthew beat her to the punch by blurting out of the blue, "Cass might have a job lined up at Google when she finishes her program."

Cass glared at him, but it was too late. Their parents were already circling the bait, teeth glinting in the light.

"Google?" her father repeated, pushing his glasses up his long, narrow nose. "Did you know they purchase enough renewable energy to match a hundred percent of their global electricity consumption? They also offer a free shuttle bus for their employees."

"It's one of the best tech companies out there," her mother said, nodding approvingly. "I don't think you would have to worry about being laid off, not like your last company."

"There's nothing definite," Cass said, giving her brother the universal *You're a dead man* look. Because he might be the one who'd gotten their parents' hopes up, but she was the one who would have to deal with the potential fallout. "Not definite" was an understatement. Frankie, one of her old officemates at Avicom, had landed at Google a couple of weeks earlier and had offered to hook her up when she was ready to come back to California—as her brother very well knew.

"Google?" Eva repeated. Cass glanced at her but couldn't tell what she was thinking. "That sounds like an amazing opportunity."

She shrugged uncomfortably. "Like I said, there's no guarantee. I'm not even sure when I'm going back to California."

"I would hope that if Google offers you a job, you'll go back pronto," her mother said.

Cass stopped herself from sighing dramatically. She wasn't a teenager anymore, even if being around her parents made her feel perpetually adolescent. "We'll see," she said, inwardly fist-pumping at the annoyance that crossed her mother's face. That vague, noncommittal phrase had been her parents' favorite response back in high school whenever she'd asked to do something not on their list of approved activities.

But she wasn't just blowing them off. She truly hadn't decided yet if she wanted to go back to life at a tech company. She didn't love sixty hour work weeks and two hours of daily commuting, not to mention struggling to find time to do the basics like work out or watch her favorite TV show—*Supergirl*, currently. She was an unabashed SuperCorp fan, even if the CW never in a million years planned to make the Supergirl-Lena Luthor romance canon. Given that network's history with the Bury Your Gays trope, she would actually prefer they didn't make SuperCorp canon because lord knew they would probably do a spectacularly bad job.

"On that note," Maya said, "who'd like to try the torte?"

Everyone did, and the next fifteen minutes was spent oohing

and aahing over the chocolate concoction. For someone who didn't like to cook, Maya could definitely bake.

After dinner, Matthew and their dad did the dishes while Eva helped Cass and Maya put away the leftovers. That left the two moms together, which was probably why Cass raced through the clean-up. She kept glancing through the archway from the kitchen into the living/dining area, increasingly anxious as she saw Eva's mother deep in conversation with her own. What were they talking about?

When the group reconvened in the living room, the two moms were sitting on one of the couches facing each other, still talking animatedly. As Cass neared, she heard Eva's mother say, "And yet, I only want her to be happy."

"I know," Cass's mother said. "That's all we want for our children, isn't it?"

Cass almost tripped over her own feet. Had her mother been possessed by a spirit of some kind? If so, it appeared to be benevolent, not evil.

"Eva honey," Eva's mother said, and patted the couch between her and Cass's mom. "Come sit with us."

"You, too, Cass," her own mom said, shifting to make room.

Which is how she and Eva found themselves on Matthew and Maya's couch, squished between their respective mothers while the television blared the countdown to New Year's in Times Square. Every once in a while Cass would glance over at Eva, only to find her gazing back from under her eyelashes, and they would sort of smile awkwardly and shrug or even laugh because really, the situation was absurd. And yet Cass found herself enjoying the evening as it wore on, sandwiched between arguably the two most important women currently in her life while the rest of her family retold familiar stories and counted down the final hours of the old year.

She almost didn't want to leave shortly after nine when Eva's mother stifled a yawn and said, "All right, girls, I think the witching hour is upon me."

Almost, but not quite.

There were hugs all around and promises to pop over for brunch in the morning, although Cass didn't say where she'd be coming from, her studio or Eva's house, and no one asked.

"You just want me to make pancakes for you," she said as she hugged Maya.

"Um, duh, always."

Her brother hugged her next, whispering, "Sorry about the Google thing."

"S'okay," she murmured back, walloping him on the back. "I know you panic under pressure."

"Do not!" he hissed, and shoved her away.

"Sure you don't," she said. "Happy New Year, bro."

Rolling his eyes, he bumped her fist with his. "Happy New Year, little sis."

While Eva helped her mother into her coat, Cass's mom pulled her aside. "Are you okay to drive?"

"Of course," she said, slightly irritated by the question. "I only had one glass of wine."

"I know. I just worry. Some day if you're ever a mother you'll know what I mean." And then she kissed Cass's cheek and ruffled her hair. "Good night, daughter. Happy New Year."

"Good night, mother. Back at you."

Her father hugged her last. Apparently he and her mother had made a pact to shock her as much as possible because he said softly, "I'm proud of you, kid. Oh, and I like the girl. Er, woman. Eva."

"Thanks, Dad," she said, pulling away to smile up at him. "Happy New Year."

They escaped at last into the cold, and Cass was glad that her brother had loaned her the use of the Camry with its heated seats. She helped Eva's mom into the front passenger seat and then started up the hill toward the neighborhood near the freeway, watching out for drunk drivers. It was still early, so the roads wouldn't be too dangerous yet. That was another reason Sandy had wanted to go home early—she didn't like being out late on New Year's Eve, she'd said at dinner. Or, for that matter, having her daughter out late on the deadliest driving night of the year.

Yep. Moms were worriers all right.

When they reached the care facility, Cass parked in front of

Eva's mom's duplex and left the engine idling not because she was impatient—okay, maybe a little—but because the heater had barely had time to warm up. Eva walked her mother to the door of her unit and started to go in, but her mom very clearly pushed her out and gestured toward the waiting car. Then, after a final kiss to Eva's cheek, Sandy DeMarco disappeared into her home.

Shaking her head a little, Eva walked back to the car. Cass watched her approach, acutely aware that they were about to be alone for only the second time since their date the previous week.

Eva slid in beside her. "She wouldn't let me come in."

"I saw. Why not?"

"She said I should be with my gorgeous, young woman friend and not my old, tired mother."

Cass laughed. "I like your mom, and not just because of that comment."

"The feeling is mutual. Wish I could say the same about your mom."

"You can. My dad told me they liked you when we were saying goodbye." As Eva stared at her dubiously, Cass added, "I'm serious! You can totally ask him."

"Call me crazy, but I think I'll pass."

She started the engine but didn't pull away from the curb. "So. Still feel like having company to watch the Seattle fireworks?"

"Of course. If you still want to come over…?"

"Absolutely. Gotta get my Harvey fix. By the way, I can't believe you took him to Vancouver."

"Ben and Tina are in Illinois, so I didn't have much choice. He's crate-trained, though, so it was fine. Plus, it's the Pacific Northwest. People are beyond dog-crazy here."

Cass couldn't argue with that. She put the car in gear and drove carefully back to the Bowl, once again on high alert for erratic drivers. They reached Eva's house without incident, and then Cass was parking out front and they were walking up the front path together, down-clad arms brushing. Eva unlocked the door and moved to block a frantic Harvey, who seemed to be saying with his little yelps and crazy eyes, "You were gone for hours! I could have died! Can I kiss you? Please, please, please, please?"

They gave him tummy rubs and head pats before stripping out

of their winter gear one after the other. Eva stepped into faux fur slippers and asked, "Can I get you anything? More wine? Beer?"

"A beer would be great." She didn't plan on getting drunk tonight, but a little liquid courage was never a bad thing. They hadn't talked about it so she wasn't sure what Eva was thinking, but their texts all week had been extremely—affectionate, and it certainly seemed possible that they might do more than watch television together tonight.

Eva returned from the kitchen with two bottles of the Elysian's Immortal IPA. "Hope this is okay. It's Alexis's favorite."

"It's great," Cass said as she accepted one of the bottles. "I love the Elysian. I actually ate dinner there the night we met."

Eva's eyebrows shot up. "You did? So did we. Alexis and me, I mean."

"You did?" They stared at each other, and Cass started to laugh. "Oh my god, do you think that's why you seemed so familiar that night?"

Eva was laughing too. "No way. That would be too funny, especially since it turned out you did know me." She paused and bit her lip. "Can I ask, though—were you, you know, hitting on me that night? I didn't think so, but Alexis swears you had the look."

"The look?" Cass echoed, buying time as she followed Eva to the couch and sat down close beside her. Harvey immediately hopped up onto the cushion on Eva's other side, sighing dramatically as he rested his head on her thigh.

"You know, the look. The *look*," she added, as if the emphasis would be enough.

"Maybe," Cass conceded. "You really did seem familiar, apparently for more than one reason, but I probably wouldn't have come over to talk to you if you weren't so adorable."

"Aw, you think I'm adorable," Eva said, fluttering her eyelashes prettily.

"More like adorkable," Cass amended.

"Accurate." Eva reached for the remote where it rested on the low wood and slate coffee table. "Any preference among the local channels? I'm pretty much a KING5 woman myself."

"No allegiances here," Cass said. She pretended to yawn exaggeratedly and slipped her arm around Eva's shoulders.

"Smooth," Eva said, but she leaned her head against Cass's shoulder, humming softly in what sounded like contentment.

Harvey licked Cass's hand for three full minutes until Eva pushed him away, laughing. Then they settled back in together, a blanket draped over their legs and feet—"because," Eva said, "the wood floors are a bit drafty."

"I love blankets," Cass assured her. "I'm pan-blank-sexual, I guess you could say."

Eva groaned without taking her eyes off the television, where a local news anchor was interviewing people in the crowd huddled around the base of the Space Needle. "That was awful."

"Thank you. Thank you very much."

The beer mellowed her nerves even as the snuggling beneath the blanket lifted her temperature. And not just because it was fleece. Eva's body pressed into hers from shoulder to thigh, the swell of her breast occasionally bumping Cass's rib cage when they shifted just right. After a while she forgot to focus on the television in favor of watching Eva. Her hair was pulled back in a smooth bun, a few strands only now beginning to work their way loose, and she smelled of lavender and that same hint of spice Cass had detected previously.

"I like your tie," Eva murmured, fingers tracing the line of Cass's bow-tie.

"It's a clip-on," she admitted, distracted by the feel of Eva's fingertips brushing against her bare skin.

"So it won't be difficult to take off, then?" Eva asked, her voice low and—sultry. Definitely some sultriness there.

Cass tittered nervously. "Yeah, I guess not." Jesus, what was wrong with her? It was like they'd switched personalities or something.

"I missed you this week," Eva said, smoothing Cass's collar down. Then she took Cass's beer and set it beside her own on the coffee table.

"I missed you too," she confessed.

"So how committed to watching the fireworks are you?" Eva asked, her breath warm on Cass's neck.

"Not at all committed. Why? What did you have in mind?"

Eva rose and offered her a hand. "I'm not sure the tour I gave you last week was quite complete."

Cass took her hand. "No?"

"Definitely not." Eva tugged on Cass's hand, leading her toward the bedroom. "You up for a do-over?"

"Absolutely." And then she laughed, because even in seductress mode, Eva was just too danged cute.

She pouted over her shoulder. "Hey, now, I'm trying to be all smooth here."

"I got that, thanks."

"Whatever," Eva huffed.

They reached the bedroom, Harvey on their heels as per usual, and Cass watched as Eva tucked him into his crate at the foot of the bed. Then she lit a candle on the dresser, shut off the overhead light, and turned to face her.

"Hi," she said, drifting closer.

"Hi," Cass said, and met her halfway, arms slipping easily around Eva's shoulders.

"Is this okay?" Eva asked, her eyes more serious now as her hands rested on Cass's waist. "I know we haven't really talked…"

"It's good," Cass assured her. "I've been thinking about kissing you all week."

"So have I. Can I…?"

Cass nodded and bent slightly, angling her lips toward Eva's. The first touch was light, tentative, a reacquaintance after their time apart. Eva's lips were cool and tasted of beer, and Cass moved closer, pressing her mouth against Eva's more firmly. Eva made a small sound and parted her lips, and Cass followed suit. Eva's hands at her waist tightened as their tongues slipped together, hot and wet, and instantly Cass felt a pulse of desire settle between her legs. It had been a while, since before she'd met Eva actually, but sex was like riding a bicycle, she'd often thought. Except, you know, not.

Eva tugged at her shirt. "You have too much clothing on."

"Ditto, champ."

"Excuse me?" Eva leaned away, her eyes dark in the candlelight. "Did you just call me 'champ?'"

"Um, no?"

"Good answer. Shirt, please."

She liked Bossy Eva. Bossy Eva was hot.

Cass unclipped her bow tie and tossed it aside, not paying attention to where it fell. Then she started unbuttoning her shirt, the pressure between her legs growing as she felt Eva's eyes on her, watching as the panels of her shirt separated to reveal her torso.

"You can help," she said softly. "I mean, if you want to."

Eva nodded and slipped her hands inside the shirt, sliding her palms up Cass's rib cage and over her racer back bra. Cass's breath caught, and then Eva's hands were on her shoulders pushing the shirt off.

"You have a six pack," Eva said, her eyes widening.

"I work out."

Eva laughed, meeting her eyes. "Your pick-up game needs work, Trane."

"Really?" Cass gestured to the room. "'Cause it looks like it's working fine on you."

"Good point." And then Eva ducked her head and pressed her mouth against the hollow of Cass's throat, her tongue and breath painting goose bumps across Cass's skin. "Are you cold?" she whispered, kissing her way up her throat.

"No." Which was an understatement. Cass tugged at the hem of Eva's turtleneck sweater. "Hello, still too many clothes."

Eva placed one last open-mouthed kiss on the skin behind Cass's ear, making her shiver, and then pulled her sweater off in one smooth move—until it got stuck on her bun. "Crap. Um, a little help here?"

Cass tried—and failed—to hide her snicker. And then she realized Eva was only wearing a bra beneath her sweater, a lacy white push-up bra that stood out against her olive skin. She was tempted to lean forward and touch her lips to the generous swell of Eva's breasts, but instead she helped Eva pull the sweater the rest of the way off. The bun came undone, which was fine with Cass. A sudden vision of Eva kissing her way down her body, long hair cascading across Cass's skin, popped into her mind, and yeah. Hair down was totally okay with her.

"You can touch, if you want," Eva said, smirking.

Cass realized her gaze had returned to Eva's chest, and she bit her lip before placing her hands on the curve of Eva's waist and dragging her palms lightly up her sides. But then she walked her fingers around to Eva's back and paused on the clasp. "Okay if I…?"

Eva nodded. A moment later the bra came loose, and Eva allowed it to fall down her arms, catching it at her bent elbows. "You're a little too good at that."

"All the better to do this," Cass replied as she rubbed the tips of her fingers across Eva's ribs and beneath her breasts. She was curvy for such a small woman, and her breasts settled warm and heavy against Cass's palms. She skimmed her thumb over the darker areolas, feeling the skin pucker beneath her touch.

"Good point," Eva said, her voice breathy. She leaned into Cass's touch, eyes closing as Cass pinched her nipples lightly, rolling them between her thumb and forefinger. "Oh my god."

Cass smiled. And then she gave in to her previous urge and dropped her lips to Eva's chest, kissing and sucking her way to one of her nipples. She took the bud into her mouth and sucked lightly, flicking her tongue against the tight skin and slowly increasing the pressure as Eva's breath caught.

"Nnn," Eva moaned, her legs buckling slightly as she pushed closer to Cass, hands threading in her hair. "Holy shit, you're good at that."

"Thanks," Cass said, straightening up. She grasped Eva's elbows and began to back her toward the bed. "What do you say we get a little more comfortable?"

Eva snorted. "Seriously with the pick-up game."

"Did you say pick up?" Cass asked, and suddenly she was swinging Eva into her arms bridal style.

"Cass!" Eva squealed, gripping her tightly around the neck.

"Sorry, I thought you wanted a ride. My bad." She lowered her onto the bed and stood above her, grinning.

"Now that you mention it," Eva said, voice deepening into that same sultry tone, "I wouldn't mind a ride with you, Ms. Trane."

The tone as much as the words made a beeline for Cass's already tingling core, and she dropped onto the bed beside Eva, stretching out along the length of her body. "I think that could be arranged, Professor DeMarco."

Eva rolled onto her side to face Cass and kissed her deeply, tongue probing for entry as her fingers threaded through Cass's short hair. Cass kissed her back, licking up into her mouth, and soon Eva was half-lying across her. They kissed for long, luxurious minutes, noses bumping and teeth clicking as they learned each other's rhythm, but Cass was amazed at how natural it felt to kiss Eva. The other woman was different from what Cass had expected, less inhibited than she seemed on the outside. Here in her bedroom she was sexy and daring, her fingernails skimming across Cass's skin, teeth teasing at her ears and neck and, at last, her nipples, sucking and biting her through the thin material of her bra.

At last Eva pushed the material up, exposing Cass's small breasts. "Mmm," she said dreamily, and resumed lavishing Cass's nipples with her tongue and teeth.

"You're pretty good at that yourself," Cass said as she pulled the bra off over her head, hearing the breathiness in her own voice but too intent on the sensations coursing through her body to care.

"'Anks," Eva murmured, vocal vibrations teasing the sensitive skin of Cass's breasts.

Eva slid her knee between Cass's legs and pressed, softly at first but harder as Cass arched up toward her. "Tell me what you like," she said, her hand smoothing across Cass's abdomen to toy with the waistband of her dress pants.

"Everything," Cass all but gasped, closing her eyes as Eva's knee rubbed against her clit.

"Is that so? I guess we'll have to see." She unbuttoned Cass's pants and pulled down the zipper, her movements slow and deliberate, maximizing the contact her hand made with Cass's body. She tugged at the waistband, and Cass lifted her hips, momentarily mourning the loss of Eva's knee. But in the next moment Eva was shedding her own pants and climbing onto Cass, her knees braced on the bed on either side of Cass's hips. She paused momentarily to tie her hair back with the scrunchy on her wrist, the movement briefly lifting her beautiful breasts. Cass lay immobile beneath her, barely daring to let herself believe that this was really happening. She and Eva were really doing this.

Hair secure, Eva placed her hands on Cass's breasts, palming her nipples, and at the same time ground her pelvis against Cass's.

"Okay?" she asked, her voice husky, eyes almost black in the dark room.

"Okay," Cass nearly croaked, resting her hands at the top of Eva's thighs, her thumbs fitting neatly into the indentation of her hip bones.

"Good." Eva's eyes fluttered shut, and holy shit, she was rubbing herself against Cass in a way that felt so, so good. Cass arched her hips trying to get more pressure on the spot that needed it, but her pubic bone was in the way. That didn't seem to be the case for Eva, who was breathing faster now as she literally rode Cass, their skin separated only by the thin cotton of their underwear.

Watching Eva grind against her, eyes closed and neck arched, was beautiful, but the position was going to be the death of Cass. After another minute of exquisite torture, she grasped Eva around the waist and, with a slight growl, flipped her onto her back. Then she levered herself over Eva, her weight mostly balanced on her hands, and slipped one leg between Eva's. There, that was what she needed. She rocked her hips into Eva's but not too hard. She'd been told her hip bones could be sharp.

"Okay?" she asked, and Eva nodded, her eyes closing again as she arched her back and lifted her hips to meet Cass's downward stroke.

"Good," Eva said, brow furrowing in concentration as they set a rhythm. "So good."

Time slowed and crystallized, and soon all Cass could seem to see was the white bed and Eva's dark skin and her eyes, when she opened them, glinting up at her in the candlelight as they ground together. Cass wanted to slip Eva's underwear off over her hips, wanted to stroke through her soft wetness and bury her fingers in her heat, but it was too late. She could feel her orgasm building, building, and there was no way she was going to stop now if she didn't have to. Eva's hands dug into her waist, propelling her on, and then, suddenly, Eva was arching her back one last time, limbs going taut.

"Fuck," Eva breathed, her hands squeezing Cass tightly.

Cass was almost there too, and she pushed against a tense, unmoving Eva until—there. *There.* That was it. "Oh my god," she gasped, holding herself up, elbows locked as she shuddered in release.

"Oh my god," Eva echoed, and then she was laughing, her limbs loosening as she clutched at Cass.

"What?" Cass asked after a moment, her voice raspy as the waves receded. She collapsed onto her side, one leg still intertwined with Eva's.

"That was intense," Eva said, eyes still alight with laughter. "Especially considering we never got around to getting completely naked."

Cass glanced down and noted their underwear—black fitted boy shorts for her, white lacy briefs for Eva—wrinkled and out of place but otherwise intact. "You're right," she said, and glanced back up into Eva's eyes. Reluctantly she smiled. "I feel like I should apologize. That was like a college hook-up."

"Well, you are a student," Eva said, still smiling as she poked Cass in the chin and slid her finger down her slightly damp neck.

"And you are a teacher," Cass said as Eva traced a path down her chest between her small breasts and onto her muscled midsection.

"That is so not our trope," Eva said, pressing her palm over Cass's navel.

"Not our trope...?" Cass started to ask.

But Eva's hand had reached her boy shorts and was beginning to inch beneath her waistband, a clear question in her eyes as she gazed at Cass, no longer laughing.

"Never mind," Cass said, and promptly shimmied out of her shorts. "Your turn."

Eva quirked an eyebrow at her and reached for her briefs. "My pleasure."

There was plenty of time to talk tropes and theories later, Cass thought a moment later as she pulled Eva onto her, relishing the feel of skin on skin. For now she was more interested in a little more hands-on mentoring.

CHAPTER ELEVEN

"I've been thinking of doing that all week," Eva confessed around a bite of cookie.

They were lounging in sleepwear on the couch in the living room, drinking beer and munching on Trader Joe's chocolate chip cookies. Cass's face was still flushed from their earlier activities and her hair was standing up in odd places, but Eva thought this might be her favorite iteration of Cassidy Trane: smiley, loose-limbed, unabashedly goofy. Then she remembered Cass leaning over her less than an hour earlier, lips trailing fire across her breasts while her hands did amazing things... Maybe that was her favorite Cass yet.

"You mean drink beer and eat cookies?" Cass asked, eyes on the television. The fireworks would start at midnight, which was only a few minutes away. "Or watch KING5 with me in our skivvies?"

When they'd roused themselves from bed, they'd gotten cleaned up and pulled on just enough of Eva's clothing to be decent. Her living room blinds were closed, but not all the windows in her house had drapes. Besides, it was sort of hot to see Cass in her old high school debate club T-shirt and a pair of silk pajama shorts. Cass had drawn the line at wearing the silk top.

"Drink beer and eat cookies, obviously."

"Oh, I thought you might mean the sex."

She nudged Cass with her elbow. "Of course I meant the sex, doofus."

"In that case, me too."

"Really?"

"Really. Actually," Cass added, "longer than just the past

week. If we're being honest."

"How long?" Eva asked, licking chocolate from her fingers before Harvey could. He'd whined so pathetically in his crate—she had totally spoiled him by letting him sleep in her bed for the past year and a half—that they'd finally let him out and returned to the living room to watch the fireworks on local TV. Now he was seated beside her, head on her blanket-encased leg waiting for cookie crumbs to fall.

"Would it be creepy if I told you I'd been thinking about having my way with you ever since we walked in the arboretum?" Cass asked, her gaze never leaving the television.

Eva's breath caught. "Seriously?"

"Seriously."

"As long as we're being honest, then yes, that is completely creepy."

Cass's head whipped around and she stared at Eva, eyes wide.

"Sorry!" Eva said quickly. "Just joking. I also may have been harboring inappropriate feelings for you for some time now."

"That wasn't funny," Cass grumbled.

"I'm sorry," Eva repeated, softening her tone. She leaned in and kissed cookie crumbs from the corner of Cass's mouth. "Forgive me?"

Cass turned her head so that their lips almost touched. "I suppose," she said, and then they were kissing again, the taste of beer and cookies mingling—until Harvey pushed his way between them, slobbering on both of their chins and whipping his tail so hard the bag of cookies fell to the floor.

By the time they'd sorted the chaos, the countdown was upon them. They stood up and chanted the countdown along with the TV announcers and then, as the first fireworks exploded off the top of the Space Needle, they turned to face each other.

"Happy New Year, Cass," Eva said, smiling up at her.

"Happy New Year, Eva," Cass replied, smiling down at her.

The kiss was sweet and slow, with a promise of more to come. Or maybe that was just in Eva's head.

They watched the fireworks show, oohing and aahing at the colorful display and at the amount of smoke wafting across Seattle Center. Then they cleaned up their midnight snack and returned to the bedroom, where they crawled under the covers and snuggled together, Harvey lying between their extended legs.

"Is this okay?" Cass asked after Eva had turned off the bedside lamp and curled back into her side. "I mean, I can still head home if you'd rather."

"No, it's fine. Unless you'd rather go home?"

"I'm pretty happy right here," Cass said, and kissed her hair.

"Me, too," Eva admitted. She stretched, feeling the energy still flowing through her body, that post-orgasmic glow made up of equal parts joy and laziness. She was looking forward to sleeping in tomorrow, though with Cass in her bed, she wasn't sure how much she would sleep. Not just because there were far more interesting things to be doing other than sleeping, but also because she hadn't slept beside a human being in a year and a half, not since Alexis had temporarily moved herself in.

Alexis. Holy crap. She was going to be so excited. When Eva had turned down her invitation to watch the ball drop at her and Tosh's house in order to spend the evening with Cass's family instead, she had instantly crowed, "You're totally getting laid and meeting the family, all in one night! I told you: this is kismet, and nothing you can say will dissuade me."

Eva actually felt pretty kismetty right now. In a good way, of course. Until Cass's voice came out of the dark: "I have something I feel like I should tell you."

And just like that, the joy and laziness retracted, leaving the usual low-level anxiety rumbling in its place.

Eva leaned over and flicked the bedside lamp back on. "That sounds ominous."

"It's not, really," Cass said, but then she stared down at the blue and green comforter Eva had bought after Ben had left, picking at a stray thread.

Never one to handle silence well, Eva filled it. "You're not about to tell me you're in a relationship, are you?"

Cass looked up quickly. "God, no."

"STD?"

She shook her head. "Nope. I've been lucky on that front. You?"

"Also lucky. Although I feel like this is a conversation we

should have had a few hours earlier."

"I think if either of us had been unlucky on that front, we would have had to have this conversation sooner."

"Good point," Eva allowed. She squinted slightly. No secret girlfriend and no STD. That left... "You're taking the Google job, aren't you?"

Cass blinked. "No. I mean, there's no actual job at this point, just a vague offer from a friend to hook me up. I didn't tell my parents that because I didn't want to burst their bubble. I haven't exactly given them a lot to get excited about, not like my brother, and anyway, I still haven't made any plans for after school. At this point, I'm just focusing on getting through the rest of my program."

There was that hope rising again, the one that whispered that maybe Cass would stay here and find a job in the Seattle area instead of returning to California. Eva banished it and sat up, scooting back against her pillows. Harvey immediately followed, and she scratched his fuzzy, wart-like chin. "So back to this life-changing reveal you wanted to share."

"It's not life-changing," Cass said. Then she stopped and laughed a little as she sat up beside Eva, leaning against the pillows on her side of the bed. "Actually, it is. But not in the way you mean, I don't think. Okay. So you probably noticed at dinner the way my parents fawn over Matthew and not so much me."

Eva frowned. That wasn't how she would have put it, but this was Cass's family they were talking about, not her own. "I guess so."

"Well, that's not just related to my recent fuck-ups. I sort of have a habit of disappointing my parents."

Okay, now she'd lost her. "What do you mean, your 'recent' fuck-ups? Like what exactly?"

"Like getting laid off and moving into my brother's garage. Not exactly winning at adulting over here."

Eva stared at her. "That's how you see yourself?"

Cass stared back. "It's not how I see myself, Eva. It's who I am."

She shook her head. "Come on, Cass. You're a smart, talented person with so much to offer. Why do you think the dean depends on you so much? You must know how rare it is for someone in his position to trust someone in yours with so much responsibility. It's because he knows you'll rise to the challenge. Same with University Computing. They don't hire every student who comes along, you know."

"Actually, that isn't entirely true," Cass said. "The IT department relies on student workers because they're cheaper and often more technically proficient—"

Eva waved a hand. "That's not the point."

"No, I know. Sorry. Look," Cass said, toying with the loose thread again. "It's sweet of you to say all of that, but none of it changes how my parents see me."

"Which is what?"

"The same way they always have—as an intellectually inferior fuck-up."

Eva squinted at her. "I mean, I definitely see where they worship the ground your brother walks on, but that's only because he's chosen to follow in their footsteps. Intellectually inferior, though? I just don't get that."

"That's because you don't..." Cass hid her forehead against her knees for a moment. Then, her voice slightly muffled, she announced, "I'm dyslexic."

"Dys—you are?"

"Yep. Surprise." She peeked out at Eva, her shoulders hunched.

This really was big, Eva realized. At least, it was for Cass. Eva touched Cass's arm. "Thank you for telling me."

Cass shrugged. "I thought I probably should. You know, so you know what you're getting into."

"It doesn't change anything, as far as I'm concerned," Eva said, her throat tightening as she saw the way Cass looked at her.

"It doesn't?" Cass asked, her voice as wary as her gaze. "Really?"

"Really. Being dyslexic has nothing to do with intellect, you know," she said softly.

"Tell my parents that."

Gladly, if she ever had the chance. Because if the Professors

195

Trane didn't realize how bright their daughter was, then they were fucking idiots. But all at once, everything clicked into place—why Cass had never been inside the local bookstore before; what that strange font had been on her computer; why her parents had gotten so excited at dinner at the idea of Cass being a reader.

"I take it they didn't respond well?" she asked, trying to sound neutral.

"They did the best they could," Cass said. "I just never felt like I measured up. Matthew says he feels the same way, though, so it probably wasn't all about the dyslexia. Sometimes—no, a lot of the time, actually, it felt like they cared more about their work than us."

Gazing at Cass now, her brash confidence winnowed down, Eva understood that her tattoos really were armor aimed at holding the world away, keeping her separate from the disdain and criticism of the people around her, including (especially?) her own parents. At least Eva had always felt special in her parents' eyes. They may not have known quite what to do with her, but they had made certain that she knew how proud they were of her every step of the way. Made sure other people did, too. For years after she had moved away, her father kept the newspaper articles about her scholarships up on the bulletin board at the dealership. At the time, it had been a little embarrassing. Now, though, she could see how lucky she was.

"I'm sorry they made you and Matthew feel like that," she said, pressing a kiss to what Cass had called her Wonder Woman tattoo, peeking out from under her T-shirt sleeve. "Sometimes people can be incredibly book smart and yet complete morons when it comes to other people."

Cass let out a short laugh. "You know what? You're totally right about that."

"You said before they didn't react well when you came out. Is that part of the problem you're talking about?"

"Probably." Cass sighed and leaned back against the pillow. "My parents are these devout liberals, so they say they don't really have a problem with me being queer. Instead they point to a whole litany of other behaviors."

"Like what?"

"Like they don't understand how I can live the way I do.

They're total planners, and, well, I'm not."

"No," Eva said, pretending to look askance at Cass.

"I know, hard to believe, isn't it? But the rest of my family are these total rule followers. I'm not like them not because I don't believe in rules but because most of our culture's rules don't have anything nice to say about me." Cass glanced over at her. "You know what I mean?"

Eva nodded. Cass was a genuine outlier: not only queer in both gender and sexuality, but with a brain that functioned differently from the majority of other human beings. Eva had read a little about dyslexia, enough to know that dyslexics struggled with phonetic decoding. To read a word, a person with dyslexia had to identify squiggly lines, translate them into a sound in their mind, and then string the sounds together to compose a word. For the 15 to 20 percent of the population who were dyslexic, it took a huge amount of energy just to identify a single word. In a culture where reading was a benchmark of intelligence, being dyslexic could literally be dangerous. She couldn't remember the exact statistics, but something like half of all adolescents in alcohol and drug rehab were dyslexic, as were more than half of all juvenile delinquents.

"'Why can't you be more like your brother?' our parents used to ask when we were younger," Cass said, closing her eyes. "Why couldn't I stop 'acting out,' as they called it? Why couldn't I be respectful and simply do what was asked of me? Later, when I graduated from Vassar and moved to Europe to play rugby, they kept asking what my long-term plan was. How would I ever afford a house, they wanted to know. What about a car?"

"What did you tell them?" Eva asked.

"I recited Max Weber at them," Cass admitted, smiling as Eva laughed quietly beside her. "I told them I didn't need their instrumental rationality or their bourgeois accumulation of money and material objects."

"No, you didn't," Eva said, still laughing.

"I totally did. I was this self-righteous liberal arts major in a family of scientists and mathematicians. What else could I do?"

"Oh my god, that is pure gold. How did they react?"

"I'm pretty sure they considered defaulting on their remaining Vassar loans."

Eva nodded. "Sounds rational. Also, that way they could hold on to more of their money."

Cass snickered. "I hadn't thought of that."

They were laughing and looking into each other's eyes, and it was so easy. So right. Eva knew it must have been like this with Ben at some point, back in the beginning when they were younger and living the life of intellectuals in the city that never sleeps, but she couldn't remember that part anymore. The only thing she remembered now was the ending, the terrible sharp, bitter pain that had consumed anything good left between them.

Her laughter faded and she looked away from Cass, absently scratching Harvey's chin whiskers. His eyes opened just barely and his tail thumped the comforter cover, and she smiled down at him. He was such a sweetheart. Thank god he was only five. Barring illness or accident, he should be around for a while.

"Anyway, enough poor me. How are you?" Cass asked.

"I'm good," Eva said, and wiggled her eyebrows suggestively.

"While I am pleased to hear that, you know it's not what I meant." When Eva didn't say anything, Cass added, "How are you doing with the whole baby thing?"

At dinner, Cass's parents had—naturally—wanted to talk about their future grandchild. Matthew and Maya had just attended the 20 week ultrasound, so there were pictures on phones that the senior Tranes had proudly shared with Eva and her mom, even though Cass, Matthew, and Maya had tried to steer the conversation in another direction.

"It wasn't easy," Eva admitted, turning her face into her pillow. "Especially given my history with Maya."

"Your history?" Cass asked.

"She didn't tell you? She was working the night Isabella was born. She was with us the whole time."

"I had no idea," Cass said, her voice low. "I'm sorry. I never would have—"

"Hey, it's not your fault," Eva said, reaching for Cass's hand. "I would have cancelled if it was too much. In a way, it was actually sort of nice to shift the narrative, you know? To make her the new protagonist and me the background character. Only where my story was a tragedy, I'm hoping hers ends happily."

Cass held tight to her hand. "Do you want to talk about it? I mean, you don't have to, of course."

Eva tilted her head, considering. This was a new year, and one part of her thought she should leave the story of Isabella's short life in the past, start the year fresh and focused on the present and future. But another part reminded her that her daughter would always be with her. Isabella would always be in her heart and memory, and that was a good thing. Eva didn't ever want to banish her to the past. She wanted to carry her with her always.

"Whereas you have dyslexia," she said after a moment, "I have been cursed with an incompetent cervix."

Cass's brow furrowed. "A what?"

"It means my cervix won't let me carry a baby past the second trimester. The fetus could be perfectly healthy, like Isabella was, but I still wouldn't be able to make it much past twenty weeks—unless they stitch my cervix closed, and even then the only guarantee is a high risk of infection."

"That sounds awful. I can't imagine having a needle in there." Cass looked a little pale, and Eva regretted going into such detail.

"Sorry. Suffice it to say, I won't be carrying any more babies." She didn't tell Cass that medical risks aside, the biggest block for her was the thought that it could happen again. That she could grow this tiny human being inside her womb and then have to deliver her too soon and hold her while she died. She had been powerless to save Isabella. She couldn't do that to another child. Frankly, she couldn't do it to herself, either.

Cass ran her thumb over the back of Eva's hand. "I hope you don't need me to tell you that it wasn't your fault."

Eva expelled a breath. "It might not have been my fault, but it was my responsibility."

"I don't see that."

"She was inside *my* body. It was *my* job to protect her, to keep her safe."

"Okay, but it's not like you went out and shot up with heroin. Your body failed. Bodies do that. They're basically these flesh-encased machines, like cyborgs only without the metal, and they all break down. You're not responsible for what happened because you didn't do anything to make your cervix—what was it?—

199

incompetent."

Eva pillowed her chin on Cass's shoulder. "Intellectually, I agree with everything you just said. Except maybe the cyborg analogy. But what I think and what I feel in this case are two very different things. My therapist calls it magical thinking, and I get that it isn't rational. Doesn't mean I don't still feel it."

Cass nodded. "I get that part, I think. I can tell myself until I'm blue in the face that learning to read late doesn't reflect on my intelligence, but I still remember how embarrassed my parents were. How ashamed I felt. Matthew was so sweet. He would hold my hand on the playground and tell me he knew I was just as smart as he was. He still has my back now, too. I got lucky with him."

"You got lucky with each other."

"I hope he feels that way. Sometimes I'm not so sure."

They were quiet for a little while, and then Eva said softly, "It wasn't just my body, though. Sometimes I wished I wasn't pregnant with her."

Cass's eyes had drifted closed, but now they shot open again. "What do you mean?"

"I used to lay awake at night beside Ben, listening to him snore and feeling the baby growing inside, and I would panic," Eva admitted, running her fingers up and down Cass's muscled forearm with its tattoo sleeve and the fair hairs that offered a downy covering. The softness of her skin contrasted interestingly, Eva thought, with the fierce tribal ink that darkened her skin.

"Panic how?" Cass asked.

"Ben actually left for a little while after the first miscarriage, an indication that handling crises together was maybe not our strength," Eva confided. "Given that parenting is like this series of slow-moving crises, I worried about the emotional damage we would inflict on our child if we eventually split up."

She didn't tell Cass that Ben's parents had divorced when he was eight, and he'd always called their break-up the single worst event of his life. At least, until Eva went into premature labor with their second child.

"I used to wonder if my anxiety caused the miscarriage," she said, her face turned into the pillow again. Cass stroked her hair and made a small sound that might have been disagreement, but it could have been sympathy, too. "I used to blame myself and I thought Ben must, too, even if he never said so directly. I don't anymore," she added, turning her head to look up at Cass. "Alexis convinced me to see this therapist friend of hers, and it took many, many sessions—and months of anti-depressants, too—to convince myself that my body had failed due to physiology, not because I occasionally wished the pregnancy would end."

"Magical thinking," Cass said.

"Exactly. Even now it sometimes comes back, especially late at night when I'm just lying here listening to Harvey snore and trying not to wonder—" She stopped and turned her face away again.

"Trying not to wonder?" Cass prodded gently.

Could she say it? She'd never even said this aloud to Ben: "Trying not to wonder what Isabella would be like now if she had lived."

"Oh, Eva," Cass said, sighing as she slipped her arm around Eva's shoulders and pulled her closer. "I'm so, so sorry."

"So no, I don't begrudge your brother and Maya," Eva whispered. "I really don't. It's just sometimes hard to be around them, that's all."

"I totally get that," Cass said, her breath warm on the crown of Eva's head.

"You do?"

"Of course. Sometimes I don't want to be around people who aren't dyslexic. I mean, y'all just pick up a book or read a sign and have no idea how good you have it."

"It's all relative, isn't it?"

"Yep. Completely relative."

A few minutes later, Eva turned out the light again and they slid back down onto the pillows. Cass held out her arm and Eva closed the distance, tucking herself against Cass's side. She'd never slept well with Ben touching her, but Harvey had been training her for the last eighteen months, so maybe snuggling would be different with Cass. Everything else so far seemed to be.

Just as Cass's breath started to even out, Eva whispered, "I can't believe you quoted Weber at them."

Cass laughed softly, her breath teasing Eva's hair. "They

couldn't either."

Eva didn't doubt that for one second.

***

"Happy New Year," Alexis said as Eva opened the front door. Then she did a double take and whistled. "Damn. That is some fine sex head."

"Shut it," Eva said, ushering her in and closing the door quickly to keep the January chill outside where it belonged.

Alexis handed Eva the Cupcake Royale box she was carrying and bent down to give Harvey a kiss. Then she hugged Eva, shrugged out of her jacket, and kicked off her shoes all in one go. "I guess I don't have to ask you how your night went," she teased as she followed Eva into the kitchen where the coffee had just finished brewing. "She's not still here, is she?"

"No, she went home for brunch with her family," Eva said, placing the Cupcake Royale box on the counter.

"And she didn't invite you?"

"She did, but I told her about our New Year's Day tradition. You know, sisters before—well, not misters anymore, but you get the point."

"Aw." Alexis reached for her favorite coffee mug, a decent sized cup with an old-fashioned San Juan Islands post card painted on the sides. "That's so sweet. You're my favorite too."

Eva poured coffee into both of their mugs and set their cupcakes on plates. Then they headed back into the living room and took up positions at opposite ends of the couch, legs extended toward each other. Harvey, naturally, squirmed his way onto the couch and nestled between Eva's knees.

"So?" Alexis asked, gazing at Eva over the top of her mug. "You're all glowy. I take it your new year started off with a bang?"

"Lex!" Eva started to throw part of her cupcake at her friend but wisely decided against it.

"Okay, sorry about the dirty pun."

"No you're not."

"No, I'm not. But seriously, was it worth the wait?"

Eva smiled into her coffee mug. "Definitely."

"So, tell me everything! And by everything, I do not mean the nitty-gritty, just so we're clear."

"The sex was great, seriously," Eva said. "But it wasn't serious at all. We had fun together, you know? She's the queen of cheesy jokes. I actually found myself laughing in bed with her."

"That is so important," Alexis said as she finished her cupcake. "That's how I knew Tosh was it for me—we laugh at all the same things, and we have fun even in bed. I don't think I could have done that in my twenties, you know? I was so uptight and insecure when it came to my body, let alone anyone else's."

"I know what you mean." With Ben, once she had finally relaxed, sex had been satisfying for the first few years. The middle years, too, when they could find the time. But by the end, sex had felt—heavy. Would she get pregnant? Did she even want to get pregnant anymore with him? "You know the best part about last night, though?"

Alexis shook her head.

"I didn't have to worry about birth control, or what would happen if it failed again."

"Way to rub it in."

"No, really. I didn't think about Isabella even once, not until afterward when we were lying in bed talking."

Alexis's teasing smile faded, and she tilted her head slightly. "Did you tell her about Isabella?"

Eva nodded. "Well, yeah. I'd already mentioned her before, the day we met for lunch."

Alexis leaned forward and squeezed her foot. "Sweetie."

"What?"

"Don't take this the wrong way, but are you falling for her?"

Eva laughed, even though it wasn't really funny. "What? No." But she knew even as she uttered the word that it was a complete lie. For her to sleep with someone, it had to be serious, which was why she could count the number of people she'd had sex with on one hand.

"I thought you said she was going back to California in a few months?" Alexis asked, frowning.

"As far as I know, she is."

They looked at each other, Harvey thumping his tail at the

sudden rise in tension, until Alexis said, "Well, fuck."

Alexis almost never swore, but this time, Eva had to agree, the curse word seemed warranted. Because she, Eva DeMarco, had just slept with a woman who would be moving away at some unknown but far from distant point in time, leaving her—what, better off having loved and lost? That platitude, like most, was utter bullshit, in Eva's experience. Losing love hurt, period.

"Anyway," she said, pushing away the anxiety starting to snake its way through her bloodstream, "tell me about your New Year's Eve. Were Tosh's parents any better?"

"I wish." Alexis rolled her eyes and settled back against the couch cushions. "Although I guess his mother didn't mention Christine quite as many times as the last visit—only twenty-nine occurrences this time—so that's something. Yay."

Eva winced. Christine was Tosh's ex-wife who, according to his parents, still could do no wrong even though she and Tosh had been quite happily divorced—and happily remarried to other partners—for years by now. "Christ, I'm sorry."

"I know, it sucks. Now let's talk about more important things. Did you watch Kathy Griffin or Ryan Seacrest?"

"Um, hello, Kathy Griffin."

"Good call. Tosh's parents insisted on watching Dick Clark, even though I pointed out that he's been dead for a while now."

"Wait. Dick Clark died?" Eva asked, reaching for her phone.

Alexis gazed at her, smiling. "You are so bad at celebrity trivia."

"You say that like it's a bad thing." She stared at her phone screen. Sure enough, Dick Clark had died back in 2012.

"Trust me," Alexis said, "it's definitely a bad thing."

Eva thought about tossing a throw pillow at her, but realized Alexis might spill her coffee all over the fawn-colored couch—purchased to match Harvey's fur color. Instead, she picked up the remote. "What's our movie plan, lady? Rom-com, foreign, or thriller first?"

"Ooh, let's start with thriller! I haven't seen that one with Anna Kendrick in it yet, but I've heard good things."

"Thriller it is," Eva said, and pulled up the rental guide on her cable. She rarely watched TV, but Ben had been a sports fan so they'd always had digital cable. He'd been gone for close to two years, and she hadn't bothered to change the plan. Maybe it was time she thought about doing so.

The first day of the year passed the way the six previous first days of the year had passed, ever since she and Ben had moved to Seattle: with her and Alexis lazing away the hours watching movie after movie, sharing pizza and beer and store-bought sushi that Eva had picked up at Whole Foods the day before. And cupcakes. Couldn't forget the half dozen cupcakes Alexis had brought from Madrona. And yet, this day was different from all the others because this time, Eva was exchanging regular text messages with Cass.

"Hi!" Cass wrote shortly before lunch time, just as the thriller they were watching neared its eventful climax. "Hope you're having fun with Alexis. Tell her hello for me!"

Eva paused the movie, ignoring Alexis's frustrated groan, and typed, "Hi! Just finishing movie #1. She says hi back." She paused, and then she added a smiley face. That was acceptable, right? Not too mushy, not too standoffish? She hit send and unpaused the movie.

A couple of hours later, Cass texted a selfie of her and her brother in running gear on the patio of the Eagle's Nest. "Wish you were here!"

Eva responded with a selfie of her, Alexis, and Harvey swaddled in blankets on the couch. "No thanks. But wish you were here!"

Cass's answer came before Eva had a chance to restart the second movie, a rom-com with a predictable story arc that didn't make it any less enjoyable, she and Alexis had agreed. The text contained a single emoji: a heart.

Eva stared at it, trying to deduce its meaning. Had Cass sent a heart because she loved blankets, as she'd professed the night before? Could it be for Harvey, which would be totally understandable because who wouldn't love him, really? Or did it hold a different meaning, the one Eva hoped it might? She typed the same heart emoji and hit send before she could think too much, and went back to the rom-com, heart racing at least as much as it had during the thriller that morning.

The third text arrived late in the afternoon just as the two main characters in their foreign film kissed for the first time. The two female main characters, because Alexis had suggested they watch a foreign *lesbian* flick, and Eva had been only too happy to track it down on Amazon.

"Oh my god," Alexis said when Eva paused the movie mid-kiss to read Cass's latest text. "You are so smitten!"

"Am not," Eva said, but her defense was weak because she was too busy looking longingly at Cass's photo of leftover lasagna.

"I could be there in five minutes...." the accompanying text read.

Eva glanced up at Alexis. "You're heading home for dinner, aren't you?"

"Unfortunately, much as I hate to leave the comfort of our New Year's Day tradition, Tosh's parents leave tomorrow. So, yes, after this movie is over, I'm out." She sat up a little straighter, frowning at Harvey's obvious attempt to hold her in place with his humongous head. "Why? Are you making plans to see her again?"

"She offered to feed me," Eva said, and showed her the photo.

"You are so lucky," Alexis said, and sighed.

"I am, aren't I?" Eva said. Then she typed, "Make it an hour and five minutes?"

"Fine," Cass said, her feeling about the wait conveyed clearly by a grumpy face emoji. But that was followed by a blown kiss, so she couldn't be that grumpy.

"Man, oh man," Alexis said, shaking her head, "I can't believe you're falling for a student."

"Shut up!" Eva said, slapping her friend's shoulder. "You were the one who said I should date her!"

"I know," Alexis said, laughing. "I was right, wasn't I?"

For now, Eva had to admit, she was. A few months down the road, though, the answer might be very different.

Harvey lifted his head, his tail thwacking against the blanket, and she scratched behind his ears. Then she hit play on the remote, and the two beautiful Swedish women, one dark-haired and one fair, went back to kissing in a dark island forest.

***

"Is this too soon?" Cass asked when Eva opened the front

206

door to see her standing on the porch, lasagna pan held out in front of her.

Probably, Eva thought. "No," she said, and tugged Cass inside, kissing her before she could even take her jacket off.

"Good," Cass said against her lips.

And it was. The leftover lasagna was pretty great, too.

CHAPTER TWELVE

Winter break ended a few days after the new year began, and Cass half-expected her affair with Eva to follow suit. After all, Eva had made it clear that her main commitment was to her career. But as the first week of classes blended into the second and then the third, Eva didn't stop texting her or inviting her over after school. In fact, she even showed up on Cass's doorstep a few times late at night after the rest of the neighborhood was asleep. They started spending time with friends and family too, sharing cupcakes and coffee with Alexis and more than a few meals with Matthew and Maya. Cass was the designated family chef, after all. Two Saturdays in a row they went along on each other's standing dates—Cass with Alexis and her family for movie night, and Eva with Matthew and Maya for game night. They didn't talk about the future, but Cass could feel Eva becoming more and more enmeshed in her life as the weeks passed.

The nights they spent together didn't always involve sex, either. More than once they skipped straight to the cuddling portion of the evening, or they studied together or even, occasionally, watched a movie. Those nights in particular reminded Cass of the brief period back in Oakland when she and Alyssa, her ex, had spent nearly every waking moment together, cooking and eating and talking about work and rugby late into the night. They too had existed for a time in a cocoon of sex and togetherness, though with jobs and apartments in different parts of the Bay Area, they'd had to work a little harder to see each other.

And then, during the third week of classes, came the winter quarter's all-college meeting. Cass attended as a regular grad student this time, not as a presenter. During announcements, Steve pulled up the new Arts and Sciences blog that Cass had recently completed, highlighting its updated college calendar on one side of the home page and the inaugural faculty research profile splashed across the center panel: Sociology's very own Eva DeMarco.

"Nice job, Trane," Jace MacKenzie said, reaching across Zach Abbott, Cass's grad officemate, to smack her arm.

"Thanks," Cass murmured back, glancing around the room. She could hear whispers rippling through the audience, particularly among a cadre of middle-aged white men seated near Linc Anderson, but in general the response seemed positive. Cass finally located Eva seated between Gwen and Scott Karoly on the far side of the student center's multi-purpose room, and tried to catch her eye. But Eva didn't seem to notice her.

Which was fine, Cass told herself, turning back to face front as Steve continued the announcements. She would catch up with her later. Eva wanted boundaries, but that didn't mean they couldn't be friendly, did it?

Immediately following the meeting, Cass and several of her classmates approached a group near the back of the room that contained Eva, Tina, and Ben, among others. Cass had paused automatically, a smile already forming on her lips. But Eva had only nodded at her politely and returned to her conversation with her ex-husband and his current girlfriend, rebuffing her with a studied coolness that left Cass breathless.

That didn't hurt, she told herself, blinking rapidly as she continued past. It didn't hurt at all to have her place in Eva's world publicly disavowed, even though Eva had spent the previous night in her bed. Eva had asked for these rules, and while Cass hadn't explicitly agreed to them—somehow needing to think about Eva's boundaries had turned into ignoring their very existence—she couldn't pretend to be surprised when Eva froze her out in front of the rest of the college.

That night, when Eva texted to see if she wanted to come over for dinner, Cass texted back that she couldn't. "Sorry," she added with a blowing kiss emoji so that Eva wouldn't suspect anything. Even after what had happened that afternoon, she still longed to jog up the path to Eva's porch and knock on the door, to be let into the fire-lit house where Eva would press a kiss to the corner of her mouth while Harvey leapt and whined at her heels. But tonight, she didn't think she could see Eva without revealing how hurt she'd been when Eva looked right through her as if she was a stranger. Or if not a stranger, then at least someone she couldn't possibly care about as much as Cass cared about her.

Crap, she thought as she sat at her kitchen table, her lesson plan for her thesis project spread out before her. She was totally Amy in this scenario. Amy, who had unfriended her on social media and still hadn't responded to any of her texts or emails.

The comparison wasn't something she wanted to contemplate for long, so she turned her phone face down and went back to prepping for the third class in her writing curriculum for homeless queer youth. This week they would be exploring the theme of place. She would provide a set of prompts the students could use, or they could come up with one of their own. They could write prose or poetry or something in between, share their thoughts in paragraphs or stanzas or even lists, just as long as they ruminated on the meaning of "place" in their lives. The six youth in the class were residents of Presley House, a transitional living program for 18 to 22 year olds who identified as LGBTQIA, and by the end of the seventh class, each would have enough original writing to stitch together a thematically linked narrative. Or, at least, that was the plan. Whether or not the enrollees would all complete the program was anyone's guess, but it helped that the grant from the youth center paid each student ten dollars per class plus all the pizza they could eat. So far, their attendance had been perfect.

The following morning, she ignored her first text of the day from Eva as she headed cross-campus to work on a website permissions issue for the Physics Department. Matthew hung around the administrative service manager's office heckling her, which Janet, the manager, appeared to tolerate more than Miranda, Steve's assistant, probably would have. It really was nice to have her brother so close, Cass thought for the umpteenth time as she laughed at one of his silly astronomy jokes: "I was up all night wondering where the sun had gone... and then it dawned on me!"

Janet laughed too, which only inspired Matthew to continue: "Why does a moon rock taste better than an Earth rock? Because it's a little meteor!"

They laughed again, even though Cass totally knew better than to egg him on, and he said, grinning, "Never trust an atom because they make up everything!"

Cass's phone beeped again, the telltale ring tone she'd chosen as a joke for Eva: the first few bars of *The Office* theme song. Before she could stop her brother, he grabbed her phone from the outside pocket of her bag and checked the notification still lighting up the screen. "Hey, you have a text from…" He stopped, glancing up at her and wiggling his eyebrows.

Cass had told him and Maya that she and Eva were keeping their relationship (if it could be called that) quiet at work. So far he hadn't blown their cover—at least, as far as she knew.

"Thanks," she said, and kept clicking through Drupal modules to find the one she was looking for.

"Gee, don't sound so excited," Matthew said.

"Leave it alone, Matthew," she warned, her eyes narrowing.

"I think I'll go grab a coffee," Janet, the manager, said pleasantly, and vanished through the office door with a swirl of her Indian print skirt.

"Oops. Sibling rivalry strikes again," Matthew said.

Cass stared at the computer screen, willing her brother to go away, but her psychic powers were apparently confined to reading his mind. She could no more move Matthew with strongly worded thoughts than she could make campus Drupal users read the help files on their systems.

"Seriously, Cass," he said, voice quieter, "is everything okay?"

"Yes," she said. Then, as she felt his gaze continue to bore into the side of her face, she sighed and pushed back from Janet's desk. "Or, no. I don't know. We're sort of not speaking."

"Does *she* know that?" he asked, nodding at the phone.

"Apparently not."

"Dude, you can't just ghost her."

"I'm not," Cass insisted. "Well, maybe a little. But I have my reasons."

"Such as?" he asked, his forehead furrowed.

She knew she shouldn't involve him, but the words just sort of burst out of her, propelled by the still-fresh memory of the previous day's humiliation. "She doesn't want anyone to know about me, Matthew. I'm like this dirty little secret, which I thought would be fine. But I don't know now. Maybe it's not."

He nodded. "Maybe it isn't. Have you told her how you feel?"

"No."

"Why, because that would be reasonable?"

"Says the man who refused marriage counseling with his pregnant wife."

"Come on, you know she didn't actually mean it. Besides, I think in order to succeed at therapy you *both* have to be mentally competent."

Cass laughed ruefully. Maya's hormones really were all over the place, making her sob for hours one day and practically burst with joyous excitement the next. Her emotional instability was so bad that Cass had been researching different foods that might help balance her out. Not that she had any intention of telling Maya that until well after the baby arrived.

"Fine, I'll text her back," she told Matthew. "Now get back to work so I can do the same."

"Okay," he said reluctantly, and pushed away from the wall to drop a light kiss on her hair. "Come find me later if you need to, got it?"

"Got it," she said, mock saluting him. But as she watched him walk away, a surge of affection drove away some of the hurt Eva's texts had triggered. Cass would forever be glad she'd accepted Matthew's invitation to move to Edmonds—even if she ended up going back to California with her heart broken all over again.

She didn't text Eva. Her writing class was scheduled for five-thirty at the Seattle Queer Resource Center, only a couple of blocks from Presley House on the south side of Capitol Hill, so after working out at the gym and logging a few more GA hours, she headed into the city. Parking near the resource center was as crazy as ever, but she still made it to the conference room in time to set out extra pens and notebooks before anyone else arrived. The students got there just after the pizza boxes, and for the next fifteen minutes, Cass munched cheese pizza and shot the shit with the kids she was starting to get to know better through their writing.

There was Hannah, the girl from Spokane whose slight frame vibrated with tension through 99.5 percent of class; Ryan, the non-binary kid who was getting their life together finally after six months at Presley House; Killian, the red-haired gay boy who had spent his teen years on the streets of Seattle after his parents threw him out of their Enumclaw home; Maria, the Latina trans girl who didn't speak much but wrote beautiful poems about her childhood in Puyallup; Charmaine, the girl of color who wore her queerness proudly after nearly a year at Presley House; and Kyle, the Latino boy who identified as pansexual and clearly had an unrequited crush on Charmaine.

They laughed and joked and sniped with the ease of people used to sharing community space, all except Hannah who had only arrived at Presley House the week after Thanksgiving. Her case manager hadn't been sure Hannah should participate, but in the end he and Cass had decided that maybe writing her story would help her in a way that group and individual therapy had yet to do. The other kids tried to include her in their in-jokes, but Hannah resisted their overtures and hunched her shoulders as she read through her journal from the previous class. Poor kid. Cass didn't want to think about what had happened to make her so profoundly incapable of relaxing her guard even for a moment.

As usual, the pizza didn't last long. Soon the boxes were stacked in one corner and the students had spread out their pens and notebooks at the conference table. Cass waited until they'd quieted. Silence made an incredibly effective teaching tool, she'd learned while volunteering at the Oakland LGBTQIA youth project. She had started out co-teaching the writing course with the woman who had developed the curriculum, which meant she mainly observed the other teacher in action. But teaching, as she and Matthew often said, was in their blood, and eventually she was leading her own classes in Oakland.

One of the things she especially liked about the writing curriculum was that there was no right or wrong answer. Whatever the student felt like writing that day was fine—as long as they wrote. Fueled with carbs and comfortable in the space, most of the youth spent their forty-five minutes together scribbling away at page after page. Or at least thoughtfully sketching out what they wanted to say. Ryan had to be kept on track, especially when their phone kept buzzing with notifications from "buds," and Hannah had the habit of laying her head down on her arms supposedly "to think." But even with those minor hiccups, the class went well. And, as usual, almost too quickly. Soon enough it was six forty-five and the kids were packing their things to head out again.

Cass stowed away the extra pens and notebooks as Ryan lingered, chatting her up about the dyslexia font she'd mentioned during class. "There are open source versions," she explained, "and Chrome even has an extension that renders the text on any page more readable."

"Dang. I gotta get my hands on that," Ryan said, shaking their head. Then they paused, eyes on the open doorway. "Wait. Who is that?"

Cass followed their gaze expecting to see another youth or possibly an older volunteer out in the hall. But no, unless she was seeing things, the dark-haired woman in the wool pea coat leaning against the wall outside the conference room was, in fact, Eva.

"Crap," Cass breathed, suddenly regretting her failure to text Eva back.

"Is she waiting for you?" Ryan asked, their eyebrows rising toward their mostly shaved hairline. "Don't tell me that fine woman is your girl."

"She's—a friend." While *illicit fuck buddy* was technically more accurate, Cass had no intention of revealing that particular truth to anyone, let alone a youth in her class.

Eva, who had been staring at her phone, glanced up. As she caught Cass's gaze, she offered her signature awkward wave.

"I hope I have friends that look like her when I'm old like you," Ryan said.

"Watch it, kid." Cass started to smack them on the shoulder but thought better of it. Even play violence could trigger past trauma in kids who had lived on the streets.

"See?" they said, smirking. "I knew you was more than friends. Otherwise you wouldn't be getting all uptight and shit."

Cass shrugged into her puffer coat and started toward the door. "Call me if you have any other questions about the font, okay?"

"I'll let you know," Ryan said, and held out their fist as they reached the doorway. "See you later, Cass. Have fun with your lady."

Cass bumped their fist and waved them away. No use claiming that Eva wasn't her lady. Ryan wouldn't believe her, anyway. She paused in the doorway and gazed at Eva. "Hey."

"Hi," Eva said, and then bit her lip. "How are you?"

Cass stared at the woman who had looked right through her only the day before. "I'm fine. What are you doing here, Eva?"

She pushed away from the wall. "Okay, I know it looks like I'm stalking you, but I was in the neighborhood."

"Really?" Cass didn't even try to keep the skepticism out of her voice.

"Really. I had a meeting with Alexis at Seattle Central," Eva said, shifting from one foot to the other.

Seattle Central Community College really was in the same neighborhood. Cass glanced down the hallway, but they appeared to be alone. Good. That meant no one else had to witness this awkward encounter.

"Look," Eva added. "I just wanted to say I'm sorry about yesterday."

"It's fine." Cass shouldered her messenger bag and started down the hall. "Sorry I didn't get back to you. I've just been really busy."

They were in the front entryway when Eva caught her wrist and stopped her. "So what, you aren't avoiding me, then?"

Cass gazed down at her, aware of the giant rainbow flag decorating the wall directly behind them. "No," she admitted at last, her voice low. "I have been avoiding you."

Eva nodded. "I know what I did at the meeting was... Anyway, if you want to stop seeing me, I get it. I just—if that's the case, say the word. But please don't just shut me out."

Was that the case? Did Cass want to stop seeing her? She thought about never again witnessing one of Eva's soft smiles or her dorky waves or the way her glasses slid down her nose when she got really excited. She thought about never again being kissed the way Eva kissed her, like she was about to burst from emotion. She thought about Harvey and his kisses, his tail thwacks and his head butts. Was she ready to give up all of that?

No, she realized, she wasn't. Not just yet. Not even if it hurt sometimes. That was a fact of relationships, she'd learned by now: Everyone hurt each other, whether they meant to or not.

"I don't want to stop seeing you," she admitted, gazing down at the tile floor. "It's just, yesterday was really awful."

"I know, and I'm sorry. Honestly." Eva paused. "I know I'm the one who said it had to be like that, but maybe there's another option."

"We could pretend to be friends," Cass offered. "You know, instead of totally avoiding each other?"

Eva nodded. "I was actually thinking the same thing."

"You were?"

"Yeah. Assuming you ever spoke to me again." Eva smiled up at her, the look in her eyes soft and open. "I really am sorry, Cass."

"I know." And then, because they were at queer central in the gayest neighborhood in the gayest city on the West Coast—other than San Francisco, of course—Cass leaned down and kissed her. To her credit, Eva kissed her back.

Immediately, a chorus of voices rained down on them.

"Get it, Cass!"

"Woo hoo!"

"Yeah, boi!"

The voices came from the stairs to the second floor, from which her students were apparently spying on them. Cass pulled back and waved at them, narrowly keeping her middle finger in line, and then said to a blushing Eva, "Sorry. Youth."

"What can you do?" Eva said, and waved at the Presley House kids as they ducked out the front door.

Out on the sidewalk, Eva leaned into Cass as they headed toward the main road a few paces down. It was dark out and the south side of Capitol Hill could be sketchy, but it was also queer friendly. Cass didn't hesitate before wrapping her arm around Eva's shoulders.

"Where are you parked?" she asked.

"Near the Elysian," Eva said, gesturing to the north. "If this went well, I was hoping to persuade you to join me for dinner."

"I already ate pizza," Cass said, "but I could probably be persuaded to have a drink."

"Excellent," Eva said, smiling up at her, eyes lighting up behind her glasses. "By the way, you were really good in there. Those kids really look up to you."

"Wait—you were spying on me?"

"Stalking and spying," Eva agreed. "The door was open, so I couldn't *not* listen."

Cass shook her head. "You wouldn't be saying such nice things if you'd been here a couple of weeks ago. But the kids are settling in, I think. All except Hannah. She's definitely struggling."

They chatted about the program and her students as they walked. Cass had told Eva about the class before, and it was nice how engaged she was now, asking all the right questions at precisely the right moments. Cass wondered if she was trying extra hard to win her back and thought about telling her she didn't have to. But then she realized this was just Eva—at least, it was Eva when they were alone. Eva at Edmonds was a whole different ball of wax.

Cass pushed away memories of the all-college meeting. Tonight was the first time they'd gone out in public since they'd started hooking up. As they waited for a table in the crowded entryway of the Elysian, Cass couldn't help being proud of the glances they elicited, some covert and others open. Eva was lovely and gazing up at her with obvious affection, which was reassuring. She wasn't embarrassed to be seen with Cass or suffering from latent homophobia. She was simply worried about failing to achieve the promotion she'd been working her entire adult life to earn. Her worry seemed a bit excessive to Cass, but as much as Cass wasn't a fan of the back-stabbing, grandstanding nature of academic life, Eva was her own person. If she wanted a life in the academy, Cass owed it to her to respect her choices.

Once they were seated with Eva's dinner order in and pints of the brewery's IPA before them, Eva gazed at Cass over the top of her glass. "Thanks for giving me another chance."

"Thanks for stalking me."

"Hey, it wasn't really stalking," Eva protested, laughing. "I mean, you told me when and where your class was, so…"

"Valid." Cass sipped her beer, enjoying the smoky taste. Seattle's beer and coffee were far superior to San Francisco's, in her humble opinion. Seattle also had Eva DeMarco, another major plus in its favor.

"When did you say rugby starts?" Eva asked.

"The third week of February."

"Are you excited?"

"Definitely." Cass took a sip of beer. "You're not much of a sports fan, are you?"

"What? I like sports. I've always liked sports."

"Really?" Cass asked. "Because it doesn't really seem like it."

"I guess I still think of myself as a football fan. In coal country, the NFL is like its own religion complete with relics and rituals. People hang Steelers flags outside their houses and businesses, and on Sunday after church, everyone barbecues and watches The Game."

"You mean in the fall?"

"No, I mean all season. I used to think it was perfectly normal for men to dress up in plaid parkas and hunting caps and go outside to barbecue chicken in the middle of a snow storm—until I went away to college and learned how the other half lived, that is."

Cass couldn't imagine going to an Ivy League after the childhood Eva described. "You said before that Cornell was a culture shock."

"Right." Eva hesitated, and then she admitted, "I had a perm and bangs when I got there, but they were gone by the time I went home for Christmas."

Cass could tell she was embarrassed, so she stifled her snort of laughter and merely nodded. "Well, I had a ponytail when I got to Vassar, so to each her own."

"I can't picture you with long hair."

"Yeah, not my favorite look."

The conversation paused briefly as the server delivered Eva's turkey burger, and Cass watched in amusement as she separated the burger and fries and very carefully squirted ketchup onto one corner of the plate. Even her dining habits were adorable.

"So do you actually like watching football?" Cass asked.

"I don't mind it. Ben is a huge Bears fan, so I have definitely watched my share of Monday Night Football."

"That's right," Cass said, remembering the navy and orange Chicago Bears fleece she'd seen Ben wearing around campus on assorted occasions. Matthew had asked him if he was a Broncos fan once, and Ben had gone nearly apoplectic before he realized

Matthew was joking. "His family is from there, aren't they?"

Eva licked ketchup from a finger. "Yeah, Evanston. His dad is an econ professor at Northwestern and his mom's an investment banker."

Investment banking—thus the money that had purchased Eva's current house. Cass wondered if she'd thought of selling it after the divorce, but probably she was waiting to find out about tenure. No use in buying a new home if she'd only have to turn around and move to the next university town.

"Matthew and Maya usually host a Super Bowl party, so—" Cass broke off as Eva looked down at her plate. "You've been to one of their parties, haven't you?"

"Two, actually."

"Ah." She paused and then forged ahead. "I know it might be weird, and there will definitely be other Edmonds folks present—including Ben and Tina, probably—but would you maybe want to come to this year's party? Just as friends, of course," she added quickly.

"I would," Eva said, but Cass could hear the hesitation in her voice. "But I don't know. Can I think about it?"

"Of course," Cass said, and took a healthy gulp of her beer. "So, Pennsylvania—does that mean you're a Mario Lemieux fan?"

Eva looked at her blankly, and Cass laughed. So much for being a sports fan. "Hockey," she explained.

"Oh." Eva made a face. "I don't really see the attraction."

"Fair enough."

Cass changed the subject, guiding it to safer topics such as the perennial favorite: outrageous things students had said or written. Eva had a treasure trove of Stupid Student Quotes, and Cass ended up laughing so hard at one point that she snorted her beer and had to visit the restroom to get cleaned up. On her way back to the table, Cass watched Eva picking at her salad, a slight smile teasing her lips. No resting bitch face for her. Maybe that was why students at Edmonds gave her such high ratings—she seemed approachable to a degree that not a lot of professors did. Cass knew that she offered more office hours than was required, and that she made herself available to students whose work or class schedules conflicted with her office hours. Eva cared about people, and that was partly what made her such an excellent professor.

If she didn't get tenure, Cass knew, it wouldn't be because she didn't deserve it. But academia wasn't a meritocracy. Success in academics depended on who you knew and how savvy you'd played your political hand prior to your tenure review. Dating a grad student who was not only the same sex but who had also pissed off one of the most powerful men on campus? Definitely not a savvy political move.

But Eva was her own person and fully capable of making her own decisions. If she thought Cass was worth the risk, then who was Cass to tell her otherwise? Still, it didn't stop a niggling worry from setting up shop at the back of her mind. She genuinely cared about Eva. She would hate to be the reason she didn't attain a lifelong dream.

"What's that look?" Eva asked as Cass dropped back into the seat across from her.

"What look? This look?" Cass asked, and crossed her eyes. Then she rolled them around, knowing from experience that it looked like her eyes were rolling in opposite directions. Or maybe that she was having a seizure. Probably the seizure.

Eva laughed and threw a french fry at her. "That is totally creepy! Stop!"

So she did.

A little while later Eva paid the bill—"You didn't even eat anything, Cass"—and they headed back outside, where they lingered on the lamp-lit sidewalk.

"Do you have homework to do?" Eva asked.

"Always. Do you have lessons to plan?"

"Naturally."

They gazed at each other, and Cass could see one of Eva's eyebrows quirking like it did when she got an idea.

"Want to go to the Thistledown?" Eva asked.

"Totally," Cass said, and held out her arm. Eva hooked it with hers and they were off, laughing as they skipped across the broken, haphazard pavement.

The same grouchy bouncer from the summer was working the door, but inside the bar this time. She nodded at Cass and eyed Eva a tad suspiciously before waving them through with a cursory check of their IDs.

The bartender ignored them as they approached, until Cass cleared her throat. "What can I get you?"

"An Elysian IPA for me," Cass said, and glanced at Eva.

"I'll have the same, please."

While Cass dug in her wallet for her credit card, Eva touched her arm and said, "I have to pee. I'll be right back."

Cass nodded and watched her leave, knowing her smile probably seemed a little besotted but too content at the present moment to care. Her thesis project was going well, Maya's pregnancy was entirely without complications (if you didn't count her hormonal psychosis), and Eva—well, Eva was still willing to try to make a go of a relationship with her, despite the attendant complications. Life at the moment was genuinely good, and Cass was—dare she say it and risk pissing off the gods?—happy.

The bartender slid the beers to her and Cass handed him the credit card. Then she moved to a nearby table, a little farther from the speakers. She hadn't been sitting there long when her video chat notification went off. She hit accept, grinning as her brother's face appeared on the screen.

"What up, bro?"

"Just checking on you. You didn't come home after your class tonight."

"I know. Eva showed up, and we decided to stick around Capitol Hill."

"Oh!" He perked up. "Awesome. That's really good."

"It is," she agreed. A movement caught her attention, and she realized Eva was approaching. "Dude, I have to go."

"Okay. Have fun," he said, sounding mildly envious.

"We will. Next time you can come out with us, okay?"

"Sweet. Later, Crater."

"After a while, Anglophile."

Eva paused next to the table, squinting down at Cass. "Excuse me, but you look familiar. Do I know you from somewhere?"

Cass gazed up at her, biting back her grin. "Um, no, I don't think so."

"No, really. Do you come here often?"

"That's not what I said and you know it," she protested, laughing. "I asked if you hang out here a lot."

Eva slipped into the seat across from her, eyes dancing. "Pretty much the same thing, babe."

"Don't 'babe' me," Cass said, even though she secretly liked the term of endearment.

"Fine." Eva gulped down a prodigious amount of her beer. Then she leaned across the table, caught Cass's chin firmly in her hand, and kissed her.

At first, Cass was too surprised to react. But as Eva's tongue flicked against her lips, she startled back to life. She opened her mouth slightly, allowing Eva access, and leaned into the kiss.

A few moments later Eva pulled back, looking flushed and self-satisfied.

"What was that for?" Cass asked. "Not that I'm complaining."

Eva shrugged. "I just really wanted to kiss you."

Cass licked her lips, thrilling at the way Eva's gaze dropped to her mouth again. "Professor DeMarco," she said, pretending to be shocked.

"Ms. Trane," Eva said back, the swagger still in her voice and face.

And yep, Cass decided an hour later when the Uber dropped them off at Eva's house to continue neglecting their classwork together, forgiving Eva had absolutely been the right decision. Because while Cass wasn't sure where they were headed, she was definitely open to finding out.

CHAPTER THIRTEEN

"Are you ready for some football!"

Eva barely managed to refrain from rolling her eyes as Jack Keller, a pocket-protector-wearing physicist, greeted the latest arrivals with what he had apparently decided was going to be his catch phrase. But she kept her snarky side in check because not only was Jack a generally decent guy, but the latest arrivals just happened to be her ex-husband and his new girlfriend.

Although really, she thought as she smiled over Matthew's shoulder at Ben and Tina, didn't the fact they'd been together for a year and a half and living together for all but six of those months qualify Tina for the role of plain old girlfriend? Which, speaking of, queer people clearly didn't have a monopoly on U-Hauling.

"Hey," Tina said, coming over to give her a hug. "Where's Harvey?"

"In the kitchen with Cass," Eva said. *Dang it.* She hadn't meant to say her name. She was already a little nervous about this social outing, given they were still trying to keep their relationship under wraps. But in the past week, they had started spending more time together on campus. Cass had stopped by her office to chat a few times, and they'd even had coffee one morning at Ed U Brew. Hanging out off-campus around other Edmonds folks was the next logical step, but still, it felt a little risky to Eva. She had only recently managed to step out of the faculty gossip limelight. Did she really want to step back in? But she had told Cass she would try, so here she was, trying.

To cover the first of what would probably be far too many blunders, she whistled. A moment later she heard her dog's toenails scraping the kitchen tiles. And sliding on the hardwood dining room floor. And, finally, gaining purchase on the area rug in the living room.

"Harve!" Ben said, opening his arms.

Even Eva could admit that it was adorable the way her—their—dog whined and leapt into Ben's embrace, licking his clean-shaven chin frantically. Her ex caught her eye over Harvey's wriggling head and nodded. She nodded back. They'd chatted that morning and agreed that Harvey would go home with Tina and Ben for a night or two. This would be Harvey's second overnight since Christmas, and Eva suspected there would be more as springtime approached, now that she and Ben were on better terms. Whoever said that time healed all wounds was mostly correct. Maybe not all wounds, but a significant portion of them. The fact that she and Ben were both in relationships helped, too—even if Eva's current relationship was only temporary. And secret. Whatever. It was good, and she was happy. For now.

Living in the present moment, she reminded herself. LIVING IN THE PRESENT MOMENT.

Cass emerged from the kitchen to add a tray of chicken wings to the already impressive spread covering the dining room table, which had been pushed against a wall of windows to make more space. There were mini pizzas, nacho chips and guacamole, pigs in a blanket, and a giant pot of veggie chili. She had been cooking all morning, and there was a smear of guacamole near her dimple that Eva wanted nothing more than to walk over and lick from her—

Whoa, girl, she thought. Keep it together. There were three more hours to get through, possibly more, without revealing their intimate knowledge of each other.

"Hey, Cass," Ben said, smiling at her.

"Yo, Sweetness," Cass said.

Because even though the Bears had lost a prodigious amount of games that season (as per Tina), Ben was of course wearing his favorite retro Walter Payton jersey that he'd picked up in a thrift shop near Wrigley.

"Tina," Jack said, grinning, "you're just going to let her call him that right in front of you?"

Oh, for fuck's sake.... Eva caught Cass's eye. "Do you and Maya need help cleaning up the kitchen?"

"No, that's o—" Cass stopped, squinting at the significant

look Eva was shooting her. "I mean, actually, that's a good idea. Wouldn't want to miss any of the game, would we?"

As they escaped into the kitchen, Maya looked up from the sink where she was washing a cutting board. "What are you guys doing? I thought Operation Just Friends precluded disappearing into adjacent rooms together."

"You're here, so it doesn't count," Cass said dismissively.

"I'm not sure that's true, but okay." Maya glanced at Eva. "Had enough of the football talk already?"

"It's not that," Eva said. "It's just, *ugh*, compulsive heterosexuality is so nauseating!"

"You know," Maya commented, "most Super Bowl parties aren't big on discussions of compulsive heterosexuality."

Cass snorted. "Obviously you've never been to one in the Bay Area."

Maya inclined her head. "Now that is completely true."

She paused to massage a spot in her lower back, and Cass immediately leapt forward. "Why don't you get off your feet? Eva and I can get this."

"No, it's fine."

"Maya," Cass said in the warning tone that sometimes made Harvey pee on the spot.

Maya actually hesitated, which Eva had not expected. Then: "Fine. Thanks for treating me like an invalid, I guess," she said, her tone grudging as she pulled out a chair at the table under the window and lowered herself into it.

"Personally," Eva said, "I was more than happy to let other people wait on me, and I wasn't nearly as pregnant as you are. Are we sure it isn't twins?"

"God, no!" Maya burst out, and Cass laughed.

As she passed Eva a towel to dry, Cass lifted her eyebrows in a gesture Eva easily interpreted. Eva nodded back. She was okay. The more she was around Maya, the easier it got. By the time the baby came, she was hoping she'd be able to be around him or her without more than an occasional twinge of pain. Him or her— Matthew had decided he didn't want to know the baby's sex ahead of time, so even though Maya couldn't not know (reading ultrasounds was one of her many professional skills), she was keeping it a secret. At least for now.

Secrets, secrets, everywhere.

Harvey, however, hadn't received the relationship-concealment memo. When the game started and Cass finally left the kitchen to settle on the couch between Matthew and Jack, Harvey immediately jumped up onto her lap, spun three times, and settled down with a long sigh as if to say, "*Finally.*"

Laughter rippled across the room, and Bridget Endover, a Psychology Department pal of Tina's, said, "Looks like true love."

Cass glanced up at Eva, her eyes wide. Eva stared back at her. Well, damn. She hadn't thought of this particular situation when Matthew encouraged her to bring Harvey to the festivities. Their gazes held probably a little too long because Cass only looked away when her brother elbowed her unsubtly.

Eva tried to focus on the TV screen where two teams she didn't care about were facing off for the NFL championship. But Cass was absently stroking Harvey's head, and Eva couldn't help but remember how Cass had pinned her to her bed the night before and had her way with her not once, not twice, but three delicious times. She blinked and stared hard at the television, praying her face wouldn't flush. Jesus. They might as well have cartoon bubbles over their heads that read, "We're sleeping together!" Coming to this party had been a terrible idea.

And yet, as the day went on, she was glad she hadn't missed it. The food was plentiful, the company was excellent, and even the game was entertaining. Or, at least, the commercials were. Matthew and Maya's house was a bit larger than hers, as Cass had said, and Eva had always enjoyed its perfect bungalow-ness with its large, framed windows and open rooms that flowed one into the other. The original oak woodwork hadn't been painted over, and it gleamed in light from mica fixtures and Tiffany-style lamps. Maya and Matthew had decorated the walls with old maps and blueprints, which added an interesting, eclectic flair to the Arts and Crafts interior. Hanging out at their house made her feel like her own was slightly unpolished, but she wasn't sure how long she would be there, so redecorating after Ben left hadn't been a priority. If she got tenure, though…

Aargh. The closer her review date came, the harder it was to wait.

She wasn't the first person to leave after the game ended, but she wasn't the last, either. Still, by the time she'd reached the porch, she could already see Cass turning the corner onto her street, following her home for a work session as they'd planned.

Cass's cheeks were pink and her eyes bright when she opened the front door and let herself in. They'd started leaving their doors unlocked when they knew the other was coming over, and as a result, Eva might be anywhere in the house when Cass arrived. Tonight, though, she was waiting in the front room, her back to the gas fireplace, soaking up heat after the chilly walk home.

"Hi," Cass said, stripping out of her coat.

"Hi." Eva hesitated. "Did anyone—no one saw you follow me, did they?"

Cass's movements stilled momentarily before restarting again. "No. At least, I don't think so," she said. Her eyes were a little less bright as she turned away from the coat tree, and Eva wished she could dial her question back. Honestly, she wished she could dial back her paranoia, but that was probably not going to happen anytime soon.

They regarded each other across the room, and then Eva stepped toward her. "Thanks for inviting me to your party," she said, wrapping her arms around Cass's waist and resting her head against her strong chest.

Cass's arms closed around her and Eva felt her sigh, sensed the tension draining out of her. "Thanks for coming to our party. Did you have fun?"

"I did. The game was even mildly interesting, considering what it had to work with," Eva added, smiling into Cass's neck. "My dad used to say that. You know, like, 'Nice job on your art project, kid, considering what you got to work with.'"

"Dad humor," Cass said. "Sadly, my father does not possess that gene."

"But is it sad, really?" Eva asked, reluctantly backing away from Cass's warmth. Cass tried to catch her and bring her back, but Eva twirled out of her reach. "Nope. Work time, missy. Your thesis isn't going to write itself."

"Wouldn't it be cool if it could, though?"

"I think that would be some form of plagiarism. Academic

dishonesty, at the least."

"You know who we could ask about that, don't you?" Cass commented as she opened her backpack and lifted out her padded laptop sleeve.

Eva tilted her head. Then she saw Cass's smirk and they said in unison, "Linc Anderson." She was fairly certain it would never not feel good to rip on that douchebag.

They settled in at the dining room table to work, full from the steady grazing each had partaken in at the party. Every once in a while one of them would stand up and stretch or go lay down next to Harvey on the couch for kisses and belly rubs. But for the most part, they worked straight through for the next two and a half hours. This, even more than sex with Cass, made Eva happy—their ability to work together in the quiet living room, firelight flickering in the background, Harvey snoring nearby. Well, maybe not *more* than sex, but right up there. Ben had needed noise and distractions to work, last minute deadlines and the pressure of almost failing to make him finally park his butt in the chair and do the work. Cass seemed to approach scholarship more like Eva did, slow and steady and without the need for procrastination. Eva wondered if her work ethic was innate, or if she had cultivated stability to combat her dyslexia. Matthew, Cass had told her, was more like Ben, so maybe it could be chalked up to temperament.

The sky outside had been black for a while when Cass dropped her pen and leaned back in her chair, scrubbing one hand through her hair. "I'm hungry," she announced. "What do you have to eat?"

Eva looked up at her over the top of her glasses, eyebrows raised suggestively.

Cass smirked. "Yes, but what sort of caloric substance can you offer me so that I don't bonk in the middle of said sexy times?"

"I thought bonking was the point of sexy times," Eva said, laughing at the look on Cass's face. "Fine, I'll feed you first. Pasta or frozen pizza? Or cereal?"

They decided on Cheerios with applesauce and dried cranberries because it was quick and easy. Then they hightailed it to the bedroom where they lit candles, stripped off their clothes, and climbed under the comforter, shivering at the touch of cool sheets against their skin. It was strange not to hear Harvey snorting in the crate at the end of the bed, but Eva pushed the thought away and focused on the beautiful woman before her.

"Come here," Cass said, her voice low, and pulled Eva on top of her. They lay for a few minutes like that, warming each other up, until Cass touched her cold foot to Eva's leg.

"Ouch!" she yelped, which only made Cass laugh at her. So, naturally, Eva kissed her.

They made love slowly that night, taking their time with each other, scooting back up the bed to kiss again and stare into each other's eyes. Eva felt so relaxed with Cass, so safe, and by now they knew each other's bodies—what one liked, what the other didn't. She honestly thought Cass might be the most attentive partner she'd ever had. It only took a word or sometimes a gesture to tell her to go slow or to speed up, to press harder or to be gentler. Sex with Cass wasn't perfect any more than it had been with anyone else, but it always felt good.

A little while later they were spooning when Cass murmured, "What are you doing on Valentine's Day?"

"Nothing."

V-Day fell on a Tuesday this year, and Eva rarely planned anything social during the week when school was in session.

"Would you like to come over for dinner at my place?" Cass asked. "I thought I could cook you dinner, you know, recreate our first date? Only without the star-gazing portion of the evening."

"Sure," Eva said, after a moment. "Why not?"

"Gee, such enthusiasm," Cass said, but she sounded more amused than offended.

"Sorry. It's just, Valentine's Day feels like a Hallmark holiday." She and Ben had always agreed on that much.

"I swear, academics," Cass muttered, her breath tickling Eva's neck. "One would think you might actually do some research before making such a pronouncement, but no."

Eva turned in Cass's arms until they were facing each other. "Excuse me?"

Cass was smiling, and reached up to bop Eva lightly on the nose. "Your pal Siri would inform you that Valentine's Day has been celebrated since the fifth century, and is based on the Roman festival of Lupercalia held to celebrate the start of spring. But the Christians had to come along and outlaw the old ways and give them new names. Oh, and demonize the Romans, of course. St. Valentine was supposedly a temple priest who was beheaded for marrying off poor, persecuted early Christians."

Beheaded? That didn't exactly scream romance. "You have an oddly vast knowledge of the history of Valentine's Day."

Cass shrugged. "My parents called it a Hallmark holiday too."

"So this was your revenge? Kind of like quoting Weber at them?"

"Exactly like quoting Weber at them."

"Wow, you must have been a fun kid." Eva leaned forward and kissed Cass's dimple, sucking on it lightly. "I hope if you ever have your own—" She stopped, hearing the teasing words only after they were out.

Cass smoothed the moment over: "Even if I don't, I totally plan to make Matthew and Maya's kid a mini-me. I mean, what are aunts for?"

"I don't think turning their sibling's progeny against them, but that might just be me." Eva kissed Cass's nose and slid out of bed.

"Where are you going?"

"I have to pee," she said, and pulled on her robe as she left the bedroom.

The hallway wood floor was cold and creaked familiarly in the otherwise quiet house. Yep, still strange not to have Harvey's sweet, goofy presence somewhere nearby. If anything happened to him... But it would, she reminded herself. He was a dog, and dogs did not live for more than a decade and a half. He would leave her, just like... She stopped the thought. *Not tonight, Satan.*

She shut herself in the bathroom, peed—because she really did have to—and washed her hands in hot water. Then she left the water running and stared at herself in the mirror. Her face was flushed and there were shadows under her eyes, but the pallor and dark rings of two years earlier had mostly receded. Her mother had commented on it at tea the previous morning, alluding unsubtly to Cass's role in her recently improved outlook. Eva had denied it, but now she wondered: Would her good mood remain after Cass finished her thesis and went back to California?

She splashed her face and turned off the water. Back in the bedroom a minute later, she slipped naked between the sheets, shivering slightly from the drafty hall.

"About this V-Day date," she commented, burrowing closer to Cass's warmth. "Would your brother be involved this time? Because I'd really rather it just be the two of us."

"Shut it," Cass said, placing her foot on Eva's leg again. Only this time it backfired because she was warm while Eva most definitely was not.

A little while later Cass had warmed her up considerably, and Eva was just about to drop off when she heard herself ask, "Do twins run in your family?" She froze as she realized where the question had come from. Specifically from the fantasy of Cass miraculously deciding to shirk California for Washington and, well, for her. It wasn't a daydream she spent a lot of time on, but she couldn't seem to stop her stupid brain from getting its hopes up.

"They do. On both sides, actually." Cass paused, and Eva stared intently at her collar bone, barely daring to breathe. "Why?"

"Oh, just curious. I've never dated a twin." Which was one hundred percent true.

Once again Cass didn't press. A little while later she got up to pee, too. As Eva waited for her to return, she wondered why that was. Why didn't they talk about the future? Why didn't they discuss their relationship? Maybe she was just as scared as Eva was to rock the boat, to ruin what they had. Because what they had was pretty freaking great, even if they did spend most of their time together sneaking around behind closed doors. Actually, that might be one of Eva's favorite things to do with Cass—be on their own away from the gossip and low-key malice of campus politics.

Maybe that was why, for once, she was actually looking forward to Valentine's Day.

***

This was what happened when you made a plan for Valentine's Day, she thought the following week as she drove up the hill as fast as she could without endangering herself or others. The plan inevitably got pummeled.

The call had come just as she was about to leave for dinner with Cass. She had run out to her car with the flower bouquet she'd gotten Cass still in hand, tossed it into the passenger seat, and driven off without Harvey. So much for their romantic Valentine's Day.

The spot next to her mother's unit was open, so she parked quickly—possibly a bit crookedly—and ran up the walk. She knocked on her mom's front door, waited exactly two seconds, and inserted her key in the lock.

"Mom," she called as she closed the door behind her. "Where are you?"

"Eva?" Her mom came around the corner from the kitchen, wiping her hands on a towel. "What are you doing here, honey? I thought you had a date with Cass." She stopped and coughed, a deep, phlegmy sound that made Eva cringe slightly.

"The front desk called to let me know you didn't show up to dinner tonight and weren't answering your phone. Why didn't you pick up?"

Her mother's eyebrows rose. "I didn't know they called."

Eva sighed. "Mom, is your phone unplugged again?"

"Oh, shoot. That's right. I wasn't feeling well last night and I didn't want any of those telemarketer calls. I'm on that national Do Not Call list and I swear, I still get those danged calls all the time."

At the sight of her mother upright and speaking—and complaining about telemarketers, no less—Eva's heart rate began to calm. "Did you skip dinner tonight because you weren't feeling well?"

Her mother waved her hand dismissively. "There's a cold going around. I've had my pneumonia and flu shots. I'll be fine."

"Okay. Well, I'm here now. Do you want me to make you something for dinner?"

"I can take care of myself," her mom said. But her delivery was ruined when she launched into another coughing fit.

"I assume you have soup in your cupboard?" Eva asked, heading into the kitchen.

"You know how I like my Progresso."

She opened her mother's soup cabinet and smiled at the sight of half a dozen rows of soup, three cans deep and two high. At least she knew where to come if there was a zombie apocalypse. Or, say, an earthquake, which was far more likely given where they lived.

Once the can of chicken noodle was heating up, Eva ducked into the living room to call Cass and fill her in on what had happened. Cass, predictably, was worried about her mother and encouraged Eva to take her time. Dinner wasn't going anywhere.

Eva bit her lip, listening to her mother coughing in the kitchen. "I don't know how long I'll be here, though. We should probably just reschedule."

Cass was quiet for a moment. Then she asked, "Are you sure?"

"I'm sorry," Eva said. And she was, but she still couldn't resist deadpanning, "I know how you feel about the whole headless guy celebration."

Cass laughed. "That's okay. It's only a Hallmark holiday, right? The ravioli's just as good reheated, which is all that matters."

"Thanks," Eva said, wishing she was there in the studio with her about to consume an amazing meal that Cass, obvious romantic that she was, had made just for the two of them.

"No worries. Give your mom a hug for me. And if you feel like coming by for dessert, let me know. I'll be here."

"Okay. I'll call you later."

They hung up, and then Eva's phone buzzed. Cass had texted her a string of every heart emoji known to man. She smiled to herself and replied back with a single heart.

When she returned to the kitchen, her mother was at the stove stirring the soup and muttering about "damned stubborn Italian blood."

"I can hear you, you know," Eva said as she checked the cupboard where her mother kept her medicine. The bottle of cough syrup was almost empty. Looked like a run to the drugstore after dinner was in order.

Soup and toast wasn't quite the meal Eva had hoped for tonight, but she was glad to see her mother perk up as they ate together. After she'd washed the dishes, Eva headed to the Walgreen's near the care facility. She loaded her basket with cold supplies and then paused in the greeting card aisle. Should she get a card for Cass to go with the flowers currently wilting in the Subaru's front seat? *Aargh*. She wished she were better at navigating relationships. Ben had done the pursuing in their eventual union. All she'd had to do was say yes.

When she let herself back into her mother's unit, her mom was waiting for her, arms folded across her nightgown, raised chin making her seem taller than her five feet.

"If I promise to take my medicine and call the doctor in the morning, will you please try to salvage your date?" her mother asked. "You can even call me later to check on me yourself, now that you turned my phone back on."

Eva hesitated. Cass had hinted that she might try her hand at tiramisu again… But her mother obviously didn't feel well, and Eva still remembered the phone call about The Fall, still couldn't quite shake the guilt that her mother's injuries could—*should*—have been prevented.

Her mom moved closer to where Eva hovered in the entryway. "I really am fine, honey. Please trust me on this."

Eva gazed into her mother's eyes, as yet able to focus on the world around her—but for how long? Her mother was already losing her independence one retinal cell at a time, Eva realized not for the first time. Having her daughter swoop in to take care of her when she probably did only have a cold must feel like adding insult to chronic injury.

Eva hesitated, and then she relented. "Okay. But call me if you need anything, okay? And leave your phone on."

"I will," her mother said, and tugged her into a hug. "I love you, Evie."

"I love you, too."

"Oh, and tell Cass I'm sorry I ruined your dinner."

"You didn't ruin anything," Eva assured her.

The hard thing, she thought a little while later as she drove back down the hill more slowly than she'd raced up it earlier, was balancing her own emotional needs with her mother's. She and her therapist had talked about the ways that losing her father and Isabella—and the unnamed baby—in such close succession manifested in her life now, both consciously and unconsciously. Eva knew she was much more fearful now than she'd been a few years earlier. She worried that calamity would strike at any moment—an earthquake, an accident, a mass shooting. All Ed-U faculty and staff received training on what to do in an active shooter situation, and there had been moments when she was on leave that she'd realized how relieved she was not to have to worry about a deranged or simply enraged student walking into one of her classes with a rifle.

"Are those rational fears, though?" Gayle had asked her one morning when the sky was bright and Eva could hear birds singing. Gayle saw patients in a small den at her home, a split-level ranch in Magnolia directly across the street from Discovery Park.

"Yes?" Eva had hazarded.

"They may be rooted in logic," Gayle had allowed. "But does worrying about those things change anything? If someone is going to bring a gun to your class, can you really do anything to prevent it? Or an earthquake. What does worrying about an earthquake—or a car accident, for that matter—achieve?"

Nothing, other than maybe convincing her to make an earthquake kit, which was still sitting half-completed in her basement. Eva had understood what Gayle meant, but she wasn't sure it was that easy to reprogram her brain.

Matthew and Maya's street was higher up the hill than hers, which meant she had to pass it on her way home. But instead of driving past, Eva found herself turning onto their block, the image of tiramisu spurring her on. Cass had said she should let her know if she wanted to come over later, hadn't she? The Camry wasn't in the driveway, so she parked on the street and walked up the drive. As she approached, she realized the studio seemed darker than she'd expected. Standing on tiptoe, she looked through the window set into the front door. The television was paused on the fantasy video game Cass and her brother liked, but there was no sign of Cass herself.

The door was unlocked, so Eva turned the knob and started to step through. She was about to call out for Cass when she heard her voice coming from the couch where she was presumably lying down out of sight: "Her name is Eva."

She froze in the partially open doorway, even though she knew she should step inside and announce her presence. Somehow she couldn't seem to make her limbs cooperate.

A tinny voice sounded from what had to be Cass's phone. "So that's why I haven't heard from you lately! I knew you were going to fall in love with some woman up there and never come back."

Eva stayed where she was, heart fluttering in her chest. *Fall in love?* Could that be how Cass felt about her?

But no: "It's not like that," Cass said.

She shouldn't be listening to this, Eva thought. She really, really shouldn't be listening to this. But still she didn't move. For the first time, she understood the impulse that led drivers to slow down and stare long and hard at an accident on the freeway.

"What's it like, then?" the other voice asked.

"I don't know, but we're not a couple," Cass said.

They weren't? Then what were they? Even as she started to slink back outside, Eva heard the other speaker say, "Well, good. Then you won't have any reason to stay in Seattle, will you?"

"I guess not," Cass agreed.

Eva backed outside and pulled the door shut as quietly as she could, her pulse roaring in her ears loudly enough to drown out the caller's next words. As she retreated down the driveway, the bouquet she'd picked up for Cass earlier in the day now clenched in her fist, she swallowed against a sudden surge of nausea. She couldn't believe she'd listened in on Cass's private conversation with a friend. Then again, she'd gotten what she deserved. What was the cliché about eavesdropping? Those who do it rarely hear anything good about themselves. Check, and check.

She drove home in a blur, replaying the conversation in her head until she wasn't really sure anymore what she'd heard. Cass had clearly been talking to someone in California. She may not have come right out and said she wasn't in love with Eva, but it had been implied, hadn't it? Either way, Cass's last few words kept ringing in her ears: *I guess not.* Eva had known from the start that Cass was planning to return to her old life, but some part of her had thought that maybe, if things between them continued the way they were going, then it was possible that Cass might change her mind. That she might actually decide to stay.

Why hadn't she knocked before opening the door? If she had, they might be sitting down at this moment preparing to eat the dessert Cass had made them. They might be holding hands and smiling, or drinking wine and discussing Eva's mom's health. But she hadn't knocked and now they weren't doing any of those things. Instead, she was running away because that was obviously the mature, reasonable thing to do.

She parked in the space off the alley and trudged toward her back door, feeling heavy and exhausted the way she used to during the early days of her family leave. Harvey met her at the door, whining and dancing as usual. She picked him up and trudged into the bedroom, collapsing on top of her covers without even taking off her jacket. He whined more and struggled to lick her face, and she worried for a moment that he might accidentally pee on her. But really, wasn't that the least she deserved for eavesdropping on Cass? Cass, who may or may not have made her tiramisu and was still waiting for her call.

Fishing her phone out of her coat pocket, she pulled up her messages app and stared at her ongoing thread with Cass. A string of heart emojis greeted her, and she almost threw her phone across the room. Instead, she took a calming breath and typed, "I think I'm going to need a rain check for dessert, too. Sorry!"

Cass's reply only took a moment: "No worries. Text me tomorrow and we'll figure it out! ♥"

Eva hesitated, biting her lip. "I'm actually busy tomorrow. Late meeting on campus and then I need to check on my mom."

Cass's reply took longer this time and was noticeably lacking in exclamation points. "Okay. Let me know when you want to try again."

Eva sent her back a thumbs-up emoji. She couldn't bring herself to add any hearts.

Cass didn't respond this time. And honestly, Eva thought as she roused herself to put the flowers in water and let Harvey out to pee, why would she?

As she lay in bed in the dark a little while later, Harvey snuggled up to her side, Eva thought again that this was what happened when you made a plan for Valentine's Day. What had she called it earlier, the headless guy celebration? More like heartless. But it wasn't like she had anyone but herself to blame for her current eviscerated state.

Harvey, ever the sensitive one, whined and kissed her ear. Eva sighed and hugged him closer, his wriggly body warm against hers. *Cass*, she thought, and stared up at the ceiling, waiting for what, she didn't know.

CHAPTER FOURTEEN

Cass stared at the text Eva had just sent her. It was Wednesday night, and even though Eva had already said she would be busy checking on her mom tonight, Cass had thought they might be able to make a plan to get together tomorrow. But no. Turned out Eva intended to spend two nights in a row grading papers from her visual methodologies class and looking after her mother.

"Is your mom okay?" Cass typed back. "I thought it was just a cold."

"She'll be fine. I just don't want her to be alone."

Which was totally understandable. But still, this would be the longest Cass had gone without seeing Eva since coming back from Southern California. She couldn't help feeling a little grumpy about it.

"Just warning you, the ravioli probably won't survive much longer," she typed, trying to maintain her usual cheerful tone.

"Duly noted," Eva replied. "Talk on Friday?"

Friday? Since when did they go all week without talking to each other?

"Sure," she replied, and added a thumbs-up emoji.

The delivery icon popped up, and she set her phone down and tried to go back to work. But she couldn't focus. She kept peeking at her phone and rereading her message history with Eva. Had something happened? Even if Eva was busier than usual this week, they had made late night visits to each other's homes before. What they hadn't done since New Year's Eve was spend more than two consecutive nights apart.

By five-thirty, she gave up working on her writing class lesson and checked the driveway. Maya was home from work. Cass should probably go check on her. At 27 weeks, Maya's belly was the size of a small basketball, though from behind you couldn't really tell she was pregnant. Not for lack of eating. Her appetite had rebounded early on in the second trimester, which was why Cass wasn't surprised to find her seated at her kitchen table snacking on apple slices slathered in almond butter.

"Hey," Cass said, reaching for an apple slice only to have Maya smack her hand away. "Okay. Didn't realize there weren't enough apples in the house." She glanced pointedly at the fruit bowl in the middle of the table, overflowing with apples and bananas.

"Sorry," Maya said, and pushed the plate toward her. "Reflex reaction. Are you headed over to Eva's?"

"No," Cass said, and jammed a large apple piece in her mouth so that her lack of elaboration would seem perfectly normal.

"Oh. Is she coming over here?"

Cass shook her head, still chewing.

"Really? You two have been attached at the hip for weeks now." As Cass snickered at her word choice, Maya rolled her eyes. "It's an expression, Cass. Grow up."

"She has midterms to grade," she explained. "And her mom is sick."

"Midterms and a sick mother?" Maya repeated, giving Cass the side-eye.

Her tone made Cass's stomach dip, because when she heard Eva's excuses repeated, they sounded like just that: excuses. Still, maybe Eva was just really busy. Or maybe she was freaking out about something other than Cass. As spring quarter and her tenure review drew ever nearer, her anxiety had grown commensurately. Sex seemed to calm her nerves, though. Endorphins were awesome, and running wasn't the only physical activity that could trigger a natural chemical high. Maybe she would change her mind and call Cass for a late-night visit...

Cass chomped on another apple slice, trying to redirect her mind. Somehow it felt inappropriate to be having thoughts of a sexual nature near a pregnant woman. And yes, she saw the irony given that most pregnant women had engaged in acts of a sexual nature in order to achieve their current condition, but emotions weren't logical.

Just then, Matthew burst through the front door and ran through the house calling, "It's here! It came!"

"No way," Cass said, standing up to high-five her brother. "I thought it wasn't coming until next week!"

"So did I, but here it is. David Cantor from Facilities brought it in his truck. Come see!"

With an apologetic look at her sister-in-law, Cass followed Matthew out to the driveway where a burly guy she recognized from campus was unstrapping four large boxes resting in the back of his Ford 350.

"Um," Cass said, glancing around, "is it just the three of us?"

"Don't worry," Matthew said. "The boxes are lighter than they look."

She was pretty sure she'd heard similar unsubstantiated claims from her brother before, but it was his observatory.

For Christmas, their extended family had chipped in to help Matthew buy a SkyShed Personal Observatory Dome (POD), a portable dome to house the fancy telescope array that had been sitting in a corner of the main house's attic ever since they'd remodeled the detached garage. The POD was slick. Even Cass, a liberal arts major, could admit that. It was versatile, too, and could sit anywhere reasonably flat. Matthew had said he wanted to build a standalone deck for it in the backyard, but that hadn't happened yet.

"All right," she said. "Where to?"

Matthew just looked at her. "Um."

"You don't have a plan?"

"It was supposed to arrive next week!"

"You know next week is only seven days away, don't you?" She shook her head. "Come on. Let's put the boxes on my deck and cover them with a tarp in case it rains. Then we can come up with a more permanent solution later."

"Good idea," he agreed, nodding quickly.

Sometimes he could be such a miniature clone of their father: able to see what was directly in front of him and what was light-years away, but with little idea of how to bridge the gap. Unlike their father, though, Matthew had kept his hair—so far.

At least he was right about the POD's disassembled weight. The three of them easily moved the boxes to Cass's deck, and while she looked through the backyard storage shed for a tarp and covered the boxes, Matthew paid the Facilities guy the agreed-upon fee for his assistance: a case of beer. Then he rejoined her on her deck, fussing over the tarp in a micro-managery way that almost earned him a smack to the back of the head. But Cass reined in her violent urges and dragged him into the main house instead.

"Where's Eva?" he asked as Cass set about going through their fridge and cupboards to see what she could make for dinner.

"At her mom's. Is Mexican okay?" she asked over her shoulder.

"Yes, please," Maya said.

"No bossing me around," Cass said, pointing a bag of wheat tortillas at her sister-law.

"I wouldn't dream of it," Maya said innocently. And then she and Matthew both laughed. Because right. *That* would happen.

As she made quesadillas, Mexican rice, and homemade refried beans, Cass observed her brother and his wife. Matthew had popped beers for himself and Cass and a bottle of organic ginger ale for Maya, and now they were seated at the kitchen table talking about their work days. He took turns rubbing her feet, which hurt after most of her shifts even when she wasn't pregnant. Since she'd begun growing an actual human being inside her body, the foot pain had only increased.

"Did you sign us up for that birth class?" Maya asked.

"Yeah," he said, rubbing her instep. "But are you sure we need it? I mean, you are kind of an expert at the whole birth thing…"

"Oh, baby, it's not for me," she said, her tone affectionate. "It's completely for you."

"That makes more sense," he said, and they shared the same intimate smile they'd been sharing since they first met.

Cass loved being around them when they were like this, quiet and caring and not bickering over money or, say, where personal observatory domes should go. And yet, right now, she almost wished they would snipe at each other because witnessing what they had together only made her more lonely. Would she ever have what they had? With Eva she'd thought she might. But now she wasn't so sure. It wasn't just the fact that Eva seemed to be pulling away. It was also that Eva had gone to such lengths to hide their relationship from her colleagues, as if she was ashamed of being seen with someone like Cass.

And cue twin telepathy in three, two, one...

"So what's this about Eva's mother?" Matthew asked, changing the subject. "I thought she only had a cold."

Cass applied cooking spray to the huge non-stick frying pan their parents had given Matthew and Maya at Christmas a few years ago and placed it on the gas burner, wincing as it made a bit more noise than she'd anticipated.

"She does only have a cold, but Eva didn't want her to be alone because she's a good daughter, okay?" Cass said, and tossed a tortilla into the pan to brown.

"And she has midterms to grade," Maya added, her voice needling in a way that Cass was absolutely not going to rise to.

She lasted for thirty seconds before saying, "Two hundred level sociology classes have a major writing component, you know."

"And that's why science rules," Matthew said, comparably predictably.

"Dude, I've seen your tests. Grading twenty-five short answers takes just as long as reading a paper. Do you know how many filler words sociology students use? It's probably the same amount of content, except that your students are more concise."

"Ha! You said it, not me," Matthew gloated.

Cass heard the sound of glass bottles clinking together and looked over her shoulder at them. "I don't have to finish making your meal," she pointed out.

"Sorry." Matthew held up both hands. "I take it back. Sociologists rule and physicists drool."

She shot him the finger and turned back to the stove. No way would she stop cooking mid-meal, and they all knew it.

When dinner was ready, Matthew washed his hands and helped Cass serve their plates while Maya kept her sore feet up. Soon they were seated around the kitchen table, chatting about recent news. There was always something to talk about given the current state of the nation, and talking politics with her brother always took Cass back to their childhood, when their parents invited various scholars to the house and engaged in "spirited debate," as they called it.

This was nice, Cass thought. Familiar and cozy, with minimal critique from the actual Mexican-American in the room. Maya had passed along some of her family's favorite recipes, and besides, anytime she didn't have to cook after a long day at work handling the bodily functions that attended the birthing process, she had said more than once, was fine with her. But still, as pleasant as the meal was, Cass couldn't help wondering what Eva was doing at that moment. Was she making more soup and toast for her mother, or had she picked up meals for them from PCC on her way up the hill? No way of knowing for sure, though, because her phone stayed silent throughout the meal.

At a break in conversation, Cass asked, "So what about this deck you wanted to build for the POD?"

"Oh, right. I think we should build it this weekend," her brother said. "It's not supposed to rain, and it might actually be warmer than last weekend."

"This weekend?" Maya's voice rose. "Are you joking?"

"No. You knew we needed a POD deck. Which is different from a POS deck," he added, laughing at his own joke.

"Hey," Cass said, "does this make us POD people now?"

"Good one." Matthew gave her another high-five as his wife shook her head.

"But, seriously, bro, you could have had a hot tub and you went for the astronomy set-up instead? Talk about lame."

"That's what I said," Maya put in.

"Excuse you both, astronomy is not lame. But just for that, see if I invite either of you to watch the next lunar eclipse with me."

"As if anyone in Washington State will be able to see the next lunar eclipse," Cass scoffed.

"Speaking of future astronomical events...." He trailed off and looked at Maya, who nodded expectantly. "Okay," he said, and turned back to Cass. "So hey, Cass."

"So hey, Matthew," she said, and took a sip of beer. What was this about? There wasn't anything wrong with the baby, was there? But no. They both looked too relaxed for that.

"Maya and I have been talking," he said, "and we were wondering if you might want to stick around longer than originally planned. You know, to help with the baby."

Cass stared at him. That was not what she'd expected. "Um."

"We know you want to get back to California," Maya said, "which I do not blame you for in the least, by the way, but my leave is only six weeks. We thought if you stayed just until summer, that would be enough to get us through until Matthew's spring classes end."

"You have to finish your thesis anyway," he added, "and it would only be until mid-June. This way you could do your defense in person instead of over Skype, which I've heard can be a challenge. What do you think?" Matthew smiled his hopeful little boy smile at her that reminded her of all the times he'd had her back when they were kids. From the womb to the tomb....

"I'll definitely think about it, okay?" she said, reaching over to muss his hair. "I can't say the thought hasn't crossed my mind, especially in the last few months. But thanks for asking me, you guys. It means a lot, really."

"Of course," they said in unison.

Cass glanced down at her plate and took another bite of rice and beans. If they'd asked her a week ago, she probably would have jumped at the excuse to stay longer. But now that Eva was blowing her off—if that was what she was doing—her old California plan didn't seem all that bad. Boone had called her just the night before. Her roommate was moving out of their two bedroom apartment in Oakland in a couple of months, and Boone was hoping Cass might want to be her new roommate—assuming she was still coming back. Cass had started to tell Boone about Eva, but then she'd realized she couldn't really tell her San Francisco friends what was going on. They weren't bi-phobic, but they wouldn't understand why she would choose to go back in the closet for a woman who had been a practicing heterosexual for the past decade.

Except Cass wasn't really going back in the closet, was she? Eva wasn't hiding their relationship from her friends or family, just from the good ole boys network at Edmonds that possessed the power to make or ruin her career. While Cass understood the nuance, she was pretty sure that her friends in San Francisco, none of whom came from academic families, wouldn't see a difference. Or, even if they did, approve.

First Boone, now Matthew and Maya. It was nice to be wanted. It was just that Cass couldn't help wishing that Eva was the one doing the wanting.

Cass's plate was almost empty and her stomach already more than a little full when Maya said, "Okay, what gives, Baby B?"

"I don't know what you're talking about," she deflected, spooning her last bite of rice onto a bite of quesadilla.

Matthew and Maya exchanged a look.

"Come on, Cass," her brother said. "Is this about staying? Because there's no pressure from our end, really."

"No, that's not it."

"Then what is it?"

She stared down at her plate a second longer, and then she sighed. "I think Eva might be blowing me off."

"Why? What did she say?" Maya asked.

"Nothing, really. It's just a feeling."

"In that case, maybe you should give her a little space," Maya suggested. "Sometimes people just need a little alone time."

"No way. Definitely talk to her," Matthew countered. "If marriage has taught me anything, it's that it's better to communicate than not."

"Sometimes," Maya agreed. "But conversations about emotions before, say, the other person has had their coffee? Definitely not better than not communicating at all."

"When have I ever tried to talk to you about emotions before coffee?"

"Friday, before the alarm went off."

"Okay, that's totally different. I had never seen the baby's elbow—"

"It was their butt."

"—sticking through your skin before! I think it's perfectly normal to be excited about that."

"Ew," Cass said, overcome by another *Aliens* flashback.

"Through your *skin*? Is that really a thing?"

Matthew frowned at her. "Don't 'ew' my child. It's the miracle of life, okay?"

"Ignore him," Maya told her. "There are very many things about pregnancy and childbirth—and children in general—that contain a high 'ew' quotient."

"You're ganging up again," he said, and stood up, reaching for their now empty plates.

"Sorry, not sorry," Cass and Maya said in unison, laughing as he huffed and headed for the sink.

"But really," Maya said, watching him as he started to load the dishwasher, "your brother is probably right. Communication usually is the better choice."

"Eva said maybe we could talk on Friday."

"Well, there you go. Maybe she just needs a few days to herself."

A few days—that wasn't too much to ask, Cass thought as she got up to put away the leftovers. Like Maya had said, sometimes people just needed their space. But even as she tried to convince herself there was nothing wrong, Cass couldn't shake the feeling that Friday's conversation with Eva was probably one she would rather not have.

***

Cass had barely left her Jeep the following morning when she ran into Jace MacKenzie in the student parking lot.

"Congrats, dude!" he said as they bro-hugged. "I just want to point out that I totally called it."

She already didn't like where this was headed, but she tried to tamp down her paranoia. "What did you call?"

"Eva DeMarco," Jace said as if he were stating the obvious. "Last fall, at the potluck."

"What?" She lowered her voice, glancing around. "What are you talking about, Jace?"

His brow furrowed. "Are you not seeing her?"

"That's not—Where did you hear that?"

"A bunch of places. People have seen you hanging out, and you know how this campus works."

She did, actually, because all campuses everywhere were exactly alike. As soon as two people were seen grabbing a coffee or attending the same Super Bowl party, the rumors started flying. Except that in her and Eva's case, the rumors were accurate. Was that why Eva was pulling away? Had someone mentioned the rumors to her, too?

"Awesome," she said, and started toward central campus. "Just perfect."

He fell into step beside her. "Sorry," he offered.

"No, it's fine," she said, even though it absolutely wasn't.

It was impossible to stay irritated around Jace for long, though, and soon they were chatting about University Computing and their thesis projects, program credits, and life after graduation.

"What are you going to do after you're done?" he asked.

"No idea yet," she admitted.

"Yeah, me neither. Something good always comes along, though. You just gotta be open to it."

They reached the library a moment later, and Jace held out his fist. "Later, Trane. And sorry again about before."

She bumped his fist. Jace could be clueless, but he generally meant well. "No problem," she said. "I appreciate the heads-up, actually."

"Cool. See ya!" And he trotted off, his ruck sack bouncing with every step.

Even though she'd spent more time the previous night worrying about Eva than thinking about schoolwork, her thesis meeting with Gwen went well. She was making real progress, both with her Presley House students and with her research summary. Maybe the day wouldn't be a total loss after all, she thought as she jogged down the stairs to the ground floor and started across campus. Steve had asked her to stop by and see him this morning, which was good because as faculty and staff members had gotten used to Drupal and Canvas, her workload had begun to shrink.

"He's waiting for you, Cass," Miranda said, not looking up from her screen.

"Thanks," she said, and headed into his office.

"Cass." Steve rose from his desk to join her at the conference table. "How you doing, kiddo?"

"I'm good," she said, slipping out of her jacket. "How's your week been?"

"Excellent. Mary and I tried a hike up at Baker Lake on Sunday. Have you been there?"

"No. Where's that?"

"Up north in Skagit County."

They discussed winter hiking, Matthew's personal observatory dome, and Steve's eldest daughter's progress in her environmental sciences PhD program at U-Dub. Then Steve said, "So. Miranda and I are working on next quarter's budget, and we need to know soon: Are you sticking around through spring, or are you leaving us?"

She answered more quickly this time. Apparently the third time really was the charm. "I don't know yet," she told him. "I've been so focused on completing my research that I haven't really made a plan for next quarter."

He gazed at her across the table. "If you could start thinking about it soon, I would appreciate it. I've got those discretionary funds that would finance one more quarter of your assistantship, but if you're planning on leaving, I'd like to funnel the dollars elsewhere."

"I'll think about it and get back to you," she said, even though this felt like exactly the wrong time to commit to a plan for spring quarter. Then again, she wasn't sure there ever would be a right time. "When do you need to know by?"

"In the next couple of weeks."

She nodded. "Got it." At least by then she should know which way she and Eva were headed. One way or another.

"So how's the writing class going?" he asked.

"Good," she told him, and launched into a description of the previous week's session, relieved to think about something else.

After that, they moved on to the Arts and Sciences blog, and Steve made a suggestion for another profile, a biologist this time who had been using drones to monitor Elk populations in the Cascades. It actually sounded really interesting, and Steve thought there might be some compelling video footage she could use.

"You could produce a short video, couldn't you?" he asked.

She nodded. "Absolutely."

A multimedia project sounded like the perfect note on which to end her graduate assistantship—assuming she didn't stay on campus next quarter.

"Excellent," Steve said. "Sounds like a plan. Is there anything else you want to talk about, Cass? I hope you know my door is always open, should you need it."

She blinked. "Um, no, I don't think so."

"Okay." He paused, but he didn't make any move to stand up or otherwise dismiss her. "I was playing racquetball the other day and your name came up."

"It did?" *Oh god*, she thought, picturing Jace's grin from that morning as he congratulated her on dating Eva. *Please don't let that be what Steve is talking about...*

"Martin Van Lyden from History mentioned that Linc Anderson is still holding a grudge against you because of last quarter. He has friends in high places, including the Board of Trustees, and Martin said he's been rattling some cages."

"Seriously?" She'd forgotten how entitled white men responded to having their power challenged: with extended temper tantrums.

"Martin said your brother's name came up, specifically in reference to the Arts and Sciences tenure review committee."

Cass felt her face flush as a combination of dismay and rage flooded her system. Who the hell did Linc Anderson think he was? She had a mind to drop by his house tonight and let him know just who he was messing with—

"But don't worry," Steve added, reaching out to tap her wrist once. "You and Matthew have plenty of friends in high places, too."

"Do you really think he would go after Matthew?" she asked, her voice tight. And if he did, what would stop him from targeting Eva? Because it was only a matter of time before the gossip about their relationship reached him.

"I don't know," Steve admitted. "Mostly Linc is a blowhard who likes to hear himself talk. That's always been his greatest flaw. However, I will say that I think a meeting between the three of us with me mediating could help resolve some of the tension. Would you be open to that?"

Cass's immediate reaction was *hell no*. But then she thought about the tenets of rugby she'd learned and preached over the years—taking responsibility, facing your demons, being the best you could be for those you cared about. Matthew and Eva didn't deserve to have their careers jeopardized by her pride. Because that's all it was between her and Linc: He needed to feel like the alpha, and she didn't want to give him the satisfaction.

She sighed and rubbed her forehead. "If you think it'll help, I'm willing to try."

"Good. I'll set something up, and we'll see if we can get this nipped in the bud."

"All right. Thanks, Steve. And I'm sorry. You shouldn't have to deal with this."

"You have no reason to apologize." He rose and held out his hand for her to shake. "You and Linc both report to me, so it's actually my job to deal with this. And with the power dynamic being what it is, I think it's important that you have an ally speak up for you. You said it yourself—part of the reason University Computing picked you for that presentation is that grad students make easy cannon fodder. If they hadn't put you in that position, we wouldn't be having this conversation at all."

"I guess this is why you get the big bucks, huh?" she joked weakly, following him to the door.

He smiled. "I guess it is."

As she left the dean's suite, Cass had to admit that she felt better knowing Steve was on her side. But then she pictured Matthew's face when she told him about Linc. Would he and Maya rescind their invitation for her to stay for spring quarter? And Eva—this was the exact reason Eva had wanted to keep their relationship quiet. Cass had thought she was overreacting, but she should have known to trust Eva's instincts. After all, Eva had been playing university politics for more than a decade while Cass had been in the supposed real world, chasing down her next rugby match. Eva had tried to warn her, but Cass had gone after what she wanted without any thought for the potential cost.

Eva's words from their first date came back to her: "While you might not be planning a career in academics, I very much am."

Damn it. Everyone would be better off if she just went back to California and networked her way into a job at Google or some other Bay Area tech firm. Matthew's tenure trajectory would be safe, Eva wouldn't have to worry about gossip or political repercussions, Cass's parents would be thrilled with her financial and career outlook, and her Bay Area friends would be happy to welcome her back into the fold. So corporate life felt soulless and unfulfilling. That was a first world problem and, as such, one she was lucky to have. There was always coaching rugby and volunteering with queer and at-risk youth to give her life meaning. Maybe someday down the road one of those could provide her with an alternate career path.

She headed toward the gym, intending to literally exercise out her demons before going home to finish her lesson plan. How had everything turned so quickly? A couple of weeks ago, she'd been cautiously optimistic about the way her life was unfolding. Now her brother's career was under fire because of her, and she wasn't sure if Eva wanted to be with her anymore. Cass couldn't blame her. After all, she was starting to think that maybe they never should have been together at all.

***

This was the first Friday Cass regretted not having an excuse to be on campus. Maya and Matthew were both at work, so there wasn't another person nearby to distract her. With half of her credits this quarter tied to her thesis project, her reading workload had been cut in half. That meant she didn't even have massive amounts of reading to focus on. Instead, she threw herself into her research summary, which was a surprisingly effective way of keeping her mind off her own drama. Writing about the Presley House kids reminded her that no matter how difficult any given day might be, her life was a paradise of privilege compared to that of so many others. These kids had suffered years of emotional and physical abuse, much of it at the hands of their biological parents. While Cass's parents might have been tough on her and Matthew, they had provided a safe, comfortable home and all of the financial and educational advantages anyone could ask for.

Killian and Charmaine had both described their dreams of one day attending college, while Ryan and Maria would probably give anything for a chance to work at a company like Google where gender neutral bathrooms and transgender-inclusive health insurance coverage were standard. Reflecting on what life had been like for the youth in her class kept Cass from dwelling too much on the fact that she still hadn't heard from Eva.

By late that afternoon when Eva finally texted her, Cass still hadn't decided what to reveal to her about her conversation with Steve. She had, however, decided that whatever Eva wanted to talk about, she would follow her lead. If Eva wanted more space, Cass would give it, no questions asked. If she wanted to go back to full-on secrecy, she could do that, too. She just didn't think it would help the existing gossip situation. Or the potential Linc Anderson situation, for that matter.

"Can I stop by after work?" Eva texted a little before five.

Stop by, Cass noted, her heart sinking as she parsed the implication. Not come over, hang out, eat dinner, or work together. Definitely not stay over.

"How about we meet at your house?" she replied. "My place doesn't have Harvey."

Eva's reply took a little while. But finally she answered: "Okay. Twenty minutes?"

"See you then."

No emojis, no exclamation points, just all business. Cass rose from the kitchen table and stood in the middle of the studio, hands folded on top of her head. God, this sucked. So much for getting her life back together in Edmonds. At least her shoulder was mostly back to normal, and it looked like she would be walking away with a graduate degree. Those were really the only solid goals she'd had when she applied to the sociology program, so—yay.

As she pulled on her jacket, Cass reminded herself of her litany of blessings. She had a brother and sister-in-law who loved her, and soon she would have a niece or nephew to adore. She had a beautiful home close to said family, and her parents were both healthy and still working. She had food in her refrigerator and money in her bank account. She had her dream car, a nice bike, and her health. She had everything she needed in life.

She stepped outside and locked the studio door behind her. She could do this. She'd faced far worse situations than breaking up with someone she'd only been sleeping with for a couple of months. She'd survived rotator cuff surgery, six weeks in a sling, excruciating pain that shadowed her every move. This? This was nothing.

Matthew and Maya were still at work, but she sent her brother a quick text: "Off to talk with Eva. See you later to discuss the POD deck building plan?"

He replied a second later. "Good luck!! And yes, chat later r.e. deck. M. and I will plan to cook our own dinner tonight." He added a sad-faced emoji.

"Save me some? I have a feeling I won't be gone long..." She added the same sad face.

He replied with additional unsmiling emojis, including—was that a pirate? Smiling a tiny bit, Cass tucked her phone into the back pocket of her jeans and started down the driveway.

Poor me, she thought, adding in a solid *When Harry Met Sally* moan for good measure. Look at the real-life love stories chronicled in that movie. Some people took more than one try to get things right. Maybe that would be the case for her and Eva. She already knew that what she felt for Eva wasn't just physical. From the start, she'd felt drawn to the person Eva was, her self-conscious smiles and the habit she had of pushing her glasses up her nose when she got nervous, her passion for sociology and her kindness toward her students, the steadfast goodness she radiated even when she was trying to seduce Cass.

That wasn't to say Cass didn't appreciate her physical attractiveness, because she definitely did. She loved kissing Eva and had become enamored with the softness of her skin, the curve of her hips and breasts, the way she arched unabashedly into Cass's touch. She loved being with her, and she couldn't believe that the previous Sunday, a seemingly average weekend night when they'd made love leisurely, teasing each other and laughing throughout as usual, had likely been their last time together.

Made love—usually she hated that phrase. But that was what sex felt like with Eva. The truth was Cass cared too much. Too much to stay with her if she didn't feel the same; too much to jeopardize her career if she did; just way too much.

This was probably the last time she would walk this route under the streetlights and dark sky, she told herself. The last time she would turn this corner, count the houses from the end of the street, walk up Eva's front path, and step onto her front porch while Harvey barked like a ferocious guard dog instead of the friendly goofball he was.

Before she could knock, Eva opened the door as if she had been standing just inside, waiting. "Hi," she said, not quite meeting Cass's eyes, and stood to one side. "Come in."

Normally Cass would have stepped out of her shoes and left her jacket on the coat tree, but today she only knelt down and hugged Harvey so that she wouldn't have to look at Eva. It hurt too much to look at her beautiful eyes, her soft skin, her lovely dark hair tucked up into its usual bun, when she knew what was coming.

"How are you?" Eva asked.

Or maybe she didn't know. Cass squinted up at her. "Fine. How's your mom feeling?"

"Oh, um, she's better."

Silence fell, and Cass scratched Harvey's chin whiskers one last time before rising to face Eva. "So," she said, and cleared her throat. She hadn't spoken much that day. "You said you wanted to talk."

Eva bit her lip and looked away. "Right. I, um, I've been doing some thinking, and, well, the thing is, I'm not sure we should see each other anymore."

Cass had been fully expecting these words, but they still slammed into her chest and made her nearly gasp. It was like taking a body shot in rugby. There wasn't anything you could do but wait for the initial impact to fade.

Eva's gaze returned to her. "I mean," she said, and swallowed audibly, "I just have a lot on my plate right now. You know, with my mom's health issues and tenure review coming up. I think I need to simplify things so that I can focus better."

Cass meant to nod and follow Eva's lead. She really did. But what she heard herself say instead was, "Is this really what you want?"

"Yes," Eva said, her voice unwavering. "It is."

Well, then. What could she say to that? "Okay," Cass said, even though the solitary word felt hard and bitter as she made herself utter it.

"It's not that I don't care about you," Eva rushed on, clearly sticking to some previously rehearsed script.

But Cass stopped her. "It's fine, Eva. I get it. Really. I'll miss

255

you, but—"

"But you were always going to leave," Eva said, and then looked away again, scuffing the wood floor with the toe of her sock.

Wait. Was *that* what this was about? "What do you mean?"

"Nothing. Never mind. Look, I have to meet Alexis, so…"

"No," Cass said, surprising herself again. "Say what you mean."

Eva stared at her, something that looked like anger tightening her mouth. "I already have."

Their staring contest lasted only long enough for Harvey to grow flustered and dart between them, whining. Cass shook her head and moved toward the door. But that was not how she wanted this to end.

"Don't worry," she said, turning back one last time. "I won't make things awkward for you at school. For what it's worth, I don't think badly of you, Eva."

"Good. I mean, thank you," Eva said, smoothing her rumpled bun and fiddling with her glasses. She looked less put together than Cass was used to, her wrinkled clothes and the circles beneath her eyes hinting that she hadn't slept well recently.

Cass hesitated. She wanted to ask for a hug, wanted one last embrace for closure, but Eva's eyes were bright with unshed tears and her chin was trembling just a little, so Cass contented herself with a nod. "Take care of yourself, Eva. I hope you find what you're looking for."

"You, too, Cass."

Her throat tightened at the finality in Eva's tone, and she looked down at Harvey, who was still looking between them anxiously. "Bye, buddy." She knelt down and kissed his smooth head, turned her head and let him kiss her cheek. Poor guy. He kept getting left by people who loved him.

"Wait," Eva said suddenly, and Cass looked up at her, hope flaring. "I still have one of your sweatshirts." She gestured toward the bedroom and took a step away as if to go retrieve it.

"Keep it," Cass said, because if she didn't leave right this minute she wasn't sure she would be able to keep her composure. She kissed Harvey again and rose to her feet. "I'll see you around,

Eva. Good luck with everything."

"You, too," Eva said, her voice cracking. She held the door open, not meeting her eyes. "Bye, Cass."

"Bye." And then she was brushing past Eva and walking away. Harvey didn't bark this time. In fact, once the door closed behind her, the house remained eerily silent at her back, as if it was holding its breath.

This is the right thing to do, Cass told herself as she turned for home. It was what Eva wanted and what her career needed. It was for the best, god damn it.

Unshed tears turned the world around her into a blur of greens and grays, but she waited until she'd left Eva's street to rub at her eyes. They hadn't touched at all, had they? She hadn't even taken off her coat. How long had she been there? Five minutes, maybe? Talk about the fastest lesbian break-up in queer history...

A strange sense of hollowness settled over her, but at the same time her limbs felt heavy as she made her way back to her brother's house. This was really it. She and Eva had really broken up. All the "last times" she'd imagined on the walk over were no longer hypothetical. She and Eva were done, and now Cass wasn't sure what to do with herself.

Both cars were in the driveway when she got back to the house, and she sighed in relief. Thank god she wouldn't have to be alone right now. Alone like Eva—except she had Harvey, and he was a much better snuggler than Matthew or Maya. She was really going to miss that dog. Eva, too. She already missed her. Then again, she'd been missing her all week.

"Cass?" Matthew called when Cass let herself into the front door, his voice coming from the kitchen.

"Yeah," she called back as she slipped out of her coat and shoes, her voice rough from not crying.

"Hey, little sis," Maya said, coming down the stairs that adjoined the right side of the living room.

"Hey," Cass said, and then she collapsed into her sister-in-law's arms, face crumpling. "She broke up with me, Maya. She doesn't want to see me anymore."

"I'm so sorry," Maya murmured, her fingers gentle against Cass's neckline as she smoothed her hair down.

And then Matthew was there hugging them both, and Cass felt so safe and so protected but still so fucking sad. She thought he would make a joke because that was how Matthew handled most things—she did too, if she was being honest—but he only rested his chin on her shoulder and said, "I'm sorry, Cassiopeia."

"So am I," she said.

"This is exactly what I was afraid of," he said, his voice rumbling against her shoulder.

What? And then she realized: When Matthew had warned her away from Eva in the beginning, he'd been trying to protect his sister, not his friend's ex-wife. All this time Cass had thought he was worried she would hurt Eva, but it had been the opposite right from the start.

Her tears didn't last long. After all, they were adults and she had been through worse. Soon she rubbed her face dry and traipsed into the kitchen with them, where Matthew handed her a beer and ordered her to sit down. While he and Maya put together a quick meal of pasta and salad, the working family's standby, they drew the story out of her. She told them about Jace, too, and what Steve had said about Lincoln Anderson's threats.

"Do you think that's why Eva ended things?" Maya asked while Matthew continued to mutter curses into the simmering red sauce.

"Maybe. I don't actually know," Cass admitted. "She said I was always going to leave, so maybe that was part of it too."

Maya and Matthew exchanged a glance.

"What?" Cass asked, holding her cold beer bottle against her flushed face.

"Nothing," Maya said soothingly.

"It isn't nothing." Matthew glanced at Cass. "Just, we hope you don't feel like you have to go back to California because of this. Because of her."

She looked down at the table and swiped at a breakfast crumb. "I won't be making any decisions this weekend, but I do have to give Steve an answer soon."

"What your brother is trying to say," Maya put in with an affectionate scowl at her husband, "is that we understand if being on campus spring quarter is uncomfortable for you, and we support any decision you make."

"You wouldn't have to pay rent," Matthew volunteered. "We could trade lodging for help with the baby." Maya gave him another look, considerably less affectionate, and he turned back to resume chopping peppers for the salad. "Sorry. I'll shut up now."

"It's okay," Cass said. "I'd be freaking out about becoming a parent if I were you, too."

"Annnd, she's back," her brother said, and tossed a slice of red pepper at her.

After dinner, which involved a second beer in quick succession to treat her emotional pain, they retreated to the living room to watch a movie of Cass's choosing. She picked Rogue One, even though Maya hated the ending, because—spoiler alert—a blinding white screen of doom seemed perfect right now. Maya only sighed and sat down beside her, and Cass felt just how much her sister-in-law loved her.

Midway through the movie, Maya moved Cass's hand to her belly. "The baby's really active right now," she whispered while the characters on screen continued to fight to the death, driven onward by the merest scrap of hope.

Cass could feel the tiny creature inside Maya spinning and twirling against her hand. "BabyCenter says she'll be too big to move like this in another few weeks."

"She?" Matthew asked from her other side.

"Just playing the odds, bro."

Maya smiled beatifically, and for a moment Cass convinced herself that the baby really was a girl. Then Maya glanced back at the screen and made a face as yet another good guy succumbed to the forces of evil.

"Can we at least turn the sound down?" she asked. "I'm not sure cries of anguish are the best sounds to expose them to at this point in their development."

A little while later, Cass leaned down and pressed her ear to Maya's baby bump. As she listened to the baby move around, swimming in the sea inside their mother's body, Cass found herself thinking that maybe she could still stay through the spring, after all.

CHAPTER FIFTEEN

Eva watched Cass until she disappeared around the corner, and then she dropped onto the couch and held Harvey to her chest. He licked her face steadily, cleaning the salt of her tears away almost even before they fell. Finally, she pushed his snout away and lay on the couch, her dog curled against her while the gas fire flickered and the night grew darker beyond the windows.

She had done it. After three nearly sleepless nights and twice as many vacillations, Eva had done it. She'd broken up with Cass. Cass hadn't fought it, which told Eva everything she needed to know.

"You what?" Alexis asked an hour later as they sat across from each other at a sushi restaurant in a Greenwood strip mall halfway between their two homes.

"I ended things with Cass," Eva repeated. She said the entire sentence again on the theory that the more she said it, the easier it would become. So far, she hadn't collected enough data to determine the theory's validity.

"Why would you do that?" Alexis asked, face screwed up in what seemed to be genuine confusion. "Last I heard you were excited about Valentine's Day for basically the first time ever since I've known you, and now you're breaking up with her?"

For a moment, she considered lying to Alexis. But then she remembered how Alexis had stepped up after Ben left, and she knew she would always and forever owe Alexis the truth.

"Okay," Alexis said after Eva had relayed the conversation she'd overheard, "so it doesn't sound great. But Cass is crazy about you. I'm sure there's some kind of context we're missing, that's all."

Eva stared at her. "Did you not hear the part where she said she wasn't in love with me?"

Alexis leaned away from the table. "That's not what she said."

"Yes, it is."

"No, it isn't. I swear, Eva, if you really believe that woman isn't in love with you, I don't even know what to do with you."

Eva pushed up her glasses. "But I would know if she felt like that about me."

"Right. I forgot how advanced your lesbian whispering skills are."

Eva resisted the urge to flip off her best friend. "What about when she said she didn't have any reason to stay?"

"Why would Cass think you wanted her to stay when you don't even want anyone to know you're together?"

A car pulled into a spot just outside the restaurant, its headlights momentarily blinding Eva. When she could see again, Alexis was watching her across the table, a sad smile turning up one corner of her mouth.

"Look, I'm sorry if I pushed you to do something you weren't ready for. But the truth is, Eva, it got real and you got scared. I don't blame you. Love is terrifying. But you have to decide what you want. If you'd rather be alone with your work and Harvey, then I support you. I really do. I just want you to be clear about what you want."

"I don't know what I want," she said, ducking her head.

"Okay. Well, tell me this. Would you have broken up with Cass if you hadn't overheard that conversation?"

"No," she admitted, and took a sip of miso soup, the liquid warm and salty on her tongue.

"Sweetie," Alexis said, and shook her head. "Why do you keep doing this to yourself?"

"I don't know." She hunched her shoulders and warmed her hands on the cup. "Can we please talk about something else? Like, anything else?"

Alexis didn't answer at first, but then she sighed and said, "Fine. Shall I entertain you with the things my stepdaughter said to me this week, specifically about how lucky I am to be black because I don't have any idea what kind of pressure society puts on

Asian Americans to succeed?"

Eva flinched. "Ouch. What did you and Tosh do?"

"We held a family meeting and gave her a reading list."

And even though Eva mostly felt like crying, she laughed. Because of course they did. She wouldn't have told Alexis this, but sometimes she felt a little sorry for Carly. Not when she was being racist, of course. But having brilliant parents wasn't easy, as Cass had more than demonstrated.

Alexis offered to come back to Edmonds with her after dinner, but Eva sent her home, promising that she would be okay. This wasn't like after Isabella when her marriage was falling apart and so was she. Cass hadn't been around long enough to become fully entrenched in her life. And yet, when she got home, the house felt too quiet even with Harvey's habitual snorts and the click of his toenails against the wood floor. There was something—*someone*—missing.

Sleep eluded her, just as it had done all week. Only tonight, instead of lying awake worrying about what to do about Cass, now she stared up at the ceiling trying in vain to catch her breath. The old hurt from Ben and Isabella had circled back around and was now sitting just below a new, sharper pain, a stabbing inside her chest she swore she could almost touch. Was this what a heart attack felt like? Had she literally broken her own heart and now she was going to die in bed with Harvey sleeping beside her, completely unaware? As her pulse pounded in her ears, she made herself count her breaths until the dread sweeping over her became more familiar than frightening.

Of course. She was having a panic attack. That was all this was.

She closed her eyes and recited her mantra a half dozen times, and then she got up and found her bottle of Tylenol sleeping aid pills. She hadn't needed to take them in a while, but there was no shame in getting a little chemical assistance here and there.

Hopefully, she thought as she crawled back into bed beside her dog, the pills would do the trick. Because she really, really needed to sleep. Everything would look better after a good night's sleep. Or, at least, so the cliché went.

While she was waiting for the pills to kick in, Alexis's words came back to her: *"I'm sure there's some kind of context we're missing."*

Could Eva really have gotten everything she'd heard Cass say so wrong? But bias, she knew, regularly made people see and hear things that didn't exist. Why should she be exempt from its effects?

***

Eva awakened to Harvey's snores, the sky still dark outside. For one deliciously forgetful moment, she wondered just as she had the three previous mornings if Cass was in the bathroom or already awake and making Dutch pancakes or some other breakfast food. Then, just like the other mornings, she remembered that Cass wasn't there at all.

Her mother, she learned over tea, was inclined to side with Alexis.

"I don't understand," she said as they sat at their usual table by the window overlooking the ferry terminal. "What do you mean you decided not to see each other anymore?"

"It's complicated," Eva said, blowing on her tea. The sleeping aid had worked, but as usual it had left her feeling foggy. She was betting that black tea on top of black coffee would make a firmer dent. If it didn't, maybe she would go climbing at the gym. Cass had only come with her a couple of times, so it shouldn't feel like something—*someone*—was missing.

Her mother turned her head, watching her carefully. "Try me."

Eva sighed and set her cup down on the blindingly white tablecloth. "I told you at the start that there would be political ramifications if I got involved with a student. I'm just not willing to take those risks anymore."

"You also told me that there is no actual conflict, since she isn't *your* student."

"Yes, well, it's not that easy, Mom."

The server delivered their meals, and Eva hoped that the interruption would distract her mother. That hope, like so many recently, did not achieve fruition.

"But you love her, don't you?" her mother asked as she cut her fried egg into small, gooey bits.

"Excuse me?"

"Oh, honey, anyone with eyes can see that you love her and she loves you. Even those of us with sub-standard eyesight can see that."

"I'm not—I don't—that's not the point," she stuttered.

"I would argue it's the only point worth considering," her mother said. "But then again, what do I know?"

Eva jammed a bite of omelet into her mouth and chewed harder than was truly necessary, wishing she'd had the foresight to cancel their Saturday morning tradition. But her mother's cold was nearly cured by now and there was no good reason not to take her to her favorite dining spot.

They made it through the meal by talking of other things—the weather, old friends her mother still kept in touch with, the books currently sitting on their bedside tables, and politics, their old standby. Like many of their neighbors in Lackawanna County, Eva's parents had been staunch Democrats. Otherwise, she probably would have refused to discuss politics with her mother at all. But railing against the corruption of the current US Congress, among others, was an easy point of connection that Eva was only too happy to exploit this morning, as long as it meant she didn't have to talk about Cass. From national politics she segued into an article she was reading about the political nature of queer romance writing, where crafting a happily-ever-after was a revolutionary act for a community that had long been denied positive representation in literature and film.

At this, her mother looked at her pointedly, but Eva ignored the non-verbal jibe. She could be happy without a partner. Hello, *feminism*.

Her mother went along with her evasive tactics until Eva dropped her off at the care facility. Then she turned to her daughter and said, patting her face, "I know you already know this, but losing those sweet babies wasn't your fault, Eva. You don't have to keep punishing yourself."

And then, before Eva could even think of responding, her mother slid out of the car and started up her front walk.

Eva put her car in gear and drove away, angry tears stinging her eyes. How dare her mother say such a thing? Of course Eva knew that her goddamn incompetent cervix wasn't her fault. Of course she wasn't punishing herself for something over which she had no control. There were simply forces at play here that her mother, with her lack of familiarity with academia and the way universities operate, couldn't possibly be expected to understand.

She was definitely going rock climbing, Eva decided as she swept into her too-quiet house. And if she fell and hit her head and woke up with amnesia like the heroine in one of the novels on her and Alexis's current reading list, all the better, really.

***

"You sound upset with your mother," Gayle said a few days later, scribbling something in her notebook at their regular bi-weekly therapy session. "Would you like to talk about that?"

Eva huffed, easily rekindling the anger that had lain just below the surface since Saturday, and repeated her mother's infuriating comment. "I mean, why does she think it's okay to presume to know how I feel about something so private? Losing Isabella didn't happen to her. It happened to *me*, god damn it."

"I can see how that might feel presumptuous to you," Gayle allowed. "But I have to admit, I'm curious. What was she talking about when she said you were punishing yourself?"

Eva swallowed. "She was talking about me blaming myself for losing the babies."

"I think that's evident. I'm just wondering what would make her say that you 'keep' punishing yourself. How, specifically, does she think you do that?"

And, crap. Eva had walked directly into that one. "Oh. Well, I believe she may have been referring to the fact that I decided last week to stop seeing someone from campus."

Gayle's eyebrows rose. "You were seeing someone from campus?"

"It wasn't serious," Eva said, picturing Cass's studio, unlit candles on the dining table, the television frozen on a video game world where the player's life meter, a row of hearts, could be easily replenished by food or fairies. "We weren't really a couple."

"Apparently your mother doesn't agree with that assessment," Gayle commented, pen hovering expectantly above her notepad.

Eva wavered. Did she open up her relationship with Cass for Gayle to poke and prod, or did she shut down this obvious opening and run for the hills? But running was what she'd been doing for the past week, and at this point, she was getting tired. Besides, wasn't this what therapy was for? To expose her obvious faults and make her thoroughly comprehend her own complicity in her recurrent unhappiness?

"Fine," she said. "It was supposed to be casual, but it was anything but. Happy now?"

"I think it's your path to happiness we're discussing, not mine. What happened to make you stop seeing this person?"

Eva expelled a frustrated breath. "I heard her talking on the phone about me." Spoken aloud, it sounded pathetic. No wonder her mother and Alexis had regarded her with such pity. And Gayle—yep, make that all of them showing up for the pity party.

"If we're going to talk about this, Eva," Gayle said, setting down her pen, "I think you know I'm going to need more context. So? Do you want to talk about this relationship or not?"

Eva hesitated, looking down at her hands folded tightly together in her lap, one foot tucked under her leg on the couch cushion. "I don't want to, no. But I think I probably should."

"All right, then. Why don't you start at the beginning?"

It took longer than she'd expected to tell the story of Cass and her. She kept getting sidetracked by subplots, like Cass's previous friends-with-benefits relationship, her presentation and Linc Anderson's attacks, the way she reacted when Eva pretended she didn't exist at the winter quarter all-college meeting. She found herself describing Cass's thesis in detail, her parents and their exacting expectations, her brother and Maya and the happy little household they seemed to have, complete with a baby on the way. But all that was set to end as soon as Cass finished her thesis and went back to her old life in California.

"So Matthew and Maya are having a baby," Gayle said when Eva finally stopped talking.

"They are. Maya is due in May," she said, keeping her voice even.

"Ah," Gayle said, and jotted down another note.

"Ah, what?" Eva asked impatiently. "You don't think I broke up with Cass because of the baby, do you?"

"Did you?"

"No," Eva said, feeling her cheeks flush. "I absolutely did not. Matthew and Maya are lovely and I'm thrilled for them, okay?"

"Okay."

She was so fucking calm, and it made Eva want to storm out and—

"Why did you break up with her, then?"

Eva folded her arms across her chest. "I told you. Because of the phone call."

"That's your story and you're sticking to it?"

Once again, Eva considered walking out of the office and never returning. But: "Fine," she all but spat. "Alexis and my mother think I got scared."

"And you? Do you share their opinion?"

"I don't know."

"Do you really not know, or do you just not want to know?"

Eva rubbed her forehead. Obviously it was the latter, and she was fairly certain they both knew it. But really, she was tired of all of this. Tired of worrying about her career, tired of worrying about giving away how much she cared about Cass, tired of worrying that Cass didn't feel the same and was going to leave her—what had Maya said?—*as soon as was humanly possible.* That exhaustion was what had led her to cut Cass out of her life. She really was trying to simplify things. Only she hadn't counted on the gutted look on Cass's face when she told her she didn't think they should see each other anymore.

"Why doesn't she want to stay?" she finally asked, her voice small. "Why am I not enough?"

Gayle crossed one leg over the other. "Are we still talking about Cass? Because I seem to recall you said something similar about Ben."

"Great. So I keep attracting people who will leave me," Eva said, refolding her arms across her chest.

"I don't think that's accurate," Gayle said mildly, steepling her fingers. "Was it you or Ben who ultimately ended your marriage?"

"You know it was my call. It just didn't work anymore. Plenty of people split up after losing a child."

"That's true. But why did you 'kick him out,' to borrow your phrase?"

"Because he didn't want to be with me anymore."

"Did he tell you that?"

"Well, no. But he blamed me for Isabella, I know he did."

"Did he tell you *that*?"

Eva blinked. "Not in so many words. But he wanted to be a father and I couldn't give him that. Besides, he'd already left once."

"That's right. He'd already left you once."

"Yes. And?"

"And you worried he would one day leave you again, didn't you?"

"Of course I worried he would—" She stopped, recognition flashing. *Fuuuck*. This was why she hated therapy sometimes, and yet it was also why she kept coming back. "You're saying I pushed Cass away just like I pushed Ben away, so that they wouldn't have the chance to hurt me first." She sighed and bent over, elbows on her knees. "I can't believe I pay you to make me realize what an emotional disaster I am."

"Technically, your insurance company pays me, so..."

Eva glanced up, mildly outraged, only to see Gayle smiling at her.

"What's the worst thing that could happen if you tell Cass how you feel about her?" her therapist asked.

Eva straightened up. "She might not feel the same. She might leave me."

Gayle gazed at her. "And how is that any different from what's already happened?"

Right. It wasn't.

"Now let me ask you this: What's the best thing that could happen if you tell her how you feel?"

That was easy. "She says she loves me back. And, well, she stays."

Gayle leaned back in her chair, nodding. "That's what your mother was talking about, Eva. That's the decision before you— whether or not you're ready to let yourself be happy. Let's talk more about that next time, hmm?"

Next time? She glanced at the clock on the wall. Whoops. Her time had been up for a while.

"Thanks, Gayle," she said, rising and collecting her things.

"You're welcome, Eva. You can do this, you know. You're

stronger than you give yourself credit for."

She wasn't sure about that, but at least Gayle, who knew her darker side better than anyone else in the world, seemed to believe in her. Then again, Eva was paying her to say such things. Or her insurance company was, anyway.

Freaking therapy, Eva thought as she walked out to her car in Gayle's driveway, songbirds calling out their early spring songs in the park across the street. It was absolutely the worst.

***

She could hear Matthew's voice from the hall, excited as a little kid's as he and a similarly enthused student discussed various applications of thermodynamics and kinetic theory. At least, that was what Eva thought they were talking about. She leaned against the wall just outside his office, scrolling through Twitter in an attempt to keep herself distracted from what she was about to do. Except that Twitter was pretty much guaranteed to elevate your heart rate anytime you signed on, so she switched to Instagram and began scrolling through assorted cute kitten and puppy feeds. Much better.

She was still chuckling at the sight of a tiny kitten lying on a pit bull's giant head when the student emerged from Matthew's office. The girl smiled shyly at Eva and ducked past her, and Eva checked the time: four thirty-five. Matthew's office hours had officially ended five minutes ago.

Now or never. Actually, never sounded kind of good. She started to turn away—she could do this tomorrow, couldn't she?— but she'd only taken a step when she heard Matthew's voice behind her. "Eva?"

"Oh," she said, turning around and pushing up her glasses. "Matthew. That's right. Your office is on this hall, isn't it? I was just..." She trailed off. "Anyway, I'm glad I ran into you. Do you have a second?"

He already had his jacket on and his briefcase in hand, so she wasn't surprised when he said, "No, not really."

"Please?" she asked. "It's about Cass."

He stared at her for a moment longer, and then he turned back into his office, flicking the light on as he went. "Fine. You have two minutes."

Why did people always give other people two minutes to make their case, she wondered as she followed him into his office, warmly lit and overflowing with plants. How exactly had two minutes become the general cultural currency? She would have to look it up sometime.

"What about Cass?" he asked, dropping onto his desk chair and swiveling to face her.

She balanced on the edge of a battered love seat covered with a fleece tartan blanket that reminded her of Cass. "Right. Look, I know I messed up badly. I'm actually hoping you'll help me try to make it up to your sister."

He frowned in disbelief. "Why should I help you? You broke her heart, you know. You let her believe she wasn't good enough for you, and then you walked away as if she didn't even matter."

Eva blinked. "But I didn't—I never said—"

"You told her you didn't want anyone here to find out who she was to you, Eva. How do you think that makes someone like Cass feel? Someone who grew up feeling like she could never measure up because of how her brain functions, not to mention who she is in the world?"

"But she's Cass," Eva said. "I mean, she's amazing and talented and so, so smart. If anything, she's too good for me. How does she not see that?"

He squinted at her. "Why did you break up with her, then, if you think she's so amazing?"

"I got scared," she admitted. "I got worried that she would leave me. I'm not proud of it, but, well, I'm kind of a mess, it turns out. I just want to make amends, Matthew. Well, that and ask her to give me another chance. If she decides not to, then I'll live with that. But I have to at least try."

Matthew gazed at her a second longer, and then he expelled an irritated breath. "You can't hurt her again. I know you've been through a lot, but Cass isn't as tough as she seems. She just isn't."

"I didn't realize that before. She seems like such a badass on the outside. With those tattoos and the way she carries herself, I think I thought she couldn't be hurt."

His gaze sharpened. "But you know she can now, right? And that you did?"

She nodded. "I know. I'm a total jackass. I am fully prepared to deal with the consequences of my actions, Matthew. Really."

He waited another moment, and then he nodded. "Fine. I'll help you on two conditions. Number one, you can't hide who she is to you. I mean it. You have to actively tell people on this campus about your relationship. No sneaking around anymore whatsoever."

"That's easy—I was already planning that," Eva told him. "What's the second condition?"

"Oh." He shrugged. "I don't actually have one. I just thought two sounded better."

She shook her head, smiling. She'd missed his sense of humor, mainly because it was just like Cass's. "How about this: If she agrees to take me back, I'll crash Gwen and Steve's weekly meeting and tell them we're together. Would that satisfy your first and only condition?"

Matthew leaned back in his chair, which squeaked distressingly at the motion. "I think it would."

"Excellent. I have a plan," she told him, resting her elbows on her knees. "It just needs a little technical assistance."

As she shared her idea with him, Matthew started to smile. When she was done, he reached over and smacked her on the shoulder. "You're a good egg, Eva. I hope my sister realizes that."

God, did Eva hope that, too.

CHAPTER SIXTEEN

There was no way around it. Matthew was acting weird.

"No, I'm not," he protested when Cass accused him of slinking around after dinner Saturday night. They'd almost been finished cleaning up the kitchen when Matthew had vanished upstairs, where Cass was pretty sure she heard him on the phone. But when he came back down and she asked him about it, he claimed the voices she'd heard had come from a YouTube video.

"You're such a bad liar," she said as she finished wiping down the counter.

"No, I'm not," he repeated, though with considerably less vehemence.

"You kind of are," Maya said with a look that Cass couldn't parse.

They had been doing that all day, too. Again Cass worried there might be something wrong with the baby, but again, they didn't seem alarmed, just preoccupied and overly concerned with her plans for the evening. The previous weekend, Cass had distracted herself from the break-up by helping her brother build a floating deck in the backyard, assemble the POD, and add in the telescope array. This weekend, however, loomed emptily, which was why she had practically moved into the main house.

"Okay, what gives?" she asked, leaning against the kitchen counter. "I've told you five times I don't have any plans tonight. What do you think I'm going to do, go find someone to have rebound sex with?"

Maya's head snapped back her way. "You're not, are you?"

"Gross," Cass said. "Eva and I only broke up a week ago. I don't move on that quickly."

Had it only been a week? Ugh. She couldn't wait to be done with this part of the break-up. The first few weeks of any break-up were awful—battling the urge to call or text your ex, especially when you were tipsy or overly tired. With Eva, there was the added complication of avoiding her at school. Fortunately, Cass hadn't met with Gwen this week, nor had she been called to the fourth floor of Old Main for IT assistance. She'd kept her head down the rest of the time and only gone to campus when she absolutely had to. All in all, Operation Avoid Eva had enjoyed surprising success.

That didn't mean Cass missed Eva any less, because she didn't. At least once a day she checked her phone and email hoping to find a message from Eva saying she'd changed her mind and asking Cass to take her back. She didn't actually know if she would take Eva back, but still. It would be nice to be asked.

Who was she kidding? She would take Eva back in half a second. Maybe. She would definitely take Harvey back. The crazy mutt had wormed his way into her heart, and she was tempted to text Eva and ask if she could have Harvey visitation rights like Ben. (Which, excuse you, was totally not a thin excuse to be in touch with Eva.) So far she'd refrained, but there was no guarantee she would continue to do so.

Matthew's phone buzzed and he glanced at it. Then he looked at Maya and nodded subtly.

"You know I can see you both, right?" Cass said.

"That was Jack Keller," he announced. "He actually needs a hand at school. Can we run up there for a sec? He needs some technical help."

"With what?" Cass asked, but she was already reaching for her jacket.

"I don't know. He just said to bring you if you were around."

"Fine," Cass said, secretly pleased that she wouldn't have to spend the next three hours trying to focus on a movie or video game and not wondering what Eva and Harvey were doing.

The drive to campus only took a few minutes. Matthew seemed oddly quiet, but Cass chalked it up to male hormones, which Maya had recently convinced her was an actual thing. He parked the Camry near the Physics building and led her past it, continuing on toward the observatory. They nodded at the student worker stationed at the front desk, and soon Matthew was unlocking the door to the planetarium. They stepped inside, but it was empty.

"Huh," Matthew said. "I thought he was meeting us here. Let me just check the projector."

She wandered down one of the aisles and stared up at the dome as constellations began to twinkle into existence. She hadn't been back since the night she'd brought Eva here on their first date. At the memory of that perfect night, when she and Eva had kissed for the first time and she'd realized that her attraction to Eva was considerably more than an adolescent crush, Cass closed her eyes. God, she missed her.

"Hi," she heard from behind her, the voice like something out of a dream.

Great, now she was hallucinating Eva's presence. Cass sighed at her brain's folly.

"Cass?"

Okay, so that sounded real. She turned to see Eva facing her from the opposite aisle, one side of her face in shadows, the other barely lit by the light of the half-moon shining from the dome overhead.

"Eva?" she said, and then caught a glimpse of her brother waving at her from the doorway just before he vanished back into the observatory.

Oh. So *that* was why he and Maya had been acting so strangely. Jack Keller wasn't coming. Cass was here because Eva and Matthew had conspired for—what, exactly?

"What is this?" she asked, watching Eva warily.

"Will you sit down with me?" Eva asked, waving at the center seats where they had first sat together all those weeks earlier. "Please?"

Cass paused, taking in the room's atmosphere. The constellations were shifting infinitesimally across the dome overhead, but there was no Neil deGrasse Tyson voiceover this time, only a faint classical soundtrack made up of cheerful, harmonious string and wind instruments.

"Why?" she asked finally, her voice raspy with emotion she was trying to hold in check. She wanted nothing more than to sprint to Eva and sweep her into her arms, but Eva had hurt her more than once now, and not just a little. While she understood that no relationship was free from hurt, at some point you had to ask yourself if the pain was worth it.

"Because I owe you an apology," Eva said. "And also I brought cupcakes from Cupcake Royale. You can even have the salted caramel if you want."

Cass's stomach rumbled so loudly she wouldn't have been surprised to learn that Eva could hear it halfway across the planetarium. It wouldn't hurt to hear her out, would it? She started to move slowly toward the center seats.

"I might be open to an apology," she allowed. "Depending."

"On what?"

"On what exactly you're apologizing for."

"Oh," Eva said, mirroring her approach from the opposite aisle. "Well, first of all, I wanted to apologize for eavesdropping on you."

Cass stopped. "Wait. What, now?"

"I came over on Valentine's Day, but you were on the couch talking to a friend," Eva admitted.

Boone, Cass thought, and then realized suddenly what Eva must have overheard. So *that* was why she'd called off their relationship! No wonder.

"I didn't mean—" she started.

But Eva held up a hand. "You don't have to explain, Cass. I'm the one who messed up, not you. I should have stayed and talked to you, but I left. So number one, I'm sorry about that."

"Okay," Cass said, and started moving toward the center seats again. "Apology accepted."

"Thank you," Eva said, resuming her own trek toward the middle of the room. "Number two, I'm sorry for hiding our relationship and making you feel like you weren't important to me. I should never have asked that of you."

"No," Cass agreed. "And I should never have gone along with it. Hiding in a closet, even if it's someone else's, isn't any way to live, not even if you understand perfectly well why the closet exists."

Eva nodded. "Asking you to do that was unfair and insulting and most of all, disrespectful. And I really, really respect you, Cass.

I always have, even if I've done a terrible job of showing it."

Cass was starting to like this apology thing. "All right. Apology number two accepted."

"Thank you," Eva said again. "Number three, I'm sorry for being scared. This entire time, I have been so worried about what would happen if you left that it didn't occur to me to ask you to stay. In case you didn't know, I'm crazy about you, Cass. And if there's any chance you might be thinking even a little bit of not going back to California—for you, not because of me—I am all for that. But even if you're not, I'm open to figuring out how to keep what we have going because I really, really care about you. I mean, assuming you're willing to consider trying again."

Cass reached the center seats, and a moment later Eva did, too. Cass gazed down at her, taking in her neat bun, her glasses currently perched perfectly on the bridge of her nose, the hoodie that Cass could now see read "All Blues" in a familiar script.

"So you're asking if we can get back together?" she clarified. When Eva nodded, Cass was tempted to blurt out a blind acceptance. But something made her hesitate. "I don't know, Eva."

"You don't?" Eva asked, her shoulders slumping a little.

"How do I know you're not going to get scared and vanish on me again?"

"You don't," Eva admitted. "But my mother would probably disown me and Alexis would definitely stop talking to me, so I really don't think you have to worry about it."

That was sort of reassuring. "If we do get back together, it can't be like it was. I can't do that anymore. If we're going to be together, then we're going to be together, regardless of any potential consequences. Are you sure you want to take that risk?"

Eva looked up at the stars overhead and sighed. "Honestly? It makes me nervous to date a student. I can't pretend it doesn't. But I'm tired of being afraid of what *might* happen. I want to be with you, Cass, and I want to treat you the way you deserve to be treated. That means no more sneaking around, no more lying, no more pretending that I'm not super freaking lucky to have you in my life. And Harvey's life, of course."

Aw, Harvey. At the mention of the dog, Cass almost caved immediately. But: "How do I know you won't change your mind again?"

"Because if you agree to be my girlfriend, I plan on telling everyone, starting with Gwen and Steve right on up to the president. Of the university, not of the United States."

"Girlfriend?" Cass repeated, feeling a smile bloom deep inside her chest.

"Girlfriend," Eva said, eyes luminous in the light from above. "Cassidy Trane, will you do me the honor of consenting to be in a committed, long-term relationship with me?"

Cass waited another second, just to draw out the suspense that her own heart could barely withstand. Then she nodded. "Yes, I will. But I think I owe you an apology, too."

Eva's smile dimmed slightly. "For what?"

"For not telling you that I don't want to move back to California. I want to stay here, Eva. I have for a while. Not just for you, but for Matthew and Maya and the baby, and for me, too. I like it here."

"Really?" Eva's voice sounded almost fragile.

"Really," Cass said, nodding. "Oh, and also, I should have fought harder when you decided to end things."

"Why didn't you?"

"Linc Anderson," she admitted. "Steve told me he'd been making noise about sabotaging Matthew because of me, and I worried he'd hear the gossip about us and go after you, too."

"What gossip?" Eva started, but then she waved a hand. "You know what? It doesn't matter. Can you really forgive me, Cass?"

"Yes," Cass said, starting to smile down at her. "On one condition."

"What's that?" Eva asked, beginning to smile back.

"That I come with you to San Francisco over spring break."

Even in the relative darkness, Cass could see how Eva's eyes lit up. "Are you serious?"

"Completely. No way is my girlfriend going to the Bay Area for the first time without me to show her around. I mean, assuming you want me to," she added as she heard how her fake bravado sounded.

"I would love for you to come with me," Eva said, stepping

closer. But then she hesitated. "Are you sure, Cass?"

Cass wasn't certain to which part Eva was referring—forgiving her, getting back together, or accompanying her to the conference in California. But since her answer was yes to all three, she nodded and reached for Eva, slipping her arms around her shoulders and tugging her closer.

"Totally sure," she said, and then she lowered her head to kiss Eva. It was just like their first kiss in this same spot so many weeks earlier: soft and chaste and filled with the sense that something amazing was about to begin.

"I can't believe you got Matthew and Maya to help with your scheme," Cass said a little while later when the kissing had paused and the cupcakes had been eaten.

"You mean my grand gesture?" Eva asked with a smile Cass didn't quite get. "It took some convincing, but once I assured them I had your best interests at heart, they came around."

"So being with you is in my best interests, is it?"

"I was talking about Harvey, not me."

Twin telepathy was definitely a thing because at that moment Cass's phone buzzed.

"Do you hate me??" Matthew had written.

"No," Cass typed back, laughing at her brother's ridiculousness. "I love you, idiot. And I love her, too." She added every heart emoji known to humankind, arranged in as close to a ROYGBIV rainbow that she could make because she knew it would make her brother smile.

"You're such a dork," Eva said, her chin on Cass's shoulder and her eyes on Cass's phone screen.

"And you're such a nerd," Cass replied, her heart rate picking up as she realized what Eva had probably just read.

"I love you, Cass," Eva said, pressing a kiss to the corner of her mouth.

"I love you, too," Cass said, joy rising sharp and sweet inside her as she turned her head and pressed her lips to Eva's.

A moment later, Eva squeaked as Cass lifted her onto her lap, but then she slipped her arms around Cass's neck and settled herself more comfortably.

"You taste like caramel," she said.

"All the better to kiss you, my sweet," Cass replied, wiggling her eyebrows.

Eva rolled her eyes, but Cass's cheesy joke didn't stop her from kissing her again.

A little while later, Cass whispered, "Did you see stars?"

"Only about a million," Eva whispered back.

They laughed together as the constellations continued to drift by overhead, ever so slowly.

CHAPTER SEVENTEEN

Eva stretched her neck and checked the time on her phone. It had been a couple of hours already. Maybe they should head to the cafeteria and get some food in their systems. She stole a glance at her girlfriend, whose legs were jumping spasmodically as she chewed her fingernail and stared at her Kindle. Yeah, they wouldn't be going anywhere anytime soon.

Cass hadn't turned a page in close to five minutes, Eva was pretty sure, and it wasn't because she was having trouble reading. With the dyslexic font enabled, Cass's brain managed phonetic decoding well enough that she positively flew through books these days, especially with the freedom she now had to read whatever she wanted. Well, not *whatever* she wanted. The 100-level Sociology of Gender class she was teaching at Seattle Central Community College was keeping her busy, as was the writing portion of her thesis. But at least she wasn't slogging through mountains of course material every night.

Right before spring break, a friend of Eva's at SCCC had mentioned that the instructor they'd had lined up to teach an intro to gender course for spring quarter had jumped ship. Did she know any sociology adjuncts or grad students who could fill in, particularly someone who identified as trans or non-binary? Eva had asked Gwen if she thought it was unethical for her to offer up Cass's name, but Gwen had said that as long as Eva was open about their relationship, there shouldn't be a problem. After all, she and Steve hadn't had an issue with her and Cass being a couple.

The head of SCCC's sociology program had been fine with Eva and Cass's status, particularly after she heard about Cass's work with the kids from Presley House. Since Cass had already decided she didn't want to be on the Edmonds campus that spring except for the occasional meeting—and rugby, which she was still very much coaching—the class had provided the perfect excuse to turn down Steve's offer to extend her graduate assistantship. Now, six weeks in, the class seemed to be going well, and the director of the program had hinted that there might be more work for Cass at SCCC both with the sociology department and with the queer studies program. Mike, the Ed-U rugby coach, had mentioned that SCCC had been talking about starting a women's rugby club for years, so there might be an opportunity there as well.

"See?" Eva had teased Cass one night recently as they sat at her dining room table grading papers together. "You can't escape a career in academics. It really is in your blood."

"I don't know," Cass had said, leaning back in her chair and fidgeting with her red gel roller pen. "Are you sure you aren't embarrassed to be dating a community college instructor? After all, you are a self-professed academic snob..."

"No, I mean, not—I only meant—" Eva had faltered, wondering why she'd had to confess that particular fault and not the dozens of others Cass was still in the process of learning about her.

"Just kidding," Cass had said, laughing. "I'm a total snob, too. But as much as I hate to admit it, I really like teaching, and since there's no way I'm about to get a PhD, Seattle Central is perfect."

Cass's new teaching career wasn't the only thing they'd had to celebrate this quarter. Steve had managed to fill the two open seats on the college Tenure and Promotion committee with younger, more progressive professors, one of whom happened to be married to a mystery novelist. Steve claimed not to have known that the English professor's wife was an author of popular fiction, but either way, Eva was fairly certain that she had him and Gwen to thank for the committee's vote to recommend tenure for her and three other Arts and Sciences candidates. She still had to survive the university-wide review in the fall, but since Academic Affairs and the university committee relied so heavily on college and departmental recommendations, Steve and Gwen were both confident that the official announcement was only a matter of months away.

Today, though, she and Cass were waiting for news of a different nature. Maya had gone into labor the night before, and

Matthew had called shortly after Sunday brunch to invite them to the hospital to meet their new niece or nephew. They had raced up the hill and were seated now in the birth center lobby, waiting to be called back to Matthew and Maya's birth suite.

"Why is it taking so long?" Cass fretted, shutting off her Kindle and rising to pace the waiting area for the twentieth time since they'd arrived.

"It takes as long as it takes," Eva said, quirking a brow when Cass mock-glared at her. "What? It's not my fault there's no rushing the process."

She knew Cass was worried that something had gone wrong; the thought hadn't escaped her, either. The last time she'd been in this hospital had been to deliver Isabella—not exactly good memories, by any stretch. But while American infant and maternal mortality rates might be high compared to other developed nations, most births in the US were still without complication. The odds of significant problems at birth for mother or baby were very low, especially for Maya, who had closely followed every recommendation made by her OB/GYN in the past ten months. Maya's baby would be fine, and so would she.

As long as Eva kept telling herself this, she could believe it was true.

"How are you doing?" Cass asked, stopping and squatting beside her chair.

"Fine," she said. Then, as Cass squinted up at her, concern evident, she added, "Really. I promise."

"Okay." Cass didn't look convinced, but before she could press any further, her phone beeped. She grabbed it from the chair and read the screen quickly. "Oh my god! Oh my god, Eva, we can go back. Come on!"

The staff buzzed them back into the birth wing, and Eva hurried down the corridor beside Cass, trying not to remember the days and nights she'd spent in this very place in a futile effort to keep Isabella inside her body just a little longer. Today wasn't about her or her child, she reminded herself. Today was about the Tranes and the new member of their family. Her family? Since Cass had decided she wasn't going back to California, that she was going to stay in Edmonds and focus on teaching and coaching instead, the Tranes had started to feel like Eva's family, too.

"It's a girl!" Matthew crowed when he met them at the door of the birth suite.

Cass hugged her brother and pounded him on the back while Eva surveyed the room, trying to manage the memories threatening to overwhelm her. Maya was lying down with her hospital bed in the up position, her face flushed, hair a mess, arms cradling a small, mewling newborn with a full head of dark hair that peeked out from under her blue and pink striped baby cap.

Her. They'd had a girl, too.

Maya looked up at Eva. "Come meet your niece," she said, and in her eyes and voice Eva could hear the love and understanding Maya was extending to her, the same caring she'd offered that night two years earlier when Eva had sat in a similar hospital bed in a room just down the hall, cradling Isabella in her arms. "Come say hello to Anna Rosita."

"Anna Rosita," Eva repeated, drifting closer to the bedside.

"We're going to call her Annie," Matthew said, his arm coming around Eva's shoulders.

"Annie." Cass's voice was thick as she moved to Eva's other side and slipped her arm around her waist. And just like that Eva was surrounded by Tranes, their joy and love buoying her up and giving her the strength to smile through her tears.

"Annie," Eva echoed. "I love it. Congratulations, you two."

"Thanks, Eva," Matthew said, his hold tightening for just a moment.

A little while later, Maya placed the sleepy baby into her arms, and Eva held her close and silently promised to do everything in her power to keep her safe. She was strong, Eva could feel it, her limbs struggling already to move, her eyes blinking in wonder at the new world around her.

Seated beside Eva on the day lounger, Cass kept one arm around Eva's shoulders and placed the other beneath her arms, helping to support the baby's weight.

"I love you," she murmured, and Eva couldn't tell if she was talking to her or to their niece.

Probably, she decided as she leaned over to kiss Cass's cheek, it didn't matter. But just in case: "I love you too," she murmured back, and was rewarded with the radiant smile she thought she might never get used to.

Honestly, that was more than okay with her.

ABOUT THE AUTHOR

Kate Christie lives with her wife and daughters near Seattle. A graduate of Smith College and Western Washington University, she worked in academia for many years as a marketing and communications consultant.

To find out more about Kate, or to read excerpts from her other titles from Second Growth Books and Bella Books, please visit her author website at www.katejchristie.com. Or check out her blog at katechristie.wordpress.com, where she very occasionally finds time to wax unpoetically about lesbian life, fiction, and motherhood.

To receive updates on future titles, including book four of the Girls of Summer series, sign up for Kate's mailing list at https://katechristie.wordpress.com/mailing-list/.

Made in the USA
Middletown, DE
03 March 2019